MAFIA BOSSES GOT ME

THE DARK MAFIA ROMANCE COLLECTION

JUST BAE

CONTENTS

CLYDE

MICHAEL

NICO

JIMMY

CLYDE

CHAPTER 1

When the urge to travel overtakes, it should be tempered with at least a little practicality and logic. That wasn't exactly how things had gone in Ella's case but, oh well.

It was how she found herself bouncing around bars and hotels all over the world. Sure, she had her little studio flat in Glasgow as a base, but in recent years she was hardly ever there.

Instead, she was as close to settled as she had been for a long time. In a pompous hotel in Boston. It also happened to be where she met someone, she'd call her closest friend and unofficial landlord of sorts - she'd been crashing at his for as long as she could remember now, reassurances it was fine despite her attempts to get moved out the way.

"Bentley, event room six." the familiar voice called as she hung up her coat in a locker, turning to catch James staring from the doorway, doing his level best to hide the smile as she groaned in exaggerated annoyance "Another day, another group of businessmen who skimp on the sommelier," she commented, trading in the almost brash rumble of her accent for the tilt of light Scottish lilt that seemed to keep the customers happy and the tips appearing.

"Nope, for once they know their wines and Dean has just got done setting up their selections for the meal." James soothes her, an almost cheeky smile at the way she seems genuinely surprised. It tends to be she gets the well-paying but rough parties, namely because she can handle it - but still, it's nice to get a civilized group who won't be asking for fancy jaeger bombs by the end of the evening. "I'm working with Dean. Ooh, joy, he's always great banter during the downtime." Ella spoke brightly, briefly giving him a one-armed hug "But you're by far my favorite of the night staff. Including myself." she added with a soft laugh that was lost in the din of the bustling staff corridors.

Speaking of the devil, Dean popped into the back for another bottle of wine just as Ella was about to head through to behind the bar. "My favorite forest!" he greeted - a nickname that stuck early for the pair. Unfortunately.

As James made a beeline for the next fire to fight, even at this late hour, Ella followed Dean back behind the bar of one of the event spaces. Giving a nod to the server, the young waitress stepped towards the long table to inform them they could now place cocktail and spirit orders.

Dean leaned a hand, heaving up the ice buckets so he could lean close and bring her up to speed on the group "Local… politics, DA, upcoming lawyers, those sorts," he summarized picking up on the barely raised brow that broke through her 'customer service face'. Thankfully, it remained in place for the most part as a shadow appeared across the bar, Ella stood quickly as she expected the young waitress.

Instead faced the vaguely tilted head of one of the guests and a gaze that felt like he was seeing into her damn soul. It took every ounce of composure for her not to shudder.

"What can I get you, sir?" she asked cheerily, watching as the accent landed and prompted the barest hint of a smile from him "I was going to ask about whiskeys, but it sounds like I should trust a recommendation."

Ella didn't let her thoughts show on her face, as if everyone from Scotland was an expert in shortbread and booze, before turning to the section of wall behind her for spirits. Stretching to reach one from the top shelf, she spans a couple of ice cubes in the glass to cool it and leave just a trace of water before pouring a healthy measure "Small batch, single malt - Borough, though we're one of only two stockists in the city." she informed him pleasantly, managing a small smile despite everything in her head screaming 'these are not good people, minimizes interaction, the tips aren't worth it.'

His gaze doesn't leave her as he takes a sip, apparently mulling it over before he gave an approving smile and saunters back to his seat, moving unhurriedly as he picked back up on the table's conversation.

Barely moving her lips as she fidgeted with the garnish trays, Ella kept her voice low as she caught Dean's slightly wide-eyed gaze "That look never means good things, what's wrong?" the sommelier shifted along the bar behind her. "Former dirty DA, now... crime boss who keeps his hands clean. Does a lot of business here." Her comment carried on a breath and was loaded with sarcasm.

"Great…"

The night managed to go much the same, quite quiet for the sheer number of folk they had. Sure, there was the occasional ripple of raucous laughter, but it was mostly like any other event. Even when James appeared, checking in with the group, there wasn't much out of the ordinary. "Frank, a pleasure." the former DA's voice rang out from the end of the table, fixing him with a level stare and easy attitude that the manager didn't react to. "Mister Stewart, we're pleased to have you with us again. I trust everything was to your satisfaction?" he enquires smoothly, ever the professional even as he notes the way the man's gaze flits behind him to the bar with a slow smile as he downs the last of his whiskey "As always, Frank. You've really got an eye for staff, I'll say that."

There's a barely discernable tick in James's jaw as he smiles politely, "Well, a business is only as good as its staff." he comments simply, a tone as if Clyde should be able to relate.

A slow nod of agreement as the bearded man gets to his feet steadily, James politely gesturing to the doors as the party leaves, most talking among themselves but Clyde content to hang back and speak with James as if they're old friends till the doors click shut behind them.

From just over her shoulder, Ella hears Dean release a breath, calling over the waitress to give pointers on where she could improve and the like - the poor thing only started a few weeks ago and they're already throwing her to flying solo at private functions, must be the day manager's idea of a joke. Though, if it continues this way, she should be fine - the night staff looks out for their own, so she'll learn quickly without someone biting her head off as a driving factor.

"Hey, kid," the girl startles visibly as Ella speaks up, despite how soft the woman tries to keep her voice "You'll be okay. You handled it well, for a trial by fire." at least the friendly smile Ella aims her way is returned with a noticeable easing of the waitress's shoulders as they finish clear up and return to the staff halls.

* * *

Later, Ella can be found just inside the staff door, obnoxiously twirling her car keys around a finger as she waits and says her goodnights to the leaving night staff. Finally, trailing behind the last of the night shift, comes James. "Ready? Wouldn't want to get stuck in that rush-hour traffic?" she jokes, earning an amused groan from her friend as he slings an arm around her shoulders with a heavy exhale that makes her surprised, he's not straight up leaning on her. "Yes, please. Let's not top off a long night with traffic."

CHAPTER 2

It only happened because, despite offering her a place to crash, James started to feel bad about finding her curled on the sofa - a relic of the manners that had been drilled into him most likely. She'd lasted one night in his bed, despite his best efforts to hide the stiffness in his back from sleeping on the sofa, she'd noticed it on the drive to work. Noticed the way he winced ever so slightly when they hit a pothole.

It had made for an awkward conversation at the end of the shift - her near begging him to switch back, him stubbornly refusing to 'let the lady sleep on the sofa', till Ella reached the end of her patience. "Oh, for fuck's sake, it's a damn king, there's plenty of room for both of us." she'd huffed, folding her arms loosely as he approached her with a slight frown. Well, not quite a frown - she could read him like a book, he'd quite obviously got the wrong end of the stick, earning him a deadpan expression as she spoke dryly "Frank, relax, I'm not trying to fuck you." His response was an awkward and almost relieved noise of amusement.

Since then, it was just a thing. Sure, some days that meant spooning with her best friend but there was nothing there. They'd tested it as a theory at one point, more out of drunken bad decisions than anything. But even after multiple drinks deep, they still concluded that while the other was objectively good-looking to them and a person they liked, there was a distinct absence of any attraction there.

A point only emphasized by the fact Ella was rudely awoken by the alarm and the slap of an armed landing across her head as James attempted to fumble the clock into silence. "Tell me again why you won't just move the damn thing to your side?" she grumbled, reaching to switch it off with practiced efficiency as she hauled herself from under the covers. "For the hundredth time, there's no plug for it on this side," he muttered with a yawn, padding off for a shower as she disappeared to get coffee brewed.

A practiced routine that meant they switched and soon he was at the door with her keys in hand as she wandered out jamming the last few pins into the twist in her hair in an attempt to hide that she'd run out of time to get it all the way dry.

* * *

Predictably, the day manager was waiting to give James the run-through as they walked to clock in and stow away their stuff. He was oddly smug about a client booking one of the suites as he added that they had booked the lounge for a private function till midnight. "Special request that she serves them," he added with a nod at Ella over Frank's shoulder. Leaning around her friend, she managed a small but sickly-sweet smile as she bit out the response of "Mixologist, not waitress." She nearly slammed the locker door shut. "You may want to get her to rein in that attitude once you see the room." he drawled, handing a printout to James before he left without so much as a backward glance.

There was the sharp hiss of a breath pulled between teeth that got her attention, reading over his shoulder "Stewart. I don't like sending anything less than a duo where he's concerned, especially not that far from everyone else." referring to the lounge on the floor below the suites, fairly regularly used by occupants of the suites above it but not usually with such specific requests.

Ella frowned for a moment, knowing acutely that there was no saying no. It was, technically, a reasonable request and he was one of their more well-known regulars in the city. Namely, people still trusted him, he still held sway with local law and despite no longer being a DA he was still someone the bosses wanted to keep happy. "Barback." she spoke suddenly, dragging his piercing gaze to her "Fulfill the request, send me with a barback. I can grit my teeth and play waitress for the night, but we'll still have numbers."

It was obvious from his expression that James didn't like this, but it was the safest solution either of them could see. Calling over one of the back-of-house staff, Ella had to wonder if his choice had been deliberate given that young Sam was training for the fire department so looked suspiciously like he could be a bodyguard.

Escorting them personally to the lounge, he didn't miss the slight quirk of Clyde's brow at the addition of the barback - holding the former DA's gaze until he'd backed out the room with the usual respectful incline of his head and gentle click of the doors.

As Ella directed Sam to sort ice and make a start on garnishes, Clyde spoke up from the middle of the half dozen or so companions seated around him, "Frank seems intent on keeping a man at your side." he commented smoothly, watching her with that same easy confidence as last time "Anyone would think he doesn't trust me around you." there were a couple of chuckles from his suited buddies as Ella grabbed the pad and pen from behind the bar, approaching with her best attempt at polite and cheerful "Health and safety. We all take our jobs very seriously." holding his gaze stubbornly before letting it swing round the group "Drinks?" never dropping her eyes too long as she noted the orders.

The night went along much the same way. In the downtime, she would quietly teach Sam some basic bar skills, the numbers gradually dwindling until it was just Clyde and them waiting out the clock.

The second the clock hit midnight, Ella was quietly covering the trays and setting up the clean glasses. Clyde watched intently as he leaned his forearms on the bar, eventually extending a large hand towards her "Where're my manners? I'm—" it likely wasn't her smartest move but she cut him off as politely as she could, shaking his hand as briefly as could be considered polite before trying to retract her hand "Mister Stewart. We're briefed on all suite guests." her customer service persona slipping just slightly when he didn't release his grip on her hand. "Please, call me Clyde. I didn't catch your name?" despite his charming tone, Ella couldn't help but feel like offering that information was a terrible idea. "Bentley," she answered quietly, not about to give out any more information than he could get from the name tag pinned neatly to her waistcoat.

Tags only ever displayed surnames, perhaps a first initial in the very rare cases where they had multiple staff with the same surname. Ella had never thought to ask why, perhaps it was just a personal preference of the bosses or maybe they had decided it was more professional.

Finally releasing her hand, Clyde chuckled "Bentley and Frank?" though Ella didn't respond beyond a tight smile as she motioned for them to leave, locking the doors quietly once everyone was out. Trying to ignore the way Clyde leaned on the doorframe - objectively, still a reasonable distance from her but personally far too close for her liking.

Swallowing the mix of suspicion and annoyance, she imitated James's respectful little nod with a politely spoken "Goodnight, Mister Stewart" before leading Sam back along to one of the staff lifts so she could check in with Frank and Sam could get back to his work.

When her friend saw the slight frown furrowing her brow, he motioned her behind the front desk "Are you all right?" concern and a protective tone dripped from his words as she waved off his question. "I'm fine. He's just very... intense. It's the constant feeling of being watched, studied, it's exhausting," she responded almost tiredly, briefly rubbing at her face with her hands before she pulled herself back together to ask, "Where am I needed for the rest of the shift?" which only got a response of it being a slow night so she could man the main bar, but it was unlikely she'd have much actual work to do.

CHAPTER 3

You'd almost be forgiven for thinking that 'work issues' could stay neatly contained at work. But the world isn't so black and white, plus whatever power writes the script of reality has a seriously twisted sense of humor.

That was the only explanation Ella could fathom as she strolled through the market, easily navigating with an arm full of bags, for encountering the main work issue of Clyde Stewart and his disturbingly astute gaze.

She had been mid-way through her usual chipper banter, carefully adding the new items to her bags "No Frank today?" the elderly man asked cheerily. He was met with a brief chuckle from her, an endearingly gentle sound like a warm blanket "Not today. Work has been hectic, and he needs the rest - though he'll probably perk up the second he smells this. Seriously, you outdo yourself with every new batch." she complimented with genuine warmth to her that Clyde had yet to see, noting how broad her accent was compared to within the hotel as the elderly man bashfully waved her away.

"Surely a woman like you could perk him up - though the bread is a nice touch." while his voice was smooth and light, it still had Ella focusing on keeping her breathing slow as he easily fell into stride with her. Without giving her much room to argue, he took advantage of a bottle-neck in the crowd to scoop the bags from her arm into one hand, like some play to make sure she talked to him.

"Whatever you're assuming, Mister Stewart, I'm fairly certain you've got it wrong." just because she wasn't at work didn't mean she could talk without filter, one wrong step could still cost her an earful from the bosses. "We out in the world, just call me Clyde," he reminded her, a hint of amusement lacing his next comment "Oh? Was assumin' from his territorial behavior that you two were a thing."

"All right then, *Clyde*," she deliberately, almost sarcastically, drowned it in emphasis "No offense, but I don't see how that'd be any of your business, either way." a heavy arm draping casually around her shoulders as they walked, Ella fighting her instinctive reflex to slap his hand away from where it rests over her far shoulder, thumb brushing the side of her neck.

"Call it curiosity, it happens when you've been doing business at the same place for so long. You want to know what makes them tick." his tone is deliberately light, thumb shifting to rub insistent circles in the tense muscle under it.

The clatter of keys in her hand as they near a little car has him shifting slightly to walk at her back. Nearly crowding her as she opens the boot and reaches for the bags with a polite but detached 'Thanks' - instead, he sets them inside himself, reaching with next to no effort to briskly close the boot, not moving his keen gaze from her. "I imagine I'll be seeing you again soon, have a nice day, *Ella.*"

It's not till she's sat in the driver's side, huffing in annoyance, that it hits. He called her by her first name. How in the hell did he find that out? Tamping down the flare of panic and anger as she drove home, she'd deal with that little issue at work, but she couldn't raise it yet without basically ensuring James would be an insufferable mother hen for goodness knows how long. He still maintained that while she had grown up in a 'rough area', the sort of people who frequented the hotel was another kind of dangerous altogether.

A couple of days later, a rare night off.

"What's your trouble with Stewart?" Ella asked as nonchalantly as she could manage, leaning on the island as he cooked. It wasn't that she couldn't cook, but she found nowhere near the same joy in it as James did -

much more content to tick off a list and lug ingredients back. If she hadn't been watching so carefully, she probably would have missed the way he stood up just a little straighter before responding without even glancing back at her "He's a regular client of the hotel - I just struggle to get a read on him, it makes me nervous." he admitted simply, finally casting a glance at her over his shoulder "Why the sudden interest?" it wasn't accusatory but Ella could already hear the concern edging into his voice.

"Ran into him at the market, the one near work with the bread you like..." she muttered, trying to keep her voice as if she was talking about something as mundane as the weather but he still turned slowly to lean on the counter facing her "He seemed interested in what we were, called me Ella. I don't know, it feels like he sees so much..." while the comment about him knowing her name had made him briefly frown in worry, the final comment prompted a nod of understanding as he mumbled something about it being the lawyer in him, constantly observing.

"Ella, are you all right?" he asked kindly, rounding the island to wrap his arms around her shoulders, letting her rest her head back against his chest - hence being able to feel her nod before she hummed, "I'm fine."

There was a dragging silence, punctuated only by the steady low simmer of the pot before James broke the silence after pressing a kiss to the top of her head. "He probably got your name from the day manager. What a prick," he said so casually that Ella couldn't help the snort of laughter as her expression shifted to one of agreement, neither thinking that highly of the day manager and his bizarrely pompous attitude. Nor his superiority complex regarding the night crew.

* * *

It's another quiet week of shifts before James is seeking her out in the main bar with a sympathetic half-smile. "Again?" Ella almost whines, casting a glance back down at the bar knowing full well it would have to be heaving for him to justify a 'no'. It's met with a discrete nod as he escorts her through reception to the function room next to the restaurant. A reassuring hand on the small of her back as he speaks softly, "I'll be at the front desk, barring any major disruptions, and it's a formal meal so there's a duo of wait staff."

The fact it seemed to be more of a private event and less of some intimate gathering did well to soothe her, along with the comfort of working in a team. Normally, she didn't get rattled, but something about how familiar he was, had left her on edge.

"At last," Clyde speaks up from the head of the table as Ella steps away to move behind the bar. "Gents, you're in for a treat tonight. Especially the whiskey lovers among you." he's so casually confident in his attitude, fixing James with a slow smile. "Thank you, Frank, that's all for now." her friend gave a tight nod and a final glance to emphasize his reassurance from earlier. He returned to his usual post at the front desk, the doors closing behind him with an almost inRolls Royceble click.

After a while, she almost relaxes, content to make small talk with those who approach for cocktails, apparently with zero self-doubts even if they're enjoying the brightest fruity drink she can make. It's nice - they're eager to share stories of holidays with their wives as she works, sometimes asking for recommendations if they were to stay there.

As the night wears on and the atmosphere becomes jollier, she's soon part of what seems to be a game. The guests coming up with increasingly obscure cocktails to try and stump her - so far, she's yet to be caught out. Clyde seems to be watching with amusement, even when he's pulled into a conversation, she's uncomfortably aware of his gaze.

Though not as aware of his presence, as it turns out when she realizes too late that it's him who has sidled up to the bar.

"Workin' so hard and not even breakin' a sweat, quite impressive." His small smile was unexpectedly endearing as he leans his forearms on the cool wood surface to get just that little bit closer.

"Glass of Borough... and one for yourself." his offer was met by the scripted reply that she can't due to this and that in the code of conduct. "Shame. You'll just have to join me for one when you're *not* working then." The assumption that she doesn't get a say in it rubs her up the wrong way.

A lot does about Clyde. He's not bad looking, he seems polite enough but the observing kicks in her fight or flight. The focused attention makes her nervous, jittery - but she can't be completely sure as to why.

CHAPTER 4

"You don't need to do this every time." James is watching from the doorway as Ella wrangles a fresh set of bedding on, despite the fact he only changed the damn thing yesterday. As she spots a rouge hair clip or t-shirt, she launches it to him and continues. "Well, yeah, I do. Look, put it down to the mysteries of women or something, but trust me, all right?" she's sporting a smile as she collects her things, tossing them on the sofa as she passes them, right on top of the pillow and neatly folded blanket.

He watches, almost marveling, as she pins a loose shirt to the inside of her jacket, all the essentials for a night in a motel disappearing into the pockets like some modern-day Mary Poppins bag. "Right, I have got the details of every motel and hotel within a fifteen-minute walk and in my self-imposed budget. Just in case." she's slipping her mobile into the pocket of her jeans, shaking her hair out the plaits it had dried in as he laughs.

Fixing him with an accusatory glare, glancing in the mirror to see what he finds so funny as if she's flashed him or something. When he composes himself enough, he collects their coats, approaching with a smile to pull her into a hug that's more like a headlock "You take this wingman thing entirely too seriously." though he appreciates it, generally not the most social it's nice to have a close friend who 'gets' him. Ella ducks out of his hold to be able to speak clearly, practically herding him out the door. "Anything worth doing is worth doing right."

It may be a wine bar sort of club but it's about the only place they agree on, Ella resisting anywhere that essentially requires a dress to get past the door, James screamingly out of place in the pool halls and dive bars she doesn't mind.

As usual, he needs no help to get flirting, Ella's presence more a confidence booster than anything else - he usually feels sleazy going out to deliberately pick up women, but her reassurance that there are almost definitely women out doing the same, helps soothe that.

It's no surprise when he finds her at the bar to say he's going, the whole 'checking on his friend' thing doing wonders for the woman waiting with a lip caught between her teeth.

Now she's flying solo, she chances the club down the street. Louder, busier, and generally the perfect place to get lost in your head and good music.

This is exactly what she gets to do, an easy smile on her face among the crowds of people moving like an ocean to the music. It's close quarters, bumping into others isn't exactly a rarity, but it's the deliberate tap on her shoulder after a while that has her pausing. Turning, she finds herself face-to-face with someone who looks like security. Quirking a brow, knowing she's done nothing to warrant getting kicked out, she waits for the muscle to speak.

"Ella?" He leaned to her ear so she can hear him, prompting a slow nod from her before he continues, "Boss wants a word. Follow me."

Well, shit, that's not good. But Ella follows, familiar enough with the place that she's not going to find herself stuck in a hall somewhere, but skimming through her list of if she even knows the owner. Maybe he's been to the hotel or something? Did he maybe own that bit on the restaurant street she did some shifts at years ago?

The whirr of thoughts came to a screeching halt as she stepped up the small staircase into the VIP section and Muscles McGee finally stepped to the side to reveal his 'boss' reclining on the couch. All that time in the city and yet now she couldn't seem to shake the bearded bastard.

"Ella…" losing a battle to hide the slight smile that was probably helped by the booze in her system, tone a mix of amusement and something that spoke to her noting how he kept appearing. "No company tonight?" he asked, a teasing tone as he pats the seat next to him, holding her gaze stubbornly.

"Take it that's rhetorical since you seem to know a

shockin' amount about me." Her response was more casual than she'd usually allow with someone she barely knew, sauntering over to drop into the seat and taking a moment of pride at the expression on his face. Like the comment or delivery had caught him off guard.

Clyde recovered well though, dropping an arm from along the back of the seat to turn more towards her. "Well, knowledge is kind of key to the job," he responded. "Former or current?" came her quick wit response. He wasn't expecting her verbal parry like that, but he couldn't say he didn't enjoy it. A breath of laughter laced through his words as he responded slowly, "Both."

"Little overdressed for a nightclub, aren't you?" Ella says, propping her head against her hand as she leans on the back of the seat. Clyde responds with a shrug, the hint of an easy smile just noticeable through the beard, "Business. It's not all cocktails and fancy dinners." Clyde's voice is tinged with good-natured humor, though he can't confirm if the candid attitude is because he doesn't have someone higher in the food chain to fear or because her company is loosening him up.

"A hard life for some..." Ella teases, one of those smiles that looks on the verge of laughter pulling his gaze from hers to focus on her lips in a way that has her suppressing a shiver. It certainly sobers her up faster than a bucket of ice over the head.

Thankfully, she regains composure, tactfully nudging the conversation to his time as a DA, figuring getting him to talk about himself is a fairly safe zone. Absentmindedly sipping the drink, a server brings by at one point, taking longer than she cares to note to realize he's either very astute or she's easy to read in that Clyde had correctly guessed rum and coke as her poison.

She was gingerly accepting a second glass when Clyde started with the questions about her time before the hotel - seeming near fascinated by how casually she appeared to treat all the traveling, but thoroughly confused why she'd stayed in Boston of all places. It was because it was his hometown, but Ella had no such prior connection to sway her time there - it seemed to take him by surprise that the city and its people had grown on her. She stayed because she didn't feel that pull to go be somewhere else, at least for the moment.

An hour later

It was late as they stood outside, Ella turned up the collar of her coat against the cold as she bid goodbye, and turned to start her walk - scrolling through her options on her phone to start calling someone. "Ella," her name called along the pavement startled her slightly, stopping to turn back. "It's late, get in the car. I'll drop you off on the way, where to?"

Ella huffed as she strolled back. "I don't know yet, probably the first motel along the way that has vacancies."

Clyde looked thoroughly confused for a second before folding his arms when he leaned back against the car door. "A vacancy?" earning him a joking roll of the eyes. "Motels, huh? Gotta give Frank his space to get his groove on."

Clyde seems much less intimidating when he laughs, more regular. Stepping to leave barely a couple of inches between them, he's holding her gaze again. "Or…maybe you can come back to my place."

Ella checks out Clyde before her gaze drops under the guise of checking her phone before he adds, "There's a guest room at my place that hardly ever gets used." He looks at her lips as Ella's bottom one is stuck between her teeth in thought, her expression revealing rough ideas of naughty things she could do. But a bad thought occurs to cancel the rest out - her bosses would be pissed that she's socializing with one of their top clients. She'll be out of a job when word gets around. Still, a better offer than faffing around finding a motel room. Ella nods, getting into the car as Clyde holds the door for her before shutting it with more care than she thought possible from the broad-shouldered man.

CHAPTER 5

Clyde caught Ella's slight surprise, "Hmm" as she got out of the car, staring up at his place with a vaguely-amused frown. Passing her a little closer than was necessary, he quirked a brow.

"Not what you were expectin'?" a hint of teasing to his tone as she shrugged when they stepped into the elevator.

"Kind of? Your type tends to favor tradition. They show up in nice cars that are classics. When they talk about homes, it's some big mansion in the suburbs," Ella says it offhand, more thinking aloud than anything else. He turns, hands casually in his pant pockets as he speaks in a low voice "My type?" Ella can vaguely hear a warning in her head that she's said something she shouldn't have, gotten too cocky - but the part of her brain that's been drizzled in rum is running the show now, prompting her to turn her head to him briefly "Crime lord, mob boss, however, you want to dress it up." by her tone, you'd be forgiven for thinking she was discussing something as mundane as the weather.

A huff of laughter as he guided her out of the elevator with a light hand between her shoulder blades reassured her a little that she wasn't immediately about to end up dead or jobless. "Well, aren't you just full of surprises..." he chuckled, Ella subtly shaking a little of the tension from her shoulders as she followed him through the open-plan space. "It's not quite Borough, but it's pretty damn good." his comment brought her attention back as he set two glasses on the counter in front of him, his gaze flitting up to hold hers, almost looking out from under those lashes "Believe you owe me a drink."

Ah, fuck.

Don't make bad decisions, don't make bad decisions, don't make bad decisions...

A simple drink stood leaning against the counter - turned into deeper conversation and little nudges - which eventually ended up as easy banter on the sofa. Clyde reclined like a king on his throne as Ella sat sort of side-on, legs curled under her as she rests her shoulder against the back of the cushions. Eventually, probably when he'd leaned to laugh about some comment she'd made, Clyde dropped the hand of his arm along the back, drawing nonsense patterns on her shoulder with his fingertips. A move Ella was well aware she should have handled at the time, but she found herself not minding it enough to care.

"I'm doubtin' your bosses care that much about what

happens with guests if you're not on the clock." Clyde spoke up, his voice a low rumble, whether intentionally or not "'Sides, I can't be that bad if you're here." he teased lightly, looking at her with that slight quirk of a smile as if waiting for the reveal of some secret.

"You're un-nerving," she speaks with a smile, and he nearly chokes on his drink containing a laugh, his expression prompting her to continue as his touch becomes firmer on her shoulder, straying to the side of her neck "You just casually stroll straight into familiarity with people." Clyde can't help but smile at how the drinks have loosened her tongue, sounding more and more like the easy-going Scot he'd witnessed at the market "Plus, you look at folk like you can see everything." there's laughter laced in her words as she seems to realize how much she's rambling. "Not quite everything," he muses, picking vaguely at the sleeve seam of her t-shirt; her face heating as her brain catches up. "You're proving my point, Clyde," she comments quietly, the hint of amusement in her voice as she shakes her head.

He shrugs, it's a gesture done with such ease, he quite clearly has very little cause to worry about how he comes across, he's practically oozing self-assured confidence. "Not a clue what you mean, I'm just enjoying a good drink and some gorgeous company." keeping his tone light, he lets his hand rest cradling the side of her neck, thumb brushing over her pulse point almost possessively.

It takes every ounce of her remaining ability not to shiver, the only giveaway he's gotten any reaction to is a slightly longer blink and a shaky breath pulled sharply through her nose. At this point, Ella would be surprised if he couldn't feel the way her heart is running a mile a minute, despite her calm demeanor, she was sure she must be practically vibrating like a hummingbird.

Despite all the moving, she's never been involved with a guest or a co-worker. No matter how easygoing she behaved that was one rule that always seemed to stick with her. But Boston was blurring that line. She and Frank were friends, they were both crystals clear about that, but they'd had the chance to be friends a while longer than anywhere else she'd lived - hell, they were close enough for people to assume they were a couple, as evidenced by Clyde thinking exactly that. Was time an excuse to loosen her rules a bit? Or was it just the haze of a tipsy brain speaking?

A hand on her knee pulls her out of those spiraling thoughts that had prompted a small frown to grow on her expression, pulling in a steadying breath as she realizes just how much closer he is. It wouldn't take much to just reach out and...

Her fingers trail through his beard till he's pressing his cheek into her palm with something like a sigh. That does it. The thin thread of restraint snaps as she closes the gap, leaning to brush her lips teasingly along his, gently catching his bottom lip briefly between her teeth before letting it slip free as she leans back slightly. It's more to gauge his reaction than anything, the way he chased telling her she's not about to make a complete tit of herself for misreading the situation.

There's haste, and desperation, in how they narrowly dodge noses to lock the other in a kiss. The grip at her knee was firm but careful as he uses his hold to ease her across till, she straddles his lap, large hands splaying over her back to drag her tightly against his chest. She doesn't fight it, a hand weaving into his hair as the other slips under his jacket to map the hard plains of his chest under his shirt.

A roll of her hips has him grinding out a drawn-out "Fuck..." between clenched teeth, his head falling back over the cushions as she hides a gentle chuckle by unhurriedly lavishing attention on his neck. Ella can't lie, that reaction is a hell of an ego boost. A hand at the nape of her neck pulls her up as he starts speaking as calmly as he can "We've had a few drinks-" but Clyde is pulled up short when he locks his gaze with her, her eyes focused and clear.

He'd been ready to play the moral and polite gentleman. To bemoan their drinking and express how much he wanted her, but sober enough to remember every second of it. That little plan was quickly going up in smoke - taking with it the finely crafted demeanor he used in public, true nature bubbling through like a pot on high heat.

Shifting them, he near slammed her back into the cushions below as he pinned her with his weight settled between her thighs. Ending up tangled and grinding against each other like a pair of horny teenagers, him having been taken slightly by surprise at the speed she'd shucked off his jacket.

"Someone's eager." his rumbling teasing prompted a gentle chuckle from her as she made to prop herself up slightly, Clyde smoothly pulling the arm out from under her to press her hand into the arm of the sofa above her head. "Let's get you to bed," it near groaned into her throat as he brushed his beard against the skin of her clavicle, smirking at the barely hidden whimper he pulled from her. "Dinner?" his question was collected and controlled, Ella taking a moment for her brain to catch up and nod when she didn't trust her voice.

Smiling slowly, he stood, extending a hand to pull her to her feet as he led her down the corridor to the guest room. Standing at her back in the doorway, he noted the shaking breath she pulled in, speaking softly against the shell of her ear "Get some rest. We'll go out for dinner, do it right, then I can take you apart piece by fucking piece till you don't even remember your name."

Well, fuck. That's one way to shut up the usually quick-witted smart-arse.

"Thank you," it came out much weaker than she'd been aiming for, clearing her throat quietly to try and sort her voice "For letting me stay tonight." the hum of thought behind her almost sounded amused before he moved away, steps retreating to his room as she closed the door and leaned back heavily against it.

CHAPTER 6

Clyde woke the next morning to Ella wrestling her way back into her boots while muttering a string of colorful threats at the hem of her jeans that keep getting stuck in the teeth of the zips.

"Morning, someone seems chipper for how much they drank." he greets with amusement as he passes where she's sat on an ottoman, going through the habit of setting the machine with a pod to sort his morning coffee. Once it's brewed, he turns to lean against the counter, watching her over the rim of the mug, the edges of his eyes crinkling with a smile.

Ella sits up finally once her boots are zipped, greeting him with a slight breathy "Mornin'." and a bright smile as she stands, "You may have the size advantage to process that much, but I have the genetics. Scots may get sunburn on a rainy day, but we don't get hangovers." she comments proudly, only half-joking as she notes a shrill alert from her phone that her cab is there, making towards the door.

Clyde catches her gently by the elbow, maneuvering till she's between him and the wall. "We still on for dinner?" he asked with that soft gravel to his voice that has her swallowing thickly as she nods "Excellent. I'll text you the details," he responds with a small smile as he opens the door for her, relishing the way she doesn't seem to trust her voice to speak as she leaves.

* * *

By the time Ella gets home, she notices the bedding in the wash basket and the set she took off back on the bed. There's the telltale sound of running water and she's glad Clyde had an en suite because she'd hate to be feeling grotty and have to wait for God knows how long for James to be done.

She's just about to leave the room when she spies a very specific box poking out from under the bed as if it wasn't put back properly, making a mental note to torment the hell out of James at least once today as she heads through to put on some coffee and wait sat on the counter of the island as she works her way through a large glass of cold water. The smell of brewed coffee lures him down the hall in a towel, startling slightly when he sees her perched on the counter wiggling her eyebrows at him. "Good night, Pandora?" she teases as he makes a coffee to take back to the room while he dresses. Despite the flush she can see creeping up his neck, he plays it cool "Mhm, we're getting drinks next week." James responds, taking a long sip of his coffee before tilting his head slightly and asking off-hand, "Where did you end up staying?"

Barely managing not to react, Ella waves off the comment "Unimportant, you two are going for drinks? Isn't the date supposed to come *before* the kinky sex?" the cheeky smile stretching across his face telling her exactly what he was about to say as he left to go get dressed. *Prim and proper Frank? Yeah right.*

Her phone goes off as the bedroom door clicks shut, Ella is immediately grateful that James can't see the way she's biting her lip as she reads the message from someone whom he's not a massive fan of.

"Thursday, 7 pm, Rossi's. Meet you there."

She's jostled by the soft pad of footsteps, James rounding into her sightline as he finishes buttoning his shirt. "Out with it, where did you stay?" he smiles triumphantly when she blushes. "What poor man's soul did you suck out?" he nudges her knee as she leans next to where she's sat, earning himself a sharp swat to the shoulder.

"None. I went to a club after you went home, met someone, crashed at his, no hanky-panky and we're out again on Thursday." As much as Ella hated even just omitting information from him, she was hoping it would satisfy him and she could move on with the day. The look he gave her was framed by a subtle frown, obviously more suspicious because she was being unusually cagey when they were usually almost uncomfortably open with each other. "Who's the guy? It's not exactly reassuring if you can't tell me," his voice was soft with a tone of concern.

Ella said it so fast and so muttered he could barely tell she was speaking, carefully prompting her to try again with a reassuring hand on her knee as she took a deep breath. "Clyde Stewart..." to his shame, his first reaction was the working code of conduct that didn't exactly look kindly on staff fraternizing with guests. Though, it was quickly followed by personal concern given his affection for Ella and his wariness toward Stewart.

Arranging his features to what he hopes is minimal judgment, he squeezes her knee "Keep it professional at work... and text me while you're out so I know you're not in a boot or a hospital bed somewhere, okay?" he speaks quietly, a gentle smile at the way she visibly relaxed and pulls him into a hug. "Promise," she murmured, slightly muffled by his shoulder.

* * *

A couple of shifts pass without incident, just the monotony of manning the main bar through the night and one incident of an irate guest who ordered a 'gin and tonic, but make sure it's grey goose' who then refused to listen and caused a scene when she explained that Grey Goose wasn't a gin. According to the guest, she was an idiot who didn't know what they were talking about.

Not the worst she'd had, by far, but she was still snappy by the end of her shift and James ended up bribing her with fresh pastries from the deli around the corner to put her in a better mood when she woke up. Neither of them was happy when she got pulled in for the Wednesday day shift, but she muscled through under the understanding she'd get the next two days off - no hustling to come in for days and any night shifts they'd find a cover for.

It was worth working the hectic day shift for that.

* * *

"James," Ella had her eyes down, fixed on her phone as he glanced up from the sofa, doing a quick double take as he noted how she was dressed, the beep of his phone barely pulling his attention away as she looked up "I've shared my location with you, just so you know I'm not dead. Not going to lie, probably not going to be back tonight."

She almost sounds nervous, so he chooses not to make it worse with judgment or his own opinion of Clyde as he quirks a brow with a cheeky smile at the little black dress, flattering but pretty modest, her hair up in a nicer version of the twist she's so fond of. "You look nice, relax." he soothes, earning himself a kiss pressed to the top of his head as she passes.

* * *

It would usually be a manageable walk, but she's not about to risk it in heels so springs for a cab. Thankfully, it's the right call, judging by the rain that sweeps in when they're about halfway there - the short dash to the door a lot less hellish than if she'd got caught walking in that weather.

It doesn't take much to spot Clyde, watching the door with a spirit in hand. Ella tries not to smile as she makes her way over and she sees the slight frown flit across his expression for just a second before he's standing as if he didn't recognize her at first glance.

"Ms. Bentley," her smile breaks through at that as he presses a kiss to her cheek, pulling out her chair in a move that would usually have her rolling her eyes. But with him, it doesn't come across like a ploy to come across better, it comes across like habit or another subtle example of the power he oozes - it's almost endearing.

"No need to be all formal now, Clyde." There's a teasing edge to Ella's voice, though her nerves are well hidden to the average person it comes with the territory of crime that he can pick them up a mile away, that less polished side of him admittedly enjoying it probably a bit too much.

"You look gorgeous," it's almost growled, Clyde catching her gaze because he knows it'll get her to blush, even if she manages to keep her other reactions in check.

"Thank you... It's high praise coming from you, handsome as ever." he can't help the way his smile grows at that, almost able to see it on her face as she cringes as if her words are 'too much. "Sorry, I'm a little rusty..." it's almost a grumble, the slightest hint of amusement laced through it like humor is her go-to defense as she distracts herself with the menu.

"Surely, you're not out of practice at dating. Aside from the endearing personality..." he makes a discrete sweeping gesture at her that prompts a brief chuckle from her. "I'm surprised you could make the time for me."

That earns him a laugh, even if she keeps the volume down. "Truthfully, it's been years since I went on a date. It's a hazard of work." He makes a noise in his throat that sounds like he knows all too well what she means, the stuffiness finally fading away again.

* * *

Thankfully, by the time they leave, the weather has cleared up somewhat - it's no longer raining at least. As they step out into the street, Clyde has a firm arm around her waist, glancing questioningly at his Rolls Royce almost to ask if she's coming with him or waiting for a cab. When she makes no effort to disentangle herself, instead almost tucking herself more firmly against his side, he feels the slight rush of achievement. Things rarely don't go his way, but he's still proud this was something that stayed true to that statement.

CHAPTER 7

A near-perfect gentleman the whole drive - aside from the hand resting heavily, easily, on Ella's knee like it was the natural thing for him to do. The walk up to his apartment is much the same, polite hand on the small of her back to guide her, but it's settled just a smidge lower than could be deemed safely good manners.

As Clyde closes the door behind them, she's shifting almost awkwardly in the hall as if unsure of where to go - or even what to do with herself, if he's assuming correctly that the thing, she does with pressing at her wrists is a nervous tic - but he's all too happy to lead, jacket hung up and loosening his tie as he steps around her leisurely.

"I believe I made you a promise," he may have only tested it a couple of times, but he assumes right that it has a blush slowly burning despite her keeping her expression and stance calm, prompting a small smirk as he moves to ease her against his chest by his grip at her waist. "You play the ballbuster well, but I'm beginning to like the real you more." He feels her bristle slightly at the idea the burning-faced tongue-tied bag of nerves is the 'real' her, a breath of a chuckle against her neck as he casually cages her between the wall and his firm chest.

"Make no mistake Stewart, I 'play' at nothing. Just because you caught me on the back foot a few times—" He cuts her off with a demanding kiss, tongue teasing along the crease of her lips as he coaxes her to let him in, wasting no time once she does in deepening the kiss and making her head spin. Clyde can't help the smirk that tugs ever so slightly at his lips when he feels her knees go weak, relishing the way one of her hands grazes the back of his neck before sinking into his hair with a gentle tug.

Caging her in his arms, pressing her tightly against his chest, he lifts her just that little bit to where she can barely skim the ground, walking them both with determination and purpose into the bedroom. When he finally lets Ella get her feet properly on the floor again, pulling back only slightly to nose at where the neckline of her dress had firmly kept any cleavage under wraps but given him free rein of every inch of her throat and clavicle, something he takes advantage of in the form of the occasional nip of his teeth.

* * *

It takes a second, but he notices the drag of her hand down his chest, teasing over the buttons of his shirt as she passes until she cups his aching crotch in her palm, eliciting a sharp inhale from him before he's mouthing at the sensitive point behind her ear as one large hand easily circles her neck, exerting the barest amount of pressure but it's enough to pull a mewl from those lips.

If only based on her face, she seems floaty, heart hammering at giving over control. But her hands tell a different story, working with measured assurance to release him from the confines of the fabric. Clyde can't help but grind out a low, "Fuck..." nipping at her earlobe when she takes him in hand with the same confident finesse, he's watched her wield behind the bar. Palm twisting over the sensitive head to slick him with the pre-cum and ease the strokes that have his chest heaving as he shucks off the shirt

When they reach the edge of the bed, he tries to turn the tables, but a firm plant of her heel has him pausing. Almost allowing her to nudge him till he drops to sit on the edge, planting slow worshipping presses of her lips along a shoulder, taking her time as she moves lower, the hand from his hair trailing to follow the same path until the gentle noise of one knee then the other hitting the rug perks his ears.

The way Ella's looking up at him through her lashes is anything but nervous, stroking his ego when he remembers just how flustered he can make her. Another reminder, though far from needed, of his power over those around him. But his mind quickly decides there's something more important to focus on as he feels the slow stroke of her hand that's joined by the drag of her tongue before pulling him achingly slowly into the heat of her mouth. The urge to shiver when he feels nestled deep in her throat, nose pressed tight against his pelvis, is strong - but as she starts to move, his focus is on the hand that fists in her hair, the other still laying around her throat as he feels himself move within her.

Without exerting much pressure, it spurs her on, the steady swirl of her tongue making his grip tighten in her hair as she moves faster, hollowing her cheeks as the hand cradling his sac feels them tighten, taking him as deep as she can when he unravels, swallowing around him as he comes in ropes down her throat. "Fuckin' hell...." the hand in her hair moves to smooth through the strands as she seems in no hurry, tongue dragging gently along the underside until she releases him with a quiet pop to sit back on her haunches.

Cradling her cheek in a hand, dragging his thumb along her bottom lip, he watches that slightly dazed look flit across her eyes. "More than just a gorgeous smile, good girl." the edge of the growl to his voice has her barely hiding the sharp intake of breath.

"Up," Clyde's command is firm, steadying her by moving his grip to her waist as she gets gingerly to her feet, near dragging her to stand to flush against him between his knees, carefully easing down the zip of her dress as slow as he can, purely to feel the way her excited trembling increases as he nears the end of the zip. A tug at the end of the track has it pooling around her feet, though she doesn't seem that fazed to be left in heels and the silky Brazilian cut knickers. "Well, that's a pleasant surprise..." his words are muffled against her skin as he drags open-mouthed kisses over the swell of her breast, shamelessly holding her to him by a firm grip at her rear. The only crack in her composure is a moan carried on a breath when he catches a nipple between his teeth just on that line between pleasure and pain.

It's oddly graceful, the way Clyde pulls back and twists, bringing Ella to land on the bed and allowing him to hover above her. "Shh, I've got you," the words send a shiver through her that has her sinking her teeth into her lip as he eased the silky material down her legs, shuffling out the last of his barely-hanging-on clothes. The warning she got was a firm trailing of hands from her hips, down her thighs till they rested on her knees - the next she knew, he'd manhandled them apart and settled his shoulders between her thighs as he proved his tongue wasn't just talented as a wordsmith. It was almost embarrassing how quickly he had her tumbling over that edge of bliss, a firm suck at her bundle of nerves finally prompting an almost choked whine of his name as she tensed, trying to re-muster the brainpower to move away as he kept up his sweet torture despite her sensitivity, dragging another mind blanking orgasm from her with a huskily spoken stream of encouragement "Come on, you can give me one more.", shifting to press himself more tightly against his nook between her thighs as he built up to a third - only then drawing back with a self-satisfied smirk when her voice sounded on the verge of sobbing. "Too much, too much. Please, Clyde, stop," a chuckle washed over her skin as he climbed her body to catch her in a dominating kiss that felt like it set every nerve in her alight.

Clyde swallowed down Ella's high-pitched moans as he worked a finger into her heat, swiftly adding another as he worked to make sure she could handle him. That consideration didn't last long as he flipped her, Ella moving fast enough to messily get her knees under her and an arm to stop her face from hitting the mattress at least. That stability was short-lived as she heard the crack of skin on skin, jolting her forward slightly as he moved behind her, making a pleased hum at what she assumed was the already red mark on her backside from his handprint.

Clyde was in no hurry as he slid his cock into her, a firm grip on her hips as he took a second to savor being buried to the hilt rather than watching her from the other side of the bar. He walked his knees apart, nudging hers together before he set an almost brutal pace, his ego relishing the way she babbled his name amongst wanton moans and pleas not to stop. One hand slid up her spine, pushing her shoulders lower before winding into her hair to tug it slightly and prompt a hiss-of-not-pain from her before he felt her flutter around his length, taking all his self-control not to fill her up that damn second as he chased his release, the speed of his thrusts increasing.

But just as he felt that wave of pleasure cresting, he

pulled out sharply, pulling a breath through his teeth as he gave a slight tug on her hair to direct her to lie down, head tilted back off the edge of the bed. Despite the flash of annoyed expression at him directing her like a damn horse, Ella quickly got the message, relaxing her throat as she wrapped her lips around the angry tip of his cock as he fists it before nearly slamming his pelvis against her chin. His movements were forceful, firmly chasing his pleasure as she let him dictate the speed, swallowing him down as he came and nearly collapsed forward onto her - it only took a couple of insistent taps at his hip before he with Clyde so she could sit up and swallow to get her breath back.

'Sitting up was probably a generous description, more propped on the elbow of a shaking arm as he joined her back on the bed, sucking marks lazily along her neck and clavicle as she clung to him, the slight drag of nails on his back threatening to overwhelm his exhaustion. He quirked a brow as she made a move to get up, dragging her back against his chest by an arm around her waist and a low-spoken "Where do you think you're going?" the breathy burst of laughter from her making him smile slightly where he'd buried his face in her hair. Propping himself up to catch her gaze, his back to that level of observation that unnerved people and made him as successful as he was. "You're goin' nowhere sweetheart." the husky tinge to his voice had her chewing on her lip, unable or unwilling to tear her eyes from him "Get some rest, I'm not done with you yet."

If she'd been more coherent, she'd probably have caught the ominous note to that. Instead, she was all too happy to listen, prompting a rumbling noise of amusement later when she woke up first and got a little creative with his wake-up call - not that he was complaining.

CHAPTER 8

It was late the following evening before Ella eventually made it home, already curled up and dead to the world by the time James came home from work. Admittedly, he may have curled up a little tighter to her, glad she was home safe and sound despite the reassurance of her location just a click away on his phone.

* * *

It was a few days later while pottering around the city doing long procrastinated errands, that Frank eventually broached the subject of her date - using the ins of her excitedly asking about his. "How'd it go?" he asked carefully, relaxing slightly at the snort of laughter that bubbled out of her.

"Well, despite being rusty as hell - it didn't go too bad. We had some laughs, and went somewhere nice for dinner that was surprisingly low-key..." she shrugged, fighting a smile as he fixed her with a look like he expected her to continue.

"C'mon, I doubt you want all the details." it came out laced with laughter as she nudged him with her shoulder as they made their way along the narrow sidewalk.

"Is it bad that I kind of do?" James asked, at last, keeping his eyes firmly ahead with a very slight frown on his face. "Someone I care deeply about is getting cozy with a mob boss. Surely, you can understand my concern?" there's a resigned sigh at the end of his question, prompting Ella to clutch his hand tightly.

"Thank you. But I'm a big girl... You don't have to worry, all right? You just focus on wooing that stunner some more - only you would manage to pick up a date *after* a hook-up, who also works nights." Her laugh is infectious, prompting James to jokingly look bashful, at least somewhat reassured.

Failing all else, she at least wasn't shutting him out, so he'd have plenty of opportunity to keep an eye on her. Plus, he'd already seen that Stewart had future bookings, so he'd be able to work to try and get a read on him as well.

* * *

Three further months, four hurried coffee dates, two encounters in the back of that damn Rolls Royce, and every extra shift Ella could get her grubby little mitts on.

That's what got her to the place to be able to tour the Starling Properties' new apartments, having finally decided to move out as a push to James to get serious with his lady. The same one who had since met Ella, and who had been incredibly accommodating about giving Ella a chance to make herself scarce or dragging Rob back to her little studio.

She'd packed her bags, told Rob her plans, his lady was moving in - all was going to plan. Till she got the call on the walk to work. There was a delay in construction, they would have to push back her move-in date. When James instantly jumped at the suggestion, he halts his plans till they could give her a new date, she almost aggressively refused "Worst case scenario, I'll get a long stay Airbnb. It'll be fine, it'll be grand." she responded firmly on their way out the staff locker area, unsure if she was just trying to convince him or herself as well.

Never one to dwell too much, Ella took advantage of the quiet nighttime at the bar to prop her phone out of sight and casually browse listings. She'd either find a month-to-month or bounce between motels and Airbnb until the property managers got their damn construction back on schedule and could give her a new move-in date.

A smooth voice snapped her gaze from the screen to the speaker, hurriedly worn customer service expression faltering slightly at the bearded face smiling cheekily back at her "Good evening, Mister Stewart." keeping her demeanor professional as always, "What can I help you with, sir?"

Clyde enjoyed Ella calling him that far too much, apparently breaking from habit to opt for brandy as he cast a glance back at the small group seating themselves at a table, adding on a round of beers for them.

He remembered how excited she'd been, finally getting a place when she'd let him for coffee after doing the paperwork. Once he knew it was one of the Starlings, he chanced his luck - calling in a favor to Alto Starling to come up with a way to stall the move. It'd give him the perfect chance to swoop in like the hero, bring her just a little more under his influence and it wouldn't be half bad to come home to someone after a long day.

"Looking forward to moving? Been meaning to get you a housewarming gift - maybe a nice set of tumblers," he said reaching to brush his fingertips along the back of Ella's hand as she set his glass on the bar. Ella let out a slow exhale, shoulders dropping a little.

"Delayed, I'll sort something in the meantime though. It'll all be worth it when I get to move into my bright little space with its views," she smiled brightly, the excitement still bubbling just below the surface despite the bad news.

Clyde arranged his features into the picture of sympathy, taking a sip of his drink as he appeared to think for a moment before speaking slowly, casually. "You could stay at my place, in the meantime. I'm sure there's enough storage in the guest room for your things," he added the second half at the way the color blanched slightly from her face.

Ella seemed to stumble over her words, frowning slightly as she focused on pulling the table's beers and setting them securely on a tray. "You sure? Wouldn't want to intrude…" she'd barely finished speaking before he was waving off her comment with a slight smile

"Of course, you won't be at all. It'd be a much shorter walk for you after a good night's sleep, as a bonus."

She tried to convey with her expression what she couldn't say at work - which would have been to admonish him for being a dirty bastard while she was trying to work. Rounding the bar, he followed her to the table as she put on that polite smile and set the glasses down in front of each of the men, grateful that they continued their conversations and essentially allowed her to move unnoticed. Only a couple of them silently took note of the way Clyde caught her elbow on the way past, dropping his head to speak close to her ear before she was briskly making her way back behind the bar, a flush fading from her cheeks as he joined them.

The group would thankfully be gone not long after, meaning that the bar was once again quiet when James wandered through for his break and a probably unhealthy amount of espresso. Letting the machine whir and brew, she leaned her forearms on the bar with a grin "Mean-time accommodation is sorted, so you now have no excuses to move in with that gorgeous girlfriend of yours." Ella commented happily, setting the cup filled with rich coffee in front of him, and returning to the inventory stock list she'd been busying herself with most of the night.

He perched at the bar; eyes closed as he took a long sip before apparently having the energy to interact. Perhaps it was a focus problem instead, it was archive-clearing night and that was always a bore - even for a star employee like James. He quirked a brow, watching her over the rim of his cup as if prompting her to continue, "Clyde offered his guest room." she had been expecting concern, but the scoff caught her off guard "Chance to move you in... and he offers the guest room? He's keeping his bloody options open?" There's a coldness to his voice the wariness had given way to firm dislike at some point.

Ella bristles slightly, a gentle frown tugging at her expression, "Or maybe, he just knows fine well that this is a temporary thing, that I'm far too excited for my new place to even entertain moving in with him?" there's more bite to her words than she originally intended.

Huffing out a sigh, she softens her features. "Sorry... didn't mean to snap," she murmurs. James suddenly leans across the bar to catch one of her hands in his, his gaze saying he's sincere when she raises hers to meet it. "I'm sorry, that was out of line. Perhaps I just think so highly of you, nobody is going to be 'worthy' in my eyes." Clyde's gentle smile coaxes one from Ella in return. As he finishes his Joe, James flicks through the day's newspaper as Ella sets about turning all the displayed bottles the right way around.

CHAPTER 9

"She'll be fine." the reassurance came from the woman who hopped down to wrap her arms around him, speaking against his back. Logically, he knew she was right. It was just the 'Stewart' variable to the equation that had him unable to stop it from ruminating in his head.

She was met in the below street garage by Clyde who was dressed unusually casually considering she'd only ever seen him in a suit and well... nothing. Admittedly, more than a little distracting. She must not have hidden her look of confusion very well because he chuckled as he leaned on the room, essentially blocking the open door - Ella guessed intentionally since he didn't seem to mind how she had to move against him just to get out of the damn seat. "Good manners figured would come help with your things," he explained, following close as she moved to the boot.

A couple of clatters and she was jumping slightly to grab it to sling it shut again, stood between two large rolling suitcases, a garment bag draped over her arm with the hotel logo on it. "You didn't need to Clyde, I've moved just fine on my plenty of times." he raised a brow, gaze lifting from the cases as if asking where the rest was. Ella looked vaguely amused as she shrugged "Sill not out the habit of living light I guess." was all she offered by way of explanation, putting them back-to-back as she extended the handles, pushing the pair with ease, stopping a few feet from the lift when she realized he was still leaning on the car like his brain was catching up.

* * *

He'd slung her a key, she'd shared her shift schedule with him, and she was unpacked in under an hour before they relaxed on the sofa with a takeaway to iron out the details.

"Rent." It wasn't a question, thankfully sat shoulder to shoulder so avoiding a staring contest over the terms.

"None." "Clyde." *"Ella."*

Silence stretched as she resisted the urge to comment, relenting to being the first to turn her head as she nudged her shoulder against his, prompting him to meet her gaze as she smiled.

"All right, *every couple weeks I have some guys over for poker night... personal bartender would be a nice touch, deal?"*

Shifting slightly, he slung an arm along the back of the sofa, discretely drawing her closer as he settled. "I know you were worried about your night shifts disturbing me," he was speaking carefully, not wanting to spook her but also well aware there was a perfect opportunity to draw her a little further into his net by appealing to her caring side. She nodded slowly, encouraging him to continue as he dragged a hand down his face in a tired manner, slowing over his beard "But, I don't exactly work nine-to-five either, I may need to ask some favors." he felt frustrated and groan before he heard it, a muttered comment of how that phrase never ended well.

Sitting forward, cutting all physical contact with him, she turned slightly with a serious expression "Such as?" " *People at the bar must talk to you a lot, and may need you to listen out for trouble. Or patch up some minor scrapes."* he said it so offhand, watching her reaction carefully as her shoulders relaxed and she settled back with a small 'oh, all right then'

Wait, no, that wasn't the reaction he was expecting. The confusion must have shown on Clyde's face because Ella was talking as if it were obvious "Oh, were you expecting pearl-clutching? Didn't always work in fancy hotels, you know. Only got the fancy mixologist title when I came to Boston." not noticing the way he was watching her like he was properly seeing her for the first time. Clyde had assumed she bounced between upscale hotels, a bit as Frank had done before settling in Boston. She carried herself in such a way that she didn't seem out of place there. It threw him for a bit of a loop to learn that her work history was a bit rough around the edges.

Trailing his fingertips up her neck, watching her shiver with a small smirk, Clyde couldn't help but chuckle at the change. The more he uncovered about her that painted her as a tough workaholic, the more his ego preened at how flustered he could make her. She seemed alone, happily so, aside from James - it was like good luck was serving her up on a silver platter for him.

It was a rare weekend night that she wasn't working, Ella having taken full advantage of a quiet apartment to relax on the guest bed with a good book - foregoing the usual sweatpants and hoodie for an old t-shirt and cotton shorts. It was probably a little weird, he'd seen her all shades of naked, but they were essentially flatmates - so she'd just automatically started behaving accordingly.

Until there was a tired but loud knock on the door, rousing her from the dozing she'd slipped into. Not all the way awake, she goes to the door, surveying Clyde leaning against the frame through a squint as her eyes adjusted to the light. That was when she saw the stain on his shoulder, not immediately obvious given the dark grey of the suit.

"Fuck sake, what sort of state have you gone and got

yourself in?" her voice weighted with sleep, accent thick as she gently steered him through to the main space. Clyde sank onto the edge of the sofa as she fetched the first aid kit from the kitchen (as per usual, having to hoist herself onto the counter to reach it.)

"Well, I'm not the one who made the mistake... that would be the other guy. Or, was the other guy." he near grumbled, surprised by how gently she guided his limbs out of his jacket and shirt, leaning close to get a good look at the injury.

When she made a little disgruntled noise, he raised a brow before she carefully cleaned it down with what smelled like alcohol wipes "I'll do my best when putting on the sticky stitches, but that ink might end up a bit wonky." she explained, tracing the small bit of his tattoo that had taken a little damage from the very edge of the cut. She was perched with a knee on the seat next to him, trying to move as carefully as possible. Ensuring she was steady as she unwrapped the sticky stitch strips. Dragging her across till she was sat firmly on one of his thighs, he was met by a roll of her eyes as she set to work trying to stick the strips as accurately as possible to minimize the damage. When she leaned back, double-checking her work, she made to get up but a firm hand at the back of her neck kept her in place. Pulling her towards him till their foreheads rested together, this was very much 'hands-on, don't fuck with me - Clyde', not the easily charming side that he'd been showing her the majority of the time so far.

"Get some sleep…" Ella's comment was kind, even if she sounded blunt due to being tired. The hand at the back of her neck trailed firmly down her spine until a splayed grip on her rear had him tilting her hips against his. There was something like annoyance crackling under his cool self - while he'd settled the scales about the guy who'd dared to stab him, his ego was still smarting a bit. There was a very thin thread keeping his full rage side in check, right now he just needed to reaffirm his standing, and state his need for control.

"Stay…" It wasn't a request, it wasn't a question, it was a statement of how it was going to go. Ella nodded as she got up, not holding him up but hovering close just in case. Far too often she'd seen folk who were 'fine', crumple like a paper cup once the adrenaline wore off. Keeping the sympathy off her face, she helped him mechanically out the rest of his clothes and into his bed, pausing when he caught her wrist with a pointed look. The expression she shot his way practically screamed 'really?', a disgruntled sigh of his name before she slid in next to him, rolling her eyes when he shifted to almost tucking her under him, not missing the shiver when he breathed out a rumbling thanks. Much to the approval of his fast-recovering ego, he relaxed, holding her possessively as he pulled the covers over them.

For better or for worse, there were perks to being a person who took what life threw and adapted. For better, it made for a pretty stress-free time; for worse, it could be a very dangerous trait around someone like Clyde.

CHAPTER 10

"No, it's eight like usual, isn't it? Oh, for fuck's sake, no, the day manager failed to mention he'd changed that booking. I can make that start, it's fine it's not fine. I can make it but that little shitbag is getting a piece of my mind when he comes in for his shift. Rob, I drive a banger, zero issues hitting him with it."

Ella was cradling her phone to the side of her head with her shoulder, slowly brewing a mug of tea as she stretched her stiff limbs. "You know what, give me ten or so minutes. I'm going to ring the dayshift manager - if we stay for an event, it's double time. If they have to bring me in early, it's time and a half. Going to hit him where it hurts, right in the spreadsheets - plus, he'd be on his fourth write-up for excess staffing costs and turnover, maybe they'll finally replace him with someone who can do the job." There was the telltale pad of feet behind her, promptly followed by the whirr of the coffee machine.

"Yeah, you too fucko, catch ya later," her words were laced with a chuckle as Ella fired off some quick texts to sort the event staffing while she slowly sipped at her mug.

"Problems?" Clyde asked, leaning back against the counter next to her as he drank his coffee, watching her gaze stay firmly on her phone as she made sure she wasn't going to get roped into extra hours.

"Hmm, not really. Just the day manager being his usual self - an ass." While her tone was mostly indifferent, there was an edge that this was a common thing. Finally lifting her gaze, it flits from his face to his shoulder. "How're the lines matching up?" Ella asks with a small girn. Clyde looks vaguely amused that her concern is aimed at the mark and not at him.

Rolling his shoulder almost to emphasize his point, "Almost good as new. Just in time for poker this weekend."

That gets her attention, laced with just a hint of alarm at the shift in his attitude as he faces her side, firmly running his fingertips down her spine.

"You take special requests?" he asked smoothly, earning himself a very deadpan look from her as she nods.

"Good, I'll pick you up something to wear − a bit nicer than your uniform."

It'd be easy, to pass off the extended exhale as not out of the ordinary, unless you're dealing with someone whose work relies heavily on being good with non-vocal cues. In which this case, their ego has a great time getting a reaction.

"Ominous..." she muttered, earning a chuckle as she wandered off to get her work things sorted out and try to check a few items off her to-do list.

* * *

"This is insanity! Even by your standards," James muttered. Ella, kept her eyes firmly on the road as she swung her car through the streets to work.

"I'm working. It's just... at home rather than the hotel." Her calm words were teamed with a shrug. "It's a poker night, Rob, not a mobster meetup. Relax..." A hint of a laugh weaved through her words.

He shifted in his seat, trying to phrase things delicately. "I just don't want you getting hurt."

Leaning heavily on the horn as some idiot cuts her off. "Okay, now you're being ridiculous. I can handle myself fine and you know full well that friends are the extent of my emotional connection." Pulling in tight to the curb outside the staff entrance, she huffed, "Not asking you to like or trust him... just me."

* * *

"I'd almost have preferred paying rent over agreeing to this." Ella was busy fast icing bottles of beer and checking she had gotten out the basic spirits, Clyde long done by the way he'd been dragging out setting up his table. "Here, I was thinking you'd like your lil outfit." he teased, standing behind her as she chopped limes at the counter, and rolled up the sleeves of his black shirt showing just the edges of some of his half-sleeve ink.

"It feels good, I'll give you that." Blouse silky and off-white, shiny black leggings that were thankfully quite thick. "But it screams touch it, consider this a forward warning that I'm not above dumping ice in someone's crotch for getting too close. Obviously, present company excluded." She near felt the laugh that rumbled through his chest, apparently taking it as an invitation before his hands trailed along her sides. He nearly spoke up to reassure her, none of them were dumb enough to touch something of his.

Despite the evening ticking along nicely, it wasn't until half the table was well on their way to drink that an issue reared its head. She was taking two minutes, chatting with a semi-familiar face from the hotel who turned out to be Clyde's driver slash bodyguard slash wingman when she realized he'd been the one who 'fetched her' that night in the club. He'd been the one to ask when he came through, why she'd kept a glass of ice but no drink with her the entire night - letting out a boom of laughter when she explained, that had gotten the conversation rolling smoothly.

"Another scotch, doll face," the slurred voice from behind her spoke up, the roll of her eyes turning to glare when he slapped her backside. You could hear a pin drop, the way the crack rang through the space. Smoothly, without saying a word, she hooked a finger in his waistbands before pouring the entire glass of ice into his underwear. Security, or 'Dixon' as he'd insisted, she calls him, broke the silence (outside of the man's angry spluttering) with another round of laughter. Where the rage-fueled man turned to Clyde to deal with it, probably expecting the feared boss to terrify her like he'd do any of them, he was met by a soft look of amusement from over the cards in his hand as Clyde continued as if nothing had happened.

"Boss," the man appealed, apparently trying to toe the fine line between aggressive and not wanting to provoke Clyde's aggression. He was met with a level stare before Clyde spoke like he was irritated he even had to voice it aloud. "Don't touch what isn't yours, you should know this by now. Be grateful it was just some blue balls." the corners of his lips tugged up just slightly at the attempt at humor. While the rest were silent and angry man huffed, Dixon and Ella were both pulling their lips between their teeth in an attempt not to laugh.

Thankfully, the last couple of games went by without incident - Dixon almost seemed to make a point of making a sizeable dent in the angry man's stack of chips.

It was only after, that things got tense. Ella had taken the opportunity to at least pack up the items on the table, wrangling rubbish and dishes into the bin and sink, while Clyde showed his guests out. She was startled out of her buffing of clean glasses by a harsh smack on her backside that knocked her hips almost painfully into the counter. But as opposed to the man from earlier, this time there was a high-pitched noise of surprise followed by her trying to calm her breathing as Clyde settled behind her, his voice low, Ella unable to pinpoint exactly what made her blood run cold at that.

"Remind me to fuck you senseless before the next time. My hickeys on your neck should tell them to keep their hands to themselves." The little bubble of giggles was out before Ella could think to stop it, prompting him to turn her sharply so Clyde could squeeze her jaw in a hand, holding her gaze with every inch of his work self "I'm not joking. You're fucking mine."

Ella couldn't recall when she'd agreed to that when she'd even been consulted, but she couldn't find it in her to care.

Clyde watched her pupils blow wide, a rush as he saw the sharp switch. She was a little rough around the edges, a workaholic with a short fuse, someone who could look after herself. Then he gets his hands on her and she surrenders – a singular focus on making him happy, handing over control willingly, much softer. "Fuckin' hell, maybe moving you was a mistake—" He put his hand in the depths of her hair, tugging back her head to give him easier access to the sensitive skin of her neck "—cause now I just want to keep you for my entertainment," punctuating the end of his words with a sharp nip at her neck.

"A pretty woman in my bed, on my arm..." he wasn't about to lie and make it seem all soft, getting the impression for the past few weeks that that wouldn't land with her anyway. "Can handle herself around my associates but submits to me…" Tentatively, her hands found purchase on his chest, attempting to ease him back and away from her as she frowned.

"In the nicest way possible, I'm not interested in being someone's lil girlfriend." She figured out how quickly she could get the hell out of dodge if he took this the wrong way.

Tucking a curl behind her ear, Clyde's smile was slow.

"No, more like…. friends who fuck and you play arm candy for a mob boss." he clarified, gravel to his voice as he stepped back into the space, she'd nudged him out of, prompting a roll of endearing laughter from her as she shifted her hands. One rake through his beard to cup his jaw, the other shamelessly trailing along his chest, dipping to cup the bulge growing in his jeans as she spoke.

"All right, I'm in." Her words cut off with a shriek of surprise as he hoists her over his shoulder, seemingly very intent on the 'friends who fuck' section of the plan.

CHAPTER 11

"Come on, Rob, hold it still!" Ella was wobbling on the ladder as she adjusted her balance for the umpteenth time, having agreed to come around and help with some projects while his girlfriend was on a trip. It was supposed to be a nice surprise that she'd come back to him done with his 'honey do' list and a lovely candlelight dinner. It had also included greeting her with a luxurious bath, but Ella had managed to talk him into setting up a shower and leaving the bath till after, throw in a massage and she'll be in heaven.

"How do you know her, apparently better than I do?" he'd asked, just done with re-skimming the wall in the hall ready for painting later, splatters of plaster mix nearly head to toe. "It's the ritual," she responded in a dramatically spooky tone, pressing the nail gun into the upturned stool again as she replaced the padding and fabric.

"Women talk. I may have low-key got her to tell me while asking about her trip, steered it gently towards doing something similar at home to relax, which led to asking what her ideal relaxing night in would be for the sake of comparison and ideas." When she finally raised her gaze, Ella was grinning, proud of herself at the way Rob was regarding her in an impressive way.

It was comfortable, and she far from minded spending one of her days off helping a friend - especially knowing his lady would be over the absolute moon to finally have the things are done that had piled up while they were both busy. Mara was an amazingly sweet woman, who got along with Ella like a house on fire - unfortunately, she was only mildly less concerned about Ella's life. Sometimes it felt like they were trying to parent her. Which just made it all around ick.

It was during a break as James and Ella scoffed down some rolls from the nearby deli, that James finally started prodding again.

"Don't you feel a little... I don't know, it doesn't seem like your speed," he offered weakly, not appreciating the burst of laughter from her in the face of his concern. "We're friends, for now, we're roommates, he calls me in as arm candy, and I call him in to get wrecked after a long week of working." Ella's calm tone had her watching as

James caught up with what she'd said, choking on a bite of his roll as he stared at her wide-eyed.

"That isn't the image I'm imagining in my head," he muttered, nudging her with his elbow where they sat.

"Tough titty. Less talking, more snacking - there's a finite amount of time left and we're nowhere near done," Ella said almost annoyingly energetic as she busied herself making sure they had everything to paint and starting to tape off/cover what they needed to avoid a mess.

* * *

"Big families' lunch, normally we'd go somewhere else for daytime things but... the oldies are creatures of habit," Clyde spoke through the door, surprised she was even still standing. She wasn't long home, having finished a shift as close to the wire as she could, collapsed on the bed in her room without even attempting to take her uniform off and power napped for maybe four hours before necking a shot of espresso and waking herself up with a cold shower. Now, Clyde was leaning against the doorframe, listening to the muttered chorus of colorful language from the room as she got dressed. He'd recently resorted to handing over his card and letting her kit out a wardrobe specifically for 'him' and 'his events' - though he'd been amused to get that month's statement and see it much less than he was expecting for the number of bags she'd brought home.

"S'long as you don't expect me to be all smiles and charm when the manager inevitably fucks up, then it's fine," she muttered, opening the door as she adjusted the clip holding her hair twist in place.

There was a slightly weird moment between them.

Ella realized it was probably as normal as she'd seen him outside of... well, gym and other workouts; or maybe polos were a regular thing, and she just hadn't noticed.

Clyde was far more impressed than he'd expected to be by her in a sundress. An expression she wrongly interpreted, turning as if to head back into the room.

"I can change..." Clyde caught her around the waist with a hurried *no* as he steered them out.

* * *

Aside from a couple of associates who recognized her from the first little event, she'd done with Dean for them, there thankfully weren't any major hiccups.

That was until the day manager caught her coming back from the restroom, steering her firmly by the elbow towards the bar as he spoke hurriedly about being understaffed for the big luncheon. "Yeah, I'm aware it's busy." she yanked her arm from his grasp, her voice like the crack of a whip as a few on the tables closest to the door glanced over.

"If you know it's busy, then get to work. Don't be selfish." he snapped, reaching for her arm a split second before she cracked him in the gut with her fist. Quickly, she pulled the handkerchief from his breast pocket and stuffed it against his face with a little more force than was necessary to cover the commotion as a sneeze.

Dixon was almost instantly in the doorway, blocking the view for the most part as Ella took advantage of the added privacy. "First, you're not my boss. Second, don't you ever lay your fuckin' hands on me again? Third, you're going to fuck off to your office and I'm going to go back to the luncheon... with the rest of the guests," she hissed pointedly as he glared at her before heading off briskly, handkerchief balled tightly in his hand.

"What was that?" Dixon asked with a chuckle, walking at her shoulder to half-herd half-protect her.

"I've been wanting to punch him for years, you think I was about to let a prime opportunity to do so just slip past?" came her reply, barely about a whisper as she tried not to move her lips too much, smiling politely as they reached the table, Ella slipping discretely back into her seat.

At least, she thought she was discrete until the man on Clyde's left, whom he'd been in rapt discussion with, was leaning around him to get her attention. "That was an excellent hook," he whispered as both leaned to speak behind Clyde. Ella did not notice the way Clyde's jaw clenched.

Though not happy with being out of the loop, Clyde would at least wait until the drive back to ask about it, Dixon relishing recounting the incident as Ella tried to look quiet and guilty as opposed to highly amused and not an ounce of regret.

Dragging his hand down his face, there was the noise of Dixon snorting from the front of the car before he caught sight of his boss's expression in the rearview and promptly went completely silent, posing professional and blank-faced.

The switch in the atmosphere in the car had Ella frowning, a ripple of panic shooting up her spine as the rest of the journey passed in heavy silence. The silence weighed until Clyde damn near slammed the door of the apartment behind them.

"When it involved people like that, why do you even still work there?" The question was spoken through grit teeth as he strode towards her, crowding her against the kitchen island as she let out a shaking scoff.

"It's my job. Grit teeth through the bad bits to keep the bills paid." Ella attempted to sound steadier than she felt but it failed somewhat.

Clyde slid his hands off the counter to firmly grip her waist "Or let me." He hitched her up with a squeal of surprise from Ella. "You're mine anyway, might as well get all the perks." Her hands on his chest made to shove him away, but it was like pressing on a brick wall.

"Come on, you know where you're meant to be."

Yes, in her apartment with a job behind the bar. Ella had put down his possessive talk to a kink or something, but Clyde was stone-cold sober and very much not being hurtled towards an orgasm, which made the words land like a ton of bricks.

Could James have been right to be wary? Had Ella found herself in the lion's den?

CHAPTER 12

"Clyde..." Ella's voice was low, the barest hint of warning to her tone as he unclipped her hair, one large hand holding the back of her neck as he brushed his nose against hers.

"We've talked about this."

Ella was under the impression that those talks had been highly effective in setting clear boundaries on what they were. Apparently not, or she had been deluding herself into seeing the red flags as flags.

"We did, but I think some concessions should be made." It was low, gravelly, and breathed against her neck before he sucked an angry mark into the point where it met her shoulder.

"Would it be so bad? You already know how well I'd take care of you," he said dragging her to the edge of the counter by her hips, wedging his hips between her thighs as she tensed in an attempt to draw them together.

"That's not the point, you're essentially gunning to own me." There was more bite to Ella's voice as she landed a blow against one of Clyde's shoulders in an attempt to get some space, wincing when he caught her wrist before she could land another.

"Don't be so dramatic," Clyde said nearly rolling his eyes. He pressed his lips against the inside of her wrist as he rubbed the skin to ease the sting from his grip "I want to look after you, appreciate you, and show you to the world...like my Rolex." The slow smirk did nothing to lighten Ella's mood as she shifted back a little, beginning to understand too late just how well her rules had served her till she bent them in Boston.

There was a frustrated huff of breath, her shoulders dropping just a fraction as she muttered something to herself about how she should have listened to the warnings. There was a questioning hum from him, head tilted like he expected her to speak up. Ella tried to rustle up as much composure and confidence as she could. "I thought folk was scared of losing their job pissing off a VIP... starting to think it was more fear of you." There was only the slightest, easily missed, flicker of shame in his expression.

"I keep the balance. Sometimes that means being a little morally gray." Clyde's response was slow, deliberate, with not an ounce of uncertainty to it as he shifted his hold, cradling her jaw in his hand as he brushed his thumb along her cheekbone. No longer boring into hers, his gaze was drifting leisurely as if taking in every minute detail of her face, her expressions, her reactions. It was disarming.

The fire of offense, of stubborn independence, felt like it was dying by the minute. Would it be so wrong? Would it make Ella so weak, to let a man take over? Her life always seemed to be in so much upheaval and uncertainty she'd convinced herself that she was better off alone. It was exhausting. When she stopped, she could feel it in her bones like a weight that told her to drop, let it all just pass her by.

"You don't need to move or work till you're dead on your feet. You're cleaning up the messes of some overpaying assholes…" Clyde's beard brushed along her skin as he spoke against the shell of Ella's ear, noting the way she was trying not to react, but her body betrayed her as goosebumps erupted across her skin and her breath hitched just slightly. A dominating kiss that left her dazed, the insistent brush of his tongue to coax apart her lips. It gave as she did, slowly relaxing, submitting.

His thumb on her jaw curled under her chin as he broke away, smirking at the way she swayed slightly almost to follow him before his hand settled with a firm grip around her throat. "For the future, keep that fight for me - in public, you let Dixon take out the trash, all right?" Clyde's tone and power were on full display. Ella had only ever overheard him use it with his men. When Ella couldn't utter a response, she resorted to a hurried nod, his grip relaxing to fidget with one of her dress straps. "Good girl."

Fuck.

Who was Ella kidding? She had no damn plans for the future, aside from holding the hands of others through theirs. Maybe this was her route - a backup role, an ornament.

"I can't give up what I have." It came out shakier than she'd intended, taking a second to level her voice before she continued despite his teasing attempts to see just how much help he'd have to give gravity to get her dress off. "I can't leave in the lurch, I'd have to stay at the very least till they find someone to replace me…"

Clyde took the path of her thoughts as a good sign, there was no reason for that to be on her mind unless she was considering it

"And I'm not switching to days in the meantime, not a chance in hell!"

Now that sounded more like Ella's usual self. Clyde made sure he observed her determined gaze.

"I respect your loyalty... and I won't ask you to leave without a replacement." His tone was business-like, just the hint of a smile as he continued, "And after today, especially, I'd much rather have you answering to Frank than getting into fights with your asshole day manager."

If he hadn't grown used to her little quirks, Clyde may have taken the long exhale and the way the tension melted from her limbs as defeat. Rather than what it was, merely a signal that Ella's thoughts were no longer a hurricane in her head and instead had settled into something like an ordered list.

"Okay." Her response was simple, brisk, as she shifted back to the edge of the counter, fingertips trailing over the skin just above his belt. "No problem, give up working at the hotel and keep the first-aid kit stocked. Anything else, you demand?"

Quick enough to surprise her, Clyde hoists Cella up, legs tightening automatically around him to avoid falling - not that he'd drop her. Shamelessly, holding her up by her thighs under her flirty skirt. "Just a couple of conditions, but nothing too taxing," he muttered, en route to his room.

CHAPTER 13

It's gradual. How she leaves. How slowly a new mixologist is a familiar face on the night shift.

What wasn't gradual, however, was James's reaction when she tells him. Roaring in his ears, resignation held limply in his hands as he speaks as carefully as he can "Are you sure? What's going on?" his frown of concern had been met with a small but reassuring smile, Ella nodding as they walked the staff halls to start their shift.

"I'm sure James. But I won't be going anywhere until you can find a replacement." she heard the unspoken question under his words, shrugging slightly "Nothing. I'm just... tired."

✳ ✳ ✳

When her last shift comes, Rob has pulled more answers from her but he's still doubtful of her claims of wanting to settle down and put down roots, but he's past the point of dwelling over it at this point since her mind is made up.

He walked to work but hadn't prodded too much into how she'd got in that evening. Strolling out the staff door, his arm holding her tightly to his side as he planted a kiss on the top of her head, he was only slightly surprised with how familiar you were with Clyde's right-hand man.

"Dixon? Oh, c'mon, I got the damn bus here, I can do the same on the way back." there's a slightly frustrated sigh to her voice, despite having agreed to all this, it's still taking some adjusting to someone who relied on only herself for most of her life.

"Change of plans, tomorrow's meet is today, and our stuff is in the back." there's a sympathetic edge to his voice as Ella wrenches open the door and hops up into the seat with a grumble, an arm shooting out to catch the door. "Rob, need a lift?" she calls, a small smile on her face as Dixon looks slightly worried. "Oh relax, Frank, he's seen me naked before. Jesus." it does little to sway the deadpan expression she gets in return as he rounds to the driver's side and James gently shuts the door after he's seated beside her.

"So, this is the wildlife you're leaving us for?" he asked softly, suppressing a chuckle at Ella wrestling herself out of her casual clothes and into the simple dress, leaning to zip it when she twists in her seat

"Yup, look pretty, and don't punch people." she recites in a chipper tone, prompting a snort of amusement from the front seat and an actual laugh from Rob as she settles back to talk animatedly with her best friend.

As they round the corner to Rob's place, he huffs out a breath, hugging her tightly to his side. "Just... we're here if you need anything, all right? Or, you know, if you change your mind." His voice is deliberate and hushed, apparently still not entirely convinced she's not being blackmailed or sort of kidnapped. It prompts a bubble of chuckles from her as the car pulls up to the curb and Rob steps out with a final thrown joke about sending him a ransom note.

As the car starts moving again, Dixon catches her eye in the rearview mirror. "You, okay?" he asked eventually, Ella managing a weak smile in response, more focused on plaiting her hair neatly out of the way.

"Yeah, it's just... adjustments. Don't know how to feel about it all," she admitted, leaning forward slightly to speak candidly with him.

"Try me - what's tripping you up?" he asked with that slow smile, for how scary he looked for his job, she'd found him to be a right softie so far.

"I feel like a hooker..." Ella muttered, at last, knowing full well if there was anyone she could speak freely to, it'd be him. "Or, an escort is a better comparison."

There was an unexpected burst of laughter from him that startled her before he calmed enough to speak in a soothing tone as if it was the most obvious thing in the world. "Look, doll, I won't sugarcoat it. I don't know if the boss is even capable of fluffy feelings - but he trusts you, values you, and yeah that means he wants to show you off sometimes." He was slowly pulling into the park, slotting in behind the Rolls Royce. "Trust me on this, you're not just a pretty face with some nice tits, that he's paying for. If it makes you feel any better, if you had a dick, you'd probably be working alongside me." That prompted a very unladylike snort of laughter from Ella as they stepped out of the vehicle.

* * *

Sitting next to Clyde, as was tradition, all the women sat just a smidge further back from the table. It was meant to be some order thing, but Ella was focused on the great vantage it gave her of her surroundings. Meaning, when the men were almost done with their business and indulging in some cocktails, she had a clear view of the cart the bartender rolled up to the table.

A small frown touched her expression as she watched him work, switching shakers mid-way through as if it was nothing. But it was only for the final guest, plenty of extra still in the shaker as he set it down. Something that had a soft grinding noise catching her ear as she glared at the bartender.

Leaning forward, she tried to discretely signal Clyde by a hand on his elbow, but he simply covered her hand with his as if she was playing the part of the doting partner. Glancing around for Dixon, she spotted him with his attention on the bigger security picture instead.

Dammit.

Standing swiftly, she plucked the glass from the guest's hand, mere inches from his face. "I wouldn't advise drinking that. Best case, the balance is completely off - worst case, there was something in that shaker that shouldn't be there." the way Clyde had caught her closest wrist when she stood had tightened to the point of pain as she spoke, now his grip hung loosely around her wrist as he gently guided her back behind him, Ella settling the glass on the edge of the table as she passed.

The guest had her fixed in a stare, a quirk of his finger calling over his security whom he whispered to before they went to check the cart.

In the silence, you could cut the tension with a knife. The security team returned with a small glass jar in their hand, the bottom still sporting the large amount of glue that had held it in the bottom of the shaker.

He brushed away his security to go 'fix things' before his gaze turned to Clyde, a small smile curling his lips as he spoke with a heavy Brooklyn accent "Should I be suspicious that your bird is in on it?" he asked carefully, prompting a slow and almost proud smirk from Clyde as he pulled her to his side by an arm around her waist "Course not, she's a mixologist with high standards," he commented with the slightest shrug. It seemed to calm things as they said their farewells and filed out to their cars.

While Dixon hopped back into the taller car Ella arrived in, Clyde steered her firmly towards his Rolls-

Royce. The drive was silent and painful, Ella eventually speaking up as politely as she could manage "I'm sorry if that was out of line—"

"Don't. You tried to warn me, I brushed you off." His response was a snap that had her barely flinching back into the seat before he settled a hand heavily on her thigh "You did good, don't worry." His tone sapped the tension from her body.

* * *

No matter how much it became her usual get-up, Ella never lasted long once the front door was shut. The heels would be off before she was even out the hall, any fastenings or hair trinkets were undone by the time she reached her room. In next to no time, she'd be back out in something much comfier.

Today was no different, aside from being a little slower. When she'd gone to set everything away, her uniform had caught her eye, sliding it from the hanger and tossing it into the bottom of the closet to deal with later.

Jolted abruptly out her thoughts when she pads through the living area, all too aware of how the low hum of conversation died near instantly, hurrying her steps towards the kitchen to grab a bottle of iced water and get the hell out of the way as efficiently as she could manage.

That plan went up in smoke the minute she heard Dixon call out a bye before the front door clicked shut behind him. Barely out of the little kitchen area before a broad chest blocked her way - startling her for more than one reason. It wasn't fair that one man could make sweats and a t-shirt look so damn good.

"Dixon was just telling me about an interesting conversation that you two had." Clyde didn't sound pissed off, a small smile confirming that when he heard her muttered 'clypin bastard' comment.

Running his hands down her arms until he could pull her close by her waist, Ella was shamelessly watching the flex of his muscles and the couple hints of ink on his skin. "Don't get me wrong, the sex is absolutely a plus. But I asked you to do this because you have such a way with people." His tone was business-like and sincere, grip not notably tight but still making it clear he wouldn't put up with her walking away. "Outside this apartment, you're almost like a female Dixon," he said carefully, enjoying the burst of amusement from her, accurately guessing that Dixon had probably said something similar. "But inside her? Come on, we have fun, right?" Clyde doesn't do emotions well but it's well enough to handle hers.

Ella allows herself to relax, nodding like she's processing it. "Must just be the last day at the hotel getting to me."

There's a chuckle bleeding through her words as if she's trying to lighten the mood.

"Overthinking? That I can help with," Clyde sighs smoothly, thoroughly enjoying the hearty giggle as he near drags her to the sofa.

CHAPTER 14

"I was engaged... Years ago." Clyde spoke, tracing imaginary patterns on her skin as he lay behind her. "The gal… took her life, it wasn't long after that that I switched lines of work. That stalking bastard slipping through the law's fingers time after time, it probably felt like her last piece of control."

While the honesty was slightly awkward, Ella could guess it had something to do with all the jokes that bartenders were only a few steps from therapists. Annoyingly, she fit the stereotype.

"Going to guess that's got something to do with being clingy after I patched you up?" she murmured, turning her head to glance over her shoulder at him as he nodded, an arm snaking around her waist to pull against his chest.

"A woman on my arm, it's archaic but it speaks to power and stability," Clyde said, keeping his voice business-like and as casual as he could. But it was met by a knowing hum from her as she relaxed in his hold.

"Security," Ella added, helpfully, earning a noise of confirmation from him. "Well, that makes things a whole lot clearer," she commented, shifting slightly to get comfier.

"I'll admit, it was a little scummy at the beginning. Wasn't lookin' to stick my dick in your personality..." Clyde expected her fiery temper to make an appearance, but she was listening calmly. "Then I got to know you. You're...not hard as nails. Essentially, exactly what you say on the tin. It's refreshing and kind of, I don't know, relaxing to be around," Clyde internally cringed at how sappy it sounded, reluctantly loosening his grip on her as she turned to face him instead.

"So, putting it super simple, you need a companion, not a girlfriend. Rooted in trust rather than love." Ella pondered aloud, smiling slightly at his expression that told her she'd hit the nail on the head. "But it's me here 'cause Dixon doesn't look as good in a dress." She tried to keep the laughter out of her voice, but it wove anyways as he rolled onto his back with a groan, muttering something akin to that being an image he didn't want in his head.

When she made to get up, Clyde caught her wrist without even having to look, tugging her firmly back beside him. "Where you off to?" His voice laced with a yawn, his other arm thrown over his eyes.

"My room, to bed," came her amused response as if it were obvious, but it was met with a disapproving mumble.

While most of his words were lost to the tired grumbling, Ella did manage to catch "just stay" and "not that much of a blanket hog" before she exaggerated a sigh and settled down.

* * *

It took a little while, but they found a footing for her.

Clyde wanted Ella in heels, she found a solid rotation of heeled boots. He wanted her dressed feminine but not overly modest, she almost exclusively wore well-tailored jeans and tactile tops that were the polite side of revealing.

He'd let her know what sort of situation they were going into - if she needed to keep quiet and use their signals if she noticed something, if her old work banter would be well received or if it was just close associates like Dixon and she could be her regular version of herself.

Clyde came clean about postponing her apartment and Ella was pissed and let it be known - resulting in a rolling housing order signed with Starling that guaranteed six months in one of the apartments within a week of being invoked. Starling had expressed that he was surprised she'd not simply bartered for Clyde to buy her one, but she was quite clear about not accepting above and beyond 'reasonable'.

Gradually, Ella became familiar with Clyde's closest associates, helping Dixon in a sort of PA role that he'd previously been juggling as part of everything else he did.

Clyde even took a couple of days to relax after a particularly hectic week - something he'd not felt able to before, but was reassured enough to even sleep in - finally dragging himself through at the smell of breakfast as Ella slid a far-from-perfectly-round omelet onto a plate as Dixon made notes on what had to be dealt with by Clyde personally and what could be managed with just the underlings.

"This is domestic..." Clyde commented with a yawn, startling both of them as he sat at the table. Dixon was quick to give him the run-down so he wouldn't jump straight into boss mode, reiterating that there wasn't much, and it would all still be fine in the morning. "Oh, and the flesh holes will be coming in the morning," Dixon added to Ella as she set down Clyde's plate in front of him, the bearded man nearly choking on his coffee as he'd been mid-sip.

Pointing a finger at Frank, there was no room for argument. "Don't you dare stick your dick in it," she said before huffing and explaining for Clyde's sake.

"It's one of those slabs med students use to practice stitches. Figured it was worth learning some new skills that might be useful - plus, keep me sane." Leaving her job had become a running joke, Ella spending way too much of her free time on skill building and seemingly not knowing what to do with herself. Clyde, found it highly amusing given he was sure there were one hundred and one women in Boston who'd be over the moon to have him asking them not to work. As agreed by both, thankfully she wasn't one of them.

* * *

One part Ella wasn't adjusting quickly to, even after over a year, of occasions, was where she truly felt out of her depth and on the back foot.

"Stewart," the voice was so familiar, Ella frowned for a moment before she turned to its source. Her eyes widened as she caught sight of the man in rapt conversation with Clyde. When the man did a double take, trying not to let his surprise show, Clyde not so subtly tightened the arm around her waist, his hand inching down to hold her by the hip.

Just before Clyde steered them away, the other man spoke up again, this time directly to Ella. "I'm sorry, have we met before?" His face tinged with a frown of thought as he tried to recall why she looked so familiar.

"Theo, right?" she asked with a hint of a smile, her amusement growing when he nodded before the realization washed over his face like a bucket of ice water.

"Bentley?" he sounds almost panicked as he glanced between the two, finally choosing to speak directly to Clyde.

"I didn't know, boss, I swear," Ella muttered under the guise of affectionately tucking her face into his neck.

He'd flirted, badly, any time he came in. Admittedly, it was long before she even spoke to Clyde - but he wasn't about to let on he knew that it was far too amusing to make one of his men squirm instead.

"You know now, don't fuckin' forget it." Clyde's tone left no room for confusion, the cold stare enough to send him moving just a little too fast for Theo to hide the fear successfully.

"You have an uncanny ability to charm people," Clyde muttered darkly, checking his watch before steering them briskly through the crowds - exchanging a few words with the host before dealing out some good wishes and a goodbye.

As they approached the car, Ella exchanged a confused look with Dixon as he opened the door. If his expression was anything to go by, Clyde's mood wasn't anything new, but it wasn't anything good either. Her silent interaction with his right-hand man only served to make it worse, judging by the almost painful grip on her knee as he slid in next to her.

They barely made it into the apartment before Clyde near tore his jacket off, tossing it on the kitchen counter as Ella bit out a comment about why he got so moody at the very idea of another man talking to her.

"I don't fuckin' like it," he bit out his response as Ella rolled her eyes, leaning to ease off the heels. Her voice was tired, it wasn't the first time they'd gone through this damn dance, but she never hoped it would be the last.

"Clyde, not this again..."

He closed the distance in a few brisk strides, grabbing her bicep firmly, his momentum pulling her along till he dropped her on the sofa. Leaning on the back, caging her in, Clyde dropped his head level with hers to hold her gaze. "You expect me to believe you don't feel anything for me? That I'm not the only one who can make you blush?" It almost sounds accusing, a hand gripping firm at the back of Ella's neck when she goes to look away with a sigh.

"You expect me to believe I'm alone in this?" There's a flicker of a frown across Ella's features at that, there's an edge to Clyde's voice that Ella doesn't recognize.

No, she does, which just confuses her all the more.

"Clyde..." she says carefully, shifting as best she can to sit up a little straighter, risking raising a hand to gently cradle his cheek. Some of the aggression rolling off of him dampens down, allowing himself to lean into the touch.

In honesty, she didn't know. Ella had long since stopped trying to make sense of her feelings, or even figure out what they were. It was easier to shove them to the side and not look too hard.

One thing was easier to see though, three words they both longed to hear. Very different reasons, and very different tones, but three words, nonetheless.

"You're not alone."

CHAPTER 15

"You noticed the boss acting a bit.... off, lately?" Dixon asked, slouched in a chair as Ella watched the F1, silicone slab in her lap as she tried to suture without looking too closely - slow going but she'd set it as a little challenge to herself.

The question prompted a thoughtful hum, a slight frown briefly creasing her expression as she thought about it. "Kind of, but probably not in the same way you're meaning," she responded, surprised at the breathy chuckle she got in response.

Dixon sat forward, resting his elbows on his knees as he fought to contain a grin as he watched for the gears turning in her head. "Territorial, damn near Clyde me a death stare when I made a wisecrack about stopping at a cafe for that outing later, make a proper date of it."

Her grumbled response was automatic, silencing abruptly when her brain caught up. "How many times, I don't need a damn bodyguard just to pick up a dress for this stupid—wait, do you mean that deadpan stare like a pissed-off toddler?" she asked, her expression a mixture of a frown and shock when she got a nod in response. "He did the same thing when I said I was stopping by Frank's to help with some things for his girlfriend's birthday.

If an expression could more clearly convey 'Oh no', Dixon had yet to see it, because he didn't think one could fit better than the expression on her face at that exact moment.

Burying her face in her hands, she slouched in the seat with a groan, "Ah fuck, I'm such a dumbass." That had Dixon pretty much dissolving into a fit of laughter that seemed to attract Clyde's attention from his home office, padding down the hall with a grumpy expression.

"Oh, hey boss," Dixon sat up to turn in his seat, greeting him with a grin as he got to his feet under the guise of leaving. "Ella was just saying, if she can't just do it alone, she'd rather you take her to pick up that dress."

While she didn't show it in a reaction, Ella let a rush of breath out her nose as she planned to tear Dixon a new one at the next opportunity, his fate was sealed the second he leaned towards his boss as he passed to leave with a murmured, "Think she wants to make sure *you* like it - since she seems to have the hang of fitting in."

So, the actions of the closest thing to a sibling Clyde had, and a 'work friend' of Ella's - were how they'd ended up on an awkwardly quiet drive through town. "You didn't actually say anything he said you did, did you?" Clyde asked, a slightly amused sigh as they parked.

"I *thought* it," she admitted quietly, trying to hide the smile as she turned her gaze to him. "Did you, death-stare Dixon, over joking about a date?" Though Ella didn't have to wait long for a response, Clyde's facial expression said it all. That rueful smile threatened to break free, the almost deliberate pulling on of his professional control persona.

"Maybe not a death stare, but I wasn't happy about it," came his grumbled response.

It was quiet for a moment before Ella reached to squeeze his hand. "You don't need to be grumpy with Dixon..." Her voice was calm as she stepped out of the car, Meanwhile, Clyde was hot on her heels.

While Ella chatted with a woman at the counter, Clyde caught the way she brushed off trying it on. "You guys usually nail it, no need to be taking up any more of anyone's time."

An arm slowly slid from behind her, a large hand pushing the bag gently back across the counter before she heard him trot out his full charm tone.

"Actually, I'd love to see her in it. If that's all right..." the staff didn't need to know who he was to be nodding eagerly, the ridiculously high limit card on the account told them all they needed to know.

Clyde settled outside the dressing room with a barely hidden grin calling a "Need a hand with a zip or anything?" that earned him a flustered response of "No, no, I can manage, thanks." The soft thud of her leaning on the wall to slide on heels to check their length.

"Perfect as always," Ella said to the tailor as she came out, double-checking that she wasn't about to catch a shoe in the skirt any time soon. A very fitted, bandeau-sleeved number - the silky skirt and deep blue give it a very ocean-inspired look.

Whereas Clyde had just been looking for an excuse to see Ella dolled up, especially given how they butted heads on 'her spending his money (he was of the mentality of the sky was the limit whereas Ella was acutely aware of 'not taking the piss out of his generosity'), what it had done instead was make those confusing emotions rear their head. That possessive affection that he didn't even want to think of describing as love. Love only brought loss and pain.

"Gorgeous," he muttered, reveling in the way Ella kept her reaction calm aside from the betrayal of a blush starting to burn across her cheeks as she beelined back into the dressing room. She was intent on getting changed back into her clothes and getting out of there before it could get any more awkward.

They got as far as the car before it got awkward...

Ella's head rested back against the headrest as they drove in almost comfortable silence. Clyde finally being the one to break it as they waited in traffic. "I enjoy being with you." The comment stilted like he'd struggled to find a better way to phrase it, clearing his throat as he continued in the safety of the Rolls Royce where only they could hear. "You make me feel like I can take over the world, like as long as I've got you beside me then am home."

Ella gasped, deciding it was only fair to finally be more open with Clyde, given how much he'd told her over their time so far. "I don't want to lie - it's all confusing as fuck. But I want to make you smile, have your back, be right by your side..." It was like Ella could hear her heartbeat thundering in her ears, aware of every breath. This was exactly why she didn't do emotions - it was confusing, terrifying, and vast like Pandora's box kicked wide open.

Clyde chuckled before speaking in a tone that almost sounded like a relief. "I don't think either of us knows where we are, but safe to say we're there together." He reached to take her hand, holding it when he noted the barely-there tremble to it as she held his grip. It was after a few more intersections that he raised their hands to press the back of hers to his lips. "Does this mean I can take you on another date without you fighting me?" he asked with a cheeky grin, enjoying the slow smile it earned from her even as she rolled her eyes, softly responding, "Nah, still going to fight you on it. But we can go on another date."

✳ ✳ ✳

They did, though Clyde found his way around her fighting his generosity. Casual, daytime, batting cages, and lunch-truck meetups.

Clyde discovered that Ella had a shockingly mean swing, but virtually no accuracy regarding aiming the ball - not so great for baseball, but useful as a defense. To the surprise of nobody, Clyde was pretty damn good as well.

Ella had to admit, there was something nice about watching how Clyde moved with such assurance and freedom - enjoying himself without expectations hanging over his head.

He'd even been so relaxed she'd convinced him to go for a few rounds of crazy golf. Unfortunately, it turned out to be yet another thing on the ever-growing list of things he was unfairly good at.

But now, they had decided to take a walk, having picked up lunch from a food truck instead of something more formal. At least for a little while, they could pretend to be two ordinary folks, on a regular date.

CHAPTER 16

It was certainly a test of Clyde's jealousy. A meet where he'd opted to bring Ella along, having tried to avoid it once she'd gotten used to not working nights, knowing full well she'd run on fumes before saying anything otherwise.

Dixon drove, exchanging looks with his boss the entire journey in the rearview mirror, looking far too pleased with himself when Clyde fought a smile.

As soon as Frank saw a suited Frank, he knew exactly who would be following him. However, he was surprised to find he wasn't alone, a familiar brunette quite obviously trying to resist the urge to knock him over with a hug. As they went through the usual pleasantries, sorting out the check-in, James rounded the desk to show them up to the suite. The foyer was empty, so he chanced a quick hug with his friend. "Wow, you look..." he waited till he could finish his sentence muffled in her hair "...happy."

"I am," Ella murmured before they parted, wearing a

beaming smile tinged with almost confusion or surprise that this was her most content. While Dixon was doing his job, keeping himself aware of their surroundings, Clyde made it a point to hold her close.

His grip tightened slightly as Frank addressed Ella instead of him when they reached the doors. "The booking was a little open-ended-" he began, unable to hide the smile when she cut him off.

"I know, it was me who made the booking."

Both knew she'd have enjoyed doing that with the day manager, a non-violent flex to deflate his ego.

"No staff, I can handle it."

He left with the usual pleasantries and a fond smile exchanged with his friend. Once the door was shut behind them, Ella tried to keep the humor out of her voice as Clyde seemed reluctant to let her go so, she could make sure everything was 'just so' for the meeting.

"Clyde," she said turning so they were chest to chest, her voice took on a soothing edge. "Nothing personal. Just business."

She was finishing setting out the glasses, having set out a small but well-curated selection of decanters and mixers on a nearby table, when Dixon had been sent to answer the knock at the door.

Ella took up a spot and stood next to Dixon, occasionally stepping forward to fill a glass or fetch a drink for one of Clyde's associates. The 'business' side of their meeting easily lasts an hour.

At the change in tone, Dixon nudged Ella just slightly

as he stepped forward to join the men who now looked much more relaxed where they sat. The tone shifts changed his role from security to one more of a familiar face and Clyde's second. It didn't take a genius to work out that the nudge was probably to tell her she was now off-duty too.

However, she made sure to sort a round of refills first, a knowing smile when she brought a couple of glasses of that familiar malt, perching on the arm of Clyde's chair, handing him a glass as he slid easily into conversation with some faces, she recognized from the poker nights.

"You must be Blue Balls..." a younger-looking guest said smirking. Ella took a moment to realize he was talking to her as she sipped her drink.

"Can't blame him, I'd brave some ice to slap that ass, too." *That made it click, he must be buddies with the idiot from the poker night.*

"Fuck sake, that's not a moniker I want to be carrying." There was a note of exasperation in her voice, but she caught the way he reacted like he hadn't expected the voice.

"You're not from here, are you?" There's an edge of amusement to his voice as he sits forward, frowning like there's something just out of reach in his memory. "But you are from *here.*"

"Glasgow, originally. But, yeah, I worked here - bar if it weren't obvious." Ella answered slowly, gaze dropping to the hand he extended towards her.

"Call me Henry." she shook his hand, opting to introduce herself how she'd always been on her work badge. Last name only.

"Think I remember you. Used to do private events with the wine guy... uh... Mike?"

Ella slightly chuckled as she corrected him on the right name (and title, Dean would hit the roof if someone called him 'the wine guy).

"Yeah, that was probably me - think they teamed us hoping we'd cancel out each other's sarcasm or something…"

"Did that work?"

"Nah, we were snarky bastards. Just said it to each other rather than guests."

Clyde barely noticed when she shifted from the arm of his chair to the spare seat on the sofa next to Henry, only a burst of laughter later catching his attention.

"See, that's the difference. You lot order by the name even if it's blended malt piss-water," Ella said smiling in an almost cheeky way; the pair had fun throwing barbs at each other.

"Yeah? Go on then, sweets, let's hear how the orders stack up..." He quirked a brow in a way that tended to rub most folk the wrong way, that cocky attitude that came from buying your way out of trouble from a young age.

Clyde watched as Ella smiled sweetly, taking a moment to savor the last of her whiskey before she spoke with more patience than she was aware she even had.

"You're the sort to order tequila and shot it every time; cocky and with a shit tone of growing up to do."

It prompted a snort of laughter in response as he caught Clyde's eye over her shoulder.

"Clyde and Dixon?"

"Dixon's a beer guy, low percent but a tasty brew; the sort who can play the long game, patient, notices the details. Clyde drinks whiskey the right way, not watered down, so you get every layer; focused, smooth, and not to be under-estimated."

Ella shrugged, reclining on the sofa.

"You?" He knew full well that leaning any closer was going to wind up Clyde, but cocky as ever he wasn't paying that no mind.

"Straight liquor or a rum and coke. To the point, no fuss. Plus, you know, tastes light at the time but fucks ya up later," Ella said trying to keep a straight face but the snort of amusement from behind her broke her composure, catching her off guard as she hid her burning face in her hands for a moment. "And good at removing filters." her voice dissolving into a chuckle.

When the conversation died down to a low rumble, a few headed home a little less steady on their feet. Showing them out with a small chuckle at the drunken rambling, she turned to find Clyde frowning in deep conversation with someone who looked like they could go serene to feral on a hair-trigger.

"It's the fourth in as many months, that's not chance." The other man muttered darkly, the cheery casual shirt; a stark contrast to the stern expression he wore.

"Kill the root, keep it clean. I'm not about to let some strung-out rookie fuck up everything for some pills and a god complex." Clyde sounded so calm, even though it sounded like he was issuing a pretty hefty order.

"Loud and clear, Boss," the man said with a sick sort of smile as he left, a swagger that wouldn't have looked out of place in an 80s film, passing Ella a little too close for her liking as she held the door.

"All good?" she asked, stacking the empties on a tray to make it easier for housekeeping in the morning, straightening what she could to try and reduce their workload.

Clyde raked a hand through his hair, settling his hands at his belt with a wide stance. "Yeah, might have some mess to deal with later…" He watched the frown flit across Ella's expression as she stilled.

"Related to the creep who just left?" she insinuated, earning a quiet hum from Clyde as he approached.

"James? Yeah. Well, he handles shit like this—gets a lil overzealous sometimes, though."

Ella wasn't entirely sure if Clyde's explanation made things better or worse.

* * *

"Fuck off, Dixon," Ella grumbled, digging for a cloth to wipe the brownie batter off the counters at least. There was a splatter of it up the front of her apron, thankfully none in her hair though Dixon had gotten at least a spoonful straight to the face.

"It said whisk, there was nothing that hinted an electric whisk was a bad idea."

Since Clyde had a day of calls to make, Dixon was doing the legwork errands, and Ella figured now was a good time to get started on not being quite such a limited chef. Perhaps misplaced confidence in a lasagna that didn't end up a bubbling mess had prompted her to try something sweet but (in theory) just as easy, Dixon getting back not long after she'd started.

Lies.

Chocolate brownies were not easy, and the batter was a complete pain to clean up.

"Yeah, whisk gently, the thing has three settings." Dixon was barely able to speak for laughing, cleaning himself up with a damp kitchen roll as the racket pulled Clyde through from his office as he finished up a call.

There was a contented hum as Dixon ignored the warnings about raw eggs instead of wiping a dollop from his chin. "Mmm, if it helps any, think you aced the recipe, the execution was just a little... uh... chaotic."

Ella paused her whisking to briefly flip him the bird, dumping the lot into a tin and sticking it in the oven with a little more force than was strictly necessary.

The mental self-critical spiral halted abruptly as Clyde caught her around the waist, pulling her back against his chest as he moved them both to the counter, sucking on the teaspoon she'd scraped the bowl with "Frank's right, tasty but chaotic." A deep rumble of laughter rang through his chest as Ella rolled her eyes at the pair, relaxing nonetheless as she moved to get the apron off without it touching anything.

"At no point did I allude to being Betty fuckin' Crocker, all right?" Ella grumbled,

Dixon took some pity on her as Clyde scrolled through his phone with a frown. "A baker Ella is not, but she can lift a grown-ass man on those shoulders so...everyone has their strengths."

CHAPTER 17

It's going well. All too well, a matter of fact. Ella is sliding right along into the role while Clyde dislikes the amount of leering. He's had fewer problems with Henry since he got Ella to be a go-between of sorts.

There are a lot of out-of-towners that week and it's probably not far off to compare it to the E3 of crime.

But it means yet another night at the lounge, small talk with Clyde's associates' wives, and less time with Dixon having to be at her shoulder. Which is the extent of it until a knock at the door. Without much thought, Dixon answers, frowning as the employee speaks quickly. Almost instantly, he's moving quickly but calmly to speak softly in Ella's ear.

Her expression drops, only for a moment, before she excuses herself with a polite smile and tries not to run as she makes her way to the door. The door has already clicked shut behind her by the time Dixon manages to bring Clyde up to speed.

Ella is running as soon as the door closes behind her, beelining to the staff lifts as she follows the familiar employee-only halls. Thankfully, nights have low staff turnover, meaning most are well aware of what's going on and not about to question why she's somewhere she technically shouldn't be.

Rounding the door of his little office, Ella huffs out a shaking breath at his state of him. "Fuck sake Frank, what sort of bother have you gotten into now?" There's a little bite to her voice as her knees hit the floor, focusing on the first aid kit on his desk and getting the wounds clean.

"I'm not saying it's related, but we had some issues last night in the bar. A guest getting a little heavy-handed with a woman at their party. I gave them a warning; they didn't like that - though it came across like they just Stewart's been told 'no' often enough. Then, tonight, I pop out to check one of the cameras that's acting up, and... well, the rest is written on my face," James finishes weakly, the barest hint of a smile at his terrible humor.

"You know, if you want to play the hero - you could just buy a cape, they're very in style at the moment." Her attempt at humor and a smile is weak, but he appreciates it all the same.

There's a flicker of something between confusion and shock across his face as he watches her thread one of the curved needles, tidy little stitches as she frowns in concentration before snipping the end. When she notices his face, she feels a kick in her chest that it's been so long since they last spoke properly. "Wanted to expand my skills, figured advanced first aid was a good place to start. Especially since apparently none of the men in my life can keep themselves in one piece."

Once the wounds are clean, she's dressed what is needed and is patiently rubbing salve into what is likely going to be a web of bruises down his arm as he sits backward in his chair, the stained shirt tossed on his desk. Thankfully, or not, they missed his face for the most part. A split lip and a mild black eye are the worst of it that can't be hidden - knowing full well he won't hear a word of taking time off to recover.

* * *

They chatter mindlessly like they'd do in the mornings, as she helps him into his spare suit. Once he's sorted, James pulls her into a hug, prompting a confused laugh from her as they part to walk through to the foyer.

"Please, just keep your head down. I get it, you have a big heart and want to do the right thing, but please stop putting yourself in harm's way because of it." Ella's voice isn't angry, but it's clear she's concerned and a little rattled

"Call. Fuck, Rob, you know I'm always just at the other end of the phone." There's a sigh of exasperation dripping from her words as she hugs him gently, a murmured confirmation that he'll listen from Frank as he takes up his post behind the front desk again.

As she steps into the lift to head back up to the lounge, a hand darts to stop the doors before it's followed by a familiar face stepping alongside her. "That looked cozy..." Henry says slowly, smirking slightly as she rolls her eyes, stubbornly refusing to speak.

"So, what, you're Clyde's little arm candy and you're fucking the help?"

Ella closes her eyes as she pulls a long and calming breath through her nose before she speaks in a level and measured voice. "To you, they may be 'the help'," she says the term without even trying to hide her venom at his phrasing. "But to me, these people are my friends. That doesn't change just because I don't wear the uniform anymore." There's a bite to her voice, but not as much as she'd like, chewing on the inside of her cheek as she worries about what in the hell is going on. If it's worth raising it to Clyde, or maybe Frank, even if just to get the owners to support a ban or some better damn security - especially for the night crew.

Settling a hand at the small of her back, he leans closer, Ella turned her head just slightly to meet his gaze "You know, it's a bit low brow for Stewart, but I'm always down for getting my hands dirty." it catches her off guard that it's not said with his familiar leery tone. Sure, his usual cockiness is there, but it sounds like he's trying to curry favor with Clyde rather than be a horndog. Instead of potentially getting involved where she shouldn't, Ella manages a slight nod but keeps silent.

As soon as the doors open, she's huffing out a breath as

Henry exits and she hits the button and swipes the room key to go up to the suite. She's calm and collected, as she makes her way in and heads straight for the bathroom - though her hands are clean, she still scrubs just to make sure she's not walking around with her friend's blood in the lines of her palm or something. Once she's reassured of that worry, she leans heavily on the counter as she takes deep breaths. Ella can hear them shake and speed up as they fail to contain the wave of emotion, her head dropping between her shoulders as she tries to keep it all together.

The ringing in her ears, feeling like she's overheating, is probably why she doesn't notice the figure in the door. Until they're behind her, turning her gently but firmly to cage her in their arm, pressed against their chest.

"Dixon told me... you all right?" Clyde's words rumble through his chest as Ella shakes her head sharply. Nope, she's not okay, now she's slowing down it's all hitting at once. The anxiety, caring so much for folk that the concern makes you sick, the inability to just shrug everything off like water off a duck's back. It's revealing her life for what it was - running.

"You should be downstairs, that's what's important," she mumbles, trying to push away from him as she smashes shut the box of emotions. But it doesn't work, the lid slips because Clyde's arms don't. Ella hates herself for it, hates how weak it feels, but the tears are flowing before she can scramble to stop them.

Clyde doesn't comment, he knows Ella well enough to

know that she's not one to cry and drawing attention will just make her feel worse. Instead, he picks her up, walking through to sit on the sofa with her in her lap, just holding her in silence until her shoulders relax and her breaths are steady again. It's then that the muttering starts, muffled where her face is buried in his neck, but he catches enough of it.

"Fuck sake, he's fine, and yet I'm bawling like a fuckin' bairn," Ella says sitting up as she tidies her hair and tries to wipe away any trance that she's been upset. Her attempts to shift and turn to stand up are moot, she may be stubborn, but Clyde has her beat on that trait.

Catching her chin, he drags her gaze back to him as he kisses her briefly. "No, someone you care about got hurt. Go to bed, rest, I'll handle it," he says softly, soothingly, against her temple, ignoring the almost petulant noise of argument.

When he heads down to draw the event to a close, Henry makes his same offer to Clyde, despite the level of glare he receives from Dixon in the process. The others don't poke for an explanation, most more than a few drinks deep and easily ushered out by their partners or Clyde's imposing stance.

"Henry," he calls him back from the doorway. "I'll be in touch," he states simply, watching as the younger man looks vaguely respectful for once, a slight incline of his head before he disappears.

"Is it really a good idea to get involved? Or getting rich boy involved, for that matter?" Dixon asked lowly once they were alone, falling into step with Clyde as he made his way up to the suite. Taking advantage of the privacy of the lift, Clyde huffed out a long breath, frowning slightly.

"Probably not but... I don't know, Ella's a mess. I feel like I have to," he said almost defeated, confused by the very words he was saying.

"If I didn't know any better, I'd say someone has it bad," Dixon commented, shrugging slightly as he fought a smile. "Just sayin'. But having me sort it is probably a far better shout than doing nothing. Cause you know Ella'll settle things herself and it'll get messy."

It prompts Clyde's chuckle as they step out into the suite.

CHAPTER 18

Dixon heads off to his room, closest to his door, while Clyde lets himself into the master suite. He finds Ella sitting up in bed, leaning her shoulder against the head-board, legs curled under her as she talks on the landline.

"You're all right? Let me get some ice from the mini-bar...it'll help with the bruising..." Clyde says approaching quietly but had gotten waved off. He slowly got undressed and then shifted beside Ella as she finishes her call. As soon as the phone is in the cradle, Clyde hauls her back against his chest, knocking a laugh out of her, a sound that fades to a giggle as he drags his lips along her neck.

"I promise, it'll be handled..." He soothes her, feeling his smile grow as her shoulders lose their tension, shifting them both down the bed till they're settled along the mattress. There's a watery noise of grim amusement as Ella turns into his warmth.

"Thank you..." she says as she pecks his lips.

But she stops as she pulls back, both standing on a mental edge, sensing a shift between them that's both terrifying and welcoming.

It's Clyde who makes the move, a hand cradling the back of her head as they meet in a slow kiss, unhurried and like they're trying to rediscover each other through the smooth meeting of tongues and reverent hands on each other.

A shiver races through Ella as he trails a hand down her back, pressing firmly at the end till she's flush against his chest. Sinking a hand into Clyde's hair, a giggle rises in her throat as he rolls them till he's flat on the bed with her draped on his chest.

Clyde is far from discrete about slapping her ass before he's pushing up her t-shirt. He's pretty sure it was his at one point. Slowly, he sits up to pull it the rest of the way off, Ella shifts on her knees as she straddles his lap in a movement so smooth, it's hard not to notice how in sync they've become. What's less smooth is the way she shifts to stand next to the bed to shimmy out her underwear, and the very un-suave way Clyde wriggles out of his.

Noting how she's fighting a smile, he barely grunts out a "Come here," before tugging her back into his lap and trying to kiss the smile off her face. A hand cradling her cheek, he slips the other between them to hold himself steady, noticing the tremble to her thighs as she sinks slowly down his length.

Gripping her hip with his now free hand, he breathes

out a low moan against the skin of her neck, helping her set a slow and steady pace as she rolls her hips. This isn't some sprint to cum, it's not base need and lust like it usually is. This is tender and nerve-wracking, admittance to a shift they've been ignoring for a while. Something neither has been able to say.

It's attentive and almost worshipping, the way she lavishes his neck and shoulders with attention. Firm, lingering presses of her lips and brief but gentle nips of her teeth. It's enough to leave his mind blissfully quiet, arms wrapped around her back to hold her close as she rides him at a pace that reduces him to little more than moans and curses. Clenching around him in a rhythm that has tingles running through her and his breath catching in his throat.

It's not enough. Clyde flips them, using his body to press hers into the mattress, head dropping to rest his forehead against her clavicle with steady determined thrusts that have her keening under him.

Arms wrapped around each other, a mess of limbs and almost desperate kisses; it isn't long before she's near whimpering his name when she comes, Clyde following close behind as he fills her, holding her tight like he was scared she'd leave.

The only sound in the room is their quick breaths, slowly evening out as she tenderly rests a hand on his beard, thumb brushing across his cheek. It prompts a contented hum from low in his chest, catching her hand in his to press a slow kiss to the inside of her wrist.

"We don't need to talk just now; it's been a long day," Clyde murmurs against the skin of her palm, turning her in his arms with minimal fight from her. "Get some rest," he said reveling in the quiet mewl as he settles his cock deep in her cunt again, holding her almost tenderly with her back against his chest. Ella lets out a breath that seems to take all her tension and worry with it, linking her fingers with his with a soft, "all right... sleep well." He mingled with a yawn as they settle, resisting the urge to let her humor kick in about the odd brand of affection of snuggling with a little added cockwarming.

Ella usually got a heads-up before associates appeared at the apartment. It must be important because apparently, this last-minute meeting didn't have enough notice to give her some warning. She only learned of it when she pads through the living area in one of Clyde's shirts, noting the extra figures only by the time she'd neared the kitchen. Well, she'd just have to focus on making a cup of tea, because it wasn't like reacting now would do anything.

It certainly wasn't a group she expected to see first thing in the morning. Clyde, Frank, James.... but there was also Henry and one whose name escaped her, but it was hard to forget the creepy vibes he gave off.

"Eyes on me," Clyde's command sounded almost like a growl, his jaw clenched tight as he waited for them all to listen before getting back into their discussion. Ella cut through to the utility room as the kettle boiled, fishing a pair of leggings out of the drier to at least pass for dressed. Kind of scruffy, but dressed.

Eventually, brew in hand, she walks over to perch in the vacant space between Clyde and Rob. Giving her friend a reassuring smile, she let her gaze quickly scan over his injuries - apparently happy they were healing well, or at least happy enough to stay quiet aside from a very brief lean of her head on his shoulder.

"Should toots really be hearing this?" James piped up, staring a little too intently as Ella leveled him with a deadpan stare to a chorus of affirmative answers from the rest of the group.

"So, we know it was a crew for hire - find them, follow the breadcrumbs back and we'll find who got so pissed off with Frank that they decided they want to try and turn him into mincemeat," Dixon spoke calmly, already scrolling through his phone to reach out to some associates who ran in those circles before he got to his feet and stepped into the home office.

"And what happens when we find them?" Henry asked after a few beats of silence.

"Woodchipper?" Ella suggested almost hopefully, taking a long sip of her cup of tea. "Or maybe a pinata?"

James slowly tilted his head as he watched her with an unreadable expression before turning his gaze to Clyde with something to his expression that spoke to being impressed rather than horrified - like Henry, who was wearing an expression like he'd gotten a wildly wrong read on her.

Clyde huffed out a sigh, trying not to chuckle at her suggestions and instead continue professionally. "We find them, and they answer my questions. Willingly, or my way. Then we'll ensure this doesn't happen again—"

CHAPTER 19

It took just a week. A week before Dixon was crouched next to the sofa as she napped fitfully, groggily sitting up as she blinked her eyes into focus. Her vision cleared till she saw Clyde sitting across from her, frowning in deep disapproval before she turned her gaze to Dixon - who merely looked his usual self.

"James found the one who sent the crew after Frank," Clyde began slowly, Ella sitting up straight at the drop of a coin, cobwebs of sleep completely gone as she smiled slightly.

"That's good, right? So... who is Dixon going to punt in a dumpster?" she asked with a chipper note to her voice, barely catching Frank's tactfully hidden snort of laughter.

"There's the problem. James won't tell us who is it unless I agree to some conditions first." The grumbling edge to his voice said it all that he wasn't best pleased with even talking about it. "I get thirty minutes to deal with the scum, then James wants you. He wants your help doing his usual people disposal - though I doubt it helps, more his sick interest in how you'll face it." Clyde was quite obviously less than impressed with the whole thing, but her prompt nod caught him off guard.

"All right. I'm not a violent person by nature but... can't say I wouldn't want to kick this dude in the balls a couple of times and enjoy it, for the number they did on Rob." She said so simply that Clyde can't help but smile, just slightly, when Dixon lets out a chuckle.

"Just a heads up, this sort of stuff... James really enjoys it. *Really* enjoys it," Dixon mutters pointedly, "As in, try to ignore everything below waist height."

The deadpan expression gets a raised brow as Ella seems unfazed "Come on, Frank if you're trying to rattle me then try harder. Think have heard it all from the escorts at the bar, the weird shit some of the criminal crowd are into..."

While Clyde is far from happy having to concede to someone else's demands, he's a little reassured that she's keeping it together.

That was how they ended up in a warehouse downtown, James at the doors as he nodded Clyde inside. When Dixon looked like he was waiting on an order where to go, Ella nodded him inside much to Clyde's frustration.

"Not keeping your guard dog, sugar?" James said, sauntering closer with a cig in hand.

Ella managed a weak, sarcastic smile. "No, I do just fine on my own thanks." She was not thrilled with the way he was watching her as she folded her arms.

Eventually, time was up. James moved to thump on the doors, but Dixon was already sliding them open as Clyde made a beeline for the car. He didn't look too ruffled, thankfully. Frank, however, was holding his hands put towards her in a calming gesture.

"Before you go in... go easy, all right? I know how your temper can get."

Ella frowns, confused, realization dawning slowly. Whoever is in there, she's already met. Striding past him, James is already on the inside of the door, sliding it shut behind her as her vision adjusts to the low light.

When it does, the figure tied to the chair comes into sharp focus, overly cocky attitude in full effect.

"Told you I wasn't above getting my hands dirty."

If he had another stupid comment to make, it was silenced as she strode over and jammed her heel into his crotch with enough force to tip the chair. Sending him clattering onto his back, the chair rattling off the concrete floors. Crouching beside him, she was fuming. "You son of a bitch. You were behind this, and you stood there in that lift, I'd only just got done patching him up, and you acted like you had a shred of morality in that weedy little body."

Despite the slight daze from his head hitting the floor, the man smirked. "Plants aligning. Trouble enough to shake Clyde's hold on power, and since you seem to be a *sucker* for the hero type it was a bonus that it was your little friend who made himself the perfect fuse." There was a crack as her elbow came down on his nose, a curse muffled as he coughed at the blood draining down his throat.

Methodically, Ella recalled every injury she could remember. Every bruise, every cut, every graze - dealing the same to Henry till she was kneeling exhausted on the concrete as she tried to get her breath back.

Lifting her gaze to James, who had been watching it all with a steadily growing smile, she tried to steady her voice and keep it firm. "That helps, or do I need to finish the job for you?" Ella's attitude caught him off guard as she got to her feet, slowly, given the ache settling into her bones.

"Oh, that little display will be on display for days maybe weeks. Tell Clyde I'll have this cleaned up by the morning," James said and Ella nodded briefly.

It wasn't till she was dropping heavily into the back seat of the car that the adrenaline started to ease, leaving her with little but exhaustion and the shakes.

"James says he'll have it clean by morning," she muttered, ignoring the expression of concern Dixon was drawing her in the rear-view mirror.

Clyde reached to tuck her against his side, his arm firmly around her shoulders as he passed her a handkerchief to clean her forearms and face of the few traces of blood.

* * *

It's Dixon who calls later to check in with James, discretely angling for a recall of what happened. He gets it, but of course, it's in excruciating detail, deliberately tuning out the noises he can hear in the background.

He finds Clyde standing at the door of his room, watching Ella sleeping. A frown deepens on his expression as Dixon fills in the events they missed, finishing with an almost sigh. "I've seen Frank's injuries. Aside from the nut shot, it's a near-perfect eye for an eye - not a scratch more."

That soothes Clyde to hear that Ella only made things even, and didn't go full revenge rage. It speaks to her character and her strength of emotion.

"Well, if Henry was looking to unsteady you, it really backfired. Especially considering your lady keeps impressing the old guys."

Frank's comment makes Clyde smile before his face changes to one of intent thinking.

CHAPTER 20

"Don't say it," Ella muttered, smoothing out the simple dress she'd only just been able to get back into, a tired huff of breath escaping her as she made sure all her hair was pinned out of the way of tiny grabbing hands.

Clyde stepped up behind her, resting his chin on her shoulder as he rocked the bundle in his arms gently. "Don't say what?" he asked innocently, a cheeky smile growing across his face as she met his gaze in the mirror with a pointed look.

Turning to transfer the bundle to her arms, she cradled the baby boy carefully, unable to stop the little smile. She'd never been much fussed about kids or not, have felt guilty for not feeling the cozy coo'ing love she thought she should. But from the second she found out, she wanted to protect.

Sure, she may not be the mother who tears up on his

first day of school. But she'd make sure he grew up safe, to be whomever he wanted to be.

In the wake of Henry's fuckery, the practical angle had taken focus. A quick courthouse marriage for the legal protections and benefits it'd offer, which had been revisited properly a few years down the line in the form of one hell of a party.

It was maybe a year after that when Dixon was startled by an aggressive 'son of a bitch!' yelled through the apartment. She'd not been exactly happy about it but had been sharp and protective at the mere suggestion of terminating. Clyde's reaction that evening had been pure joy, but it was barely five minutes before his talk of the next one was shut down fast.

Now, it was lunch with some of the other big players in Boston - Clyde wanting to show off his healthy and happy son as well as the wife with her reputation (namely for her humor, straight talking, and calmly executed temper) in some ego-stroking exercise.

In all honesty, Ella had coursework she'd rather be doing. It may be later in her life, but she was finally studying for a degree in Hospitality & Business - distance part-time but studying, nonetheless.

But, when Clyde smiled, an arm around her waist as he stared at their son with wonder, Ella couldn't say no - even to a stuffy lunch at the hotel.

The only downside – is James's move. His girlfriend, now fiancée, had gotten a job that would be a promotion. In Sweden. But Sweden has plenty of hotels, so it hadn't taken much for Rob to convince her to go as he packed his bags, too. They were happy out there, regular video chats meant they were in the loop about baby Nate and Ella had seen her fair share of their cat Dee making an absolute menace of himself.

MICHAEL

CHAPTER 1

It had started all by accident.

Carlina's grandfather was a tailor, a damn good one at that. While his son had had his sights set on a comfortable office job crunching numbers, the elderly man had cared for his granddaughter. Keeping her safe, rolling fabric onto bolts. As she got older, that extended to ordering and stock organizing of it - especially when he started teaching her everything he knew. The only condition of the knowledge was not to come onto the floor when the shop was open.

He never said why, and she never thought to pry. Until she was older, an adult in her own right, and the long days were taking a visible toll on him. "Nonno, let me help." Her grandfather hadn't taught her much Italian, her retention for second languages wasn't great, but she never forgot the word *Nonno*. He had reluctantly agreed, on the condition, she promise to be careful - some of their most loyal customers were not people you wanted to get on the wrong side of.

It wouldn't be long before she saw exactly what he meant.

"Paolo!" a smooth voice rang through the shop, Carlina sure she could almost feel it along the floorboards as she stuck just behind her grandfather's shoulder when he greeted the man, the voice being familiar enough that she could guess it was a regular. "Where have you been hiding this one?" It took Carlina a moment to realize he was referring to her as her grandfather proudly said, "Michael, essere al settimo cielo!"

"Grazie, my old friend. Who's this bella signorina?"

"Michael, this is my lovely granddaughter, Carlina."

The man's gaze softened to warmth, as if Carlina were a member of his family, a pleased comment of "Keeping business in the family, as it should be." He smiled kindly as he shook Carlina's small hand. Afterward, Paolo moved at a shuffle to herd the men to the fitting area while he pulled his tape measure from where it had hung under his collar.

Michael, who seemed to be the 'head', was eagerly chatting away as Carlina moved in near-perfect sync around her grandfather, noting measurements given in barely more than a whisper, knowing exactly what bolt he wanted pulled based on even vague half thoughts. By the end of the selection, Michael and his men had bought at least three suits each. Before he left, he was holding Carlina's face in his old hands. "God forbid the day Paolo passes, but I think this place will be in safe hands with you, nipotina!" The man turned a smile to Paolo, patting him on the shoulder as he exited.

* * *

It continued much the same, for nearly a year. In that time, she had come to figure out that a shocking amount of such customs were part of the Italian crime families. A fact only solidified when his shop went up in flames thanks to old wiring - the revolving door of guests to his hospital room looking like a casting for The Sopranos.

While Carlina's grandfather, Paolo was too broke and old to run his tailor shop, Carlina was intent on keeping the family business going.

Clearing out her savings, she bought a hearse. When it came to bolts of fabric, she picked them with their current clients in mind, kitting it out as something like a portable workbench. She still did most of the cutting and sewing at home, on the floor of her studio apartment, but it served well enough to travel to clients and keep the bills paid.

It was doing well when her grandfather passed. Despite the distraction, her grandfather's loyalist customers attended the funeral - all wearing his designs. Carlina kept her composure, but couldn't stop the tears from running at the sight.

A year and a half later

Carlina had gotten up early to visit her grandfather's grave before her appointments. Taking the time to crouch, head resting on the side of his headstone as she spoke to him. Like she did every week. Unsure if she really believed he could hear her wherever he may be. It was times like this she envied his faith, and the comfort it must have brought him in life.

Thankfully, her first appointment of the day was the same man from her first day on the floor of her grandfather's shop. As always, the man welcomed her at the door by catching her cheeks in his hands and dropping a brisk kiss on her forehead.

"Mornin'," she greeted, a work bag hanging from her shoulder as she unlocked the door.

Something was different, there was a new face today with the old man. He didn't look much older than Carlina, but her patience was running thin at the way he was looking at her.

"This is my son. Michael Jr., this is Carlina - Paolo's granddaughter." The predatory look turned to something softer.

"Nice to meet you. I'm sorry for your loss." Michael's voice was gentle, not as rumbling as his father's, but you could hear the family resemblance.

"Not a loss. We know exactly where he is," Carlina said, helping RJ onto the folding platform as he chuckled (used to her dark humor method of coping by now). However, that day would be the start of a series of events she would later come to loathe.

Two months later

The elder Michael passed and his son took over the 'business'. Despite having gone to law school, Michael, Jr. used that knowledge in nowhere near the intended way. As the landscape of New York had changed, and the elders had faded away, he'd gradually worked Carlina under his wing. Useful, given that it meant she carried his protection like a younger sister would - and he often confided in her like an older brother may.

It was rare that Michael leveraged that relationship, aside from when dealing with women in his life (in the beginning it had been ushering out clingy flings, in later years it was advice to keep his wife sweet) or as a distraction (often, he could bring her to a meeting he wanted to go well, she was certainly more widely liked than he was, him seen as an equal and her someone to be nurtured, and could often sweeten deals with some tailoring if need be.)

Until their neighborhood had a bit of a shuffle. More fresh blood was brought in from outside the borough. No matter, it was a lot of young officers just starting in life who were easily bought off just like their predecessors. The only sticking point was their Chief - an old southern sheriff type, content with what he had and too dedicated to the job for his own good. Sniffing far too close to their work, getting under Michael's feet as he tried to expand their business - but Michael had a plan.

CHAPTER 2

"That's it, Michael, you've lost your damn mind," Carlina said briskly as her hands flew across the fabric in front of her, wielding a large pair of scissors that seemed to slide through it like a hot knife through butter. He sat wide legged on her tiny couch, quirked a brow as he sat forward, a hand smoothing over his beard. "Careful. I have limits of disrespect I'll tolerate, even from you."

Carlina huffed as she sat back on her haunches. "Sorry. I just worry about you. You have a family and business to look after, it's a lot easier to do when you're not behind bars." That earned her a slow small smile, prompting her to continue, "you said it yourself, Chief's too upright to be bought off. If you try too hard, he'll squeal, and you'll have him breathing down your neck, then the Feds." Carlina resumed cutting, neatly bundling the pieces in folders with the customer names and notes.

It was the methodical way she moved that Michael focused on, graceful and so assured.

That could be exactly what he needed.

Honey, rather than vinegar.

"You're right. I think we should welcome the new Chief as our new neighbor. What about a two-piece suit for the guy?" There was a scheming look in Michael's eye, like he always got when he thought he'd checkmate whatever opponents he was dealing with. "Hey, I happen to know the best tailor in New York."

Throwing in some flattery with a smile, Michael knew from experience had a great chance of getting Carlina. She rolled her eyes but then grumbled *yes, Michael.*

Later in the week

Deputy Chief of Police, RJ Brown, the new deputy chief of police at Brooklyn's 62nd Police Precinct had not followed in drunken father's footsteps - instead, he wanted to be a police officer. Bright-eyed and full of moral enthusiasm. That had faded over the years as he rose through the ranks and became jaded to the small community in which he'd been raised in Houston. He'd turned to drink, curb-crawling, treated it like support to prop himself up with as pieces of himself gathered dust and the loneliness gnawed at the corners of his mind - till someone suggested he ran for sheriff; an honorary more than practical role. Despite the allure, RJ realized he couldn't do it anymore.

Moved to New York, went where ever he was assigned, got sober, and traded one vice for what most would consider a better-paying option. Forget about those damn cinnamon buns from Cinnabon a block away from the precinct. It had cushioned him up a bit, or maybe that was age - either way, his uniform was a little snug when he got promoted to Chief and slung off to this precinct. One that hadn't been paid much attention till near half its staff were due to retire the same year.

Now, here he was, attempting to bring the place up to speed when it seemed even the force had neglected it for a lot longer than anyone let on.

Michael's meeting with Chief Brown

Another waste of time, pompous meeting with an overly important public figure. RJ was grateful to unbutton his jacket as he sank into the chair behind his desk, huffing as he flicked through his tasks and lists for the day ahead.

That was, until that smooth talker knocked on his door. Law school kid, extensive family, very nice car - Chief had a feeling he was the one pulling the strings on the puppets that had been trying to butter up his cops in his district. But he called for the guy to come and meet him anyway.

"Evenin' Chief," Michael greeted having a cocky smirk as they made small talk about some community projects. As RJ shifted in his seat, trying not to let on it was an attempt to shift the sharp waist of his pants, Michael saw his chance and pounced.

"That looks like a little snug, you got there? I know the feeling. My father was very cautious about the diet we grew up on…"

Chief Brown kept a deadpan expression rather than giving Michael the reward of a reaction.

"Hey, I know the best tailor in New York, even does house calls. Let 'em know I sent you. They'll cut you a nice deal," Michael said, fishing a card out of his inner pocket. He held it out between his fingers as he got to his feet.

Chief Brown took it and read over it as Michael excused himself.

"Be seeing ya around, Chief."

* * *

Chief Brown reached for his desk phone - punching in the number on the card and anxiously waited as the phone rang.

"Paolo's Tailoring. How can I help you?"

Chief could almost hear the beam in the woman's voice as he forced his brain to work, his mouth to form the right words. Clearing his throat, he was grateful to hear his voice come out unaffected. "Callin' bout lettin' out a suit? Michael Maccioni had recommended you guys."

The Chief heard a soft chuckle that made him

anxious to know more about the person on the other side of the line.

"Oh yeah! Michael and his family have been coming to the shop for years. If it's small, it shouldn't take no time at all. We could work on it later tonight and have it ready for you by tomorrow—let's say five—if that's okay?"

Chief Brown glanced to the chair where his uniform was hanging up, thanking his past self for bringing it in. "Sure, no problem. Can I trouble you to come to the station to pick it up? This is the Chief of Police."

"Sure, no problem."

Once Carlina confirmed the address, she made assurances the uniform would be finished in time. Meanwhile, Chief Brown wasted no time getting back to work.

About an hour later

At a light knock at the door, RJ answered it properly this time, eyebrows raising at the petite Italian woman with the bulky workbag standing on the other side, who he'd assumed was a shop assistant.

"Here to let out a suit?" the woman said, prompting Chief to wave her inside his office. Extending a hand, he cast a slowly roving gaze over the young woman. "You can call me Deputy Chief or RJ." It clicked into place at the name - *oh, Michael was getting a piece of her mind the next time she saw him.*

"Carlina," she said with a slight smile, setting her workbag down on the chair.

Deputy Chief Brown shrugged on the jacket, holding his arms away as Carlina slung the tape measure around him, acutely aware of just how damn close she was. "Need some help down there'?" he asked in that relaxed drawl, watching her. On instinct, she raised her gaze to his as she spoke and directly regretted it.

Normally, the kindhearted customer was much older or soft around the edges. The younger ones, who were brave enough to flirt, had all the muscles in the world and insensitive pitches. Yet, here's a guy who looks just the right amount of older, not really too much out of shape or at least that's what Carlina had supposed. He was big enough down there for Carlina not to help but think about situations which are definitely not suitable for the task at hand.

"No, no, it's fine. I can let out the pants based on measurements, so I'll be out of your hair in no time. I should have this done for you by tomorrow."

Carlina wanted to kick herself, seeing that she was dangerously close to babbling. She slid the Chief's jacket from his shoulders and folded it in her bag with the rest of the suit.

"Thanks a lot. Definitely appreciate it." Chief smiled and Carlina seemed just a touch flustered. It had been a while that any man had that effect on Carlina.

Later in the day

Carlina had torn Michael a new one on the phone,

while she ran the Chief's suit through the sewing machine. He'd listened to her little rant, huffing a bored noise when she was finally done talking.

"I see an opportunity for something good, Carlina."

"I'm a seamstress, not a damn lookout!"

"Watch your tone. I know that. If Chief's got eyes on you, he's not looking at us."

"So, what, I'm your bait now?" Carlina sighed.

"If he were hungry, you would be. He's just a nice guy from Texas trying hard to do his job in my New York—"

"I think you're underestimating him, Michael."

"I think you're forgetting your place."

Then, the line suddenly went silent.

Carlina reminded herself of just how lucky she was to have the connections she did. It was literally her job to support her family, and that came with loads of bullshit. Being an Italian growing up in New York was like living in Goodfellas the movie, but that's the perception everyone believes we live in.

"I love you, Carlina." Michael's soothing tone snapped Carlina out of that spiral of worry as she picked up the handset, turning it back off speaker.

"Love you too, Michael. I'm sorry, you're right…"

"Good girl! Keep me posted about brother RJ."

"Goodbye, Michael. You're so rude."

CHAPTER 3

True to her word, as much as the situation made her feel a little uneasy, Carlina was right back at the police precinct the next evening with a slightly less snug suit. She'd hastily stepped out when she'd prompted him to check it fit and heard the tell-tale clink of a belt - whether it was done for his comfort or hers, she wasn't entirely sure. It wasn't usually an issue. Waiting at the door, one shoulder blade resting on the frame, but the other on the door, Carlina stumbled slightly when it was opened.

Pivoting on her heel, "All good?" she asked brightly as Chief Brown strolled to sink into his chair, motioning her to shut the door behind her. Carlina perched on a seat across from him. "That's some good work, quick too. What do I owe ya?" A ghost of a smile on his lips, tone relaxed as Carlina frowned momentarily.

She replied slowly, amusement as if it were obvious weaving in her words, "Nothing, it's a small thing, really.

But if you're ever in need of a tailor, hope I'll be the first you call."

That warm charm came so easily when it was attached to her work, unlike off the clock where she fumbled with her words more often than not, feeling put on the spot.

"Don't worry, I'll be giving you a call as long as I have this weight around her." Chief Brown grabbed his stomach making Carlina blush. "Least, let me say thank you and buy you dinner."

"Hmm—maybe another time. I'll be seein' ya soon, Chief."

Chief Brown nodded disappointed that he hadn't been more pushy, but hearing the word *Chief* roll off her tongue the way that it had did had tempered his spirit a bit.

***

It continued like that over the next two months. A split seam here, a missing button there, all small things Carlina could do with her kit - all little jobs that she ended up doing just sat in his office for less than an hour.

Meanwhile, Michael was happy.

Kind of.

He had been pressing Carlina for dirt, information, anything to tip the scales in his favor.

One night at the tailor's shop, Carlina had had enough, slamming her heavy scissors on the table as she paused cutting. Taking steadying breaths, she tried to keep her tone polite as she stood. "Look, Michael. The Chief's very busy with all those crimes in the black neighborhood, okay—There's no need to go on the offensive when things are just working out the way they are."

Air was knocked out of Carlina's lungs as Michael surged forward to back Carlina into the wall, pressing his holster deliberately into her hip.

"You're not a fuckin' kid anymore, Carlina, so I'm not about to treat you like one." His hand flexed warningly around her throat, "You're like family, so you know the nature of this business. If you want the insurance it affords, you'll remember your place."

Michael then let go of her neck, stroking her cheek gently as he pressed a kiss to her forehead. "I just want to keep everyone *safe*, okay? And that includes you. Now please, just do as I tell you."

"Okay, okay… I'm sorry, Michael," Carlina gasped.

***

Safe.

It wasn't about feeling as safe as it did. Carlina had this awful feeling inside her like she was on the verge of panic and couldn't shake it loose. Something felt off, wrong, and she couldn't put her finger on it.

Maybe it was the lack of sleep getting to Carlina, strange noises at her door had been waking her up at random hours for weeks now. But she'd yet to find the source, and none of her neighbors said anything, so she was thinking it was all in her head.

Tipping the waitress on her way out of one of her favorite restaurants, Carlina pulled her jacket a little tighter, as if it would do anything against the rain. She was about a third of the way home before she heard someone pull up not far behind her, the sound of heavy boots on the wet pavement before she found herself in a patch of dry. Well, kind of. She found herself under the Chief's jacket as he held it over their heads.

"You're soaked! Get in before you become sick."

This wasn't the usual charming drawl, this was an order. This was not Michael aka I'm the fuck-in-charge rather it was the sweet Chief of Police. Not helped by the way his elbows caged her head with how he held the jacket, the heat of him close at her back as he ushered her into the car. When Chief dropped into the driver's side, he stowed his jacket in the passenger footwell before turning in his seat to face Carlina. "Where to? I'm not about to let you walk home in that shit."

Carlina had opened her mouth to argue, opting instead to snap it closed with a sigh as she rattled off her address. Waiting until they were crawling through traffic, Carlina frankly said," Bensonhurst, a few blocks from Seth Low Playground."

With the car's heat on, Carlina was now warming up. Chief Brown didn't take his eyes off the road as he responded with a vague smile. "No sweat. It ain't every day I get to play hero for a good-looking girl like yourself." His comment prompting a very undignified snort of laughter from Carlina.

"A sunken rat who was too stubborn to carry an umbrella," Carlina said, annoyed at herself as she twisted to shrug off her jacket when she felt the water soak through to the shirt underneath.

His gaze lifted, just briefly, from the road. Skimming quickly over the dipped neck to settle on that expression he'd grown unfortunately familiar with. The frown when she disappeared into her head, chewing herself out over the slightest thing like it was a heinous crime.

"Hey, none of that, okay—" Chief liked how efficiently his voice snapped Carlina back to reality. "You're being too hard on yourself." His tone left no room for arguments, the pair sitting in silence as they got closer to her place.

Chief pulled into the curb, trying to minimize the distance Carlina had had to cover to get inside, despite how much the raining had slackened up. He was rewarded with that sweet smile that reached her eyes.

"Thank you again for helping me home."

Keys already looped around her thumb, jacket in hand like Carlina was ready to whip it over her head the second she stepped out.

"No problem, any time," Chief said as he watched Carlina disappear past her front door.

***

Michael wasn't happy.

The sight of the police cruiser rolling through the neighborhood had ruffled a few feathers. His rant about the Chief, as he paced her living room, was cut off sharply.

"Can you please stop it, Michael?"

All that did was turned his frustration to Carlina with a set jaw and hard eyes as she took a breath to continue in her best attempt at being respectful. "I got caught in the rain at the restaurant. Chief was driving down the street and offered me a ride home." Her explanation seemed to soothe Michael a little, if only for the fact it confirmed the police chief had been in a different neighborhood if he was patrolling and not sniffing around.

"Seems like the Chief's gotten quite the soft spot for you," Michael said, sounding calmer.

He was met with a bitten-out response from Carlina, though.

"Maybe he's thinking like you. I'm some tool being used in some testosterone-fueled game of chess."

Carlina wasn't expecting a reaction; a noise of anger bubbling in her throat as Michael loosed his gun from the holster, gesturing with it as if it were the most normal thing to do in the world.

"Here's the thing, we all are. It's the name of the fuckin' game."

Michael looked angrier than Carlina could recall seeing him, pressing herself further into the sofa as if a few inches would make her any safer.

"Fuck!" his fist hit the doorframe with a sickening sound. Carlina jumping to her feet to grab an ice pack from the fridge. Her concern etched deep in her expression as she fussed. For her countryman, she was always the most caring.

Michael sighed, sliding his gun back into the holster to wrap his arm around her, huddling her against his chest as he spoke with a deep rumble like his father. "I'm sorry. You're right. It isn't fair to keep blowing hot air. I'll back off." He nudged her chin with his 'injured' hand, near forcing Carlina to hold his gaze as he painted a caring expression on his face. "Maybe the Chief's being straight up with you. I'll let you find out what you can. While his attention is on you, he shouldn't be a problem."

He hugged Carlina tightly, tucking her head under his chin.

"I trust you like family, all right?"

"Yes, Michael. We're family…" Carlina sighed.

Well, that meant Michael would still be watching, keeping an eye on Carlina, but this way he could keep her in his grasp. It was better than pissing her off and losing a valuable asset.

At times, Michael loved Carlina like a sibling. As his family had expanded and times had changed, it was a lot more difficult not to include her as another member of the family. It was all about what Carlina could bring to the business. The answer to that was a lot. The world may be modern, but many Italians still abided by the old ways - voices always a little softer in the presence of a woman, less likely to resort to fights, some of the older ones still struggled simply to say 'no' to her. That came in useful, especially when

Michael's criminal record was clean. He toyed with the idea of going back to law school. He was good at it and his family ties would mean he could get things done the way he wanted. A thought for another time, perhaps.

Two days later

"Officer..."

Chief Brown lifted his head at a familiar voice as he watched Carlina approach one of his officers with a clothes bag in hand, handing it over by the hanger as the officer beamed.

Approaching, Chief Brown caught the tail end of their conversation.

"Just make sure you take her somewhere real nice. Let her show you off properly, all right? Your lady deserves it," Carlina said giving the officer a smile as she squeezed his shoulder.

"Evening, Carlina," Chief Brown greeted with a slow smile, moving with measured assurance as he rest his hands at his belt.

"Chief, I was hoping I'd run into you. Got something for you." Carlina fished something out of a paper bag; a box of mini cinnamon rolls from Cinnabon. She was not hurrying to remove her hand from where Chief's finger-tips brushed her palm when she handed it to him. "As a gesture of appreciation, I heard you had a bit of a soft spot for these."

Chief Brown took a step forward just to see Carlina's breath catch.

"Yeah, bit of a sucker for these things when I can get my hands on them," he commented, gaze heavy with a subtext that had Carlina flushing despite the way her neutral expression.

Sharply breaking the gaze, diverting her eyes to the floor as Carlina bowed slightly under the guise of checking, she'd closed her bag.

"Buon appetito, Chief." Carlina's words were laced with amusement, but the Chief was focused on how elegant it sounded.

Oh, dear, the Chief wasn't going to be getting his mind off of Carlina anytime soon.

CHAPTER 4

This wasn't supposed to be anything different from Carlina's usual day at the shop.

It's a suit. She'd taken these measurements hundreds of times before. No big deal.

A two-piece, casual even.

Except Carlina could feel his eyes boring into the top of her head as she crouched to take an in-seam measurement, standing abruptly as her knuckles grazed his crotch. The entire time she'd worked, the Chief watched her like a hawk with that slight smile - it was making her highly uncomfortable, but the 'why' was still up for debate.

She moved behind him to pin the shoulders, make slight adjustments to how the collar sat, marking places for mini darts to make it fit like a glove. Without her in his line of sight, now was the time he made small talk.

"So, you and Michael…" he couldn't stop the smile as she let out a snort.

"Michael and I are like family. Like my big brother," Carlina sounded ruefully amused.

And it really sounded like siblings to the Chief. He could hear hints of how his sister and he spoke about each other sometimes, which brought warmth to his chest.

"Guessing he's not above chasing the good guys away," Chief said chuckling as Carlina adjusted his sleeve, turning up the hem and pinning it swiftly.

She responded, eyes on the task, "Michael's not my keeper. I think I can protect myself."

Carlina's self-esteem obviously wasn't as high as her confidence in business would lead someone to believe. She played the part well, but the cracks showed as Chief examined her. Behind the persona of her work, connections - there was just a woman desperate not to be alone. The possessive urge that curled in him at that, felt darker - but alluring, he wanted to lean into it. Hear that little startled gasp, feel her tremble under his touch.

He shook his head to clear those thoughts as his eyes focused on Carlina - face creased in a slight frown as she adjusted the hang of the jacket, smoothing the lapels to ensure they were even. Before his brain completely kicked in, he reached to catch one of her hands in his, earning himself a quiet but sharp intake of breath.

"Chief…"

A hint of quiet warning from Carlina's voice, not raising her head as the Chief's thumb ran along her wrist, almost coaxing her to agree.

"Let's meet for coffee. No cuffs, I promise…" he said shaking his sleeve slightly. "All on me."

"Okay, I give in. You got me for one cup at least…"

* * *

It had started as a cup, but then it had been another and then many more along with breakfast and pastries. Their exchanges had come easily, the pair rattling through the cliff notes of their life stories with little brother. Chief Brown hadn't dug too much into her in regards to her ties to Michael, listening intently when she spoke about her grandfather with that fond smile. He'd found it easy to talk about his sister seeming to get the way you could be driven up the wall but still do anything for them - even if you were adamant, you hated them.

At some point, Chief's hand rested over Clarina's on the table, thumb drawing patterns on her palm as he listened - until they were being nudged out the restaurant at closing.

* * *

Carlina wiped her hair back off her face with a guilty chuckle. "I'm sorry, completely stole one of your days off." He caught her with an arm loosely around the waist, lips quirking in amusement as he held his other hand up in a soothing gesture. "No need to apologize. Been a long time since I've enjoyed such good company." He leaned to brush his lips at her jaw, pressing firmly just below her ear.

Traitorous body, Carlina thought darkly as she fought to keep her eyes from closing and her knees from giving out. *Why did it have to be complicated and tangled in all the other bullshit?*

Why couldn't she just meet a guy like a normal person, release the tension that coiled like a spring in her, and get on with life? Nice, simple, and clean. No, instead Carlina had to navigate the near-constant stream of whispers in her ear - everyone else's agendas and expectations.

"Come on," his words broke her out of that little mental chaos, gently guiding her towards his car. "It's too late for a young lady to be walking around these streets. Let me take you home."

Without thought, Carlina agreed, apparently moving on auto-pilot at the idea of being cared for.

A comfortable sort of quiet as Carlina and Chief Brown snuck the occasional glance at each other like some goddamn kids on a first date. Well, Carlina was like a bashful teen, and Chief's look was definitely veering more towards the horny dude who folk were a little worried about.

The Chief, being the big honcho in town, even walked Carlina to her door. She felt proud that she'd been right in her assessment that he was a good person. Thank goodness that Michael trusted her enough not to interfere.

Smile slowly widening as Carlina leaned back slightly against the door frame, head dipping slightly as Chief Brown brushed the back of his knuckles along her cheek. "Know I ain't a young buck," he chuckled at the admonishing look she drew him as if he were speaking far too harsh about himself. "But what are my chances for more time with a pretty young thing like you?"

Carlina's voice was gentle, like she thought a lack of volume would hide the bashful amusement in it to appear more put together. Like a proper adult, like she normally was - an opinionated carer, "Chances are very high, Officer."

Chief dragged his thumb across Carlina's bottom lip, eyes dark as he watched it, that fucking moniker sending his urges churning, mind flooded with every inappropriate thought he'd ever had about her. Surging forward, there was the soft thud of his knuckles bumping off the wood as his lips crashed against Carlina's and the Chief cradled her head to protect it from the frame.

That could have been taken as tender nervousness, but the way the Chief pinned her in place with his hips, practically grinding his bulge against her midsection, was a little less tender and certainly not nervous.

"Oh Chief," Carlina moaned with difficulty, against his lips, breaking apart as he dropped his head to the crook of her neck, trying to catch his breath. "My neighbors will see us."

He pressed himself flush against her, prompting a sharp intake of breath. "I'm the Deputy Chief in this area. I'm here to protect and serve," he said heaving, now kissing Carlina on the neck before he finally gathered himself. He then took a step back and said, "have a wonderful evening, Carlina'."

"Thanks, Chief! You, too."

An hour later

"Looks nice…" Michael said, admiring the cut pieces set out to sew as Carlina pinned his jacket, turning gradually as she marked out the tweaks. It was practically routine at this point. "How's our favorite customer?" he asked, quirking his head as he watched her flush but keep her expression neutral, voice unaffected as she answered around the pins in her teeth.

"The Chief, you mean…"

There was a snort of derision that made Carlina's head snap up at Michael, frowning in confusion and annoyance, but he was staring straight ahead.

He then muttered, "Bet, he loved you measuring his fat ass even though you barely got your arms around him." Michael chuckled as Carlina stood to check his sleeve hems, 'accidentally catching him with one pin as she threaded it through and tried not to rise to the bait.

Sometimes, Carlina's nerves would get to her, and she needed to restart. She daydreamed about having a normal job, some roommates, and living somewhere far away. But luck was never on her side. Something always happened that vexed her, and she had yet to end up taking that big leap. The gnawing self-doubt was never quite quiet enough.

"Just be careful. That fucker is a cop," Michael's words felt soft, almost affectionate, but Carlina's patience was so thin it just sounded condescending to her ears.

"I will Michael," Carlina pleaded.

* * *

When Michael departed, Carlina rushed over to the sofa to look at the Help Wanted section in today's newspaper. She called in to a few to inquiry about part-time shifts so that she wouldn't be away from the shop.

Her intention was plain and simple; she needed to get away from Michael. He was controlling and possessive despite not having no real family bond.

This time, Carlina vowed to take things slowly in order to avoid Michael's wrath.

CHAPTER 5

A month later

Did Carlina feel bad about leading Michael on? Yes. Did she feel like absolute death as she downed yet another cup of coffee in an attempt to keep herself buzzed? Also, yes.

But chasing them around the garden to the howls of laughter from the small kids was doing wonders for her mood, face hurting from smiling so much as she flopped onto the grass. Ending up dogpiled by Michael's trio of terror as his wife watched with a grin. Carlina made sure to keep up the persona of being with *family* despite her newfound purpose in life.

The daytime was still for tailoring; Carlina was catching chunks of sleep either side of four hours at her part-time gig at a warehouse nearby. Mind-numbing work, torture on the legs, but it didn't pay too badly and the hours fit her schedule. Slowly but surely, Carlina was saving away every cent she could - no longer actively searching for new clients, not giving her usual reminders of important events to prompt bigger orders from existing ones.

Carlina had adjusted her expectations slightly. She simply wanted to move to fresh scenery, be able to afford her bills and have a regular job like most Americans. She had zero issues staying in the neighborhood, doing the occasional favor, but she was fast realizing she was burned out having it be her life. *She was exhausted. Bone level, feeling it in every cell, exhausted.*

It would be so easy to close her eyes, take a little nap on the lawn as the kids rest. But no. Hauling herself to her feet, she hugged the little family goodbye and headed home with comments about having a lot to do.

Yeah in that, Carlina needed to change, wake the hell up, and get to work.

Carlina could do it in her sleep at this point. A month only and it was second nature. The promised time with the Chief had been stolen; coffee dates when they managed, but he seemed content enough so she wasn't about to dwell on it too much - especially when he was so over the moon when he got his tailor-made suit. Contrary to his comments on having gotten soft, she thought he looked incredibly sharp in it, actually.

It was a good thing it was habit, because just keeping

her eyes open as the first whispers of sunrise crept over the horizon was proving a battle. Trudging along the sidewalk, Carlina stopped to lean against a signpost as she waited for the crossing lights to go green, pushing herself to keep walking. Just get home, then she could sleep. She could flop on the floor, it wouldn't matter, she just had to get past her front door, then sleep was hers.

* * *

At least, it was until there was a brisk rapping at the door. It was a weekend. Who in the hell bothered to seek her out on weekends? Virtually everyone was usually too busy with their own stuff to need her.

Shuffling to the door, Carlina chances a glance at the clock. Oh, that explained why she actually felt kind of rested. She'd slept the whole damn day, guiltily realizing it was after four in the afternoon. Peaking round it, she rubbed at her eyes as she opened it properly to find Leonardo, her old boyfriend, with takeaway and her favorite bottle of wine from the motherland, Barolo. "Figured I'd surprise you, since we've both been so busy lately." He quirked a brow at the uniform Carlina was still wearing. She followed his gaze, cursing under her breath as she stood aside to let him in.

"You know how to pop up at just the right time, Leonardo. Give me a minute to get myself together." Carlina gestured vaguely to herself as she slipped away, unaware of how intently he watched her leave.

* * *

When she returned, Leonardo had set out a quick meal on the coffee table, complete with one of the stubby candles she usually left on the bookshelf. "You're such a *gentiluomo*," Carlina said smiling, realizing a second too late that she'd said it aloud as she settled next to him on the sofa. He put his hand on her knee, fingertips just barely tracing up the inside of her thigh as he squeezed at her knee, handing her a glass of Barolo with an adoring look that had her running on autopilot again.

Meaning, when Leonardo slung an arm around Carlina's shoulders, she had tucked herself under his shoulder. When he'd full-belly laughed at something she said, she had let her head fall to his shoulder. Like it was habit, like it came smoothly. They'd sat like that in silence for a bit, relaxed, till Leonardo shifted slightly to face Carlina. Arm not around her shoulders raising till he could cradle her jaw in his hand, near dragging her into a fierce kiss.

She wanted to resist but Leonardo always knew how to get her going. Call it a fling or whatever…

There was a high-pitched noise of surprise from Carlina, a hand bracing against his shoulder as the other fisted tightly in his shirt. It was a heady feeling that knocked a good portion of Carlina's brain offline. To be wanted, desired, especially by someone who had snuck into so many of her thoughts since they've known each other throughout the years.

By the time the rational part had worked again,

Leonardo had eased Carlina back, sort of propped up against the arm of the sofa, his tall stature pressing her into the cushions below. The hand that had been at her cheek, trailing down her throat, moving to grip her waist firmly under her sweater. Leonardo had shifted to nip at her neck, a low growl in his throat as she arched up into him, feeling one of her hands slide down his chest to palm him through his slacks as he thrust into her grip instinctively. He dropped a kiss at the bottom of her neckline, sucking gently as their gaze met. He was almost a goner at the sweet mewl that fell from her lips, head thrown back.

Knock, knock…

Carlina missed the first knock at the door, but Leonardo didn't, gripping her thigh tightly to hitch it around his waist, swallowing the squeal as he ground against her clothed center. Until she caught the second one, murmuring "fuck," as she reluctantly slid out from under Leonardo, despite his attempts to convince her to stay. He watched her fix her clothes, tidy her hair a little, and then open the door smiling, though not as wide as she usually would. Leonardo took the chance to sprawl like a king on his throne, easing a little of the pressure over where he was achingly hard.

"Everything is okay, Michael. Just slept in most of the day - it's no biggie."

Leonardo saw Michael's face appear briefly over Carlina's head during their conversation, eyes narrowing slightly at the scene in front of him.

"Alright, well, take care. You know where I am if you need anything," Michael said, squeezing her shoulder, refusing to let her drop his gaze, as if he viewed Leonardo as a potential threat.

When Carlina shut the door, she slid the lock back on, resting her forehead against the wood with a dull thud.

"Carlina…" Leonardo said seeing Carlina appear a bit nervous. "Come here…" He patted one of his thighs with a slow smile that he'd learned hooked her in.

Worked like a charm, Carlina settled straddling his thigh as his hands slid over her figure appreciatively, one hand back to palm him as the other raked through his hair before dropping to clutch tightly at his shoulder. Leonardo dropped a hand to hastily open his fly, groaning as he released his length, not missing the shuddering snort from Carlina as her hand grabbed it. She guide the pace till Leonardo was about to explode. She changed speeds and it wasn't long before Leonardo had thrown his head back over the sofa, a string of praises low on his voice, practically crushing her to his chest by a hand on her backside and nape. A moan that almost sounded painfully ripping from him as he came, hazy brained as Carlina reached for a napkin to clean up and tuck him away in his slacks again, face buried in the crook of his neck.

* * *

Leonardo wasn't expecting that. Not how good it felt, how quick he was reduced to a mess. Trailing his fingers along Carlina's arm, he heard a sigh from Carlina - so soft, so caring, she'd make a perfect little girlfriend again. *How far could he go? The last time they broke up, it got messy. Would she give him another chance?*

"Carlina…"

Leonardo inched under her sweater to lift it. Then, he pressed down against his thigh and said, "It's time to my turn to please you, baby."

Those blunt words flustered her.

Carlina's breathing sped up as she trembled. Meanwhile, Leonardo's hands widened her thighs, gripping them so manly. His lips tormented her breasts then went downward. He kept repeating, "you're mines, you're mines…." Those words alone could have made Carlina stop. However, she came numerous times knowing that he could only torture her body and not her mind.

CHAPTER 6

Four months later

"When were you going to say something? Or were you going to up and leave without telling me?" Michael's voice was verging on a volume that would have the neighbors far and near complaining, looming over her as Carlina sat on the sofa, slowly curling in on herself. "After everything I do for you, how could you fuckin' do this to me, Carlina?"

Carlina lifted her head at that, stubbornly refusing to cry despite knowing she looked glassy eyed. "I have a job, just like you. My new apartment is even closer to you. I don't see what I've done wrong!" Michael snatched her chin in a painfully tight grip, neither taking the defeat of blinking first.

"Like me, huh? A god-damn regular job because I

have a family to support." His hard expression faded into a sneer. "You whoring yourself out now?"

Carlina reacted before she really had time to process, slapping Michael across the face. Her eyes were cold, expression stony, chest heaving with the effort to keep her temper in check, hands now clenched so tightly into fists that he could see her knuckles turning white.

"That's one. Cross me again and you'll not live long enough to regret it." Michael's voice was scarily calm as his jaw flexed.

Carlina said, "Look—Leonardo has been a light in my life, helping me when you're not around. Things happen..." she sighed before continuing, "I just want a normal life." Carlina sounded defeated and exhausted.

Michael sank into the space next to her, bundling her tightly into his arms. "I get it, you didn't choose this way of life and you weren't born into it - just a normal girl, wanting a normal life." There was a heavy pause before he finished his thought. "I'll love any child you conceive, but at least wait till you're married. Preferably not to, you know—."

He didn't miss the way she bristled slightly at that. "What would be wrong with that? For someone who practically offered me up like a steak to a wolf, you seem to have quite the problem with Leonardo now."

Michael had to suppress a frustrated noise at that. In all honesty, it was mildly entertaining to watch the aging, out-of-shape policeman chase his sister. But this? The fact he seemed to have gotten his hooks in her, not half as entertaining.

"I didn't—" the defensive comment died with a huff he tried to play off. "I just think that you could do better. Closer to your own age, Italian, you know—someone who could look after you." Michael squeezed Carlina in a hug, trying to keep back the possessive streak at losing a valuable asset.

Carlina let out a teary scoff of laughter. "All the guys my age are in your pocket. Besides, the Chief looks after me," the day in the rain flashing to the forefront of her mind and prompting an almost shy smile. "I think you're just getting territorial cause you think I won't need you anymore."

Michael bristled at that, at the idea someone like the Chief could replace him, but she put it down to sulky confirmation. "I'll always need you, Michael. We're family."

Family. They may not share DNA, but it was true.

"Remember, keep me in the loop. All of this could have been avoided if you'd just talked to me." Michael brought out that firm but sad voice, the one he knew always made her heart ache, the one that always seemed to smooth so well over the cracks caused by his outbursts. It was a finer balancing act than some of his men - firm enough to temper that defiant spark, but soft enough that Carlina remained blissfully unaware that her decisions were not her own.

It made for good practice in law. Meaning that even

as others tried to bait Michael to fumble the professional facade, he remained cocky and stoic in the court. Self-assured, in control - at the end of the day, things would go his way. He always saw to it that they did.

* * *

Michael didn't need to know that she'd asked for the Chief's opinion before buying her new place. That was just fuel for a fire she wasn't in the mood to keep from raging out of control. The only downside was the AC that desperately needed to be replaced - but she figured there was plenty of time before summer for that to be a solvable problem.

Besides, once Michael let slip about her career plans, her oldest clients had pestered her to stay. While Carlina had a fresh set of walls to look at, her work was still firmly in the hands of someone else. Admittedly, she had dropped the warehouse job in favor of a few hours each morning doing stock at a local furnishing dealer. With the added perk that she got first pick of fabrics, they got from estate sales. She'd been very conservative with that, but had got some lovely cotton in time for the warmer weather.

It felt a little less exhausting - while the dealer was a friend of a client; he wasn't a part of that life. He didn't seem to pay much heed to her ties to it, outside of fondly remembering the window displays of her grandfather's shop and proudly informing her he had helped furnish the place in his youth - both agreeing that Patrick's favorite chair didn't match but could not be faulted on craftsmanship.

When the weather got warmer, even the new machines in the windows struggled to keep the place cool - a downside of living somewhere so densely populated, Carlina guessed. Judging by the fact the station was also struggling not to turn into a furnace.

A fact she only found out by chance when her boss called in a favor. Drop-in receipts to the station, simple enough, but he'd not been handling the heat well and was dashing home early. She'd agreed quickly, face riddled with concern when he'd met her at the door looking two steps from keeling over.

He finally seemed to believe her it was no bother, tucking himself into a taxi home as Carlina continued her journey on foot - sticking to shaded sidewalks wherever possible, the shirt-styled dress already helping a fair amount with making the weather more bearable. Thankfully, as it firmly ticked to evening, it brought the temperature down just a smidge. Not far enough, though.

Letting herself into the Chief's office with a brisk warning knock. Carlina's greeting smile as she raised the envelope in explanation slid to a frown of concern when she realized he was doing paperwork (so she could speak) and looked firmly like he'd hit the floor if he stood. "What is it with men and stupid decisions?" she huffed, more to herself than him, as she darted out to soak a handkerchief before returning. He was leaned back in his chair, watching her with almost tired amusement as she skirted the desk. "Hello to you too, baby'." There was amusement laced through his words as Carlina cradled his cheek.

Her frown of concern eased slightly as she met his gaze, dabbing at his face tenderly with the damp fabric. "You're so busy with all crime in this city that I worry you forget to look after yourself," she said, loosening his tie to unfasten the button at his collar, missing the way he shifted slightly in his seat, watching her intently. The weight of his hand resting on her hip made her focus.

"Wouldn't want to miss out on this." His voice low, lips quirking slightly in a smile as he pulled her slightly closer. "An Italian SI model tearing off my clothes then wiping the sweat off my forehead?" he used his grip on her hip to tug her against him, prompting something like a giggle as she landed in his lap.

"Chief, you're still on the clock," Carlina stated, but her heart wasn't in it as he pressed a kiss against her cheek.

"It's just us here," he said lowly, breath brushing over her neck as he held her to him. "Everyone is out on patrol." He chuckled at the way she flushed at that, absent-mindedly fidgeting with a button on her dress. He caught her fidgeting hand in his, prompting her to meet his gaze. "I've been thinking, cause I want to do this right, but who would I need to be speaking to about having permission to?" The confusion written on her face was adorable until it clicked, Carlina apparently intent on looking anywhere but at him as she tried to find her voice.

"Uh.. me? I guess, Michael..." she said, acutely reminded of how alone she technically was.

There was a flicker of a frown on his face as he caught her chin, pulling her in for a kiss that left her breathless.

"I just want to be there for you."

That comment working like a charm, appealing to her deepest insecurities, earning him a gentle smile as she dropped a brisk kiss on his lips before she slid to the floor.

He tried to keep his expression curious, a little surprise, it urging her on as her smile grew. In actuality, he knew exactly what would get her on her knees for him, and she really was *never* alone - even when she thought she was.

* * *

Chief Brown grunted as Carlina pulled down his slacks, drawing her fist along the area like he'd shown her, his cock twitching in her grip. he couldn't take his eyes off her as his length disappeared between those sexy rosy lips, slightly puffy from their kiss. He cupped the back of Carlina's neck, guiding her as she bobbed as he bit back a string of curses. "Fuck, that feels so good, Baby." His growled words seem to encourage her as he felt the head bump her throat, cheeks hollowing as she lifted - corners of her lips quirked just slightly, those eyes screaming that she was trying to smile. The flick of her tongue running firmly over his length soon had him gripping the arm of his chair with his free hand with so much strength there was the telltale noise of the materials protesting.

"Carlina…" Chief stuttered out before he came, her movements slowing as he worked through his release. "Oh shit, oh my, oh fuck…"

He had a breathy chuckle as he looked down at Carlina, a proud little smile on her face as she stood after tucking him back into his slacks. His eyes watched her with a barely contained desire. "You got me," he huffed as she perched back in his lap and handed him a pen to finish his work.

"Remember women talk, so we know a thing or two about how big you black guys are," Carlina said jokingly.

"Ah, ha…" Chief laughed as he tried to focus on work on his desk. *Innocent tailor who knows how to please me and is associated with a cocky mobster?* the Chief thought. *Oh, that would do wonderful things for his self-esteem.*

Well, that was going to be an interesting conversation to have when the Chief begins writing his autobiography. For now, it didn't mattered. he was fairly sure he'd hooked Carlina so well that she'd say *yes* no matter what he did.

CHAPTER 7

To say Chief was enjoying this, would be an understatement.

Michael had come in to pick up one of his father's friends for getting drunk out of his mind and peeing in the street. Correction, he had agreed to come while his wife picked him up, as some sort of buffer to avoid her immediately killing him. Naturally, when Chief saw him milling about, he had his hands on his belt and approached with the full confidence of a Chief in his home precinct.

"DiCicco, got a minute? I need to have a word with you."

The few officers around made sure their attention was firmly elsewhere as the two men apparently sized each other up and refused to blink first.

"Sure, Chief."

Michael followed Chief to the office, closing the door behind him.

Standing wide, arms loosely folded, Michael waited for Chief to speak. Meanwhile, Chief was leaning against the front of his desk like the posturing had zero effect on him, speaking almost lazily at long last "Figure you're the closest thing to the father figure in her life," he said watching the flash of anger flit through Michael's eyes as he clocked onto what was going on. "So you'd be the one to ask for blessing before I pop the question?"

Michael's jaw was set firm as he listened and tried to keep a decent poker face. *He couldn't believe the gall of this son of a bitch.*

"Carlina is as good as a sister to me, sure you know this. So, I'll always have her back and I mean what I say. Guess you'll have the family's blessing if she agrees." Michael sounded far from happy about it, but was keeping his temper restrained.

The slight smirk which quirked Chief's lips wasn't lost on Michael. It put his hackles up as if Carlina's original warning had been right *-you're underestimating him.*

"Great, thanks again. I'll be seeing you soon," Chief said motioning towards the door as if calling a firm end to the matter and Michael's welcome in his office.

I've a feeling she'll say yes. So good to know we're on the same page, Chief muttered when Michael left.

* * *

"I don't like him," Michael said pacing the kitchen holding his youngest tightly, bouncing them ever so slightly to keep the small one quiet. "Something feels off. I don't know how he's managed to even get that close to her."

He almost missed the brief-expression that flit across his wife Orabella's face. "You know something. Course, you two are like peas in a pod when you boys gossip."

She quirked a brow as she took a sip of her cup of coffee, electing to give the PG-13 version of their conversation, he didn't need to be privy to female gossip. "He's been a real gent, makes her feel safe and treats her real well." Orabella shrugged. "Are you really surprised? Carlina just wants to feel like she matters, not just an afterthought." Her tone hardened slightly as she fixed Michael with a level stare. "Your poking and prodding around put her right in front of someone who seems to treat her like she's all that matters. Technically, this is your fault, Michael. You're guilty for making Carlina happy."

Carlina matters. Maybe, but something made Michael think it was almost at the point of obsession. There was a darkness about the whole thing Michael just couldn't ignore.

"I guess you're right," he sighed, frustration clear in his expression. "I'm just worried."

That got him a smile from his wife as she rose and put her hand on his face.

"We both are. Carlina will be okay."

Oh, how Michael hoped his wife was right.

The next day

Carlina wouldn't need to know how Chief knew her ring size. She wouldn't suspect how he'd let himself in, pressed her favorite into the slab of putty in the case in his pocket. Wouldn't have an inkling of the way he'd watched her sleep, thinking about how she'd finally take his cock when she took his name. Would have no idea how long he'd spent thinking how best to phrase moving her - encourage her to keep her place as security, a work-space - proof he saw her as more, or at least he hoped that was how she would see it.

A week later

It was firmly autumn as Chief Brown was standing leaning against his car as Carlina hurried to meet him, the sky already picking up those warm orange hues as the sun started its journey lower.

He'd not been expecting the sight. When he'd mentioned wearing something nice, she'd apparently taken it to heart. The soft navy fabric hitting at the knee, a style that vaguely reminded him of the wiggle dresses from the movies.

A low whistle escaping him as he gave her a sweeping gaze while she locked the door behind her, shamelessly staring to which she blushed deeply, gratefully ducking into the passenger's side of the car as he suppressed a chuckle. "I didn't think you could look more handsome than you do in uniform," she'd commented softly over dinner, making him pause briefly as if he wasn't sure he'd heard her correctly. "I know you hate the thing some- times, but you wear it well."

* * *

It had been on the drive home that Carlina had quirked her head at the unfamiliar streets, gaze snapping to Chief for an explanation. "Relax, baby." His arm along the back of the bench-style seat as he beckoned her, Carlina scooting closer to slot herself against his side. "Figured it was about time I showed you my place. Now it's finished, anyway. Been fixing it up over the last year."

Chief checked out her expression; a slight flush and apparently impressed when it appeared he was doing the work himself.

Chief began giving Carlina a tour of his place with an arm on her backside, hand resting on her hip, curling her to him occasionally to kiss her dizzily. "This is—" he said as he stumbled forward into Carlina through the door as he opened it, prompting one of those lovely bursts of laughter from her as he'd kept her upright.

"Our bedroom—" Carlina completed. Her lips parted like she was about to say something else, but snapped closed with a look of confusion as her face flushed, eyes widening as Chief held the small velvet box at eye level. "Had a pleasant conversation with Michael."

That did the trick, feeling her move flush against him as Carlina nodded, chewing her lip with a smile.

"Of course, Chief!" Carlina's back bumping against the door as a low grin spread across his face. "Can't wait for you to take my name, amongst other things…"

Grinding his hips against hers as Chief Brown spoke against her neck, almost missing the 'oh fuck' that came out on a breath as her head went back.

"Assuming Paolo Tailoring will stay as is, and you not feeling that I want you to close it up."

Chief was really laying it on thick as he gripped Carlina's knee to hitch her leg around his waist, hurriedly hiking up the soft fabric of her dress, prompting a laugh to bubble from her as she held his face in her hands to kiss him frantically.

"I've already said *yes*. You don't need to keep convincing me."

Chief messily gathered her hands in one of his, near slamming them against the door above her head. "I may have said it, but I'd rather hear you scream it."

Chief made it quite clear who was in control. Keeping her tight against his chest, steering her back towards the bed as he fumbled with the zip of her dress, tugging it harshly till it gave so it could drop to the floor. Carlina scrambled to get his shirt off, breathing erratically and shallow. Cute, he hadn't expected her not to be a mess, needing lead by the hand - but he sure wasn't complaining. Nor was he particularly complaining when he shoved his pants and underwear down, pausing at a small whine from her as she damn near ripped his under-shirt off.

He almost felt bad for his aggressive behavior, Carlina genuinely liked him, all of him - it was clear as day in her lusty eyes as she sat up to pull him tight against her chest, lips lavishing attention on his neck as she clung onto him.

No, Chief reasoned, it was done because he cared for her. They ended up here, that's what it meant. It was done for the good of both of them; it got them where they wanted. Maybe Carlina had her own darkness swirling in her, or maybe she would just accept him as willingly as she accepted his touch.

Carlina scrambled to ground herself at his shoulders as he tugged her underwear down her legs to sink a digit into her, a groan ripping through both of them as he added another and started a steady pace, curling to brush that point that knocked a hitched breath from her each time he hit it. It wasn't long before Carlina was a trembling mess in his grip, babbling a mixture of his name and begs in an increasingly more needy voice.

"I can't wait for you to say my name every night, letting me take this pussy till you can't think straight." He gripped her chin in one hand, holding her gaze as he sank sharply, spearing into her heat, dragging an almost pained noise from her. Once Chief was lounged fully, he held still, relishing the way Carlina whimpered, the occasional twitch in her thighs wrapped loosely around his hips. With a slight smirk, he shoved her back, hooking his fore-arms under her thighs, hands gripping tightly at her hips as he sank impossibly deeper, watching with fascination as she arched off the covers. Withdrawing slowly, he sank to the hilt again with a snap of his hips that had her choking out a squeal.

Leaning over her, Chief set a brutal pace, using his grip to yank Carlina against him with each thrust as she clung desperately to his shoulders. His name chanted like a prayer amidst blissful praises. The way her neck was bared to him, he resisted grabbing and squeezing it until Carlina's head spin. No, he'd save that for Mrs. Brown.

That thought sent him unraveling, thrusts growing erratic and fierce, the grind of his pelvic bone against her clit sending her tumbling over the edge of pleasure with a strangled scream of his name. He soon followed her, chest heaving as he damn her collapsed on top of her, lazily rutting into her as she milked him for all he was worth.

"Fuck." Chief huffed against her skin, chin resting in her cleavage as he watched her blink blearily, looking slightly dazed and drunk. "You can say that again, Chief." It came out quiet as she tried to calm her breathing, pleased amusement lacing her words. They stayed that way for a little while before he reluctantly withdrew, cleaning them both vaguely with his undershirt before hurling it into a corner. He manhandled her further onto the bed, under the covers with him as she shed the lacy lingerie - taking her time with the stockings once she noticed him watching.

He settled under the covers, Carlina tucking herself against his side, idly brushing her hands over his torso like she couldn't get enough of him - despite what he saw as his flaws. A small smile on his lips as he kissed her long and lazy, taking advantage of mapping every inch of her skin he could reach.

* * *

Orabella was the first to know; Carlina's clients at the shop, for the most part, are not so observant to notice the smooth setting on her finger. The day after the Chief proposed, Orabella was there at the shop wiping Carlina's tears away as she rubbed the ring back and forth over her leg nervously.

"Let me tell Michael first, okay…" Orabella suggested. "We'll have dinner together."

"Okay…"

Carlina's happiness was more important than giving Michael a chance to throw a tantrum.

MeanCarlina took some convincing to extend the invite to Chief, as aware as Orabella that it could be a recipe for a war around the table.

No, it would simmer, it would be a game of chicken between two men who knew the other's game far too well.

CHAPTER 8

Carlina wished she could say she was surprised, she wished she could say Michael would put aside all his bullshit and just act like her big brother for once.

Not so lucky, making excuse after excuse about being too busy, dodging even Orabella's attempts to arrange a dinner together. Till it was nearly Thanksgiving. Suddenly, Michael was the one suggesting Carlina come for dinner.

Despite trying to keep her voice low, the Chief had heard their squabbling from outside when Michael called to broach the topic. Heard the way Carlina spun from firecracker to meek kid, just confirming what he'd long suspected about the dynamic there as they'd gotten older.

"Fine, but you play nice or so help me God, I'll fuckin' whack him my goddamn self—" there was the slight creak of her leaning heavily on the drawers to calm herself as she listened to him say it repeatedly.

"Okay, Michael. My God!" Carlina sighed. "Please. You're family."

"I hope so…" Michael sighed.

* * *

Carlina went back outside and was staring out at the window of the Chief's patrol car, her hands fidgeting in her lap as he reached over to calm her.

"Are you ready to come inside?" Carlina asked.

"It's either now or never…" Chief Brown laughed.

What was a dull hum of laughter and chat, died so quickly you could have heard a pin drop. Once eyes moved from the Chief to the woman beside him, the noise resumed as Orabella made a beeline for her, closely followed by their eldest son, barreling so fast into Carlina that she stumbled back a step, caught at the shoulders by the Chief.

"It's so nice to finally meet you, Chief Brown. Especially as we'll be family soon enough. Orabella DiCicco." She was beaming as she extended a hand to Chief, him tearing his gaze from where Carlina had bundled the growing lad into her arms like he was nothing more than a toddler, animated in how she spoke to him. He shook his head slightly, a small smile on his lips.

"Sorry, please call me, RJ. Pleasure to meet you. Carlina's said a lot about you."

It didn't take long for the almost glaring figure to appear at his wife's shoulder.

The men greeting each other with a nod before Michael spoke, well aware of those nearest were listening.

"Family, you see what I have here?" he asked, feigning ignorance, as he knew those closest were likely listening. Pulling Carlina to his side by an arm around her waist, he watched Michael stiffen at him being so close to his kid.

"I'll soon be part of it," Chief said proudly, watching as Carlina let down the child to run to his father's leg.

"We hope so," Michael said, doing a good job at sounding genuine, watching as Orabella and Carlina chattered happily before excusing themselves - Orabella with hosting to do and Carlina was always on board to help.

* * *

"So, your plans for my business are…" Michael asked, offering Chief a beer that he took and sipped.

Waving Michael off, the Chief knew that people were likely listening in around them.

"You mean Carlina's business? Nothing will change. Well, not by my wishes anyway. Maybe she'll make changes when the kids come along, but you'd have to ask her, big brother." Chief watched the way something twitched in Michael's jaw at that, the layers of decisions apparently not sitting right with his need for control.

Chief wasn't stupid. He saw how Michael manipulated those around him - even Carlina. He'd built a picture of how their paths had crossed, been able to see where his influence has marked their days. Michael wasn't a saint. He knew full well his appeal to Carlina had become obsessive, but he soothed his conscience with the argument that he never bent her free will, as Michael did. No, the choices she made with him were all her own. Anything she would give him, she did, by her own volition.

Michael learned over the last few months why his cops on the payroll were leaving though - apparently Chief was cracking down and actually trying to run the precinct well, maybe angling for a political position. It also explained why more and more he was being called as an attorney rather than a DiCicco by the men in his circle.

Chief Brown mingled with a few guests. Some even warmed up to him when they saw how often he'd scan the gathering to check on Carlina.

"City Hall, best decision I ever made," Chief was pulled from his thoughts by one of the elder guests. "Met Carlina there, got the ring on her finger, and we didn't leave the house for a week."

Michael bristled, but Chief was trying to keep a straight face as he took a sip of his drink. The group dispersing as Orabella picked her way across the room. "Michael, we need to put the little ones down soon, or poor Carlina will be stuck here all night." Michael's gaze followed the flick of his wife's head to where Carlina was on the porch, his eldest sat in her lap, forehead against her cheek as she spoke softly to him, that telltale droop of his eyes as he struggled to stay awake but flat out refused to release his grip of her sleeve.

"I'll check on them," Michael reassured her, moving to sort out the kids' as Orabella turned to Chief, her face serious. "RJ, I don't know what has got you two butting heads, but you take good care of our Carlina, you hear me?"

"Yes, ma'am," Chief Brown said.

"She means a lot. None of us wants to see her hurt. Even if some show that by being a moody brute."

That remark earned her a frown, a frown of confusion as Chief responded carefully, "I don't care if Michael likes me, so long as I'm making Carlina happy."

That seemed to soothe things over, though Chief was having a bit of bother taking her seriously, knowing some of their gossip.

Meanwhile, Carlina was having a small conversation with Michael about resolving times and maybe a normal job wasn't so bad, maybe letting the old ways fizzle could calm things - Michael wasn't convinced, or too power-hungry to agree, it wasn't clear.

It took Carlina a minute or two to reach them, exchanging hugs with a few of the guests, a few of the eldest holding her face to plant a kiss on her forehead like Nonno had always done - but she eventually made it to the pair with Michael at her shoulder.

When Michael hugged Carlina at the door, chin on her head, he made no efforts to hurry, eyes on Chief till their car pulled away.

✳ ✳ ✳

Carlina was exhausted, leaning against the passenger's door, the hem of the deep green shirt dress hitching slightly from when she'd shifted to lean more comfortably on the metal.

"Carlina," it came out as a drawl, a small noise of acknowledgment rumbling in her throat in response. Apparently not good enough as he lay a hand on her knee, fingertips brushing the inside of her thigh as she moved with an effort to sit closer to him, her head falling to rest on his shoulder. He trailed his hand higher, slipping between two buttons on her dress to press his hand firmly against her skin, low on her belly.

"I can't wait to have your baby." Chief's voice was husky, breathing just a little faster than normal as he kept his eyes firmly on the road. Vaguely aware of a contented noise from her, he stiffened as he felt her shake her head.

"*Our baby…*" Carlina moaned.

Chief Brown really had traded the bottle and ladies for chews and Carlina. Whether that was turning out to be any better, vices remained to be seen.

✳ ✳ ✳

That tip about City Hall had been right on the money. A shriek of laughter ringing through the house as Chief Brown insisted on carrying Carlina through the door, kicking it shut behind him as he set her down as gently as he could. She was playfully batting as his hands as he grabbed at her hips, pulling her back flush against him. "I'm no young buck," he says, handsy like a horny teenager. Her teasing earning her a nip of his teeth at her earlobe. The pair stumbling towards one of the kitchen counters as she caught herself on splayed hands, her now-husband single-mindedly focus on getting fabric out the way rather than off. She'd been about to make a cheeky comment when it died in her throat, replaced by a choked whimper as he thrust into her with next to no warning. Carlina was trembling. She couldn't help it, head to toe. She couldn't stop it. Chief Brown was rutting aggressively, a hand curling round her throat as her head fell back against his shoulder - too far gone to control the urges and the dark that swirled in his head. Shakily, Carlina fumbled a hand from the counter to rest it over his on her hip, a string of lewd comments under his breath that she could barely decipher, none of which sounded kind or polite. Until those words that broke him. "Fuck me harder, Daddy."

CHAPTER 9

Two months later

Chief groaned, muscles aching, joints stiff as he turned under the sheets. To be greeted with the sight of already blossoming bruises.

Reaching out, he brushed his fingertips over them, realizing they fit his hands. Moving the covers to take her in completely, they were scattered over Carlina's hips, the back of her neck, and the insides of her thighs. But she was still there. Sleeping soundly by the looks of things.

Shifting to loom over her as she lay on her front, "Carlina," he drawled next to her ear as he dropped open mouth kisses against her neck. Surprised slightly by the contented moan that came out with a breath before she turned over slowly to face him. "Mornin'," she greeted him, eyes heavy-lidded as she smiled softly. "You okay?" waking properly faster than she intended with a frown of concern. Chief merely stared at her for a moment, skimming his hands over the marks before she caught his chin to force his gaze to hers.

"That's nothin'," Carlina reassured, eyes softening as she stroked his cheek.

That jarred Chief, propping himself up properly on an elbow to frown at her, a protective arm around her back, keeping them as close as possible. "I don't like my wife keepin' secrets from me." Though there was anger in it, it wasn't aimed at her, it was aimed at whatever had her looking at him like it was the most normal thing in the world.

"It's not exactly pillow talk, Chief." His hard stare was answer enough that he wanted her to tell him, anyway.

"I know what cruel looks like what dark looks like. It's not you, it's not this." Chief's grip tightened, prompting Carlina's laugh. "I've seen a lot worse."

"I know you have, RJ…"

Chief's head lowered to kiss Carlina deeply, some of the tension escaping his shoulders. Confident in the idea of making the absolute most of his couple of days off - insecurities be damned.

The following day

"Chief, what the fuck! This is way out of line!" Michael was making no effort to keep his volume down as he strode through the station, met by a bored but vaguely pissed-off expression from Chief behind his desk. "He's a kid. They do stupid shit for Christ's sake!"

"It stopped being stupid shit and became my business the second that woman screamed," Chief snapped, having hauled in the son of some big family over roughing up his girlfriend in the park. The guy may not have come out of it unscathed, but Chief wasn't about to be stupid enough to let that slip. He told his officers to make sure the kid was in cuffs regardless of who's his family.

"A lovers' tiff, hardly a police matter," Michael retorted condescending.

"Public indecency, assault, public nuisance, resisting arrest, and a noise disturbance for good measure. Sounds like a police matter to me," was the Chief's drawled reply as Michael had a derisive snort before he stormed out.

The more he got to know him, the more Chief saw Michael as nothing more than a spoiled brat who needed to start hearing 'no'. Stop having people bend to his whims. He couldn't fix his corrupt district. Maybe, he had a chance at carving out this parasite though. One neighborhood with crime in check was better than none.

* * *

Carlina let Michael rant as usual. Her attention focused on the fabric in front of her instead as she made minute adjustments to where the pattern pieces were laid, trying to get the pattern to match just that bit extra.

"This place has run just fine for generations. Now your fiance comes sauntering in to uproot it all. Expecting me to stand for it, just let him waltz in and take everything?" Michael's voice was rising with his temper as he paused his stomping pacing. An action, Carlina thought little until he was hauling her by the back of her collar, the foot or so to a chair that he pressed her over, roughly brushing her hair out the way to trace the bruises on the back of her neck. "Look at what the fuck he's done to you."

It wasn't the concern you'd expect.

It sounded less like Michael was talking about an injured relative and more like a possession that had been tarnished. That realization hurt, begging to be seen at the corner of her mind as Carlina tried to push it away.

Wrenching herself from his grip, Carlina stumbled to her feet with an expression of betrayal. "Don't you dare. You've hurt me far more than he has." "Don't you think for a second I didn't see you working behind the scenes? But I ignored it because I was so desperate to believe I wasn't alone."

Her resolve crumbled, tears welling in her eyes as she tried to keep her gaze hard. "You don't deserve them. Orabella, the kids - your father would be ashamed to see the man you've become."

Michael's booming voice made Carlina flinch, face contorted in barely contained fury. "You didn't know my father!"

Silence hung heavy for a few moments before Michael

turned to storm to the door. Carlina spoke up in a trembling voice that made him pause with his hand on the handle. "I knew him well enough to know he wanted you to do better."

Leaving with a slam of the door so strong that Carlina could see the frame jiggle.

* * *

Carlina was completely lost in her thoughts, moving on to auto-pilot as she trudged home. After pulling herself together, she'd taken some time to just reorganize her apartment—no, her workspace. It wasn't home anymore; it hadn't been for a while - not in a dark sense, but more that it never really felt like it, it felt temporary. It seemed stupid to so quickly feel more at home at Chief's than she had since—well, since her grandfather's shop.

Thankfully, she was home before Chief was, not entirely certain she could have resisted the urge to scream if anything other than peace had immediately met her. She took her time, just letting herself mull over thoughts as she moved. It was a habit at this point - pick up around the place, take a bath, enjoy some pampering time, change, and prepare dinner.

Every single damn time, Chief did the same after it all - *a soft thank you, sweetheart.* As if none of it was expected, but appreciated all the same. Just that little thing that showed he saw her?

It felt pathetic when Carlina realized how much it

meant to her. That simple fact that Chief didn't just see 'his mistress', 'the tailor', 'Michael's play sister, or 'Paolo's granddaughter' - all he saw was 'Carlina'? It made her want to do all she could to make him feel even a sliver of how it did for her.

So, when Chief Brown turned up, looking exhausted and sinking heavily into a chair at the dining table behind her, it didn't even cross Carlina's mind to not move. Easing his jacket off to hang over the back of the chair, gently taking off his tie and folding it neatly in a pocket of his leather, undoing a couple of buttons to take the tension of the collar off his neck, hands under his shirt to rub soothingly at the nape of his neck.

"How'd I get so lucky to be with you, hmm?" he said, tugging her into his lap, stroking along the silky fabric that flowed around her legs. He liked that. Carlina heavily favored a softer take on men's fashion, only ever seeming to bring out the unisex style for him - or with him, was probably more accurate.

"Could say the same about you, RJ," she murmured, leaning to check the timer on the hob before she settled to ask about his day, the tension gradually leaving his shoulders as he had a chance to process it all.

CHAPTER 10

The revelations with Michael had Carlina looking at her whole life. It seemed like as soon as she'd processed one thing, another skeleton jumped out of the closet.

The lengths of manipulation, the things she'd let slide while knowing Michael; had her heaving with panic. But the things she found out about Chief, that should have made her blood run cold, it just seemed to pale - the revelation that it was him outside her door for all those nights, should have terrified her. But for some fucked up reason, it felt comforting alongside the blatant disregard from Michael - it scared her. It felt like the means justified the end.

Which was probably why, after nearly a month of avoiding him, it was a call from Michael that set her off. Left her waiting at the dining table with a glass in hand when Chief got home, waiting, expression unreadable.

The way she silently stared at him had his jaw

twitching until he finally broke, hands slamming down on the tabletop. "What's got you all wound, hmm? I not givin' you enough?" but it sounded more like hurt than venomous anger.

"I know about the lookouts," she whispered, refusing to meet his eyes, "Talked to the manager of the building - those noises at night. It was your men."

Chief's shoulders sagged slightly, a flash of panic in his eyes as she raised her steely gaze to meet his.

"Why, Brown? 'Don't you dare start lying to me now?" Her tone left little room for argument, despite his frustration rising as that darkness swirled in his head again.

"I love you. Since you turned up at the door of my office, I couldn't stop thinkin' bout you." His voice was rising, anger and frustration bubbling over with panic and just a smidge of obsession. "But Michael, the way he was offering you up like you were nothing, just a pretty distraction, so I'd turn a blind eye. I did it for your protection."

"It's not right," Chief grumbled, moving slowly to stand behind Carlina, gripping her shoulders gently as he pressed his lips against the top of her head. "They see what you are to everyone else. They're missin' who you really are." Listening made her chest hurt. Here was a man she loved so completely, who'd essentially broken into her shop, and stalked her - a normal person would have run away a long time ago.

"Chief, your behavior. It's not okay." Her comment

was soft, shoulders relaxed in his hold. "Don't be like Michael Please. Just be honest." The crack to her voice gave her away, head dipping forward to hide the tears. Carlina felt herself being pulled to her feet, enveloped in his arms as she pressed her face tightly into his shirt and let herself cry. Too soon, her chest was heaving, white knuckle clinging to him, his hold the only thing keeping her standing - the floodgates had opened and there was no semblance of being able to close them quickly.

* * *

It was a weird week, to say the least. Customers were told Carlina was unwell, all understanding that present jobs would take longer. The furnishing shop where she worked part-time was more than happy to give her all the time she needed, so long as she rested. Even Orabella was fed the same line. Carlina couldn't bring herself to be completely honest about it all. How do you tell a friend that her husband treats her like one of his cases and that their sex life is cigar talk with his cop buddies after monitoring all their phone conversations?

Chief didn't know how to handle it. Carlina had gone through the motions while he was at work - she wouldn't hear a word of him taking time off. She seemed a little better when he came home on a Friday; she smiled at least and it reached her eyes for the first time all week. Like every night that week, she brought him a beer and curled up tightly to his side on the sofa.

"Michael's dad, Michael, Sr., I've told you about him, right?" she murmured, earning her a slow nod from Chief as he turned his head towards her. "He was ahead of his time. Treated me no different from my grandfather, who said that it wasn't gender that commanded respect - it was integrity, kindness, and honesty. Said a respectable person protects their family. I took that to heart a lot better than his son." She hissed. "One guy he did business who was his long-time associate, Tony, had ordered a suit but was rude. I thought nothing of it. He grabbed me and roughed me up pretty badly when I told him I couldn't make his suit ahead of other customers. When Michael Sr. found out, the guy never existed again. Luckily, it was no big deal 'cause the jerk didn't get between my legs," Carlina spoke so matter of fact, a rage fizzing under the surface as she stared unfocused at a corner of the room.

"Then came you..." Carlina's voice lowered as she raised her head to meet Chief's gaze. "Seemed to see everything else, never pushed, just firm enough to make me feel so safe." She chuckled weakly, shifting to brush her nose against his. "Everyone's got a dark side. You and I just have to be honest with ours."

Painfully honest.

By the end of the weekend, Chief was yawning through most of his Monday shift. Before he came in, he made Carlina come till she cried; she welcomed every dark urge from him with trust. He'd even spent hours on the edge of bliss with her above him, with the control completely in her hands as she denied him till he begged.

Probably wouldn't be considered the healthiest way to think about at work, but it kept the Chief's day going.

Chief Brown had even gotten a love-filled smile before Carlina had kissed him in the car when he dropped her off at her old place on his way to work. All signs pointed to Carlina being happier, so that was alright in his books.

CHAPTER 11

It shouldn't have hit as hard as it did, but hemming that little christening gown had Carlina gasping to breathe.

Failure. Disappointment. Relief.

That was unexpected, to say the least.

Truth be told, the idea of having children terrified her. A fear that had only gotten worse the more she'd seen her life for what it was. But that's what women were supposed to do. Good little housewives and doting mothers. For the longest time, Carlina had tried to convince herself that it was just the nerves of youth - after all, she loved her nieces and nephews and folk constantly remarked that she was so good with them. Surely, it wasn't much of a leap to her own kids.

Then again, for the longest time, she'd resigned herself to living alone. So it didn't matter for her to dwell on thoughts like that - now they refused to be ignored. She was a wife and the Chief wasn't exactly subtle in his want for a child. Yet, month after month, it didn't happen. He never hounded about it, but it still took longer than she'd like to admit to raise the topic with him.

Why? He'd never hit her, threatened her, yelled at her so loud she felt it in her ribcage - so why was she scared of him? Slowly, she came to realize it wasn't fear; it was shame - shame because she felt like she was letting him down.

But he'd coaxed it out of her one night, picking up on the way she faked sleep, laying so stiff but stuck in her own head. He'd leaned against the wall as the doctor grilled her with more questions than a police interrogation, then had a poke around for good measure. He'd felt his frustration rising as she calmly answered each question, it painting a very bleak picture she was apparently numb to.

They'd drove home in silence, Chief pacing as she settled at the dining table with a cup of coffee to calm herself. The silence, the pacing - was it any wonder she flinched when he slapped his hand against the door in frustration?

"I'm sorry," her words sounded small, his attention fully on her. "For letting you down." He had her chin in a firm grip in seconds. Forcing her head around to look around her, "I don't want to hear you talkin' like that. House is clean, it's comfortable, certainly looks after me well," a hint of a smirk curling his lips. "in every way. All I heard today were the odds are a little low - but I'm a bettin' man." He tugged her to her feet, holding her against him by arms looped around her waist. "I ain't foldin' any time soon."

True to his word, he'd barely let her finish the dishes before he'd steered her upstairs. Now, Chief couldn't speak for her - but it was the best night's sleep he'd had in a long time, buried in his wife with his head on her chest. Even if it never happened, he had zero issues keeping trying.

* * *

Eventually, when Michael was supposed to be out of town for some business, Carlina actually visited Orabella. It broke her heart to see the excited faces of the kids when she arrived, knowing full well they were likely a little confused why they went from seeing her weekly to nothing for months.

Thankfully, Orabella knew better than to pry about plans for their own kids, figuring it was likely a touchy subject. "Orabella," it came out pained, "How much does Michael tell you about the business?" that prompted a look of confusion from Orabella, pausing to think before she answered with a frown, "Not much."

"I worry, especially about the little girls - he doesn't share the same views as his father did, doesn't put much value on women outside of what they bring to him." Carlina considered being honest, completely honest, but she couldn't risk pissing Orabella off and having Michael come to settle the score. "If he does anything reckless, take the kids and I'll make sure you'l be okay. I promise, Orabella." Carlina held her breath and waiting for the defensive yelling, but it never came.

Instead, Orabella slid her hand across the table to weave their fingers together and waited for Carlina to loft her gaze.

"When you got hurt."

Orabella remembered how broken Carlina had looked, remembered hearing her sob as she told Michael Sr. how it happened - she didn't need to know the details to guess it was only business. "Michael's father did everything to protect you, did he not? There was no balancing of the scales."

Carlina nodded as the grip on her hand tightened. *Comradery in fuckery.*

* * *

"You'll be changing precincts within the month," the Commissioner said, entering Deputy Chief's office, not looking like he'd hear any arguments. Deputy Chief of Police, Brown having to clench his jaw to keep from snapping back at the Commissioner with an attitude. Instead, he took a calming approach. "Okay, if I don't agree…"

"Well, let's just say you don't have a choice in the matter…"

"I know, but you know I've not long settled the wife." Chief Brown felt shitty, making it seem like she'd be the one kicking up a fuss, but it was the only hand he could play.

The Commissioner responded smirking, "If you agree, I'll make your transfer close by. You have my word. RJ, you're doing a good job, but the Mayor stepped in on this one."

While Chief Brown gave a nod to the Commissioner, it was stiff and begrudging. This smelled so bad of corruption it was practically seeping from the walls.

Chief had relayed that message when he got home later that evening to Carlina; her frown, matching his. It would later prompt her to advertise her apartment for rent- pressing that it was better to have savings if Michael and his crew were going to try fucking with their lives. Chief knew all too well when people had power, their targets become easy. It was smart to be as far from it as possible from where the Chief had no jurisdiction.

Though, she drew the line at a firearm - citing that by the very nature of their work, Chief Brown always has a firearm and she always had 'something sharp'. That didn't stop him from cleaning and servicing his larger firearms from his days in his hometown Houston, just in case.

* * *

"We'll have some space finally unless Captain RJ keeps sniffing around these necks of the woods. Winters can be deadly, especially with the old tires on those old cruisers of theirs," Michael said it like he was ordering coffee, like it was nothing to a few of his men. It prompted only some mumbled push-back, namely around what they'd do about the widow. "She'll be taken care of. Let me worry about that."

The men shook their head knowing that this would be a mess they possibly can't ever clean up.

"The thing about guys who marry later in life, they're blinded by the pussy. I'll bet you, if RJ gets moved to the streets, he'll take my sister out on patrol with him."

How fast someone can fall from family to just another target, or perhaps it was closer to falling from useful to expendable.

CHAPTER 12

One upside, a quieter so quicker commute. But that was lost among the downsides - shadowed only by Carlina's spite. It seemed like she grew more of a spine, the more things went wrong. Chief couldn't complain, as he was quite enjoying the increasing contrast between this recent development and the other side of the scale, only he got to see.

New officers to manage, which had meant long days to start and a lot of frustration for Chief Brown, but it was thankfully a much more social station where he got along well with the new subordinates.

A 5 percent pay cut, which meant there wasn't a snowball's chance in hell of Chief even looking at a new car that year.

Suspiciously drying up work for Carlina's tailoring, meaning she sold the place and got smarter with storage in a smaller space that was much cheaper to run - flat out refusing to let tailoring junk take up space in the house.

No need for her help at the furnishing dealer, meaning she picked up a couple of shifts at a local supermarket, which had the added bonus of a small staff discount.

A little backsliding regarding Chief and booze, which had meant more than one night, she barely spoke to him.

Thankfully, Chief was no longer fueled to butt heads with Michael, growing quite content to just go to work and do his job.

A job that had dragged on far too long that day, causing him to be slightly heavier on his feet and a little too aggressive with doors. A feeling that fizzled the second he stepped into the kitchen.

Given the tighter budget, Carlina had been doing more batch cooking. Chief didn't mind one bit and was even feeling just a little more comfortable in his clothes - but she was apparently looking to spoil him that night. A tray on the table, set with a beer already, as she'd apparently intended to serve him more comfortably in the living room. She was plating up a dinner that looked like the sort of thing you'd order at a *nice restaurant*. Despite all this, he was more focused on the fact Carlina was wearing little more than lingerie and one of his longer sleep shirts. Hair falling in loose waves around her shoulders, obviously having been left after being let loose from the twist she wore to work.

Casting a glance over her shoulder, she flashed him a

smile. "Your dinner will be ready in a minute. Your clothes are set out upstairs if you want to change and the fireplace should be going okay - slippers are in front of it, just to heat them a bit."

Turned to plate up his meal, Carlina finally realized Chief was quietly staring at her. She gestured to herself. "Oh, I didn't get round to this. I'll do it while you eat." Carlina added, lifting the tray as he instead decided on taking off his tie and coat. The rest could wait till after dinner.

* * *

Once Chief was settled and Carlina made to leave, a deep "don't..." stopped her, instead slowly curling her legs up underneath her in the armchair.

Chief watched the way Carlina held herself taller, walking with more assurance than she had done when he met her. Leaning in the kitchen doorway, Chief sipped at the last of his beer as she finished the dishes. "Heard anything from Michael?" he asked carefully, noting that she no longer bristled at the name. There was a pause of silence before she answered calmly, "Orabella stopped by with the kids during my lunch break at work. Nothing from Michael..." Carlina turned, eyes hard and a fierce protective streak humming under the surface. "I'm glad you're not wasting time pursuing him anymore. Apparently, he's not above a hit."

Chief frowned as he processed that, as Carlina sauntered across the room to him with an ever-growing smile.

"That's not going to be an issue. It's only a matter of time before they all go down, anyway."

Carlina's hands ran up Chief's chest, over his shoulders to rest at the nape of his neck. He didn't drop her gaze, instead hoisting her over a shoulder as he strode upstairs smirking. "What are you up to? I saw a smirk on your face."

"Nothing baby, nothing…"

About forty-five minutes later

"Speaking of the devil…" Chief said, shaking his head while staring at his phone.

"What, what is it?" Carlina asked.

"The DA served a warrant for Michael's arrest fifteen minutes ago. They've gotten him in custody."

"Oh my God! Shit! What are the charges?" Carlina sighed.

"Looks like they're throwing the book at him and his associates; extortion, corruption of public officials, gambling, infiltration of legitimate businesses, labor racketeering, loan sharking, tax fraud schemes and stock manipulation schemes, etc…"

"I need to call——" Carlina sighed.

"Don't worry, his wife is still at home. She'll be okay. Let's get some sleep and talk about it in the morning."

Carlina sighed again as they made their way to bed. The lights went out and at least for now; they were safer than ever from Michael's wrath.

NICO

CHAPTER 1

The red and blue lights flitted around the packed street entrance and the music was loud enough to be heard from a block or two away. He felt the bass through his rubber-soled shoes.

Nico had only been to this club a handful of times, mostly because Sergei coerced him into it after a long stakeout, so they can both get laid. He doesn't enjoy it, because he knows that the place has shady deals surrounding it, which is exactly why he's here now.

The place could be worse, though. The bartenders are prompt, and the liquor isn't bad. The dance floor is always packed, just like the back booths. The back room is open for those who know what they need, and who they need to meet to make it happen. That's where Nico was headed.

He flashcd his ID, and the muscled bouncer dropped

the maroon velvet rope and slammed open the gritty steel door. He still got carded at twenty-nine, which is ironic to him, since he's seen more death, more joy, and more than half the people in this room, despite his youth. Most people wouldn't even attempt to keep it together in his position.

First stop, the bar, for a neat whiskey. He waved down a bartender and speaks, asking for a drink and about who is working. While waiting for his target to walk through the door, he made small talk. He made eye contact with a new barmaid he hasn't seen before.

You sure are attractive, but he can't get distracted now, not when he's on the clock. A hulking man has just walked through the side door of the club and heads to the back room. Nico knocked back his drink, threw his glass down with a clang on the metal counter, and stepped off the bar stool to follow the giant.

A cloud of smoke lingers in the dark hallway, maybe from high-end weed or Cuban cigars. Nico stalked in the shadows, knowing if the man looked behind him, he wouldn't be able to see him. The steel door squeaks and squeals as it opens. Before it closes completely, Nico stuck his booted foot out to hold it open.

He peered through the crack and saw the hulk sit down at a table with the man he was after Dmitriy.

Dmitriy Andreev is an underboss for one of the Brigadiers, who ran for Maxim, the biggest Pakhan in Chicago. Nico Volkov has been assigned to his case on and off for the last five years and taking him out has proven difficult.

Most people won't dare double-cross him. That's how Nico's father, Vladimir ended up dead. He thought he could pull the wool over Dmitriy's eyes without repercussions.

Thankfully, Dmitriy had never met Nico. If he had any clue who Nico is, he might shoot on sight.

Nico Volkov had been putting together a network of mobsters to take him down and the next contact had been the hulk. He knew better now, having seen this meeting take place on what he considers his home turf. If he had known Dmitriy would be here, he would have had backup come in and take out the guy so he can finish this job. But then, he would have to throw away his cover and risk tipping off Maxim that there's someone after him. The agency would probably fire him or at the least demote him after losing their main undercover agent.

The door eased close without a sound, and a shadow moved back towards the bar. Nico's long legs folded up onto a stool and his hand waved for a stiff drink.

The new barmaid came over with a smile and took his order. Nico admired the elegant features of the young woman under the blue and black lights of the club. They created harsh angles across your body where he thought there were soft curves.

"Beer. And a shot of the top shelf stuff." He points at a whiskey bottle, high off the ground. Your small frame straining to reach it was what he imagined. He'll be surprised if you don't have to get a stool from under the cabinet.

You smiled when you pulled out a pair of heels from the cabinet, not the stool, and slipped them on. "Here," you said, slamming the bottle down.

"Those look nice," he replied, nodding towards the shoes, which had bright red soles. "I'm Nick Cannon, and you are?" He smiled, knowing he can't give you his real last name, in case you're connected.

"Jessica. I haven't seen you here before. Newcomer, or not a drunkard?" The lecherous man at the other end of the bar belched as if to prove your point.

"Neither I just don't drink much. Not my scene. I prefer a quiet whiskey after a delicious sit-down meal." He took a sip of his beer, then swiped his tongue over his lips.

"So why tonight? Why here?" you got a glass for yourself and him before popping your shoes off and slipping into a pair of Vans to become four inches shorter. He can hardly hear the *glug* of the whiskey pouring into the two shot glasses over the music.

"Work."

"What kind? Or am I not allowed to know?" your eyes sparkled with mischief.

"The kind a lady shouldn't get involved in. But if you must know... I'm making connections," Nico said after you quirked your eyebrows and pursed your lips at him.

He also knows that you understand the implications of his statement if you work here.

"Ah, I see. Anything you need to know?"

"How to make you smile, perhaps?" He winked, then cracked a smile. He threw back his whiskey, waiting for your answer.

"Tough subject. Mostly inappropriate jokes and politically incorrect statements. Grand gestures." You threw your shot glass back. "My turn. I'll need to know what time you'll be back tomorrow." You slammed the shot glass down on the steel countertop and poured another for him.

"And what makes you think I'll be back?"

"No one comes in here just once. And no one gets all the 'connections' they need in one night. So, what time shall I wait for you?" you whispered conspiringly in his ear, followed by a sultry wink. The smell of the whiskey you just downed wafted over him and stressed the smoky scent of the bar that was lingering on your skin.

"You'll have to wait and see, I guess." He nodded at a customer farther down, waving a bill, trying to get your attention. "So, get back to work. I'll see you soon. Maybe." He tossed back his next shot and met your eyes boldly.

Your bitten, blushed lips twitch and a twinkle of veiled mirth sparked in your eyes. Then you spun gracefully in your red Vans and sauntered off to tend to the waving hands. He thought about all the places he knew that sell red shoes or shoes with red in them.

He tracked the swing of your hair and the sway of your ass and hips as you walk away. Then he wondered how it would look in your heels. He mentally shook himself because you're probably related to one of these jerks and he can't get involved, lest he put you in unnecessary danger. He finished the last of his beer in a few swigs, head pounding from the loud music.

He threw a money clip on the counter with a note *for Jessica*, before leaving quickly, hoping that no one recognized him as a Knight, or even as Vladimir's son.

* * *

As he drove down the highway towards the blockhouse where he and Sergei lived, and where his partner Andrei worked out, he thought about everything he's learned and put together tonight.

Nico tried to ponder the man he wanted to recruit to work for his primary target. However, his mind kept drifting back to you. He wondered what Sergei would think of you and concluded he wouldn't trust you.

Hell, Nico just met you. None of them can trust new people, really; not in their line of work. He knew the chances were high; it's probable that you only want information for your own 'contacts.'

Maybe not, though. She could be different. He entertained the idea.

Nico shook his head and refocused on the road,

avoiding the potholes in the shoulders. He thought about the group of youngins he pointed out to Andrei this morning and how half of them seemed terrified at the sight of him.

This isn't the first time Nico and Andrei have worked undercover together; nor will it be the last, as they make a decent pair. Nico reached over and turned the dial up on the radio as a rolling country song came on and he lost his thoughts about his partner and his troubles in the thudding beat and the soulful lyrics.

Soon enough, the gravel popped under the tires of the Caddy, as Nico turned into the winding driveway to the Blockhouse and saws the lights in the garage on. *'Sergei must be working on his Thunderbird…'* Nico couldn't hear the car door slamming over the ruckus of the air compressor that was working overtime. He looked out at the acres of empty land and was once again thankful for their decision to live in the middle of nowhere. Sergei had a bad habit of working in the garage at one in the morning.

"Hey. Hey!" Nico poked his foot at Sergei's legs sticking out on the creeper.

"One moment!" Sergei yelled back over the rumbling of the compressor. "Whatcha need?" The creeper rolled out from under the car with a creak.

"Nothing. You do realize it's like one in the morning and you should probably be asleep, right?" Nico's eyebrows furrowed down at the sight of his brother's greasy, oil-stained shirt.

"Uh, yeah." Sergei said, "I'll be up in a few, don't worry." And then the creeper rolled back under the car.

"When I get out of the shower, I expect you and Andrei in the briefing room, ready to show me what you accomplished today. Are we clear?" Nico shouted as he walked out of the garage, and his footsteps paused for a moment.

"Yes!" The tools clattered back into the compartments on the creeper and the floor jack squealed as it lowers the Thunderbird to the floor. Sergei grunted as he lifted himself off the floor.

Nico heard Andrei and Sergei hollering over the water and chuckled to himself. He thinks back to the first time Andrei and Sergei met. It had ended in a shouting match and a near fistfight. You'd never know it now with the way they stick together, thicker than thieves.

The hot water soothed over his sore muscles, his headache subsiding after a pain reliever. His only thoughts are about what Sergei and Andrei may have to tell him, and how to get back in that bar to talk to you more. He doesn't know what it is about you, but it's magnetic to him. You're the only one he's given a second glance to after, Jess.

He turned off the water, wrapped a worn towel around his waist, and ruffled a hand through his damp hair.

He reached for the black tee on the back of his desk chair and slung it over his head, zipping the gray sweat-shirt over his chest. He slipped into a pair of black jogger pants and slapped his gold watch back onto his left wrist.

He thudded down the stairs to stop by the coffeemaker, and then to get some paper and a pen. Finally, he reached the briefing room to find Andrei flipping through a file and Sergei toying with the laptop connected to the projector.

Nico threw his feet up on the table and crossed his legs at the ankles. "Hit me."

Andrei slid the file over to Nico. "The ones in that file are from the group I interviewed this morning, and they seemed like they had the most potential. I did background checks and none of them are connected to Maxim, so they should clear if they pass basic training and inspections." The sound of papers being shuffled fills the room and Nico nods at Andrei.

"Do we have more to pull from?" Nico flipped through the pictures, school records, and descriptions of each person. Who they know, why they stand out, and what they did in a previous life is highlighted in every file, presumably by Andrei. Nico wrote a note on a legal pad sheet to check in with them more.

"Yes, there is another group coming in the week after next, so if a few of these drops, we have a contingency plan." Andrei motioned to the calendar, which had a few dates written in red ink."

"Thank you, Andrei. Sergei, your turn." Nico turned to the screen and the multitude of charts pulled up on it.

"This is a map of the city with the current level of

control that Maxim has and whether Dmitriy or Anna are controlling the henchmen there. Side note, Anna oversees most of the commercial and downtown areas, and Dmitriy is a little further out, with the residential properties under his thumb." Sergei motioned at different shaded and colored areas.

"Good. How's the live stream looking?"

"Up and running, the program will ping to this site —" A map is flung across the screen with red dots on it after a few clicks echo from the computer—" whenever Dmitriy or Maxim are picked up on the city's radar."

"Will it pick us up if need be? Or is just tuned to identify them?"

"Yes, there is a loophole in the coding, so I can add or remove people to search for. If one of our own goes missing on a mission, we can track them using this here." Nico got up and walked to the projected screen. He manipulated the image, so it's not just a map, but a 3D version of the city right at his fingertips.

"I'm working on a projector for above the table so we can have the entire city like this," Sergei said, having seen Nico's interest in the possibilities the map contained.

"Good work today, guys. Get some rest and be ready for tomorrow." Nico slapped Sergei on the back and smiled at Andrei before grabbing the files filled with likely allies and henchmen to make his notes. He'll hand them back to Andrei with his picks before final selections, and he kept Sergei's software pulled up on his tablet to keep an eye on it.

A short while later, the words on the paper start to blur and Nico's eyes start closing on their own accord. He called it quits for the day. In the morning, he will check on the recruits, and maybe train with them for a short while before heading back into the city. His last thought was that maybe he can sneak off to the bar to see you for a few moments before he had to head back to work.

CHAPTER 2

Damn, he was fine… You poured another round of shots for the unseemly gentlemen at the far end of the bar. You delivered the glasses and the bottle because there was only a tiny bit left; they would probably blow through it before the night was out. It saddened you Nico didn't stick around, but he didn't seem like the one-night-stand type. He might not have realized who you were. Who you were connected to.

You thought about how he carried himself with quiet yet commanding dignity. Just like your Daddy had.

"Hey, can we get some more beers and martinis over here?" The shout from a woman broke you from your thoughts.

"Uh, yeah, one minute, please." The ice clinked in the cooler as you pulled out three beers. The metal drink shaker swished as you threw the drinks together, then the grit of salt on the rims. "Here you go. Holler if you need anything else," you called, handing the tray over, just as Nancy, your fellow bartender, came over.

"I saw you talking to that hot guy earlier. Why are you still here when you could be with that?" she asked with genuine curiosity.

"I don't want to have a meaningless relationship, and he said he may be back tomorrow night. All I got was that his name was Nico. And that," you pointed at the money clip laying on the shelf under the bar where you kept your tips, along with a sawed-off, just for emergencies. *'No one appreciates having their name be the talk of the town,'* you thought when you don't tell Nancy his last name.

"Ooh, fancy. What else did he say?"

"Not much, just that he liked my heels after he asked for top-shelf whiskey and I had to put them on to get it. He seems like a good guy, a little uptight but otherwise decent." You shrugged and pointed her towards the man at the end of that bar looking for a mixer.

You pulled your tips out of your pockets and grabbed the money clip, seeing a few days' worth. *'He must make good money or happens to know the right people.'* You untied your apron and folded it up in your locker before grabbing your shoes, both the Vans and Louis Vuittons.

You stalked out of the back entrance and hurried to your car. Women have been known to get snatched by unsavory people back here, and your boss didn't like it when you left by yourself.

Your car rumbled to life, and you pulled out of the darkened lot onto the main road. A few miles down the road, the silence was broken by the pulsing vibrations of your phone in the cup holder.

You swiped the button to answer. "Hello?"

"Hey, I was just wondering when you were coming home… you didn't write your schedule on the calendar like usual, so…" your roommate Heather's voice trailed off, remembering the last time you didn't come home from work at the time you had written down. There had been a lot of explaining to do about that, and that's how she found out about your background.

"Sorry," you cut into her thoughts, "I'm on the road two turns before the one for the garage. I left Nancy to close and, before you ask, I heard her mention that her boyfriend is going to pick her up. I'll see you in a few, okay?"

"Sounds good. Don't worry about sneaking in. I'm watching some Lifetime movie and I'm bored to tears."

"Okay." The phone clicked on the other end, and you set it back in the console. Your turn signal was on to go into the parking garage, and the guy behind you was creeping closer and closer to your tailgate. You turned in after a Honda and parked in your typical spot on the second floor.

The elevator dinged as it shakes down to pick you up. You stepped into the metallic box and the ever-present smell of rotten fish greeted you. Normally when you were this tired, you would lean on the rail of a normal elevator. But you had seen some sketchy things occur in this elevator, and you would rather not catch some incurable disease.

You stumbled out to your floor and knocked on the door, knowing Heather would answer and because your hands are full of your shoes and purse.

"Hey, girl!" She greeted you enthusiastically, and at the sight of your full arms, stepped aside to let you in. "How was it? A typical Friday night?"

You set your heels on the shelf under the stairs and your purse on the counter, before slipping off your heels.

"Good, yeah it was standard. I met this gentleman…"

"Oh, why are you here then?" Her face dropped as she gently closed the door.

"He's not like that. Like at all. He had a whiskey and a beer, and not once did he push for anything. He acts kind of like my dad, you know…" She nodded fervently, and you continued. "But he's not normal in looks. Taller than tall, a jaw to cut diamonds. The eyes of a stormy sky and every shade in between. And he's muscled. Not in a 'I do steroids—look at me' way, but a 'I use my body for a living, so I stay fit' way."

"He sounds nice. Did you get a name?"

"Just a first name; Nico. And he said he might be by tomorrow. Well later today, given what time it is." You pulled a root beer out of the fridge and popped it open to let it go flat.

"You go, girl. You deserve someone who cares about

you. Especially since you got treated like trash those last few months with-"

"I don't want to hear his name," you cut her off with an edge of scorn in your voice. "I have a chance to meet someone new, to start fresh. He will not get to taint my future."

"Your father would be so proud of you. Doing your own thing, living your life." She smiled, patting your hand in a manner like a caring mother.

"He would, thank you," you replied, pulling your chin up, remembering your father's strong mannerisms, and pushing your shoulders back. "Let me get showered and changed and then we can watch silly movies until we fall asleep. Sound good?" you downed the last of your root beer before tossing the bottle in the recycling bin.

"Go get done. I'll be waiting." The cushions on the couch shifted, and the sound of a blanket being whipped out reached your ears.

A hot scrub, shampoo, and a slathering of moisturizer later had you feeling ten times better.

You strode out into the living room and settled under the blanket next to Heather. You had put on your favorite movie and before you knew it, you were dozing off, Heather's snoring right next to your ear.

You tapped her shoulder, and she jolted up, muscles pulled tautly, and fists clenched. A moment later she eased and went to bed, waving goodnight to you. The sound of water running emanated from the bathroom, and the light flickered off as you pulled the sheets around your body.

The morning light cut streams through your room as you rubbed your eyes blearily.

You glanced at your alarm clock and shook your head at the time. It's after ten. *Shit. I'm late for work!* You rolled out of bed hurriedly and flattened your hair with your hand as you jogged to the kitchen.

Heather is slouched over the table, papers spread before her, laptop on her lap. "Hey, girl. Good morning!" She is five times too cheery for having gotten less sleep than you.

"Can't talk. I'm late. The alarm didn't go off." You stuffed half a bagel into your mouth and poured your coffee into a cup. Black, no cream, no sugar.

"About that… your boss called and said to come in later. He knew you had a late night, and he had someone else come in to cover the truck being unloaded." She sipped her coffee as her left hand is typing in some sort of code. "I turned your alarm off because I knew you needed sleep. So, you're welcome." She winked smugly at you.

You stopped and gaped at her. "Thank you." You frowned as you fix your cup, properly this time, with four creams and two sugars. "Let's start over. How did you sleep last night?" you sighed once the caffeine hit your bloodstream and jolted you awake.

"Fantastic. I needed a night in. What about you?" Heather looked up; her typing paused.

"Great. I think I'm going to shower and primp. Maybe shave and paint my nails. Afterward, do you want to do facials?" you spread cream cheese over your bagel before sitting down at the table.

"Yeah, hopefully, my boss will let this be the last thing he needs this weekend. The coding for this is shit. None of it works, and it has loopholes made by amateurs." She scrubbed a hand over her face, breathing in deeply.

"Well, I'll leave you to it." You took your mug into your room and laid out your outfit. A pair of heels, white with red soles, a pair of pinstriped skinnies, and a peplum top with a lace neckline. Never let it be said that you didn't have refined taste. You also pulled out a pair of maroon Nike sneakers.

Your mug sat forgotten on your dresser as steam billows out of the bathroom, the smell of nail polish following.

You called Heather into the bathroom. After a few minutes, you were both as green as the Wicked Witch of the West. She snapped a few silly selfies on her phone before helping you peel your mask off. Then you did the same for her.

She sauntered out into your bedroom and gave her approval of your outfit. "Jessica, if you're back here directly after work, I'll be very disappointed in you. I mean it." Heather eyed you with mock seriousness.

"Yes, mother. But if he doesn't push it, then I probably will be home well within my curfew." You teased.

"Whatever. Just text me when you leave, wherever you're going. Okay?"

"Of course. Now get back to correcting the baby hackers' work and being fabulous." You nuzzled her towards the door, knowing if you didn't get ready now you would be ultra late. Your boss would probably forgive you, seeing as you were never been late before, but you didn't want to miss Nico. Something about him Derek you in, despite the obvious ties to money.

An hour later, your beat-up car pulled out of the garage and onto the highway. You rubbed the tiny heart-shaped tattoo on your ribs under your bust line to ease your nerves.

A splash resounded from under your car at the edge of the club's parking lot. You parked in your usual spot under the overhead light out back.

You played hopscotch across the parking lot, trying to avoid the puddles from last night's rain. Your boss waved his greeting from over by the jukebox. All the barstools have been unstacked, glasses polished, and fresh whiskey bottles have been set on the back-lit shelf.

You stashed your heels in their typical slot along with your license and clutch. Your boss waved you over.

"Hey, you okay to close tonight?" He asked. "Nancy's going to come in for a bit, but she won't be able to stay. Something about a date night."

"Yeah, I should be fine. If there's an issue, I can call you right?" you'd memorized his number after Nancy told you about some of the stuff she'd seen go down there.

"Yeah. Though it won't be me coming to help you. Probably Stan." He flicked some catchy beat song on the speakers and walked into the back to do whatever it is he does. He always leaves right after the 'open' sign is turned on.

You leaned onto the bar, nursing a shot of Beam while playing on your phone until you hear a throat clearing vaguely in the distance.

"I'm going to go." Your boss said, not waiting around for your reply.

With him gone, the bar is open for another night.

The few hours before six aren't usually busy. A few customers trickle in looking for a hot mid-afternoon meal. They were always polite, with 'please', and 'thank you, ma'am'.

You were serving beer and hamburgers to a group of guys out for a get-together when you heard the loud rumble of an engine.

You looked up just in time to see a sleek, spit-shined black '67 Corvette roll into the parking lot. Another car followed it; a silver Monte Carlo, a bit more beat up and dusty than the former.

You straightened up as absurdly long legs unfolded from the Corvette, and you tracked their progress across the lot. By the time they reached the front door, you hid behind the bar and served the drinks and meals.

The bell tinkled, alerting you that new customers were arriving. The first to step through the door was the same one who teased you yesterday. The second is scruffy and held an air of southern roughhousing.

Nico settled himself at the farthest barstool from the door, back to a wall, with a view of the entire room. *He's paranoid or ex-military.* You noted his subtle weave through the crowd.

The second man sat at a high boy table in the opposite corner of the bar. He nodded at Nico, who eased immensely.

Nico waved at you, and you held up a finger in response.

CHAPTER 3

After you topped off your regulars, and passed around a few beers, you made your way over to the far end of the bar.

"Hey," Nico greeted you with a beaming smile.

"Hey. Uh. So, what can I get you?" You fell back on the trusty bartender line.

"A rum and coke. Light on the rum." He watched as you pulled out a glass and drinks to mix.

"Here you go." You slid the mixed drink across the bar. "You going to tell me who your shadow is?" you nodded at the bulky man sitting alone.

"That's Derek. He's the only one who could touch me during sparring, so he got out of boring shit and gets to run with the big boss." Nico motioned at his split lip as you took note of his battered knuckles.

"Sparring for what?" you asked, a hint of worry in your voice.

"Nothing important. He will appreciate one of those hamburgers you serve, even though in about half an hour this place turns into a club. Lights and all." He pointed towards the grilled sandwiches the guys further down the bar were eating.

A moment later, you walked around the bar, arms laden with a plate of cheese fries, a burger, and a cold one.

"Thanks." A thick New Orleans accent teased your ears as you slipped the plates onto the table. "I'll holler if I need anything, don't you worry 'bout that." He reassured you before you could reply.

You spun around and met Nico's eyes, nodding his approval.

"Welcome to the Shade. I'll be with you in just a moment," you shouted in the general direction of the door after the tinkle of the bell echoed through the space. The volume of the music escalated as you turned the lights down and flipped the laser lights' switch.

The people who walked in were standing at the bar. They ordered a tray of frou-frou drinks to be sent to a table. A moment later, you put the tray on the empty table and walked back towards the bar.

Nico watched you intently as you hustled about. You paused when you felt the heat of his gaze raking over your skin. You turned around to see a glimpse of his tongue, his lips glossy.

You sauntered down to his stool, almost daring him to make a comment about it.

"I'll take a glass of the top-shelf whiskey," he said, finger-pointing to the tallest shelf as he smirks. "And I want you to keep wearing the heels." His voice was barely above a whisper as you pour his drink.

Your lips pursed as he let out a deep chuckle. He spun around to face the crowd but kept his back firmly against the wall. You swayed off, hoping the floor was without cracks to trip you up.

A few drinks later served yet not drank, you saw Nico motion for Derek to come and Nico got up and disappeared in the pitch darkness of the back hallway.

Derek sat down on Nico's stool. You met Derek's eyes.

"Everything okay?" you hissed. You knew when people go down that hall, it's not for a casual smoke.

"No worries. Nico should be back out in a few," he replied as he continued to nurse his second beer. You pulled out a fresh one out and left it on the counter for him.

Across the bar, you noticed a couple along with a few other guys starting a game of pool. The dance floor is packed, and nobody's tried to throw a punch yet. *Just another laid-back Saturday night,* you thought.

A broad man took an available stool and ordered a rum and coke. He made brief eye contact with Derek, who tapped his phone screen before giving a brief nod. The man, dark-haired and scruffy, walked through the metal door before you even had a chance to mix his drink. Derek doesn't make a move to stop him.

You stopped polishing glasses here and there to make

drinks and top off customers. The unknown man walked back in later, terrified, but no worse for wear. You brushed your hand against the barrel of the sawed-off under the bar top.

Nico stepped out from behind the door and slaps Derek on the back. He stopped to whisper a quick set of instructions in his ears, then handed him a slip of paper and a gleaming set of keys. The door tinkled and through the blinds you see two sets of headlights illuminate the lot.

"And you," Nico said, turning to face you. "I'll be back in a few hours, hopefully, you will still be here, and we can talk…" Nico glanced at the lights now flashing at the building. "I best get going before he drives my car off into the night. See you soon Jessica." He gives you a few bills with a smile.

The next few hours passed as slow as molasses on a chilly day in Canada. You brightened momentarily each time the doorbell jangled. Every time you don't see Nico's now-familiar face, your stomach would drop a bit more. Just as you ushered the last of the partygoers out for closing, after the last call has long since passed, you heard a loud rumble.

You flipped the sign, locked the front door, and stepped into the chilly, polluted air. The car idled as the driver's door swung open. Nico stepping out. He changed his clothes since the meeting and was now wearing a leather jacket and jeans instead of his tailored suit and tie.

He shrugs sheepishly and explains what took so long,

in as little detail as possible. "I got held up. Derek needed something and I had to get that somewhere safe. Sorry…"

"No worries," you replied, "I'm going to go home, and you stay safe for the night." You pressed the clicker on your key fob. Your car beeped in response and the lights flicked on.

"Hey, I want to spend time with you. Can we go somewhere together or something?" He rubbed the back of his neck, a shy look peering from under long eyelashes.

"Nah, I got to get home, or my roommate will freak," you didn't wait for him to respond, resuming your walk.

"Okay. Then what time do you work tomorrow? And how do you take your coffee?" Nico's trying to reel you in, hoping you'll take the bait. Something about you is addictive, and he can't help but want more.

"I don't work Sundays. The club isn't open. Monday, I get here at noon-ish to unload the delivery truck and we open at three." You turned to face him before you get into your car. "I like it light and sweet. Four creams and two sugars." The slamming of your car door cuts the conversation.

Nico scribbled it down in his planner, triple under-lining it. *Light and sweet. Four creams, two sugars. Monday at three.*

Sunday flew by far too quickly in jolts of laughter and wildly inappropriate jokes between you and Heather. Before you know it, Monday morning rolled in, and it was time to go to work. You dressed in another outfit and drove the usual unpleasant trip for the first time this week.

The delivery goes smoothly, and you flipped the sign to open. A minute or two after three-fifteen, you spot the sleek Corvette pull up, Nico's giant form getting out with a to-go drink tray in his hands.

There was no one else in the bar when he walked in. He dropped the cups on the counter and greeted you warmly.

"Hey. How are you?" He leaned against the bar, acting nonplussed.

"Good. You?" you replied, setting down the rack of martini glasses.

"Doin' better now that I've seen you. You free for, like, an hour?" He checked his watch. "I got nowhere to be and no one to check in with." He pulled a misleading pair of puppy eyes. Sure enough, you caved and asked what he wants to do.

"I want to take you out for ice cream. Or we can walk in the park. Or just sit here and drink our coffee, after you flip the sign to closed." As he rambled, you noticed he was blushing.

"I'm too lazy to drive around the city. Or to walk around. It's humid," you said plaintively, causing Nico to raise an eyebrow at you.

"Okay… let's play twenty questions then. I'll go first." He silently treads over to the door and flips the sign and drops the blinds. "Favorite color?"

"Teal. Yours?" you replied, dangling your legs off your stool.

"Red. The color of my car's interior. I'm going to take that as your question."

"That's not fair!" you teased.

"Moving on. Favorite ice cream flavor?"

"Mint chocolate chip, slow-churned. Uh, why a Corvette?" you bare a bit of the knowledge your dad instilled in you to Nico.

"My brother wouldn't let me drive trash. It's classy, runs well, and is easy to keep up with. Plus, it matches his Thunderbird, which is jet black. I'm sure you'll see it someday." Nico shared the answer to your next question without prompting.

Back and forth, this volley continued until an hour has passed and you both have to get back to work.

"Same time tomorrow?" Nico asked at the door, throwing away the trash.

"Sounds good," you replied, smiling, throwing more beer in the cooler, and refilling the martini salt tray.

This same pattern continued for the next week and a half, always ending with the same question from Nico and the same answer from you.

Nico had asked you why you only wear shoes with red on them. You hesitated, then blurted. "It reminds me of my past. Of whom I was, and what I am. Who I want to become. I want to be a better person tomorrow than I was today, and they help me keep that perspective."

"Very philosophical. Mine are very practical and

remind me of their job. To keep my feet protected," Nico replied, nodding in approval.

You leaned over the bar to look at his shoes after laughing at his statement, and he nearly had to catch you before you tumbled over the bar top. You straightened up, realizing you're uncomfortably close to Nico's face.

The funny part is that his arms felt insanely comfortable around you. You released a deep sigh you didn't know you were holding.

Nico glanced down at your lips and subconsciously moistened his own. He suddenly released you and you fell back to land on the floor, shocked and dazed.

He reached a hand down to help you up, and you used his momentum against him to brush your lips chastely against his, in an uncharacteristically bold move.

Despite the brief contact, you tasted the cinnamon gum he had been chewing, the underlying flavor of rich dark coffee mingling with your senses.

You swore you felt a sigh of relief leave his lips against yours before separating, this time by the height difference.

He righted you on the floor, motioning for you to slip off your heels. You comply and he slides you onto the bar top, faces now level. His thumb stroked along the length of your cheekbone as he gazes at you with a mesmerizing stare.

You blushed under his gentle scrutiny, unsure of what he's expecting. Of what he is looking for. Your head dipped, trying to avoid meeting his eyes; he Derek your chin up to admire your features at a different angle.

A moment later, his breath fanning over your face, he paused. Nico's waiting for a signal; a sign that it's okay with you. You opened your eyes to a kaleidoscope of green, gray, blue, and brown hues. You subtly leaned into him, making the barest hint of contact.

Taking that as an approval, Nico pulled you in fully. Lips dancing, pushing, and pulling. You bit down lightly on his bottom lip, a groan of approval vibrating through your mouth.

Breathless seconds later, you threw your arms around his neck. His arms caged you in as his palms rested on the glossy bar top. Nico's chest heaves, mimicking your own. He pulled away slightly, giving you a moment to take in his features.

His eyes are wide, yet slightly dilated. He's out of breath. His neck is flushed, seeping down into his shirt. His lips were bitten red. You imagine not looking much different.

"Wow." The word tumbled out of you in a deep breath.

"Wow is an understatement. That was incredible," Nico said, slightly shell-shocked.

The happy moment was ruined by the loud, obnoxious ringing of the phone from Nico's pants pocket.

"Do I have to get that?" He asked in mock seriousness.

"It's probably Derek. Or someone just as important." Fabric rustled as Nico swiped to answer the call.

"He- Yeah. Yeah. Give me a minute and I'll be right there. See you there." Nico spoke in hushed, clipped sentences to a frantic voice on the phone.

"Duty calls. I'll be back here, same time tomorrow. Cool?" Nico gulped down the rest of his coffee, sparing one last glance at you before he stepped out the door.

"See you soon." You said to the door.

CHAPTER 4

The next day came and went without you seeing Nico. The following week passed much in the same manner. After two days, you had stopped looking for him and gave up any remaining hope of him showing up.

Almost a month went by with no sign of him. You wished you had gotten his number so you could call him. *Maybe he couldn't be seen with anyone because of work,* you thought.

The heavy sound of boots echoed through the empty club as chairs clack from being unstacked. You were so focused on your work; you don't see a large man entering.

"Hey," the sharp New Orleans accent breaks your concentration.

"Hey, Derek. How are you?" you said, looking up to meet his eyes.

"Doing well. How about yourself?" He replied, pulling up a barstool.

"Okay, I guess. Where is the big boss?"

"He can't be here right now. He wanted me to check on you. Make sure you're all right." Derek's face falls at your downcast expression.

"He is trying to keep you safe, not ignore you. He will be by soon and I'll let him know you want to see him. Okay?" Derek slides a piece of paper across the bar top before getting up. A flash of silver peels out of the lot.

You sighed, scrubbing your hands over your face as you pull your hair out of its ponytail. You pulled out a stool at the bar and lean forward heavily on your elbows. The paper crinkles and you smile just enough to tilt the corners of your mouth up.

Scrawled in hurried, messy handwriting is a number. Under it, is a short note. *See you soon, Red Heeled girl. ~N*

You folded it up and shoved it into your pocket, vowing later to put the number in your phone. You flipped the sign to open with a bounce in your step.

The night began with no problems, but around ten-ish, you saw a dreaded face walk into the club. 'I knew I recognized that form...'you thought.

The man gave his men instructions, and a moment later, they dotted the landscape of the club. The leader locked his eyes on you and strode over to the bar. The crowd split for him, even if they don't know him.

A hush falls over the patrons as he stopped directly in front of you.

Your eyes traced over the square jaw covered in scruff, the large nose, and deep-set, stone-cold eyes. His voice feels like cold rain upon your ears. "Little crazy, get me a drink. You know how I take it." Then he slapped his hand down on the steel bar top with a heavy thud, innuendo heavy in his voice, meant only for you.

"And the rest of you, as you were." He addressed the rest of the people standing in the bar, who seem stunned that he has appeared.

The murmur of voices nearly swallowed his next comment as he leaned across the bar into your personal space. "Sometime today, if you can handle it," he leered.

You scurried to get his signature drink, the glasses clinking as you set one on the bar. Then the glug of tequila, and the hiss of a fresh can of lemon-lime pop. Then, a salted rim and a cut lime, and a single ice cube, finishes off the drink. You slipped it on to a coaster and handed it to him.

He reached over the bar and forced you to look up at him, with a single finger under your chin. "You will address me. Got it Crazy."

"Yes, Maxim." You meekly whispered.

"What was that?" He growled.

"Yes, Maxim." You forced a pleasant smile onto your lips and blink, fake and sugary-sweet, at him. You turned away to serve other patrons and your jaw locked.

At the far end of the bar, a young gangly man slipped a note into his fold of money. *'I work with Andrei, Nico's business associate. If there is an issue, he will hear about it.'* He introduced himself as Jed, and he was a very upbeat person. Not one you would have picked, but inconspicuous for sure.

Every hour or so, he ordered a beer just so he could pass you a note. Each time, you reassured him that you were okay and that he didn't need to worry about you. You had to refill Maxim's drink more than once, and each time, he humiliated you.

You were polishing glasses, having topped off everyone and delivered everyone's food, when a man with rich brown skin, and a wolfish look on his face, stood at the counter. He cleared his throat.

You hold up a finger to indicate one minute, and he had the audacity to grunt at you. You looked up and met his gaze, unblinkingly. Maxim noticed the exchange and apologized for the man. "Forgive Mr. Armstrong, he doesn't know how to talk to a lady such as yourself."

"Maybe he should learn." You hissed under your breath, voice full of mockery and scorn.

"We will be in the back room. Bring another round of drinks if you care too." The large man was jerked away from the bar and marched like a scolded schoolboy down the hallway to the meeting room.

"Finally, they leave." Jed laughed when you mock them with sarcasm and regained your happy attitude from before. "They aren't friends I take it?"

"Not in the slightest. They are like your boss, and they bribe my boss, so they can do whatever the hell they want. I'm not excited to go back there by myself, to say the least.

Those men have a reputation." Your eyes lost a bit of their sheen as you glanced forlornly down the hallway.

"I can follow you without alerting them, so if anything happens, I can get help." Jed offered.

"I can't ask you to do that."

"The boss said to keep you safe, and I can't do that unless I can see you." You put the glasses on an oversized tray and headed towards the hallway.

Once you reached the steel door, you pressed the buzzer, knowing better than to just walk into a meeting.

"Who is it?" Maxim's voice came through the tiny speaker.

"Just me. I have your drinks." The door squealed open, and a cloud of smoke rushed out of the opening.

"Set 'em here." He motioned at the ring-stained table. As you walked in front of Gordon Armstrong, he had the nerve to slap your ass. "Armstrong." Maxim warned.

"I can handle it. Can't I, Max?" you mocked him.

"Sure can, Crazy. This one doesn't kneel unless she feels you're worth her respect. She never kneeled for me, that's how I know." His lips twisted into a cruel grimace, his version of a smile.

You set the drinks down and walked over to Gordon. You bent over and whispered harshly in his ear. "If you want to touch me, make sure you can handle the consequences. It'll be a cold day in hell before I kneel for you. Just keep that in mind." And then you sauntered off, out of the door.

"And don't expect me to bring you anymore drinks!" you shouted over your shoulder.

"That went better than I expected." You shrugged at Jed. "Any news from the boss?"

"He says Nico is going to swing by and talk to you. Unless you just want to see Derek?" you shook your head no.

"He's going to relieve me, seeing as the leader of the Devils is here. Nico wants you protected, and I can see why." Jed approved your actions in the backroom with just a few words.

"Thanks." You gave him a deep nod.

Half an hour later, Nancy showed up and took over delivering drinks to the table. *She* has no problem with the Devil boys, of course. They left just five minutes before Nico pulled in. You see, the familiar headlights of the Corvette and the Carlo.

Derek slapped Jed on the back and gave him a fist bump before Jed got up to leave. When he reached the door, he looked back at you and gave you an imperceptible nod.

"Damnit, Jessica. Why didn't you text me when He showed up? I know Derek gave it to you." Nico asked, worried.

"Because I knew you would come down here and make a scene, which is not what you need when you're trying to make a good name for yourself." You shrugged.

"You couldn't tell me you weren't going to be here for

damn near a month?" you threw your arms across your chest and stamped your foot.

"I had no choice in the matter. We were afraid something was going to happen to you, because of what happened." Nico blinked slowly at you.

"I wasn't worried about something happening to me. I was worried about you." You stabbed your pointer finger into the center of his chest, hard. "And what happened that could have affected me?" you pursed your lips and cocked your head.

"I can't tell you. It would put you in more danger. Just know it shouldn't happen again in the future." Nico deflated and smiled at you, clearly having had some of the worry lifted off his shoulders.

"Okay, I guess." You said flippantly.

"I want to tell you. Believe me, I want to, so much." Nico gave you a pair of puppy dog eyes.

You just stopped and look at him with a look akin to disbelief.

"Let me take you out, and we can talk about it." Nico pleaded.

You looked over at Derek, who nodded.

"Okay, Saturday work for you?" your voice is clipped, your fingers playing with the piercing in your left cartilage.

"Three days? Can I at least come here and see you?" Nico leaned on the bar, dimples flashing.

"Yeah, if I'm working." You turned away and went

back to mixing drinks. "I'll meet you wherever." Your tones softened.

"The little Italian place downtown. You know the one?" Nico's fingers twisted together on top of the bar, and his cheeks lit up with a blush.

'*He knows he's winning here, and he probably knows that I'm okay with it.*' You half smiled before turning back around to face him. "Yeah, I know the one. We going to do anything after?" you asked.

"Maybe a walk through the park, and a stop for ice cream. That okay?"

"If it goes the way I hope it does, that sounds perfect." You gave a cheek splitting smile and leaned across the bar and dropped a kiss on his lips.

CHAPTER 5

The next day, Nico came by the bar alone. You cheerfully greeted him, simply because he brought coffee. At least that's what you told yourself. Not because you really liked him.

He smiled with his eyes as well this time. You noticed that the corners of his eyes crinkled up with crow's feet. He set the coffee down and picked you up in a great big hug.

"What are—oh hello to you, too," you sassed, as his arms wrapped around you.

"Shut up," Nico said faux gruffly.

Three seconds into the embrace, you realized Nico doesn't hug like anyone else. For one thing, he's tall enough to rest his head on your crown. And your ear was right over his heart. And he squeezed gently but firmly, creating a comfortable band around you with his arms.

He took a deep breath, nose buried in your hair,

before he released you. "Thank you." You can feel the rumble of his voice roll through his chest. His frame loosened, and he settled himself onto a stool.

"So, what happened yesterday?" He opened the bag and pulled out a Dunkin Donuts box and a few napkins.

"Nothing major." You shrugged.

"Jed said Maxim came by." Nico narrowed his eyes.

"Oh yeah, that… it went okay. I think," you questioned.

"Was he harassing you?" Nico asked.

"No more than usual."

"More than usual?" Nico pursed his lips and raised an eyebrow.

"We have a history. I'll tell you sometime." You took a sip of your cup of coffee.

"Don't worry about it. Just promise me that if it keeps up, you will go down to the station and report him. Okay?" Nico rubbed his hand over your shoulder.

"Yeah, I'll. But I don't want to talk about him anymore. What else is happening in your life?" you smiled at Nico.

Nico chuckled. "So have I told you about my partner, Andrei, and my brother Sergei's first meeting?"

"No," you bit into a donut and waved your hand at him, in a 'carry on fashion.'

"So, Andrei is a very straight-laced guy and follows the rules to a tee. This is the opposite of Sergei, who just does whatever the hell he wants, pretty much all the time." Nico shook his head.

"I called Andrei and told him to come over to talk about something. What it was I can't remember, but anyway. So, he was like, okay, be over soon. Well, Sergei, being the man that he is, was in the garage working on his car. On the Thunderbird, I told you about." Nico swallowed a sip of coffee.

"Andrei drives over with no problems, through the gate, and up the driveway. He gets to the garage and scares the literal shit out of Sergei. Sergei dropped a wrench and scratched the fresh coat of paint on my car when he startled." You let out a cute chuckle.

"I, on the other hand, am upstairs, looking through folders and signing things, when I hear a ruckus coming from the garage. So, I go down there thinking that maybe the floor jack broke, and the car fell or something. Nope, not even close. The two of them are in the driveway throwing tools and shouting at each other." Nico started really laughing, and his dimples dented his cheeks again.

"I just stood there waiting until Andrei just walked away, trying not to laugh at the two idiots. Then Sergei went back to work and Andrei, and I had our meeting." Nico rolled his eyes.

"It took Sergei three weeks to get over his little fit. To this day, I don't know how they resolved it, but they are thicker than thieves." Nico smiled at the thought.

"They sound like great guys. I would like to someday meet them." You nodded in affirmation.

Your phone rings from behind the counter. "This is

my roommate. Give me a second?" you held the phone to your neck.

Nico nods, "Take your time." He then swiped his phone open and took a long swig of coffee.

"Heather! Yes, I'll be home on time. No, he's not here. The other one is, though. Okay, see you, bye." You answered her rapid-fire questions and promised to be home on time.

You and Nico chatted amicably over the rest of your coffee and donuts until his phone rang and the time came for you to open the club. "I'll see you Saturday." He wrapped a hand around your back and pulled you in for a deep, drugging kiss. "Text me if he shows up."

You nodded but thought to yourself about how if you did that, it would put Nico in harm's way. Maxim would surely come after Nico for trying to be with you. Even though Maxim doesn't have the right seeing as he isn't connected to you anymore.

Nico walked out the door and stepped into his car, after he waved at you. You flipped the sign on the door to open, flicked the club lights on and went back to work.

Jed and Derek swung by, on separate occasions, to check in on you.

It had been quiet, too quiet for a Thursday night. Usually there was something happening, or someone was making a deal. Scratch that, there was always something going down here. You glanced around suspiciously, wondering what was going to happen.

Fifteen minutes later, a tall, slim, red-haired woman sauntered up to the bar demanding a drink.

"I'll take one Poison Apple." Her voice flowed out like heated molasses from her painted red lips, and she looked down at you.

"A please would be nice." You retorted under your breath.

"What was that?" She leaned over the bar, and into your space, flashing too large, too white, teeth at you.

"Nothing. Just trying to remember the recipe." You fake smiled at her, with thinly veiled hatred in your eyes.

"You do know who I'm, right?" She slapped her palms on the bar. You ignored her and kept mixing her drink.

"I'm Anna. If you don't know that name, it means I have the jurisdiction of Maxim to do whatever it takes to keep his business interests in the clear. That gives me the power to turn anyone in the city against you with the flick of a fingernail." She admired her glossy red painted nails, each one sharpened to a claw-like point.

"Okay. Here you go." You slid the drink over the bar.

"Did you even hear what I said?" She ignored the drink and turned her heated gaze upon you once again.

You nodded your head. "If you're looking for peace and quiet, there is an empty table over there." You pleasantly pointed her towards the other side of the bar.

The light of your phone glowed from under the bar as you opened your messages and drafted a new one. You decided against sending it to Nico and instead sent it to Derek.

Jessica: This chick just showed up at the bar, claiming ties to Maxim.

Derek: What's her name?

Jessica: Anna

Derek: She's bad news. Stay away from her. Nico has a meeting with Dmitriy later in the week. Maybe he can talk to her there if she is there.

Jessica: She didn't hit me or anything. don't let Nico talk to her. It'll just put him in more danger.

Derek: Jessica… what did you do?

Jessica: Nothing. It's all in the past. I'm sure you will find out soon enough.

Derek: If they threatened you, I need to know.

You read the last message and clicked your phone off, choosing to ignore him.

Anna left you alone and nursed her drink for the rest of the evening. At one point, she disappeared into the back room, then reappeared with some thug on her arm. She throws back the last of her drink and her heels click-clack as she walks out onto the concrete sidewalks.

You rolled your eyes along with Nancy when Anna was out of your sight.

A familiarly tall figure walked into the bar about ten minutes before closing time.

"Last call was ten minutes ago. Sorry, pal." You teased Nico.

"I'm not here for the liquor. I'm here for the company." He quietly watched you work on cleaning up and once everyone else had left, he helped you stack the stools and restock the cabinets. Nancy left a few minutes early with her boyfriend.

"I just wanted to see you again, as I know I won't be able to until Saturday." His lips twisted up and the twin set of dimples popped out. The smile reached all the way to his eyes.

"Well, thank you for telling me. I'll enjoy my day of peace and quiet." Your voice is laced with sarcasm.

Nico held a hand to his chest as if he was offended.

"I'm kidding. I'll miss you. A little bit." You held up your fingers pinched together.

"Whatever you need to tell yourself." He bantered back as he walked you to your car.

"See you Saturday." You stood up on your tippy toes and pressed your lips to his, hoping to get just a kiss in the moonlight.

Nico, however, had other plans and grasped your waist with both palms and stroked your skin over your shirt. You could feel every drag of his fingers through the cotton of your top.

Your arms came up around his neck as you pressed yourself closer to him. Closer to his warmth.

His tongue gently swiped along the seam of your lips. You opened the slightest bit, and he took it in stride. Soon enough, he was exploring your mouth, and you were fighting right back.

You pushed back firmly, then bit down on his lower

lip and gave it a sharp tug. Nico jerked you closer and sucked in a heaving breath.

One of his hands slipped under your shirt to send goosebumps trailing across your skin. You took a gasping breath, lungs protesting the lack of air, and smelled the smoke and whiskey lingering on his skin. And underneath it, you could smell his clean scent.

He lifted you up and held you up with the other arm. You could feel his heat and the hardness underneath his jeans. You broke the kiss for air and ended up standing on your own feet as you try to recover from a hit or your own personal drug.

You held a hand up and rested it on his chest. "As much as I would love to continue this." You motion between the two of you. "I have to work tomorrow, and I'm pretty sure you have something important going on."

Nico shook his head to try to break the haze in his brain, and the fog of your kisses. "Yeah, I suppose." Nico's eyes weren't meeting yours and his kiss bitten lips were almost frowning.

"You will survive. See you Saturday." You cheerfully pressed your lips to his, chastely this time, and opened your car door. Nico took a step back and your car rumbled to life. You saw his shoulders move in a deep sigh in your rearview mirror.

Nico

Nico let out an enormous sigh before sullenly walking to his car. The engine turned over quickly and unshifted as he pulled out of the lot. A little over halfway home, the sound of his phone filled the silence of the car.

He didn't check the caller ID on the screen, just swiped it open and answered. "Hello."

"Hello, Nicolas." The gruff voice coming from the other end of the line sounded annoyed.

"Dmitriy. How can I help you?" Nico snapped his blinker light on.

"I need to confirm your attendance at our meeting tomorrow." The background noise of a pen being scraped across a paper fills the line. "You're on speaker."

"I'll be there. No plus ones. Will any of your associates be there?" Nico stopped the car on a gravel turn off.

"Yes, but not my boss." Dmitriy answered Nico's unspoken question.

"Okay." Nico scribbled a note for Andrei, about party guests on a scrap of paper, and shoved it in the console. "Well, I guess I'll see you tomorrow." Nico pulled out onto the side road.

"Farewell, see you soon." The phone clicked from both ends.

Nico mused on how he could use the meeting to his advantage now that he was sure Maxim would not be there.

The sound of an old pop station filtered through the Corvette, filling the arbitrary, almost deafening silence.

The gravel popping signaled Nico's arrival into the driveway, and the distinct rumble of the car shut off. The glow of the headlights faded, and Nico opened the side door with the pass code.

Sergei was not in the garage, so he must have been working in the meeting room or asleep. Nico slipped off his shoes and the padding of his socked feet on the hardwood floor alerted to his presence.

The light was not on in Sergei's suite or in the briefing room, so Nico carried on as usual.

A quick shower and a fresh set of clothes later, Nico nearly collapsed onto the bed. His sleep was fitful between the meeting and his thoughts of Jessica.

CHAPTER 6

At one point, he woke up from a nightmare where Dmitriy was holding her at gunpoint behind the bar, until Nico surrendered. His breaths came in great heaving gulps as his shoulders shook and his hands trembled.

When his heart rate finally slowed down, it was just in time for him to get up for the day and get going.

"You don't look so hot." Sergei said bluntly, as his eyes swept over Nico's tired form.

"I don't feel it either. Sleepless night." Nico poured himself a cup of coffee and wiped off his face after his sweaty morning run.

Sergei nodded, having had his fair share of those nights where you can't catch a break, can understand where Nico was coming from.

Andrei walked in just as Nico finished getting dressed and they hurried down to the dining room.

"Here, put this in." Andrei handed him an earpiece. Then Andrei's footsteps sound in the briefing room.

"And take this." Sergei handed him a vial of cloudy liquid. "Trackable nano bots. If you can slip it into their drinks, we can track them back to their headquarters."

"Is it permanent?" Nico inverted the glass and watched it float around.

"No, after 24 hours it dissolves, so no permanent damage is done." Sergei answered as Nico pushed the tiny glass into the inside edge of his handkerchief pocket. "Do you have the gas resistant one on or nah?" Sergei pointed at Nico's handkerchief.

"Yeah, they may be having a civilized meeting, but they are still mob bosses." Nico smoothed out the nonexistent wrinkles in his charcoal suit.

"I have the Kevlar weave suit vest on. And the shocking signet ring, just in case." Nico twisted said ring around his right pinkie in anticipation.

"Well, I think you're ready to go on my end. I know Andrei has some intel for you, probably about who is going to be there and what they want." Sergei pointed down the hallway to the briefing room.

Andrei handed over a file and spoke efficiently as Nico flipped through the papers.

"Dmitriy is there to scope out business partners for Maxim and Anna is there for the property exchanges. You were invited by Dmitriy, so don't offend him lest they attempt to throw you out." Andrei nodded at Nico.

"And if you can, try to get an invitation for the Gala,

Maxim is hosting next month. He will be there, and so will his minions. We may not be able to capture him, but we can get intel about what he is up to." Andrei took the file from Nico's hands and walked over to his computer.

"Okay, is anyone else of importance going to be there?" Nico straightened his tie and prepared to leave.

"The leader of the Sheridans, but we have no reason to be anything more than perfunctory with them. They aren't doing anything wrong, just running a chain of very successful hospitals." Andrei looked up from the computer screen. "I have Jed going with you, if that is all right?"

"Yeah, that's fine. He will arrive in his own vehicle, correct?"

"Yes. Now go get the job done. I'll test the earpieces on the way over while you're driving." Andrei loaded a program onto his screen with a loud dinging noise.

"See you soon. Later Sergei!" Nico shouted as he grabbed the keys to the Caddy on the way out.

The car rumbled almost loud enough for Nico to miss the testing call from Andrei.

"Testing, can you hear me?" There was a brief hiss of static, then clarity.

"I've got you loud and clear, Andrei."

"Okay, just don't answer me when you're talking to someone. You know the drill." Then a slight pop signaled the end of the call.

The hotel parking lot was packed when Nico pulled in. He spotted Jed's beat up Ranchero on the first level of the lot as he swung the Caddy around to park it in the next spot.

The bouncer at the door dropped the rope without even asking for his name or his invitation.

"You have been invited to sit at the table with Dmitriy, sir. You're Nico Volkov, correct?" A nervous butler averted his gaze to Nico's imposing figure.

"Yes, I'm. Can you point me towards the table?" Nico softly asked the man, aware of the figure he cut in a crowd.

"That way." The man pointed a shaking finger at the opposite wall.

Nico twisted and weaved through the crowd, stopping here and there to make small talk with the other guests. He gave Jed a sharp nod but didn't talk to him because he didn't know which alias, he was using tonight.

There was a hush over the area around Dmitriy's table, probably from the terrified grunts attempting to get something out of the man. He sent them away with a sweeping gesture and invited Nico to take a seat.

"Well, don't just stand there. Have a seat and have a drink!" He waved down a server and ordered another round for himself and handed Nico a glass of whiskey.

"Well, he seems drunk." Andrei's voice came into Nico's earpiece, filled with scorn.

"How are you, Dmitriy?" Nico doesn't skip a beat at Andrei's obvious attempt to trip him up.

"Doin' fine. How 'bout yourself, Mr. Volkov?" Dmitriy slurred as he waved his glass around.

"Great." Nico's voice came out tight with tension.

"Loosen up." Andrei instructed.

"Enjoying the gathering of our associates? Have you had any success with the leader of the Sheridans? I heard he might be here," Nico questioned.

"He is a strait-laced one, that he is. The fact that he is here is a testament to Anna's skill." The stocky businessman leered at Nico, who just smiled and nodded.

"But alas, not thus far. He is coming around, though. He is much like you were in the beginning. You're more open to the idea of working with us than you were a few months ago." Dmitriy raised his glass in a toast.

"Prod him for more information." Andrei hissed and Nico could hear him clicking away on the computer.

"I'm indeed." Nico's posture loosened and his muscles relaxed. "I was wondering what you had planned for the coming months."

"Well, I have a string of appointments planned. I never know what the hell Anna is doing. I know Maxim is hosting a big gala, and if you came to this, then he plans to invite you to that." Nico nodded along.

"Good news finally. Get that in writing." The microphone hissed.

"Can you write down when and where that will be?" Nico produced a thin notepad from his inner pocket and flipped to a blank page. Dmitriy reached over and scrawled the location and the date on the sheet.

"There you go." Dmitriy flipped the pad around to face Nico.

"Good work. Try to locate this Anna we keep hearing of. She came to the club and Jessica says she can't hold her liquor, so she is bound to be loose-lipped." Andrei sighed, and Nico nodded, even though Andrei couldn't see him.

"Where is your partner, Anna?" Nico queried as he put the pad away without looking at it.

"Around here somewhere. She said she would be back in fifteen minutes, and that was a while ago." Dmitriy set his glass on the table. "Enough dancing around. What are you here for?" Dmitriy swayed and slurred alarmingly.

"To make connections, same as you. Attempting to get into your boss's confidence, as I would like to work with him." Nico took a sip of his whiskey, letting the burn ground him.

"Well, well. High aspirations for a lowly grunt." Dmitriy sniggered.

"I happen to be the boss of one of the fastest growing intel distributors, not just a lowly grunt. I would like to work with Maxim, because, honestly, I think he would see the value in my line of work." Nico's voice sounded like a well-delivered slap.

"Good job." Andrei crowed in his ear.

"And what industry would that be?" An unfamiliar female voice floated over to greet Nico.

"Intel. I don't believe we have met. Nico Volkov." Nico bent and kissed her knuckles.

"Anna Willis." She shook his hand firmly after his formal greeting. "My boss would *love* to have someone in that field." Her voice came out saccharine, almost to the point of being condescending. "Got anything to share." Her lips twisted up.

"I happen to know who is in whose pockets and that some of your men aren't loyal. But I have shared more for less," Nico smirked.

"And I would like to meet your boss. But Dmitriy here doesn't seem sold on the idea." Nico glanced at the man.

"He just gets like that at these events. Some people aren't meant to handle the social part of these affairs, right?" She forced a giggle.

"Right." Nico blinked heavily.

"You can meet him at the Gala next month. I'll confirm your invitation." She rested her hand on Nico's arm, much to his chagrin.

"Thank you." Nico put his hands in his pockets, trying to deter her advances, but to no avail. She looped her arm through his and led him away from the semi-seclusion of Dmitriy's table to mingle and socialize.

By the end of the night, Nico had determined three things.

One, he hated Anna's voice.

Two, Jed was much more useful than they gave him credit for.

And three, the Gala was the place to be, seeing as Maxim was going to be there, in person.

He drove home, his feet aching, and his earpiece discarded on the passenger's seat. Andrei greeted him as he walked through the door with a round of congratulations and a mug of coffee to get him through his routine.

Nico slipped off his shoes and threw his suit coat on the table. He pulled out the vial of tracking nano bots, the gas mask handkerchief, and shed the Kevlar weave vest to hand off to Sergei, who put them away.

After a shower, Nico collapsed into his fluffy bed with just a passing thought of maybe taking Jessica to the Gala.

CHAPTER 7

Your alarm clock woke you up at nine-ish on Saturday, and your phone is loaded with a slew of messages from Nico.

Nico: You, okay? I haven't heard from you.

Nico: We on for tomorrow?

Nico: It's late, and I'm going to bed. Sleep well and please text me when you get up.

Jessica: Hey, just got your messages. We're still on for eleven-ish. Can't wait to see you.

The triple dots pop up on your screen, signaling that Nico is up as well.

Nico: Same here. See you soon.

You rolled over and gave yourself a beaming smile. You wondered what you would be doing, seeing as Nico didn't give you any hints, just asked for your address.

Heather came in looking for a coat to borrow and you pointed her in the right direction, cheerily.

"You're way too happy for not having had your coffee. Are you sneaking it without me?" She held a hand to her chest dramatically.

"No, today is the day." You smiled impossibly wider at her.

"Oh, my god! Date day!" she squealed.

"Yeah, it is." You nodded self-assuredly as you rolled out of bed and walked into your closet.

"Well, I would love to stay and help you get ready, but work calls. I expect details later." The door closed after you yelled back in affirmation.

You threw your favorite pair of jeans and an elegant top out onto your bed before picking a pair of Vans to wear as well.

You left the outfit on the mattress and pranced into the kitchen, singing loudly, and giggling at everything.

Your coffee tasted better for some reason, and you could take a guess as to what it is.

The sound of the toaster popping your bagel was accompanied by the rumble of the coffee machine. You finished your bagel and took a cup of coffee into your room.

After a quick shower, you blow dried and curled your hair before getting dressed and doing your makeup. Not a ton, just a hint of highlighter and eyeliner. You were putting on your lip gloss as the doorbell rings.

"It's open!" you shouted into the other room, then hear rubber-soled shoes on the hardwood floors.

You slipped your feet into the Vans you picked out and

walked out into the foyer to find Nico leaning against the railing, dressed down from the previous times you have seen him with a button-down shirt and fitted pants on.

He let out a low whistle at your outfit, and you stepped into him and leave a lip gloss smeared impression on his lips.

"You look damn good." Nico linked his fingers through yours and let you lock the door to the apartment behind you.

"I feel underdressed next to you." You blushed and smiled bashfully up at him.

"Here's a secret for you. My favorite outfit is a pair of sweatpants, and nothing else." He winked in the stairwell's darkness, and you saw the brilliant white of his teeth flashing as well.

Your mouth gaped like a dying fish as you regained your composure. The image of him in just sweatpants would be one to remember, just by the feel of his muscles. By the time you got air back in your lungs, you have stepped out of the building and on the pavement.

You recognized the gleaming black car sitting just off the curb as Nico's. He got the door for you and let out a rush of air conditioning.

You slid into the red leather seat, marveling at the high quality of the stitching and general upkeep of the almost mint condition car.

Nico got in and smoothly shifts into 1st, showing off his skills just a bit for you. You paused and smiled at the crank down windows and rolled them down to stick your hand out the window. The feeling of wind playing over your fingers was one you have missed.

"I never have time to drive just for the hell of it. Always to and from work, the endless monotony of daily life." Nico glanced over at your relaxed form in the passenger seat.

"My brother makes it a once weekly tradition. Usually on Sunday instead of church, we find some old back road and just ride with the windows and the top down. Sometimes we race the cars, sometimes we drink a beer for the ones who aren't here." Nico's eyes gazed at the road, reliving the memories.

You slid away from the window and curled up under his arm, offering your presence as a balm. Not a word is said for a few miles at he pulled out onto the highway towards the city.

"You ever ridden with the top down on the highway?" Nico looked over at you, barely contained glee in his eyes.

"No." You wiggled your eyebrows at him mischievously.

The click of the top sliding down is followed by a great rush of wind, and you threw your hands up, breaking the current.

The two of you giggled and laughed the rest of the drive, talking about random, unimportant stuff.

He pulled into a tiny Italian restaurant and put the

top back. You raked a hand through your windblown hair and collected your purse.

"Leave it here. I got this." Nico pushed it back into the car's glove box.

"Are you sure? I can cover it."

"Yes, I'm positive. If it bothers you, from here on out, you'll buy the coffees, okay?" He firmly shook your hand, agreeing with you.

His hand never left yours as he dragged you into the restaurant. The fat man at the front stand greeted Nico like an old friend and gave him a slap on the back. "The usual?" He asked.

"This one is *not the usual,* oh no. She's something special." Nico pressed a chaste kiss to your lips.

"Ah, I see. Right this way." the man led you to a secluded part of the restaurant with just one booth, clearly meant for a couple.

"Thank you." You sat gratefully and smoothed out your top.

Lunch flew by, with Nico ordering your food and conversing with the wait staff in Italian, surprising you once again with a hidden talent.

The waitress whispered something in Nico's ear to which he responded, "Lei è la mia luce e il mio amore," before nodding at you.

The waitress blushed profusely and nearly ran away, clearly embarrassed.

"What did she ask?" you nodded after her abrupt escape.

"If I was available." Nico said nonchalantly.

"And you said?" you stroked your hand over his on the tabletop.

"Enough for her to know that I wasn't." Nico pressed a reassuring kiss to your forehead before waving the other waiter down to pay.

He paid for lunch and the two of you drove to the upper end of the district, towards the clothing shops and boutiques. "First, a stop here, to get you measured." Nico held open a glass French door to a tiny alteration and tailoring shop.

"I need her measurements for a floor-length gown." Nico motioned you towards the woman, who ushered you into a back room.

After you removed all your clothes, barring under-wear, she took a series of measurements, double and triple checking them before moving on to the next one.

"Here you go. Have a lovely day!" She bustled around the shop and shoves a sheet of paper at Nico while you get dressed. Nico was leaning on the door, waiting for you, and at the sight of you, his lips twisted into a smile and his dimples popped out.

The two of you traveled around a bit more, and Nico collected random bits of trivia about you. Your favorite coffee, your shoe size, and the shade of gray you like best.

You ended up with bags of stuff as Nico refused to let you walk out of some stores without buying something. He also bought you a pair of Vans - red, of course.

The day wound out, ending with ice creams in the park. "Mint chocolate chip for you?" Nico stepped up to order, and you nodded.

"Two mint chocolate chips, cups please?" He forked over a ten and told the vendor to keep the change.

You settled out of the way in a hidden gazebo, off the path. "So, how was today?" Nico took a bite of ice cream.

"Definitely *not the usual.* Just like you." You swirled your spoon in your ice cream before taking a big slurp.

"I know we have only gone out on a single date, but it feels like I have known you forever..." Nico ducked his head, and he sucked in a huge breath before continuing, "There is a gala next month and I just found out about it, and I was wondering if you would like to go?"

"Yeah, sounds like fun." You devoured another spoonful of ice cream.

"I know we haven't known each other long, but... wait what?" Nico realized you spoke.

"It would be my pleasure to go to an event with you. You'll have to forgive my wardrobe choice, though." You patted Nico's hand.

"I'll get all the details squared away. Not a big deal." Nico heaved a sigh of relief.

CHAPTER 8

You walked into your place after your shift is over, a little over a week later, to find a large silver box, a bag, and a shoe box on the dining room table.

A note rested on top. *For my Red Heeled Girl ~ Nico* was written in beautiful calligraphic font.

"That came for you. It was in, or rather in front of our mailbox, and no one calls me their red heeled girl." Heather came out of the bathroom, toweling her hair dry. "Go on and open it. I want to know what it is." She said in a tone full of childlike glee.

You lifted the lid off the largest box and find a mountain of tissue paper. You peeled it back layer by layer to expose the beautiful gown awaiting underneath. The softness of the gown hisses against the crinkly tissue paper as you lifted it out of the box.

You held it up and admired it. The black faded to a pure white over the flowing skirt. It had a hint of embellishment over the waist area on your right side. The top was shouldered and seemed to expose a fair bit of collarbone.

After Heather examined it as well, you folded it up and reverently placed it back into the box. Then, you opened the shoe box to find a pair of heels. With red soles, and in your size, no less. They were an off white, meant to compliment the ombre dress. You stacked the two boxes with the shoebox on top.

Then you dug into the bag. Out came a few smaller boxes. Two slight ring boxes, a necklace sized one, three bracelets, and a few sets of earrings. You opened each one to find an array of unique tones and weights of jewelry. Some of the earrings are singles, without a partner, clearly meant for your cartilage piercing.

One box was a bit antiquated and had a note scrawled in Nico's messy handwriting. *'These were my mother's... treat them well'.'* You gingerly lifted out a long strand of pearls.

At the very bottom of the bag, there was a typed note. It gave you instructions to wear what you want and on how to return the rest. You flipped it over and there was an envelope stuck on the back of it. Enclosed is an invitation to the Gala Nico had mentioned a couple of weeks back, printed on rich rice paper and in glossy ink. He hadn't brought it up again, and you had wondered if he had forgotten about it.

You put all of it on the vanity table in your room before pulling out your phone and messaging Nico.

Jessica: So, you do really want me to go with you…

Nico: I would like that very much. I assume we're talking about the same thing…

Jessica: The Gala? Maxim is going to be there.

Nico: So, will I.

Nico: And my men. You will be safe.

Jessica: What time are you picking me up?

Nico: I was thinking four o'clock ish? So, we can go out to dinner and then to the Gala.

Jessica: Sounds good. See you then. ;)

Nico: See you soon.

Your phone dimmed soon after you plug it into the charger. You took a quick shower and fell asleep as soon as your head hit the pillow.

The morning came far too quickly, and you woke to the noise of Heather banging pots in the kitchen. You looked over at your alarm clock, and it was not even ten past eleven. Far too early to be up and awake.

You pulled your pillow over your head, muffling the noises for a few moments before you swung your legs out of the bed.

You got your coffee, and Heather served you a fresh omelet. "You're going to let me help you with your makeup, right?" She flipped and folded the eggs in the pan.

"Yeah, but I don't have to get ready for a while. Relax, we got plenty of time." You slumped in your chair.

"Not really. We have to get you cleaned up, primped, and painted. Nails, then hair, then makeup.

And finally, that gorgeous dress that your boyfriend gave you."

"He is so not my boyfriend." You blushed profusely. "I'm just very convenient."

"*Sure*, and he would just buy a designer gown, and Louie Vs' for a *'fly'* girl." She quipped right back at you.

You shoved a portion of omelet in your mouth, then pointed at her with your fork and gave her a deep nod. "I see your point."

"Hurry and eat. We got shit to do, so you look drop dead gorgeous. And so, you can flaunt your man and look like a boss." She wolfed her meal down and stared at you in disbelief.

A little over four hours later, you sat at the dining room table, waiting for Nico to show up. Heather took stock and checked everything off the list.

Nails and Makeup... Your nails were painted and sealed, French tips for both sets. Your makeup was done to a knife's edge. Sharp, but not attention-seeking, wings with a hint of highlight to give you a healthy glow.

Dress... Your dress fit like a glove, and you thought back to the time he took you shopping and had some lady measure you. This must have been why. He had known your preference for shoes runs expensive since he met you and you had put on a pair to get his bottle of whiskey.

Accessories... the jewelry you had chosen was light. Two different sizes of cubic zirconia for your lobes and one cut into the shape of a heart for your cartilage. A teardrop for your necklace and a stacking of bracelets.

The way your hair was pulled up draws emphasis to your neckline.

She finished your look with a clutch and a layer of gloss, just in time for the doorbell to ring.

"That must be Nico." You got up and swayed over to the door, teetering on the carpet in your heels.

The door swung open, and your jaw dropped to the floor. From somewhere in the room, a gasp came out. A second later, you realized it came from you.

He looked flawless in his tailored suit, which matches the dark gray on the bodice of your dress. The streamlined fit highlights the broadness of his shoulders and the length of his chest. The pants were ironed to a needle-sharp crease and were just tight enough to make you wonder what is hiding underneath. In his hands, there was an enormous bouquet of fresh roses.

He stepped past you into the apartment and waved at Heather.

"You must be Nico." She rushed over and shook his hand.

"And you must be, Heather. I have heard great things about you." He raised her knuckles to his lips and pressed ever so gently.

"Well, I have work to get back to." Heather rushes out of the room, her face is beet red. "Don't have too much fun, kids!" you could hear her giggling not so quietly to herself as she walked away.

Nico turned to face you after he set the flowers on the dining table. "You look good enough to eat."

"I could say the same for you." You smirked and swept your eyes over his fitted suit again.

The ride to the hotel was smooth going because of the suspension of the Caddy. Nico held himself in the driver's seat with a tension that spoke volumes about how he feels about the car.

Once you pulled into a spot, Nico offered you a hand getting out, and you accepted, seeing the large puddles formed on the pavement.

The heat of Nico's body radiated, even through the double layers of his clothing. You shivered and not from the cold.

CHAPTER 9

Nico looped your hand through his arm. "Ready to enter the fray?" He glanced down at you, rocking on his feet.

"Oh, come on." You rolled your eyes. "They can't be that bad. There are other people we know here." You squeezed his arm as you stepped forward in the line through the door.

"I'll have to introduce you to Andrei. Somehow, he got his own invitation." Nico had a glimmer of pride in his eyes.

"It would be my pleasure." You kissed Nico's cheek as he handed the papers to the bouncer, who waved him through the metal detector. Your jewelry clinked and clanked as you stripped it off and step through the arch.

Nico's fingers brushed the sensitive part of your inner wrist as he refastened the bracelets, and he pressed a fervent kiss to the top of your spine when he re-clasped the necklace.

"You look good in my mother's pearls." His breath floated over your ear.

Heat crawled over your goose-bumped skin and settled at the peak of your thighs. You thought to yourself about how it is going to be a hell of a long night if this keeps up.

"Let's go." Nico straightened up like he didn't just ooze sex appeal and strode forward toward the bar.

"A whiskey for me and a martini for the lady." He motioned at the barkeeper, then at the two of you.

The familiar clinking of ice in a glass and the shaking of a mixer could barely be heard over the chatter of voices in the room.

A tall, lean, but muscular man walked up and paused next to Nico. He murmured something and Nico gave him a half smile. "This is Jimmy Newman." He waved at the dark-haired man.

"A pleasure to meet you. You must be Jessica. I have heard some about you - only good things, I promise." Jimmy gave you an exaggerated wink.

You let out a cheerful laugh, and your shoulders shook as you attempted to fend off the lingering cold.

Nico put his arm over your shoulders, claiming your attention once again. "This is Andrei," Nico muttered into your hair, feigning giving you a kiss.

"I see. And you're an associate of Nico's, here?" you patted Nico's chest and nodded at Andrei.

"Yes, I'm. And as much as I would love to stay and chit-chat, I have a meeting to attend to, so I must get going." Andrei shook Nico's hand again and gave him a prolonged look before a subtle shake of his head.

"Should we go find Dmitriy or dance a little?" Nico's hand trailed lower and lower on your back, clouding your judgment.

"Dance, I think." He led you through the throng of moving people before taking a deep inhale of Nico's woodsy cologne.

He pulled you closer until you could feel the rock-hard planes of his toned midriff pressed against you. Your hands landed on the back of his neck, and his landed low on your hips.

A thigh fit between yours and it was slanted just right to expose the hidden slit on the side of the skirt of your dress. He pulled and pushed you along the length of his thigh until you caught on and took the initiative to do it yourself.

The front of your right thigh brushed right up against his groin, causing his pants to become a little too tight. His bottom lip was caught between his teeth, and he let out short groans here and there.

You could feel the wetness between your thighs soaking the fabric of your panties. Your rocking motions pushed you closer to the edge as turned up as you were.

You pulled away at the last beat of the song and Nico let a string of dirty talk slip into the crook of your neck. "You would look so damn good in just those pearls. Or with your dress pushed up around your waist across some high-ranking member's desk."

You dug your fingers into the back of his neck under his hair, sharply snapping him back to reality. The song changed into something with a shallower beat and a slower pace.

You struggled to beat back the part of your brain telling you to drag him to a closet and fuck him senseless, but the slow song helped kill the embers of your arousal.

After a few minutes of soft swaying and stepping in a box without going anywhere, you headed back to the bar.

You sipped at your lukewarm martini and finished it before a familiar face headed in your direction.

"Hello Maxim." Nico's hand reached around you to shake Maxim's. Once the greeting is over, Nico rested his hands on you. One is possessive, resting on your hip and the other over your stomach.

"Nicolas. Jessica. How are you faring?"

You met his eyes, daring him to say something, before realizing you had seen that look on him before. It means he was jealous and would stop at nothing to get back what he considered his.

"Well, when was that meeting starting?" Nico replied, his voice pleasantly fake.

"I came to tell you it was starting. Although, I would leave your… escort… here, so she can't snitch on you." Maxim smirked at you in a contained glee.

"You know, I don't think I'll." Nico sassed, before pulling you in for a kiss. The taste of whiskey on his lips is enough to calm your frayed nerves. "Right?"

"Right, Nico." Your fingernail trailed along his arm, clearly having an effect on him, as his pupils dilated.

"We will be there soon. Don't start without us." Nico paused in thought. "We might be late; you know how it is." Nico winked at you.

Maxim's face was set into a scowl when Nico smiled, dimples and all, at him. He turned and weaved towards through the crowd towards the shadowed door beyond.

Nico's hand wrapped over yours as he led you in the opposite direction, toward another barely lit back room.

"I'm guessing we aren't here for fun." Nico closed the door before your voice echoed around the room.

"No, we need- I need to tell you the plan for later." Nico pulled out his phone and typed a message up to show to you.

'We're being recorded.'

You nodded.

'We're going to go to the meeting and you're going to stay with me. I don't want you to go with Maxim, he was giving you a look.'

You raised your eyebrows before typing back, 'I've seen that look before. He's just jealous.'

'Anyways, we're going in. I'm going to seal a few deals, grease a few palms, and you're going to watch the other people and see what is happening. Got it?' You gave a hearty nod before typing out a question.

'What is our signal? You know, like a safe word?' You handed the phone back, and Nico makes a tugging motion on his left ear, and you nodded at him.

"You ready?" Nico shoved his phone back in his pocket and pulled you in for a kiss. "You have no idea how tempting it is to not leave this room until We're both *satisfied*." Nico pressed his open mouth to your exposed shoulder and rested it there, just long enough for your skin to rise in goosebumps.

Your lips parted in a shallow gasp, and you raked your fingers across his scalp, setting his hair askew. "Soon, we will." Your voice came out in a whisper.

Nico gently shoved you through the door, out into the open, and your heels clicked on the hardwood before being silenced by the carpet in the meeting room.

"Ah, the guest of honor arrives." Dmitriy shook Nico's hand and smiled at you.

"Dmitriy, Anna, Maxim, Sir." Nico greeted everyone in the room, including the leader of the Sheridans.

"Let's get started, shall we?" Maxim motioned at the grand round table and the empty chairs.

Nico sat opposing Maxim. The leader of the Sheridans was seated to his left, and he refused to reveal his real name. You sat to his right, and the significance of the seat was not lost on you.

Maxim had Dmitriy and Anna in the seats next to him. The table was strewn with files of different sizes and thicknesses.

Nico added his to the pile after he pulled it from inside his coat and nodded at Max.

"Each of us has our respective fields of influence, and I would like a quick run through of what is in your folder." He motioned at Anna, who stood up and opened the thickest of the folders.

"The lower downtown district is very open to developmental opportunities. The midtown's business is up since we bought that bar, and the salon, and renovated them. The Shade is well taken care of, and the apartments are full." She slid the file to her left, and Maxim shuffled with it before motioning her to sit down.

Dmitriy stood up and started to speak without his sheaf of papers. Maxim must be used to this as he pulled the medium and messiest pile towards him.

"We have brought in a new batch of recruits, and I have a new potential partner to introduce. Nico Volkov." Dmitriy sat and nodded at Nico to start. You picked at your nails, trying to appear disinterested and not to draw attention to yourself.

"I'm in the business of dealing in secrets. We have not set deep roots here yet. There is not much in there." Nico motioned to the thin file in Maxim's hand. He looked up and his lips are pursed, his eyes squinted with disapproval.

You looked around the table, scanning faces and taking in expressions. The red-headed woman is rolling her eyes and appears bored. Dmitriy looked proud of himself. The leader of the Sheridans has a glimmer of fear in his eyes and glanced warily between Nico and Maxim.

"In the coming weeks, my men will bring me more to sort through, and what I find useful, I'll bring to you. For a price." Nico took a deep breath before meeting every-one's eyes and waiting to take a seat.

"I'll be in contact soon." Maxim clapped. "Would you like to speak?" He fixed a glare on said man.

"No, I'm alright." His flat, reedy voice came out for the first time that evening.

"Well, then consider this meeting adjourned, and have a lovely evening." Maxim slapped his hands on the table before striding out of the room. Everyone else files out after him, and you stay seated, while Nico leaned on the table.

"Guess we'd better head home. Sergei will want to know what happened, and Andrei will stay until it breaks up." Nico pulled you to your feet. "And I have things to do." His eyes darkened at you, and a simmering heat started low in your stomach.

CHAPTER 10

Nico parked the Corvette in the driveway and took a hold of your hand as you stepped out. "We have to stop for a second to talk to Sergei."

Your face fell. "Okay, let's hurry." You ushered him along.

"It won't take long, and he would probably appreciate your input." Nico pushed the door shut and led you down the hallway to where Sergei was sitting at a table, typing away.

"Hey, Nico. And you must be Jessica?" you nodded, and Sergei extended an arm to the empty chairs across from him.

"How did it go?" Sergei leaned back in his seat.

Nico gave him the rundown, and you chipped in with your input here and there, and then you told him what you noticed at the meeting.

* * *

"Thank you. Nico, a word?" Sergei dismissed you, and Nico waved you into the hall.

"Go up the stairs and the last door on the left is mine. I'll be up soon." He pulled you in for a quick kiss.

Sergei

"I'm worried about you and this girl of yours." Sergei started.

"Why? She hasn't shown any killer tendencies like Roxanne, and she is supportive of this." Nico motioned at the table covered in notes and files.

"I feel like she isn't telling us something, and it is something important. I don't want it to come back and bite us in the ass." Sergei poured a decanter of whiskey.

"I understand that. But give her a chance. For me?" Nico smiled at Sergei's nod.

"I'll see you later, okay?" Sergei resumed his fervent typing.

You

As you went up the stairs, you took in the house's decor. Clearly, two or more bachelors live here, and they are not lacking in money based on the grade of paintings that were hanging on the walls.

The walls are painted in neutral colors and the furniture is sparse but looked like it is used. You wandered down the hallway to Nico's room.

The door was ajar, and you flicked on the bedside

lamp, as you can't find the light switch. Across from the doorway were a sitting area and an oaken table.

There was an attached bath, with marble countertops, and fluffy towels hanging on the racks. You took in the fancy shower, and the separate toilet, before turning back out to the room.

At the foot of the bed, there was an overfilled shoe rack, which prompted you to remove your shoes, and your toes sunk into the plush carpet. You dropped your heels and ran your hands across the mussed, but otherwise smooth sheets on the bed.

Your dress dragged across the floor with a hiss.

The pictures on the bedside table caught your eye. One was with an older blonde woman who must be his mother. There are quite a few with him and Sergei and sprinkled in among them was Andrei. There was another one of him in his cap and gown, proudly holding his diploma.

You were startled out of your quiet observance by the sound of Nico knocking on the door.

"Hey." You watched as he strips his coat off and slung it across a chair.

"Hey." He strode across the room on bare feet and pulled you tight against him. "You were perfect tonight. You know that, right?" He swayed a bit, giving you a beaming smile.

"I was unaware." You smirked at him over your shoulder.

"Cheeky woman." He spun you and took your lips as his own.

Your arms crept up around his neck and his hands settled on your waist. The heat radiating off him was setting you aflame.

"I don't know about you, but I couldn't ignore how sexy you looked tonight. *So damn sexy.*" His words came out in a growl under your ear. "And you looked like my dessert for the evening—"

"Ooh… "Your voice was broken off by Nico's mouth trailing over the open shoulder in your dress and leaving little nibbles on your skin.

His hands trailed up your back and paused at the top of your zipper. He pulled back for just a moment. "You, okay?"

"Yes, please." You nodded and scrabbled at the back of his suit.

* * *

The click of the teeth of the zipper was interspersed with moans from you as he stopped every few inches and peeled the two halves apart, sending chills down your skin.

When he got to the bottom of the opening, he kneeled and rolled the dress over your chest. The swishing of the fabric hitting the floor was accompanied by a deep groan.

"You're so beautiful." Nico's eyes met yours, full of

adoration and slightly dilated with lust.

"No, I'm not." Your arms came up to cover your chest. "Please don't say something that isn't true."

Nico straightened to his full height. "Why would I lie to you? I'm going to prove it to you, you just wait." A sparkle of a challenge glowed in his eyes before he bent down and swept you up in a daze-inducing kiss.

"Take this off." You tugged his shirt out of his pants, and he threw his vest somewhere. You raked your nails down his chest as you slowly unbuttoned his shirt. You shoved it off his shoulders and trailed your fingers over his muscles.

In the dim light, you couldn't see exactly what the design is that was inked on his chest and across his ribs.

He hiked you up and threw your legs around his waist, carrying you across the room. Your hips rolled of their own accord against the massive bulge in his trousers. You felt a slight swoop of air as he set you down on the bed and you heard the clink of a belt buckle.

The sheets you were admiring earlier were folding and rolling under you like liquid silk. You pushed yourself up the bed so your head was leaning on the pillows, and so you could watch Nico strip out of his pants.

The bulk of his thighs and the Adonis belt leading your sight downwards do not go unnoticed by you.

He kneeled on the bed, hips above yours, and found your breathless lips. Your eyes were slammed shut by the force of your kissing. You rolled your bodies, so you were on top.

Your lips trailed down his throat, over his Adam's apple, to his tats. You traced the star and sun design with your tongue and found the phoenix on his ribcage with your fingertips.

Your nails scored across his back as he pulled you up from your exploration.

"Keep that up and I'm going to blow." Nico's voice was gravelly and lust-hazed. He rolled you again, sending his muscles rippling and flexing against you, to your delight.

"Let me." He ghosted down your chest and his fingers unsnapped your bra, skillfully. A sudden suction alternates between your nipples, and your back arched up into his mouth. "Feels so good!" You moaned out.

Once he worked you up a bit, he teased down your stomach and searched for the small tattoo under your breast. "Is this what I think it is?" He traced his nail over it.

"Mmm, hmm—you're teasing me!" your skin tingled with the feather-light drag of his fingers.

He got ever closer to the burning heat at the peak of your thighs. Once he's there, though, he doesn't go straight for removing your panties, he is just standing by. His breath was floating over you in teasing waves.

"Please, Nico!" your hands grasped the sheets as he trailed a finger over the wet spot you had created.

"What was that?" Nico said, smug in his position.

"Please, Nico. Please take me…" your body pulled tense in anticipation.

He took mercy on you and hooked the lace of your panties around his fingers and pulled them off.

"So sensitive. Gorgeous. My pretty lady." Nico murmured praises into the skin under your belly button.

He rolled your clit between his fingers, testing the waters. He barely pushed into your heat, giving you up to the first joint of his index finger. Slowly, he gave you more and more until you had taken two fingers.

He scissored and stroked you from the inside. Nico knew when he hit your sweet spot because the clamping of your muscles on his fingers was accompanied by a near-shout. He aimed directly for it, or so it felt like to you.

"Going to feel so full around me." The wave of pleasure was pulling higher and higher until you were teetering on the edge of bliss.

When Nico gave you a third finger, your mind went silent with white-hot pleasure. Your hearing faded out and you thought you could taste the pleasure. He stroked you through the rolling pulsing, prolonging the waves of sparks.

Somewhere during your overwhelming wave of pleasure, Nico had taken his boxers off and went for a condom.

Your eyes were hazy and unfocused, but you could tell Nico was larger than average, as he pumped himself before settling over you. His body is a comfortable weight, much like a warm blanket.

"You ready?" He noticed the blissed-out look on your face.

You nodded, and your eyes nearly rolled back into your head at the smooth glide and heavenly stretch. He stilled and your hands curled into the bedsheets as he flexed his hips, sending little jolts through you.

"So damn tight. It's like your body doesn't want me to leave." He rolled his hips back and then pushed in slowly.

A string of curses flew from your lips.

You're not quite tall enough to reach his lips, so you settled for the salt-slicked skin of his chest.

He found a smooth rolling rhythm and picked up a satisfying pace. His bulk was being held up by the muscles in his arms, and they caged your head in from where they rested on the bed.

He stuffed a pillow under your hips and slid back home. You immediately felt the difference in angle, and the solid hits on your sweet spots sent you spiraling higher.

You noticed the look of concentration on his face and felt his thrust slowing down to rutting rolls. "Going to come. Don't want to. Feel so fuckin good…" His voice was strained.

You encouraged him to keep going and rubbed your clit as he sped up again.

You found that edge with a perfectly timed pinch, and he ground into you as you clamped and constricted around him. You could feel him filling the condom as the muscles throughout your body continued to ripple and release the tension in your core.

You could only gasp and try to catch your breath as you came down from your respective peaks. He pulled out and you moaned at the loss, and he groaned at the cold air hitting him.

He tossed the condom somewhere and picked you up, headed towards the bathroom. The swishing of the water flowing around you relaxed every muscle in your body.

Nico scrubbed your scalp and between your toes and everything in between. He paid special attention to your skin and your hands. He quickly soaped and rinsed himself before stepping out and wrapping you up in a warm towel.

You slumped onto the bed, exhausted and loose-limbed with pleasure, as he slipped an old, faded tee on your body and a pair of sweatpants for himself.

* * *

You woke up in the morning to the sight of Nico's hazel eyes gazing appreciatively over your body.

"Morning, Sleeping Beauty." Nico tucked a strand of hair behind your ear.

"Morning, why do you smell like espresso?" your voice was sleep slurred, and you vaguely saw him reach over you. A second later, a steaming cup of heaven was placed in front of you, and you nearly moaned again.

CHAPTER 11

His huge frame overshadowed yours after you walked out of the bar and over toward his car. Nico swept you up into his arms. "Hello, gorgeous."

"Handsome. Am I being held against my will?" you giggled in his arms.

"Of course." His voice held a note of mock seriousness.

"Ah. Someone help me!" Nico ran his fingers down your side, sending ticklish tingles over your skin.

"Enough's enough." Nico sealed his lips over yours. You memorized his lips again, feeling the pillowy softness of them against yours, like no other feeling in the world.

He opened the door and let you slide in before closing your door and getting in the driver's seat. Not even a block down the road, he pulled you up under his right arm across the red leather bench seat. His fingers danced over the skin on your shoulder and upper arm, almost absentmindedly.

You rested your left hand on his thigh as he drove. He pulled into a Dunkin Donuts drive-thru, and then asked you, "The usual for you?" His brows are pulled down and his eyes are glistening.

"You memorized what I drink?" your face is incredulous.

"Yeah, should I have not assumed…" Nico trailed off, and then he put the pieces together. "You're telling me that no one, not a single person, bothered to pay attention to how you take your coffee?"

"No…" You trailed off.

Nico heaved out a deep, frustrated breath before ordering through the mic. "A large expresso, one creamer, no sugar. A half dozen donuts, mixed, and a large coffee, four creams, and two sugars."

The lady handed the stuff out through the tiny window, and Nico handed you the steaming cup. The box of donuts rested on your abandoned seat, closer to the passenger door.

"Thank you." You kissed Nico's cheek as he pulled out of the lot and drove towards the park.

He threw the car in park, grabbed his cup, and headed towards the sidewalk with you following behind, hands clasped together.

"So, I wanted to talk to you about what happened between you and Maxim. He looked ready to kill you at the Gala. Is it because of me?" Nico's hand squeezed yours a bit tighter.

Your shoulders moved up and down as you steadied yourself with his touch, eager to tell him about your past.

"I'm going to tell you this, and I expect it to stay between us. For starters, it's not you." Nico nodded.

"Maxim and I almost got married. My father set us up, and we just clicked." Your voice rushed out in a rapid stream.

Nico's face was placid, and you can't tell what he is thinking about. He walked through the near-empty park, confident with you by his side.

"Maxim was interesting, to say the least. He spoiled me but never told me he loved me even after three years of dating. He wasn't faithful, but if I said anything, he had a way to bury my father. So, I went along with it." Your shoulders start trembling, your mind flashing back to that day.

"I came to meet my father at Max—His house. When I walked in…" your voice broke.

"Hey, you don't have to tell me everything right this moment. We can talk about it some other time." Nico rubbed his hands together, trying to keep some warmth in his joints.

"But I must. For you to understand me." You walked around the gazebo and sat next to him; your hands folded in your lap.

Your eyes glazed over as you drifted through your memories.

"Hey, Max! You here?" you half shouted when you walked into the main foyer.

"Yeah, Jessica. We're in the dining room." An eerie silence filled the house.

Your heels clacked on the hardwood floors as you climbed the staircase and crossed the kitchen. You came to the table, and Maxim was sitting at the head. He stood up and walked over to you.

When he took a step, his foot made a sucking noise against the floor. As he got closer, you could see the bloody footprints he was leaving. He wrapped his arms around you and kissed the junction of your neck and shoulder.

You stood stock still with shock. Your feet moved you forward of their own accord, around the table to see your father's prone form on the floor. A spreading pond of blood came from a clear, concise wound in the back of his neck.

"If it makes you feel better, he didn't feel it." Maxim tries to reassure you.

"You… you killed my father." You say surprisingly calmly, considering what has happened.

"He was in my way." You don't hear the rest of what he has to say as you walk out of the room and out of his life.

You came back to your senses to find Nico holding your hands and squeezing them in grounding pulses. "I walked out and vowed to not get involved again. I still must see him and watch as he blackmails and threatens my boss."

"I'm truly sorry." Nico's voice is low like he was talking to a wild animal that might run.

"Thank you, but I don't see him disappearing from my life unless I decide to move away from here." You looked into Nico's eyes.

"I can understand where you're coming from. This city holds a lot of memories for me, too."

You nodded and took another sip of hot chocolate and pulled your legging-clad legs up under you.

"I moved here after I graduated and moved in with my brother Sergei. You met him when you stayed over." You blushed at his casual mention of your night together.

"Life was good. I had a girlfriend named Jess. I was working a few cases here and there. Mostly desk work, no fieldwork - I hadn't passed the training for it yet." Nico paused and took a deep breath.

"Jess and I lived in this apartment building together. She was done with college as well and was working. She was a schoolteacher. This was before I paired up with Andrei, and Sergei and I worked together occasionally." Nico looked down at his hand clasped in yours.

"I went with Sergei to check out some suspicious activity that had been taking place in the darker part of the city and left her there alone." Nico's eyes welled up, and you rubbed your free hand up and down on his back.

"I came back to find her chained to the ceiling; stomach slashed open. And then as I went to call the police, the building went up in flames. Sergei. dragged me out." Tears tracked down Nico's face. You pulled him closer and just snuggled under his arm, granting him the security of your presence.

"That's how I got into the case. I quit my desk job and began freelancing. I eventually got into the mob business. Then, Andrei moved here and brought the Feds with him. When he realized I was looking for a legal way to take out Maxim, he arranged for a meeting." Nico smiled at the memory.

"A week later, and a heavy packet came in the mail from the Agency. I'm considered an agent with external capabilities, meaning I don't have to go through the office for everything. And they gave me a code last name. My real one is Knight. Protection, they claimed." Nico's gaze swung down to meet yours.

"I don't mean to say your facade isn't convincing, and maybe this is because I listen to people for a living, but I knew you weren't a true mobster. You don't treat other people like they are lower than you, and you radiate empathy and kindness."

"Really?" Nico's brow furrows, and he nodded his head in silent approval.

"Yeah, it is kind of what Derek me to you. That and you looked like you knew secrets. And I happen to be in the business of dealing secrets." You smirked and winked at Nico.

He put the coffee cups out of the way on the railing.

Then, you're boosted over his lap, knees on either side of his hipbones, breaking off your train of thought.

"Do you now?" Nico pulled you closer until your breaths were mingling and steaming up the air between you. "Bet you don't know this one." He pressed a soft kiss to your lips. Then ran his nose along your jawline.

A kiss under your ear "I."

Kiss. "Really."

The feeling of lips on the tendon in your neck. "Really." You shifted into a more comfortable position, rutting against him.

Then a slight suction and your head tilt back to grant him more room. *"Like."* A big groan was emitted from Nico as you ground down on him, this time on purpose.

His head fell even lower to end up almost under your chin. A kiss with a flick of tongue in the hollow of your throat and between your collarbones. *"You."* His voice dropped into a sexy rumbling tone, and he pulled you closer.

CHAPTER 12

Your hands flew up to rest on his shoulders as he rutted up against you, and you could feel the heat growing in your lower belly. "We should go home. Somebody will see us." Your voice broke into a moan then went extremely high-pitched as he pulled you down into him just as he rolled his hips up.

"Shall we?" His lips pressed against your neck, feeling as hot as the sun and as cold as ice at the same moment.

"If you want this to go on, then yes." You pulled at the silky, fine hairs at the nape of his neck.

"Ok, then grab the cups." His eyes were glazed over with lust as yours met them. You went to get up, and his hands gripped your hips.

"Be like that then." You sassed him, as you stacked the cups up in your hands. Once he thought you were done fidgeting, he picked you up, much to your shock.

"Ahh!" your legs wrapped around his waist and your

arms clenched around his neck. You buried your face in his collarbone, as you felt the gentle sway of his humongous steps, carrying you across the darkened park. You could smell the heavy scent of his cologne and the undercurrent of his sweat.

"I won't drop you. I promise." He rubbed your back.

You nodded.

Almost too soon, you reached his car, and he had to set you down to start it up. A second later, he wrapped his long arms around your frame, trying to keep you warm, until he could open the car and get you settled.

The ride home took an eternity and was filled with heat-laced glances and wandering, trailing fingertips.

By the time you reached the blockhouse, you were full of anticipation and longing, and he was ready to attack anyone who dared to try to stop the two of you.

You barely made it out of the car before he was hoisting you up on the trunk lid and kissing the breath out of your lungs. Your hip rolled forward into him after his lips trailed down your jaw and neck to suck a trail into the shallow line of your collarbone.

"Bed—bedroom, please." You curled your fingers into the hair on the back of Nico's head and dug in the slightest bit, trying to get his attention.

He wrapped your legs around his waist and didn't pause in his exploration of your clavicles and the sensitive spot just below the hollow of your throat.

"Come on. Bedroom." You pushed him off you and

hopped off the car to saunter away on the heels he had bought you.

You shed your black leather coat as you walked to expose the lacy back of your tank top and your back. You could already feel a light sheen of sweat developing and threatening to soak through your clothes.

Nico stood and watched your hips and ass sway, much like he did the first time he met you.

"Damn." His palm wandered down to the front of his jeans to relieve some of the pressure there.

You glanced over your shoulder just as he pulled his hand away from the front of his pants and give him what you hoped was a sultry wink.

He caught up and scooped you up in a princess hold, giving you access to his skin. You took advantage, sucking and teasing your tongue against his skin in senseless patterns. You could taste a hint of his musky cologne and something woodsy.

His chest rumbled with a deep groan. "You got to stop. You're killin' me."

He slipped his shoes off near the door, not caring where they land. "Keep yours on. I have plans for those later." He stopped you before you started to take yours off.

He bolted up the stairs in a flash, ignoring both Andrei and Sergei, sticking their heads out of the room.

The door was shut with a bang by the weight of your bodies slamming into it. "Steel reinforced door, won't break." Nico gasped into your mouth as he stripped his jacket off and threw it in the general direction of the office chair.

Your heads tilted in the opposite directions and Nico's heaving chest caged you in against the unmovable door. His tongue tickled the edges of your bottom lip before you parted your lips, and he swiped along the inside of your mouth.

Your tongue and teeth gained the upper hand somewhere along the line, and you nipped at his lips before leaving them to trail along his body. You made it to the collar of his shirt before he was sliding his hands under your tank top. You left a bruise on the top of his pec, and you felt his nails dig into your back in response.

"May I?" He plucked at the hem of your tank.

He rolled the hem of your shirt up until he pushed you to stand up straight arms up, to push it over your head.

He pauses for just a moment. "Beautiful. So beautiful. Can't believe what I'm seeing." His eyes closed in bliss and opened again just as quickly.

You ducked your head and your skin heated further down your chest.

"Can you help me with this?" you pushed at his shirt, knowing you're not able to pull it off, with the height difference.

Miles and miles of golden, toned flesh were revealed for you to touch. For you to look at. You let out a quiet whimper at the sensation of his muscles tightening and coiling under your fingertips. Your thumbs landed in the

Adonis belt and above his hips. Then you skidded and trailed up his six-pack to grip onto his shoulders.

You hooked a leg around his hip and pulled yourself up to trace your tongue around the star and sun tattoo on his left pec.

He spun around to walk the two of you over to the oversized bed. You fell back with a contented sigh, and a delighted smile graced your lips. The sheets billowed up around you in a cloud of freshly cleaned cotton.

Nico unhooked his belt and the button on his pants with a sound of relief. "Look so damn good on my bed. Again." He smirked down at you, hair fanned out, shirt missing, and lips bitten red. His hand snuck under his black boxers to pump at his hardness.

You crawled up the bed and unbuttoned your jeans, but don't take them off just yet. Nico would want the honor of doing that if the last time was any indication.

He chased after you and started tracing aimless patterns down the center of your chest with his fingers and the heat of his tongue. You ruffled your fingers through his hair, as your back arched up into his ministrations.

Every touch of his lips against your skin sent a jolting shock of heat down to your core.

His fingers trailed behind, leaving a trail of lust-fueled goosebumps in their wake. Occasionally, he scraps a single nail down instead of just the calloused pads. Your thighs came up to wrap around his stomach, chasing the height of your pleasure, and looking for friction.

He unclasped your bra and dropped it on the floor next to the bed with a soft, barely audible thud. His lips sealed over your peaked nipples and sucked. You whined out a moan, and the sheet crumpled under your fists. A nip of teeth then he gave the other one the same attention, as his fingers twisted and plucked at the first.

"Oh, Ah—Nico." Your voice came out in short little pants. Your eyes flew open when he pulled on you, and you could feel his smile against your skin.

The wetness in your panties continued to grow with every single movement from him.

After a little while, he moved on to your stomach. He rediscovered the tiny black-inked heart under your breast and traced it with his tongue, then his nails.

He kissed around your belly button and left a hickey just above it. You could feel the anticipation throbbing in every muscle of your body. Your arms and legs were pulled tight with tension.

He pulled your pants down, over the gorgeous swells of your hips, and then lifted your feet out of the heels, first one, then the other, and rolled the pants off the last bit. He stopped to admire your prone form, yet again, laid out like a sexy angel, sweaty with exertion, and the curving and dipping of your body.

"Damn, woman. You're so gorgeous." He kneeled at the lower end of the bed to have access to your core. "So sexy. So wet, all mine." His voice darkened with possession.

"All yours. Only yours." The mention of being his sent a thrill racing through your veins.

Your nails scratched his scalp and he let out a deep moan, vibrating against the sensitive skin of your pussy. He rested the tip of his nose right against your slit, over your panties. You almost missed his voice moaning out your name as you gasped for a shuddery breath.

His hands lingered just above your hip bones, thumbs stroking under your waistband. "May I?" He asked.

"Please." You were near begging at this point for any sort of friction or stimulation.

He slid the soaked garment down your legs and tossed it to the floor. His hands traced the same path back up your legs, rough calluses catching and skipping along your skin.

He paused at the meat of your thighs and kneaded the weight there. "So soft. Gorgeous."

His eyes raked down from your eyes, over the blushed swells of your breasts and the hardened peaks of your nipples, to the slight hickey above your belly button.

He finished looking at your sopping wet core. Your hips were gently undulating up off the bed, looking for friction. He bumped his nose into your throbbing clit, making you gasp out. His forefingers slipped down and hovered over your slit, not making steady contact.

You could feel his breath fanning over the wetness lingering and chilling your skin as he spread you open with his thumb and forefinger of one hand and just barely poked the pointed tip of his tongue into your entrance.

The forcefulness of your movement nearly broke his nose. A steady hand pushed you down and keeps you tight. Your calves landed on the ridges of his shoulders to get closer to his ministrations.

He took you totally off guard as he jumped right into the task at hand.

The heat and texture of his tongue delved deep into your core, stretching you open the slightest bit. Then he traced your outer lips and bumped your clit with his nose every few strokes. You whimpered and clenched your thighs at every hit.

After the knot in your center wound up a bit more, he changes his strategy.

Your bud was surrounded by blazing heat and felt like it was being slapped by his tongue. You could just barely feel his middle finger enter you and press down on that one spot that made you see stars.

A few moments later he slipped in two fingers, and you tried to arch off the bed at the stretch. He made a scissoring motion and increased his speed at the loud drawn-out moan you gave him.

He could feel you rippling around his fingers and the bed squeaked as he rolled his hips into the mattress for some relief. His breaths came out in groans and pants. The front of his boxers was sticking to him, and he took a step back and let you pull off the edge just a bit.

His belt jangled, and there is a rustle of denim hitting

the floor in a pile. You watched through lidded eyes as pre-cum formed on his tip and he pumped it over himself. Then the sound of a drawer opening and closing as his weight came to rest over yours.

He resumed his rhythm with his fingers and pulled you up to the edge before adding a third. Your voice rang through the room in a gasping shout. Your walls contracted until he feels like there was no circulation in his fingertips. Your body twisted tight, then went into a series of ripples underneath him.

He pulled them out when you went boneless with bliss. You watched him through half-hooded eyes, put them to his lips, and lick them clean, groaning at the taste.

He bent down and kissed you. You could taste yourself on his lips. The bed rocked as you move against him with the heat in your center raring to go again.

"You ready?" He kissed a firm line down your jaw and sucked a hickey under your ear as he planted himself at your entrance, after rolling a condom over his considerable length.

His legs were to the inside of yours, and his forearms were holding his mass up. His head rose to give you a quick kiss before burying his face in the crook of your neck.

You rolled up into him and released a string of curse words as he gave you a deep, hard thrust, then stilled to let you get accustomed to his girth. "Ugh!" you moaned out in a nearly undecipherable blurt.

His voice was broken and was coming out in strained groans. "So tight. You feel so good, Jessica!" He feels you tighten on purpose this time, around him.

You tapped his arm and nodded, and he began to grind himself against you, before pulling out and thrusting back into you the tiniest bit. He lengthened his strokes in growing increments. He quickly found a satisfying pace, and you were digging your nails into his back in increasing pleasure.

A few minutes later you paused him in his rhythm and had him flip your positions. Your palms are resting on his abs as you lifted yourself over his erection again and sunk in one fell swoop.

"Ah." You groaned in sync at the feel of each other.

Every down stroke ended with his pubic bone grinding right into your clit, and his head bumping into your g-spot. As he pulled out again, you could feel every ridge and vein, and it just brought you more pleasure.

"I'm getting close. I want to feel you fall apart around me." Nico reached behind your head to tangle his fingers in your hair so he could pull you down for a kiss. Then he tweaked your breasts just a bit before continuing his southward path.

He reached the sensitive bud and gave it a sharp flick. You let out a resonant moan, and he settled for slipping his forefinger over the bundle of nerves.

Three powerful strokes and you felt the tension about to break. He gave you a short pinch and your nails scored down his chest. Your voice went mute, and your eyelids screwed shut. Your lower muscles were contracting and fluttering over him.

Nico gave you one final firm thrust, then he followed you over the edge into ecstasy. His firm strokes over your clit never ceased and prolonged your orgasm. You vaguely picked up the sound of your name being groaned out among a litany of cursing and Italian words.

Your thigh muscles gave out, and you collapsed onto his sweaty chest. He pulled out of you, causing another round of sparks to ignite within you.

The bed dipped, and the sound of water ran into the other room. Nico came back, and the condom had been disposed of, and he had a warm washcloth in his hand to wipe you down with.

"Just a quick nap. Then we'll shower, I promise." Your voice was heavy with sleep when Nico tried to get you to stand up. He conceded to you and threw the cloth in the sink and pulled the covers over you.

CHAPTER 13

What was supposed to be a quick nap turned into seven hours of catching zzz's after you and Nico fell onto the bed.

Your body twinged with a delicious soreness as you rolled out of the nest of pillows and soft sheets towards the bathroom.

The sink ran in the bathroom, and the swish and spit of water could be heard in the sink. You walked out feeling more refreshed.

You stumbled down the stairs towards where you remembered the kitchen being, hoping that you didn't get lost. The smell of coffee lingered in a helpful, smoky trail for you to follow.

The machine chugged away as you searched for a mug. You found one and set it down on the wooden island, where a scrap of paper with handwriting on it caught your eye.

'*There are clothes for you in the topmost drawer of the dresser. The cabinet in the bathroom has soap and such for you. Please eat and feel free to look around. I'll be back soon.*' You could recognize Nico's scrawl by now.

You admired the hand-hewn dining table, sitting with your coffee and a package of pop tarts you found in the cupboards.

Your feet swung under the chair, and you heard the clink of glass rolling across the floor. You looked under the table and there was a tiny vial, labeled with 'BE CAREFUL' in small, blocky letters.

The glass tube felt cold in your fingers, and you put it in your pocket to give back to Nico later, and then sit back in the chair.

You risked nearly burning your tongue on your drink, but it is so rich and smooth, you didn't care.

After watching the sun rise ever higher through the trees, you finished your drink and putting the cup in the dishwashers and throw your trash away. You took the stairs, two at a time, towards the bedroom.

You cast a glance towards the rumpled sheets and dig through the dresser to find a set of underwear, a flannel over a black tank top, and a pair of stretchy jeans.

The cloud of steam billowed out of the bathroom as the sound of you singing loudly and off key bounced off the walls.

A moment of appreciation for Nico's taste in soap and towels. You swiped on a coat of lip gloss and mascara and headed back downstairs to wander through the house for a while before you must head to work.

You found the garage after hearing the loud rumble of power tools shaking through the house.

"Hey!" Sergei rolled his stool out from under the car he's working on and clapped a hand to his chest, shocked by your arrival.

"Hey." You started out, voice tinged with hesitation. "What are you working on?" you motioned to the car, and the discarded pieces lain off to the side of the lift.

"You know anything about cars?" Sergei wiped his hands on a greasy rag.

"My dad taught me a little. Is there anything I can help you with?" you tilted your head to look up at the car.

"Trying to rebuild the side panel, but it won't come off here. Any suggestions?" Sergei pointed up at the frame.

You walked over, picking your way through the parts, tools, and puddles of grease littering the floor.

"Can you hand me the metallic marker?" you could see the problem immediately.

"You should cut here and here on the frame, and It'll come off. Or you could unscrew these—" You tapped a triangle of bolts just to the right of where you made the marks for the cuts and have the same result.

"Would you cut or unbolt?" Sergei pulled the stool closer and sat down.

"Personally, unbolt. Then you wouldn't ruin the

frame, and you will have an easier time putting the next one on." You shrugged and took a careful step back.

"Thank you, I've been struggling for a while." Sergei turned back to the car, and leaves you be, but picked up a stream of chatter about random stuff.

"Football?" He tossed a wrench on the tray.

"Can't understand the point of it. Or how they play, for that matter. The players are hot though, not going to lie."

Sergei let out a deep chuckle from under the car.

"The Titanic movie? You ever watched it?" you thought back to the first time you watched it with Heather.

The car again muffled the sound of his chuckle. "Hell to the no. Chick flick. I don't do emotions." His voice was so serious you started laughing at him.

"What?" The roller came out from under the car, and he looked at you in confusion.

"Have you never…" you hold your stomach, having been perched precariously on the rolling stool.

"Watched it with Nico?" you snorted.

"Never watched it, period." Sergei started the air hose, and the air compressor roared.

"Not even for Kate Winslet?" you were taken back at his revelation.

"What? And why would that matter?" Sergei's eyes narrowed as he pulled a tool from your hands.

"She has a great… um…" you gestured at your chest.

"Or so they say." You shrug.

"Well, then… What does that have to do with me watching the movie?" Sergei's eyebrows quirked at you.

You pointed your handful of tools at him, after your head shook, "You haven't seen it, therefore, we're going to fix that."

"No, we aren't." Sergei rolled his eyes.

"You don't know it yet, but we are." You gave him a saucy wink.

"When?" Sergei tried to hide his enthusiasm and confusion behind a cough.

"That's for me to know and you to find out!" you set down the tools, and shout over the air compressor.

"Come on. Jessica! That's not fair!" Sergei gasped, his mouth catching flies.

"It is, and I'm going to go figure it out." You pointed at the door.

"Come on, don't leave yet… tell me a little about yourself." Sergei points at the stool.

"Well, I'm the only child." You started.

"Just me n' Nico. And, of course, Andrei." Sergei stated the truth. "Parents?"

"Dad, who got mixed up in shit, and a deadbeat druggie mom."

"Like our kind of shit or others…" Sergei loosened the frame of the car.

"Like Maxim took care of him. That's also why I'm hell-bent on putting him away." You supplied, knowing what people usually asked next.

"Well, he was partly responsible for Mom's death. And for Jessica. So, I understand." Sergei then shared how his mom passed and how deep Nico fell when Jess later passed for the same reason.

"Can you help? The frame is just resting here, and I want to drop it down onto this rolling rack." Sergei pointed at the carriage rack, and you rolled if under the frame.

The lift creaked as he lowered it, and he stepped back after you slid the large metal contraption away from the car.

"I should be good if you want to go get cleaned up before work." Sergei nodded at the clock.

"I have awhile, but I wanted to explore the house, so I'm going to call it quits for today." You grabbed the rag you had been wiping your hands on and wiped a smudge off his face. You stepped back and took a couple of steps towards the house.

"Shout if you have a problem, Okay?" your footsteps stopped in the doorway back into the house.

You heard the clattering of tools and the sound of a magnet and bolts colliding as Sergei went back to work.

You slipped off your shoes and washed your hands before looking for something to write on.

You found a calendar on the side of the fridge, date boxes neatly filled in and crossed out.

The last Friday of every month seems to be uncluttered, so you mark down 'Movie Night' in the next two.

Then you picked the date to decide when to expose Sergei's true feelings.

After deciding, you picked up your meandering path through the house again.

The couch cushions in the living beckoned to you, but you ignored them in favor of finding the room full of music paraphernalia and vinyl records that you passed on the way to the kitchen and garage.

You stepped through the doorway, your feet scrunching in the shag rug as you take in the room. A pair of overstuffed chairs were taking up space against one wall. The wall of full shelves, possibly the most impressive collection of records you have seen.

The turntable and record player, along with the old boom box and box of tapes, laid on the worn top of the console.

You trailed along the rows of spines and pick out the cult classics.

Your fingers paused on an album you haven't listened to since you were a little girl. You slid it out and stared at the familiar script on the cover.

You pushed it into the player and set the needle in the groove.

The first strains of 'Simple Man' float through the air and your brain conjures up memories.

Your father taking you dancing and your feet on his toes.

The long ride down an empty highway, singing at the top of your lungs together.

The antiseptic smell of the last hospital you had been in, and the last limp squeeze of his hand in yours.

Your voice rung out over the sound of the music, as you spun around the room slowly.

Your voice led Nico through the house, and he heard the record player before he saw you dancing around.

Your shoulders are relaxed, and your eyes are closed. The steps of your feet matched the beat. And your voice accompanied the sound of Skynyrd, melding and weaving a melody of your own.

You heard Nico join in on the last line, and you turned around to find him standing in the doorway, slack jawed at you.

You watched as he stepped into the room and the click of the record being unclasped alerted you to Nico's change of pace.

He put on a record and pulled you closer.

Eventually, the record stopped playing and you and Nico don't stop dancing. You're wrapped up tight in his arms, and his chin is resting on your head as you swayed and twirled to the subconscious beat.

You pulled back just slightly to gaze up at him and got a glimpse of his dimples in response. He bended just the slightest to let you brush your lips against his, light as a thread of silk.

You lingered with just your lips barely touching, the heat of his breath fanning over your face. Your fingers curled into the short hair at the base of his neck, twirling and teasing the fine threads.

You felt his lips moving against yours and you pulled away just a tad to hear him better. You glanced up, hoping to meet his eyes, but they're closed.

"So beautiful. I need someone like you beside me in this life. I might be in love with you. Scratch that. I'm in love with you." Nico's eyes and lashes flutter.

"I'm in love with you, too." You whispered into his collarbone. His chest vibrated as he murmured *hmm*.

CHAPTER 14

"Where is it? I know there were twenty five of them." Sergei slammed the drawers on the desk shut.

"Where is what?" Nico stumbled into the room; eyes hazy with sleep.

"The nano trackers!" Sergei slammed the cabinet shut again with a loud bang.

"When was the last time you saw them or it? How many are missing?" Nico stopped Sergei from destroying and cluttering the room even further.

"They were on the table. Thankfully, only one is gone." Sergei wandered out to the dining room.

"Was it before or after Jessica stayed over?" Nico asked, a farfetched thought coming to mind.

"While she was here, they were out and stacked right here," Sergei pointed at the table, "But I put them away before she left. I know I did."

"Let me call her." Nico pulled out his phone and the

tone of a dial rings. Sergei crossed his arms and tapped his foot on the floor in a rapid tempo.

"Hey sweetie. Nothing much." Nico's footsteps thumped across the carpet quickly.

"Sergei has lost one of his vials of something and we —I was wondering if you picked it up by accident?" Nico nodded and hummed into the phone.

You

"Yeah, I did. It fell under the table." You heard twin sighs of relief from the phone.

"What is it anyway? Poison?" you tucked the phone between your ear and your shoulder to mix up another drink.

"Not quite. They're trackers," Nico whispered.

"Trackers for what?" you looked across the bar at the redhead who was gleefully terrorizing your other patrons.

"You can slip them into drinks and track someone for 24 hours." Sergei's voice filtered through the line, full of hesitation and wariness.

"Would it help you out if I slipped it into a certain red head's drink?" You stopped, afraid to say more.

"That would be very helpful, and we could take care of the problem." Nico's voice was full of thinly veiled excitement.

"I'll get to it... I guess." You trailed off, unsure of what you were set into motion.

"Got to go!" you could hear the glee in Nico's voice, and a vivid image of his expression came to mind. The upwards curl of his lips, and the dents of his dimples, along with the sparkle of mischievousness in his eye.

The phone clicked off, and your eyes flitted over to the other side of the bar where she sat, unassuming and unaware of the hellfire that was about to rain upon her.

You struggled to hold back a snort as you wonder when they would ambush her.

Nico

"She had it! And she slipped it into Anna's drink! Do you know what this means?" Nico nearly ran to the briefing room and pranced around as Sergei booted up the computer.

"Andrei, get your ass down here! We've got a lead!" Nico poked his head into the hallway and shouted.

"Give me a second to collect myself." The dark-haired man rubbed the haze out of his eyes and the sound of him swallowing coffee could be heard over the fan.

"Wait, hold up." Sergei pulled up the map with four red dots on it, not just one.

"I'll be damned. Your girl is smarter than you think." Sergei flicked his laser pointer at Nico.

"I would guess she split it into four drinks, so we have Anna and three of her men." Sergei expanded the map with a twist of his wrists.

"Here, and here. They have already started showing a trackable trail. And…" Sergei stooped over the screen.

"The eyes are picking them up, so we can ID who is who." Sergei opened another window.

Andrei jotted down a quick note and rushed out of

the room to get dressed. "I'll be down in a second. Don't leave without me."

Nico observed the dots converge and travel along a seedy back road before halting.

The cameras showed the red-haired woman getting out of the passenger's seat in front of an abandoned warehouse. The three thugs followed her closely, as the rusted door swung open.

There was no film inside the buildings, but the tracking dots didn't leave the premises.

An hour later, only Anna and one of her men got back into the car and headed to what Nico assumed was her estate based on the image coming through.

Andrei called the other agent working with them, who ended up being replaced by Jed for this assignment. Derek came in as soon as he dropped his little girl off at daycare.

"Here's the plan: Four cars. Me and Sergei in one and each of you in a separate one." Nico pointed at the three men.

"I'll take point. Derek, sweep left, Andrei right. Jed, you follow us, and go through the back. Sergei will be on backup support." Sergei handed out earpieces and goggles.

"If you find those fuckers, quietly take them down. No killing. We can hand them over with her. The main entrance is here." Nico pointed to a spot on the holographic blueprints.

"Andrei, Derek. There are windows on either side of

the house that you can break without fear of noise, because of carpeting on the inside. The back door is here." Nico pointed again, and Jed nodded in understanding.

"We're going to park in different places, so if it goes haywire, we can confuse them." The men determined where they wanted to park in their heads.

"When we find her, do not shoot, or kill her. We will restrain her and call another agent to pick her up. Got it?" Nico looked around the table at the men he was trusting to carry out this mission. The men he trusted with his life.

"Wheels out in ten." Nico walked out of the room, prepping his mind for what was about to happen.

The four large cars pulled out of the driveway in a staggered time frame and took different routes to the house. Nico drove through downtown traffic as Sergei clicked away on the computer, adjusting stuff, and running footage.

The grand Cadillac was parked under a tree across the road from the house. It was thankfully surrounded by woods, so seeing anyone approaching is difficult.

The house was quiet, except for a man in the room next to Derek, who was quickly taken care of.

Derek and Jed stood guard as Nico and Andrei approached the last room in the house to be cleared.

The door was slightly ajar, and Andrei pushed it open, to show the features of Anna Willis illuminated by the light of her laptop.

"Oh, hello boys. What brings you here?" She looked up as though she was expecting them, but her voice showed a trace of fear.

"You." Andrei stepped into the room, and Nico's bulk filled the doorway.

"Really?" She tilted her head to the side, as if she was confused. "Then, here, have some fun." And she clapped her hands, and the room went pitch black.

Nico and Andrei had prepared for this instance and flipped their glasses to night vision mode, and the room lights up in scales of green.

The woman's shape was crouched in the corner, trying in vain to open the hidden safe.

Sergei's voice came through the earpieces sharp with warning. *"Duck!"*

A series of sporadic shots followed the thumps of Nico and Andrei hitting the floor, whizzing over their heads.

The click of an empty bullet chamber echoed through the room, and Nico stepped up and dragged her over to the table. The lights flicked back on, and the boys pushed their glasses to the tops of their heads.

"Look here," Nico snapped in front of her face as Andrei tied her arms and legs to the chair.

"We're going to take you in. If you cooperate, it'll be easier for the both of us. They only said you had to be alive, not unharmed. Got it?" A gigantic hand grasped her chin, and Nico's voice was full of threats.

"Yes! Fine." She slumped in the chair, defeated.

"What I'm most curious about is how you managed to find me?" Anna asked Nico while Andrei was on the phone.

"What you don't know won't hurt you. It doesn't matter how we found you, just that we did." Nico returned to his pacing.

Andrei got their supervisor on the line, and a little while later, a convoy of black-suited men showed up and took her away.

The guys congratulated the crew on a job well done. "We aren't done yet, so keep an ear out. And stay safe." Nico waved to the leader as he backed the prison transport van out of the driveway.

CHAPTER 15

"Hello, this is the Shade. How can I help you?" you pushed the phone between your head and shoulder as you mixed another drink.

"This is Nico. Can you come for dinner?" you could hear the excitement in his voice.

"Yeah, um. Sure," you stuttered.

"What happened? With Anna and all that jazz?" you slid the drink onto the tray and walked out from behind the bar with the phone.

"I'll tell you at dinner. I promise." The phone clicked off.

"Okay…" you muttered to yourself.

A few hours later, the bar was slower than usual, so you asked Nancy if she would be okay to close up.

"I want to get going. Is it okay if I ask you to close up?" you folded up the washed rags and shoved them under the counter.

"Chuck will be here soon, so go on and do whatever you have to do." She pulled a bottle of bourbon off the shelf and filled up a patron.

"It's fine by me." She shrugged.

"Okay, thank you!" you threw your arms around her chest in a quick embrace of excitement.

"You're welcome." She patted your back as you stepped back towards the employee exit.

You swiped your phone open, and the ringing tone alerted to your call to Nico being connected.

"You have reached the voicemail of Nico Knight and are being redirected to his inbox. Please leave a message after the beep and hang when you're finished." The monotone voice of the answering machine sputtered out the set of instructions at you.

"Hey. This is Jessica, and it's about 6:30 on Thursday." You checked your watch.

"I got out of work early, and I'm going home and then coming over to your place." You stepped across the lane of traffic and continue to talk.

"I shouldn't be very long, and I'll text when I leave the house." You ended the call and unlocked your car.

The radio blared as you drove through tiny backstreets and across one lane bridges towards your apartment. The parking garage was quiet, and Heather hadn't gotten home yet.

You changed out of your beer and smoke-filled clothes and into a fresh set while writing a note to leave on the counter.

You popped the trunk of your car to make sure it was loaded with the cooler and the bag you had packed.

The long gravel driveway led up to Nico's house in a circular pattern. Your beat-up Buick stuck out like a sore thumb among the Cadillacs and the Porsche parked out of the way.

The sound of the car door being slammed followed your grunt of exhaustion as you tried to carry the cooler towards the front door.

Nico met you halfway and took the cooler from you. He slipped his hand into your now-freed hand and pulled you towards the house.

Andrei greeted you right as you walked through the doorway and Sergei took the cooler from Nico.

"It's just a bottle of wine and a bottle of whiskey." You half yelled after Sergei's retreating.

Derek greeted you with a quick hug. "Good to see you."

"It'll be put to good use, don't worry." Nico murmured into your hair as you talked to Andrei.

"So, how did today go?" you asked, hoping Andrei would cut you a break and give you some indication about how it went, but to no avail.

"We will tell you when we sit down to eat." Andrei pointed towards the dining room, his face an emotionless mask.

The food was steaming on the table, and Sergei popped your bottle of wine open. The places were set, and the kitchen was cleaned.

The first few minutes were mostly quiet as everyone dug into their food. The clink of silverware against the plates, and the sloshing of drinks in glasses broke up the semi-silence.

"This is amazing!" you stabbed your fork into your lasagna and took another gulping bite.

"Who cooked?" you glanced at Nico and Andrei, who were both staring at Sergei. Sergei's face was bright red, and he met your eyes with a nod.

"It was me. Hidden talent, I guess." Sergei took another bite to avoid talking.

"You are more talented than you realize." Andrei sipped at his wine. "Like, for example, your quick thinking on the mission." Andrei leaned his glass in Sergei's direction.

"Yes. That went easy. We tracked her using the nanos - by the way, thank you for putting it in her drink." Nico smiled at you.

"Once she got to her house, we came in and only had to subdue like, what? Two guys?" Nico asked Andrei, who nodded.

"Yes, just those two. And thank goodness." Derek shook his head.

"After that, she tried to shoot us and get the bomb out of the safe."

"Is that what she went in there for?" Jed asked.

"Yeah, they opened it after she was taken in. And there were multiple letters of correspondence between her and Maxim about illicit activities." Nico explained, as the guys nodded along.

You sat stock still, wondering what this meant for the case and the ongoing investigations.

Sergei, after noticing your expression, nudged you with his elbow and muttered, "When we catch *Him*, we will take care of him. He won't see the light of day again. I swear it."

Your eyes grow slightly misty when you blink back tears.

"You're part of our family." Sergei continued. "And you make him so happy. I have only seen him this happy once or twice. One of them was the day he graduated from Yale." Sergei's voice is so low you can barely hear it.

Nico glanced over at you with a beaming smile on his face.

Thank you. Your lips formed the words you can't quite say.

Nico pulled you in closer, and the press of his hand against yours brings you back to reality. "You good?"

"Couldn't be better. This is perfect." You raised your glass in celebration.

Cheers rung out throughout the room and the sound of glasses clinking together echoed around the table. "To another successful mission, and many more."

Nico's hand rests on your thigh as you finish your meal in the warm chatter of the table.

After an hour or so, you started cleaning up, but

Derek and Jed took over, and you end up in the other room with Nico.

"You want to spend the night? I don't have anything here for you, but you can stay." Nico rubbed his hands up and down your arms.

"You want me to spend the night?" you turned and faced him, an eyebrow raised.

"More than you know." Nico pressed a kiss on your forehead.

"Well, then. I have a bag in the car with my stuff." You smirked.

"Did you plan this, you little minx?" Nico's eyes darkened.

"There was a possibility, but no. I did not." You walked out the front door and came back an instant later, bag slung over your shoulder.

Nico walked you up the stairs and pointed towards the bathroom.

"I have a meeting tomorrow. And I know you must work a full shift. So please get done so we can catch a quick nap." He pushed you into the bathroom.

"Come find me when you are done. Okay?" He pressed a soft kiss to your forehead before heading off to his bedroom.

After the wonderful pressure of the shower beat the knots out of your back, you slipped into your sleep clothes and headed off towards Nico's room.

He had his legs crossed at the ankles and a book in his hand, but only the bedside lamp was on. The opposite side of the bed had been turned down, and you crawled into the sheets.

He flipped the light off and pulled you against his chest.

"I won't be by tomorrow, so don't worry if you don't see me." His nose bumped into your neck. "Why?" you relaxed against his comforting heat.

"Meeting with my superior about the case. No biggie, don't worry." He draped and arm over your chest and pulled you closer.

"I'll see you on Saturday?" you asked.

"Yeah, I'll pick you up from work and you can stay here, if you want?" Nico's voice was laced with concern.

"Sounds good to me." You said before your mind quieted, and you slipped deep into sleep, with Nico following close behind.

CHAPTER 16

Nico walked into the bar with an arm holding something behind his back. Derek followed behind him.

Another man you do not know walked behind them on the phone. He was shorter than Nico, and reed thin. His features were sallow and pale, with deep-set beady eyes.

The unknown man searched the bar, looking for something, before lingering on you and darting away.

He put the phone to his neck to talk to Derek about something. You saw Derek's lips moving, and then the man went to a stool down the far end of the bar.

The sound of Nico's deep voice broke you out of your observance.

"Hey, beautiful." His eyes raked over you then lingered on your hips. Your outfit comprises of a dress, heels, and a three-quarter sleeve jacket. "Those the ones I gave you?" He nodded at your feet.

"Yes. What do you have behind your back?" you tried jumping around him to get to whatever it was, but he pulled you against his lanky figure with a cheerful smile gracing his lips.

"A hello would be nice." His lips swooped down to meet yours. The taste of him overtook your mouth and his slick tongue teased and pulled against yours, reminding you of what it felt like on other parts of your body.

You could taste the coffee he had this morning, and you could feel his huge hand cradling your neck.

You pulled away, just slightly, and pressed sweet kisses to the corners of his mouth before capturing his lower lip between yours and biting down the slightest bit.

His chest rumbled with a groan as you felt it. Derek cleared his throat, his skin tinted with a blush and eyes downcast. Almost everyone in the club was staring at the two of you.

You buried your face in Nico's neck, but he pulled his hand from around his back just in time for you to catch a glimpse of red and a green stem. You lifted your head up just a tad to see a gorgeous, single red rose in his hand.

"For you." Nico rubbed your back, and you just swayed quietly for a few seconds, before the bar broke out in chatter again, and noise breaks into your thoughts.

"Thank you." You twirled it around and then sniffed it as you walked behind the bar to get a beer for someone who just called for the next round.

After you wiped your hand of the condensation from

the ice-cold bottle, you inquired what Nico and Derek wanted to drink.

"What can I get you?"

"I'll have my usual, and a beer?" Nico glanced at Derek.

"Sounds good, boss." Derek turned to look at the unknown man that came in with them. His eyes were narrowed, and his lips are pursed in distrust.

You mixed Nico's drink and struck up a casual conversation with him and Derek about some nonsense lie that a recruit had told Derek.

"So, he told you he couldn't do the movement, and then you— "you pointed at Nico— "Did it just to prove a point." You chuckled at the thought of Nico fighting and showing off just to egg on his recruits, so they could do better in the long run.

Your chuckling was broken off by the appearance of a dreaded shape moving across the wall of the club.

"Go sit over there." Nico flicked his eyes to the end of the bar, commanding Derek to move, and raised his eyebrows at your expression. "Is it *him?* Or the other one?" He reached across the bar to rub the top of your hand.

"The other one." Your face was a mask of neutrality.

You saw the inky darkness of his shadow leave the wall before you heard him.

"Hello, darling." Dmitriy smoothly whipped out a silver handgun and pressed it to the back of Nico's head.

The loud click of a bullet sliding into the chamber echoed from the guns around you.

You recoiled from the sight of Dmitriy behind Nico with a pistol to his head, only to feel an alarming sensation in the back of your head. The cold press of a ring of steel warned of an impending shot.

"Everybody else out." Dmitriy shouted over the din of chairs being pushed and scraped along the floor. You saw all the patrons rushing out into the street in a horde of terror.

The last face was familiar. The scruff and the firm jaw line led up to Derek's eyes, filled with uncertainty and another emotion you can't name. You gave him a nod, and he filed out into the street, as well. Through the floor to ceiling shades in the windows of the club, you could see the headlights of the Monte Carlo whipping out of the lot and onto the highway.

You tried to make a move towards the sawed off under the counter, and Dmitriy's chilling voice stopped you.

"You make a move towards that thing you call a gun and I'll blow up his handsome little head." The muzzle of the gun pushed Nico's head forward.

"Okay." Your hands came up to rest on the top of your head.

"Much better. Now for you, Nicky. Hands flat on the bar, palms up." The sound of Nico putting his hands on the counter seemed too loud in the room's silence.

"You both are wondering what I want, I'm guessing?"

The thug behind you walked you out from behind the bar, and Nico gasped.

"You. I brought you with me and you knew he wanted her." Nico jerked his chin at you.

"So, you called him and told him." Nico nodded at Dmitriy.

"He pays better." An unfamiliar masculine voice grunted out from behind you.

"Traitor." Nico hissed under his breath, just loud enough for you to make out over the sound of Dmitriy's soles.

"Enough chitter-chatter. I need her. You wouldn't be a bad gift for *him* either." Dmitriy cocked his head at Nico.

"Why me?" you questioned.

"You still belong to Maxim, even if you don't want to." Dmitriy trailed the barrel of his gun under Nico's jaw, forcing him to meet his eyes.

"No, actually I don't." You gave Nico an imperceptible nod, and he swung his hand up from the bar and grab the gun from Dmitriy and fired the bullet in the chamber into the ceiling.

The man behind you slammed the butt of the handle into your temple and you got knocked out of your chair and onto the floor. You looked up and saw the stranger who seemed glued to his phone since he had walked in. Your head rolled to the side enough to see what was happening to Nico.

Your eyes were clouded by the impact of the gun on your head.

Tearily, you watched Nico and the mysterious guy grappling for the gun. The stranger pulled your head up by your hair to control you.

You tried to twist and jerk away as your scalp stings.

The last thing you see is the rush of blood pouring from Nico's leg before the sound of the gunshot reached you.

Your hand shot out, and you screamed.

Or at least you thought you did.

The scream could have been from Nico.

Your brain felt sluggish and unable to function.

The sound of Nico moaning reached your ears just before your head hit the floor again, and your eyes fluttered once, twice, then you sunk into the bliss the darkness welcomed…

CHAPTER 17

Nico could feel the steady drip of his blood pouring out of the gunshot graze in his leg. He didn't comprehend what was happening. He just knew that Dmitriy took Jessica.

He slouched over in a chair, a filthy dishrag held to his leg to staunch the gushing. His eyelids felt very heavy, and his head hurt. He promised himself that he would call Sergei in just a minute.

He startled awake to Derek slapping his face and Sergei sterilizing a needle.

"Boss, he's up." Derek glanced over his shoulders to look at Sergei.

"Good, give him a drink and ease him on to the bar over there, away from the broken bottles." Sergei waved his hand over the cleanest part of the bar, then went back to his task.

Derek maneuvered the bottle of whiskey to Nico's split and bloody lips to give him a drink.

After a few glugs of whiskey, Derek hoisted Nico up onto the counter and pressed his chest down with his weight as Sergei approached with the needle.

Something smooth and supple is shoved between Nico's teeth, and by the slight give of the material, he guessed it was someone's belt.

His muscles clenched at the first pull of the thread through his torn leg after Sergei cleaned it with gauze pads from the first aid kit.

After the third or fourth, he can't really feel the uncomfortable tug of the needle and the fibers of the thread, as the whiskey kicked in just enough to loosen his grip on consciousness without him floating away.

Derek removed the belt and freed up his jaw.

"You could've died, you dumbass." Sergei pulled on the thread harder than necessary. "Should've let Derek stay and help."

"And what, let him get killed instead of me gettin' injured"?" Nico took a deep breath and relaxed his muscles again.

"Maybe. Maybe not. Still a terrible choice." Sergei ties a knot in the thread.

"Whatever. It's done and over with. Can't change it now." Nico gritted his teeth as Sergei pushed the needle through again.

"Just can't have you gettin' killed out here, bitch.

You're the brains of this operation and the reason any of this is happening." Sergei carried out the next few stitches patiently.

"I need a guiding star and you're it for this mission. So don't die. Please."

"Ok, I'll try to be better about letting someone help me." Nico blinked his eyes hard as the image of Sergei became blurry, then refocused.

After about ten minutes, Sergei finished and tied off the last knot, slapped a bandage on it and declared him able to walk.

Nico hobbled out to the lot, and got to your car, intent on chasing down Dmitriy. Derek pulled the keys out of Nico's hand.

"Derek, give them back to me. Now." Nico's voice left no room for excuses.

"Boss, you ain't driving. Not on my watch."

"I need to get cleaned up and go after Dmitriy. Or one of his minions." Nico tried to step around Derek, but Derek grasped his shoulders and stopped him.

"You're going to go over to your car and We're going home." Derek pushed Nico across the lot.

"No. I'm not." Nico slipped out of Derek's grip and darted back over to your car.

"You ain't going to be any help if you crash, 'cause you passed out from blood loss."

Derek stepped into Nico's space, and he let out an exasperated sigh.

"Come on. Get in. Or I let Sergei come over here and restrain you, knock you out, and bring you home." Derek pointed at Nico's car again.

Nico got into the passenger's seat as Derek started the engine up.

"At least it isn't my Corvette. I would puke at the thought of anyone else driving it." Nico released a heavy breath.

"That and we must talk about what happened. You got shot." Derek motioned at the ruined denim of Nico's pants.

"Well, I was visiting Jessica at the club, as you know. Dmitriy came in and made everyone leave, and Jessica wanted you to leave." Nico started with what Derek had witnessed.

"After you left, they threatened us, although I don't know why. Unless Maxim wanted her back and that was the best way to get her." Nico slapped his palms together.

"He saw her with me at the Gala, and probably knows that I'll do almost anything to get her back." He rested his arm on the doorsill and leaned heavily on it, weariness clear in the heavy frown on his lips and the deep furrow in his brow.

"We'll get her back, Boss. I know we will." Derek reassured Nico, while checking his rearview to make sure Sergei was following them.

"Can you drive any faster, I got shit to do." Nico snapped.

"I'm driving as fast as I can. So, chill the fuck out." Derek gave Nico a tight, forced smile.

The rest of the ride was silent, except for the rumbling of the road, and the soft strains of classical musical playing in the background, a complete polarization to Nico's rampant anger and self-hatred.

The muscles in Nico's arm clenched and unclenched as he fought the urge to force Derek to pull over so he could get out and run back to the bar. Or punch something. Or someone.

Nico was lost deep in his thoughts about Jessica and what could happen to her while she was in Dmitriy's hold.

Among these thoughts were his plans to torture Dmitriy before he turned him over to the authorities. And he might as well add Maxim to that plan.

Sergei parked the cars as Derek helped Nico hobble into the house. Nico sat at the dining room table and motioned for his laptop and a drink.

Derek brought the computer but refused the drink, as Nico needed to be as clearheaded as possible.

Sergei sat across from Nico, tablet in one hand and a notepad in the other.

"You can go Derek. We will call you when we need you, okay?" Sergei dismissed Derek, knowing his brother needed a moment, or a day, to collect himself, but also that he wouldn't take the time off while Jessica was being held hostage.

"What do you remember?" Sergei started out helpfully.

"Dmitriy came in and Jessica knew it, by the shape of the shadows moving. I sent Derek away to watch the other end of the bar, when him and a minion came out of the shadows to threaten us." Nico took a deep breath.

"His minion was Yakov. You know, Yakov Chernov? Hopeful prospect, turned traitor." Nico's voice held a trace of hatred.

"Anyways, they made everyone leave the bar, and Jessica released Derek, as I couldn't move. They threatened to shoot me if she tried to use the sawed-off under the counter." Sergei scribbled down a few notes and twisted the pen around his fingertips.

"They pushed her out from behind the bar, and I saw an opening, and tried to take it. Chernov hit Jessica over the head with the gun, and Dmitriy shot me while I wrestle with his guy, holding me. She passed out, and I fell into the chair, and they chained me to it, so I had to watch as they bound and gagged her and took her." Nico's eyes hardened at the thought of his failure.

"Well, the good news is that they need her alive for whatever they are planning to do." Sergei grimaced.

"Bad news is that they probably took her somewhere, where there are no cameras, so I can't track her with the eyes."

"Chernov, you said?" Sergei questioned.

"Yeah, I would remember that face anywhere." Nico nodded.

"Well, she will find some way to get into contact with us, or Maxim, or even Dmitriy will, and we can trace the call to find them." Sergei's chair scraped across the hard-wood floors.

"And until further notice, you're on house arrest. And if you can't listen to and understand that statement, I'll hide the car keys. And not tell you where they are until We're done with this case. Got it?" Sergei points his pen sternly at Nico, who nodded glumly, and his bare feet slapped against the floor as he walked away.

Nico slumped in the chair and rapped his fingers nervously on the table before getting up to go to bed.

The next week passed in an exhausted blur for Nico except for the call, if it could be labeled as that, from Dmitriy.

"We have her. She isn't doing so well. Better hope Maxim gets here soon. Bye Nicky!" Dmitriy ends the call before Nico could get a word in edge wise.

Sergei had enlisted a few friends who worked around the city to keep an eye out for Dmitriy, or any signs of his minions. The eyes were up and running, but they can't catch what wasn't there to be caught.

Nico pored over his case notes as Sergei clicked away on his tablet and computer when Nico's phone rings.

Unknown Caller...

The phone rings until it goes to voicemail, then hangs up.

Then it rings again, same number, still unknown. Nico picked it up and waited for a voice to talk.

A lady's voice comes from the phone, making Nico sigh with relief.

"*Hey.*"

CHAPTER 18

You floated back to consciousness when you felt your center of gravity shift as someone picked you up. The gentle sway of your body and the swing of your legs through empty air could only mean you're being carried, but the fingers digging into your fragile skin confirmed your worst fears.

You had been taken by Maxim or for him.

Your eyes strained open to an opaque netted looking fabric over your head. Your breaths came and went much like a fish out of water. This sucked the burlap up against your face before pushing it back out.

The man carrying you must have realized you were awake because he unceremoniously dropped you on the floor, then dragged you along as you limped to keep up.

After what felt like a few thousand steps, you stopped, and other men you didn't recognize restrained your limbs. You heard the muted click of something closing or opening through the head covering, and your eyes widened trying to see anything.

You could see a glow beyond the woven material when you adjusted your eyes to the lack of light. Someone had plugged your ears with some sort of cottony fluff because you could only hear muffled, burbled noises. Your mouth was gagged and covered with a strip of duct tape.

You could feel all your fingers and toes and could wiggle them. Your wrists were bound to your ankles and your shoulders are strained. You sent up a silent thanks to whoever was listening that nothing was broken.

You could feel the footsteps approaching you through the floorboards, which must have been wood to carry the vibration that well.

A moment later, the rope around your neck loosened, and the roughness ripped along your throat, feeling as rough as sandpaper. You blinked in shock to see Yakov Chernov. He dug around in your ears and pulled out the cotton balls.

"Hey, the man awakens." He snarled. "Go get the boss. He'll want to talk to her before we have some fun."

You winced at the loud noises and examined the room around you to see walls reminiscent of a prison cell and no windows.

A door closed behind you, and you saw a stout man with a beard and a receding hairline on the edge of your vision.

You're yanked into a chair and duct taped to it. Ankles to the legs and your wrists to the arms.

"Hello, sweet cheeks. I'll bet you're wondering why you're here. No? Well, I'm going to share with you anyways." You gazed up at him, your eyes wide with fear.

"Your boyfriend, who from here on out will be called Nicky, has tried to take something that belongs to Maxim. It's up to me to get it back." You skimmed across the room, not knowing if you're going to be blindfolded again, or when.

"Oh no, you don't. Look at me." He grasped your chin and dug his nails into your jaw.

"Your job is to bring Nico here or give me the means to get into contact with him. Once you've given us what we ask, I'll hand you both over to Maxim." He let go of your chin and took a step back.

"When you finish with her, give her a dose of the new shit. You know the one I mean." He told the men and pointed at you.

Yakov walked forward, and you saw a flash of polished silver slipping between his fingers, and then the dull matte of a black rubber handle. "We're going to have so much fun together."

He trailed a fingertip over your collarbone, and you struggled, straining against your bonds. "After that night at the Gala… I just had to see more of your pretty skin." He cut the bottom of your shirt off, under your bust line.

Another thug came up behind you and you could feel

the heat of his breath fanning against your neck. "Maybe we will start with your pretty hair." Then a muffled shout left your lips, and a clump of hair was tangled around his fingers. Your scalp burned and tingled.

Yakov recaptured your focus when he slammed his fist into your knee. Your eyes watered, but still nothing felt broken. He stopped to admire your reaction, then ever so lightly trailed the edge of the blade along your thighs and the clenched muscles in your arms. "You got to relax." He let loose a dark chuckle.

Then you felt the skin on your upper arm parting, centimeter by centimeter. Then the dripping of blood over your uncut skin. An inch down, he repeated the process, again and again until he reaches your elbow, then he copied the actions on your other arm.

All of this happened without a cry or reaction from you. Yakov, clearly finished with his part, left, and let the other take over. One slapped you, multiple times, across the face. Another boxed your ears and hit the back of your head with a knife hilt. Sometime after the head blow, you passed out, blissfully floating along.

You stirred just enough to feel a needle enter your arm and to feel the steady drip of something.

You awakened in time to hear Dmitriy on the phone. "Yes, I'll be there, Of course, sir. The Carlton hotel, correct. I'll have my men bring her along the next time. I'm leaving right now." Then the sound faded out and so do you. Your head rolled down to rest on your shoulder, and your arms went slack.

A while later, you blinked your eyes open. Your head felt like it had been hit with a hammer and your eyes were burning. You tried to blink the blur out of them, to no avail. The light flickered on, and you groaned as your head was wrenched up to meet someone's eyes.

These are brown and beady. He smiled, then grimaced as he entered the room. "Hello, you must be the 'Little Crazy' everyone is talking about. And I do mean everyone. Dmitriy has been bragging about how he stole you from under the Blades' noses." He nodded in worshiping approval.

"The Blades…must mean Nico and Sergei." Your brain put the pieces together, still fuzzy on the details. You noticed the buck knife on his waistband.

"I'm Spiridon Volansky. I bet you didn't know that." He shook a finger in your direction. "I'm, however, wondering why they didn't leave you alone in this room. You look pretty harmless to me." He let out a hissing laugh.

"Come a little closer and I'll show you." You leaned forward in your chair, almost as if you were looking forward to it.

He stood in front of you and trailed his hand down your face. You could smell the stench of rotting flesh wafting off his skin. *"This must be the one they treat like a dog."* You mused to yourself. He forced your mouth open and probed it.

You waited for the exact right moment, then bit down and pulled back. The force of you in the chair and him falling knocked you over and broke the chair legs. His head slammed on the floor and there was a bloody gash in the back of his hand from your teeth.

He was still alive when you checked his pulse. The force with which he hit the floor probably knocked him out.

You slid the knife out of the sheath with one hand and slipped it between your ankles. Thankfully, when the chair fell, the legs broke. You ripped the right arm of the chair off, cut the duct tape away from your wrists, and ripped the strips holding the gag in your mouth off your face. Your jaws were sore from being forced open for God knows how long.

Your arms were bleeding again, even though at some point they had stitched them shut.

You cut strips off his shirt and tied them around your arms in makeshift bandages. The door was wide open, and you didn't hear footsteps from within the building.

You looked back at Volansky and made a choice.

You scrubbed your hands through his pockets and came up with one gun mag, a smartphone, and a syringe, full of God knows what. It was only half full, so you assumed it was the rest of whatever they gave you.

Looking down at your torn and wrecked shirt, jeans with the button ripped off, and only one shoe, you took his coat as well.

The phone had an almost full battery, naively unlocked. It was seven days from the last day you remember when you checked the date. You then swiped it open and found the dialer. You punched in a number you memorized for someone who you hoped you would never have to call from this situation.

"Hey." Your voice croaked out, sounding like you hadn't used it in an eternity.

CHAPTER 19

"Hey…"

Nico picked up the phone after glancing at the number.

Still unknown.

Your voice barely filtered through the line, injured as you sound.

"Jessica. Shit. Where are you?" Nico's feet hit the floor again and again as he paced in the briefing room.

"Whatever you do, don't get off the line. Sergei is tracing the call." Nico held the phone to his neck and pointed at the laptop and then his phone. Sergei got the hint.

"Where I'm doesn't matter. I know you were looking for where Maxim would be meeting Dmitriy." You take a gasping breath. "The Carlton hotel. I heard Dmitriy on the phone. The first meeting has already happened, but he said he would be there again. And soon." Nico could hear something squeak and then the sound of sloshing footprints coming from the line.

Then the line cut out, and Nico couldn't get the call to connect.

He scribbled down the name of the hotel and shoved it at Andrei then turned to Sergei. "I got her. She's in the abandoned warehouse just north of the city by about hundred miles." Sergei put the map on the projector screen.

"I'll get her, and you get a watch on that hotel. Effective immediately." Nico rose to his feet, quickly, and began to follow Andrei out of the room.

Sergei stood up and held up a hand and pointed at Nico. "No. You go to the hotel." Sergei pointed his finger at Andrei. "You watch him."

Nico's mouth gaped open at Sergei's blatant mistrust of him "I'll get her." Sergei grabbed his coat from the back of his chair and the keys to the Thunderbird.

"Why do you get to go get her, she's, my girl?" Nico stopped Sergei with a hand on his chest.

"Ever think she might not want you to see her like that." Sergei raised his eyebrows at Nico, before pushing past him. "And with her around, you act like a loose Volkov. It's just not safe."

A moment later Nico heard the distinct sound of the car tearing out of the driveway. His brother may be older and may have just pissed him off but Nico still worried about him.

"You ready?" Andrei strapped on his gun and folded

his trench coat over his arm and slipped into his suit coat.

"Ready as I'll ever be. I just hope she's okay." Nico's brow furrowed, and he straightened his shoulders.

"She sounds like a tough cookie. You mentioned she dated Maxim. And survived no less." Andrei opened the side door to the Caddy and shoved a case of files into the console.

"Yeah, and still puts up with his shit, even though he killed her father. Guess we want to make him pay." Nico flung the car into gear and gravel went flying from under the tires.

"It wouldn't surprise me if that's why Maxim had her taken. To get under your skin, and he knows you two are close." Andrei flipped through the files in his lap.

"Whatever the reason, she will be safe from his grasp from here on out, and I'll be able to cinch the man I have been chasing my entire career." Nico wheeled the car onto the highway and the transmission shifted into high gear.

He pulled his phone out and handed it to Andrei. Andrei opened it and dialed the central office, then put the device on speaker in the console.

The overly loud answering machine picked up before transferring the call to their department.

"This is his partner, Agent Newman. We have a lead on the Poughkeepsie case. He is headed to location, and we need backup." Andrei spoke before Nico could process what he was saying.

The lady's voice murmured from the other end of the line.

"The Carlton Hotel. We're putting a watch on the building, so we can be alerted if something occurs. Three Agents should suffice." Andrei scribbled something down on a legal pad that Nico couldn't read while he was driving. "Thank you, ma'am. Have a nice day." He ended the call and handed the phone back to Nico.

"She said they would send out the guys I asked for, one of which will be Jed. I don't know the other two, said Andrei.

The rest of the ride went by quickly, and Andrei occasionally broke the tense silence by making a comment or the scratching of pen on paper.

The men parked in the lot of a nearby bistro and ordered coffees. After the barista made their drinks, they sat in the window bar and chatted on their phones. Too casual if you looked too closely, but no one batted an eye at two suited men sitting in a coffee shop. Not in this town.

Andrei made notes of each of the vehicles entering and leaving the building and their license plates.

A little over three hours later, Nico was ordering his second coffee when his phone rang at the counter. He handed his bills to the cashier and told her to keep the change. He answered the buzzing device in his palm.

"Hey."

"I got her. She was wandering around the warehouse, disoriented, and confused. She must have been falling off the tail end of a hallucination, or a drug shot, because she thought I was you." Sergei shifted the phone between his head and shoulder.

"How is she now?" Nico covered the microphone with his hand so Andrei could hear as well.

"She seems a little beat up but otherwise fine. Wouldn't go to the hospital, but I don't think they did… *that* … to her" Sergei's voice dropped low. "She's conked out right now, in the passenger seat. Probably won't be up for a while."

"Good. Thank you, Sergei." Nico voice nearly cracked.

"No problem, that's what family does. We help each other. What's going on there?"

"Literally nothing. Not a fly landing on a piece of shit. Andrei and I are ready to go out of our fucking minds."

"I'll be there soon to help bug the place and set up surveillance. I'm assuming you want to come back to the house to be with her." Sergei's voice is tinged with anticipation.

"Yeah, I'll, but the case comes first." Nico sighed.

"Not right at this moment. You got to take care of your girl. Me and Andrei can handle the case." Sergei reassured Nico.

"Okay. Talk to you soon." Nico hung up and laid the phone face down.

"Are you okay flying with Sergei while I take care of Jessica?" Nico turned to Andrei.

"Of course, Nico. Do what you have to. We got this under control." Andrei motioned to the hotel and the notepad of car descriptions.

"Okay, when Sergei texts me that he is home, I'll leave and send him here to help you." Nico nodded at Andrei and took a hearty sip of coffee.

Andrei returns to his analyzation of the hotel and the cars, without complaint.

Nico's phone dings a few hours later, almost at midnight. The concept of time has been lost to Nico. The day could be fifteen minutes or an eternity long and he would not notice the difference. He was exhausted and just wanted to go home and comfort you.

He knew if he saw you, he would feel better. His phone dinged again louder this time. It startled Nico out of his stupor and he checked it.

Sergei: I'm at home and she is settled in the guest room.

Nico: Can I come home?

Sergei: I'll be there soon, I'm leaving now. Tell Andrei.

Nico: I'll see you soon. Stay safe.

Sergei: Will do.

"Hey, I'm going to roll out. Sergei will be here soon." Nico held up his phone.

"Okay, drive safe and tell Jessica I hope she feels better soon." Andrei sipped his coffee and bit into a breakfast wrap.

Nico shrugged on his wool overcoat and hurried out to his car. His mind wandered to how you could be, but he shook himself before he could make assumptions.

CHAPTER 20

You woke up at the sudden lurch of a car stopping. The jolt aggravated every muscle and cut on your body. Sergei shut the car off as you looked around, dazed.

"Where are we? What day is it?" Came your wary voice from the passenger seat. Sergei almost missed it as he unloaded the car, which was full of stuff from the warehouse.

"The Blockhouse. And it's still Friday." Comes Sergei's clipped answer from behind the trunk lid.

"Nico and I live here. Andrei, Nico's partner, works out here as well." He swept his arm in a wave across the expansive property.

"Go through that door." He pointed at a door on the side of the house if it can even be called that.

You pushed the door open after he told you the key code and held it open for him. He grunted with the effort of carrying the boxes and bags of evidence up the short flight of stairs into the foyer.

"Your bedroom is down here." He led you to a room containing no personal effects and a crisply made bed.

"Thank you." You turned towards Sergei; arm crossed around you.

"That's what family does for each other. We watch out for each other. Be careful of your wounds. I'm going to go call Nico, and he will be home soon enough." Sergei began to back out of the door but paused when you ask a question.

"Where is the bathroom? Or a shower?" you shivered, feeling the film of dirt and death persisting on your skin.

Sergei led you out of the room and across the hall to an oversized bath. He left you alone in the washroom, with a reassuring pat on the shoulder.

You wandered around the room, opening all the cabinets and finding tons of goodies. A fresh, fluffy set of towels is put onto the counter along with bottles of rose scented bodywash. You dug through the overabundance of drawers to find the only decent clothes are oversized t-shirts and pairs of boxers.

It'll do for now, you mused, wondering how soon you can go out to get fresh clothes. Or get Nico to go for you.

The sound of rustling clothes fills the room as you shucked your grimy outfit. You look at your naked form, eyes watering at the array of bruises on your face. Your fingers traveled over the bumps of the wraps covering the lacerations lacing your upper arms, and you wondered how long they will take to heal.

"There are bandaging supplies under the sink, as you won't want to get those wounds of yours wet. At least not yet!" Sergei yelled through the door, after he didn't hear the shower water turn on.

You pulled off the grimy, rust soaked bandages to reveal hastily sewn wounds. Not wanting to face them longer than necessary, you ripped strips of waterproof tape off the roll and wrapped lengths of gauze and plastic over your arms. You put your hair up into a bun, despite the aching protests of your arms.

'Best leave that for another time,' you mumbled, knowing how bad your hair gets when it hasn't been washed for more than two days.

The shower had a small screen full of settings and adjustments for you to pick from. The rainfall was just enough to clean your skin, and you set the misting function to run in the bathroom to soften your skin.

As you luxuriated in the feeling of being washed, the soothing heat made you groan. The wounds on your body throbbed, but you ignored them, knowing when you get out of the shower, Sergei or somebody would have the good stuff to knock you out.

Your fingers pruned up after a long while and rose-scented steam filled the bathroom. You turned the shower off and stepped out into the warm cloud.

There was a tube of moisturizer lying in the sink, and you realized Sergei must have tossed it in while you were showering. After you toweled off, you slipped into clean clothes. You don't touch your hair, still piled up in its messy bun atop your head.

You made it to your bedroom and collapsed once again into the sheets after downing the pain pill on the nightstand. You curled into a fetal position buried under mountains of blankets, feeling the waves of drowsiness cresting.

You slipped into consciousness when you felt the bed dip, and you slipped back out when nothing else in the room shifted.

You shot up, chest heaving, eyes red, snot pouring out of your nose at somewhere around three in the morning.

The feeling of Nico's arm across your midriff is grounding, after you startled awake, barely hanging on from the edge of a panic attack.

"Easy breaths, in and out. Come on, feel me, right here." He lifted your hand over the bare skin over his heart, letting the regular beats bring you back down.

"I'm right here, okay." He stroked his hand over your cheekbone and curled a strand of hair behind your ear.

Your next inhale is shuddery, and the exhale is steadier. You nodded solemnly.

His right hand grasped your left, and he used it to pull you closer. You end up curled into his chest, arms thrown around his neck and a leg across his uninjured hip. Your ear was right over his heart, thumping away to its own rhythm.

His head was resting on yours and his forearms were around you like steel bars, caging you into a safety net.

He could feel the burning heat of your tears soaking his chest, but he doesn't say a thing.

Nico knew the simple act of unadulterated crying can be a release you needed.

His palms just kept stroking up and down your back, grounding you as much as reassuring himself that you're there.

You dozed on and off until Nico pulled you even closer and it's just enough to make you comfortable.

You woke up a few hours later. Your hand reached across the bed, expecting to bump into Nico, but the sheets are cold as stone.

You rolled over just to cover your eyes at the brightness of the sunlight in the room.

"Good morning, sleeping beauty. Feeling better?" Nico's voice greeted you from across the room as he paused his flipping through the paperwork to look over at you, snuggled up in the sheets, adoringly.

"You bet. Best night's sleep I have gotten, you know, other than *those* nights." You tried to hide your face in the pillows to not reveal your blushing skin.

"Well, in that case, I guess you won't mind if I go back to work." He teased you with pretend disappointment in his voice.

"I would very much mind that. I need your help with my injuries, and I can't wash my hair." You pointed at the rat's nest on top of your head.

"My hair hasn't been washed in over a week, so please give me a hand." The end of your statement came out in an almost plaintive wail.

You pouted at Nico until he sighed and slapped his closed file on the table. The legs of the chair move and his bare feet don't make a sound on the thick carpet. "Come on." He smiled down at you and offered you a hand to get out of the bed.

When he reaches the bathroom, he shucked his clothes, unabashedly, and unworried about what you might think. You spared a glance for the sewn gunshot on the outside of his leg, already healed enough for him to shower without it covered.

Your clothes came off slower, and he had to start the process before you pushed him away gently and did it yourself.

Your hand flew up to cover your wounds and your head ducked, unable to meet Nico's eyes.

"Come on. Look at me. Jessica." You turned away from him and faced the shower. He threw his arms around you and pulled your back to his front.

"I think no less of you. It just shows me you're strong enough to survive. That you survived and that you're still alive." He pressed a kiss to the crook of your neck.

"But they are so ugly." Your eyes welled up.

"They may not be as pretty as they could be. But that doesn't matter. They don't make you. You're still my princess, who wears red pumps and can put me in my place. Do not fear that they will detract from your presence." He reached past you to turn the shower on and helped you into the water.

After Nico gave himself a perfunctory scrub down, he turned to you with a bottle of shampoo. You turned and tilted your head back into the shower before stepping in front of him.

You felt the coldness of the soap soaking into the film of filth and grease in your hair.

A second later, the pads of his fingers were rifling through the roots, trying to break up the clumps and slight mats forming.

After they loosened up, he went through with his fingernails and scraped your scalp and the back of your neck with them.

He lifted the removable head from the wall and gave you a quick rinse through. Then he massaged conditioner into your roots and the broken tips. You scrubbed the rest of your body down under his watchful gaze and the heat of the beating water.

You turned off the shower and stepped out into the bathroom, quickly grabbing a towel to hide yourself. Nico stops you. "Don't...please." He sunk to his knees and peeled the gauze off your arms and your leg.

Then, thinking he was going to rewrap you, you made to move over to the sink, but his fingers on your hips stopped you.

The feather-like brush of lips raised goosebumps on your leg.

"You're irresistible."

Kiss.

"You're gorgeous." The soft hiss of breath against skin.

"You're worth a thousand praises." The soft yet rough brush of stubble across healing skin.

Each terrible stitch got a kiss and a declaration of your strength until there were tears streaming down your face and he reached your lips. Then the salt and the heat of your mouths mix, slowly but surely. Fitting together like puzzle meant only for one another.

He wrapped your arms and leg with practiced moves and buttoned his flannel over your chest. It was so much larger than you and hung down to cover your thighs.

Then he pulled on a pair of sweatpants and picked you up, princess style, for the umpteenth time. The two of you traveled out of the bathroom and in the opposite direction of your room.

"My room is that way." You poked him and pointed down the hall.

"And mine is this way. My bed is bigger and more comfortable." He said in a no-nonsense fashion; His steps never broke pace.

"Fair enough." Your head rested on his shoulders, and the lulling, rocking motion of his walking soothed your screaming mind.

The door opened to reveal a room, much like yours but more lived in. The bed was unmade, and there were piles of clothes on an armchair. He set you down on the bed, and you breathed in the concentrated scent of him, rising off the rumpled sheets.

The sound of a phone ringing interrupted the peace as he cuddled with you. He talked hastily into the phone and then hung up.

"That was Andrei. He needs to come home and work on some stuff, and I must go into the city to fill his spot in the watch." Nico rambled.

"It's fine, Nico. It'll give me a chance to explore this giant home of yours." You laughed at the notion of getting lost in the maze of rooms.

"Okay…" The heat of his lips pressed against your forehead, and you watched as he threw on a suit and pulled himself together.

One last kiss, this one deep and drugging, and Nico left, albeit unhappily, for work.

CHAPTER 21

A week later, you were feeling much better, and your wounds were healing. You still had nightmares at night, and you suspected you would for a while yet. But you felt more normal than you had in a day or two, sitting on the couch with Nico.

"So, Sergei discharged me from house arrest." Nico trailed his fingers over your arm as you watched your favorite mafia movie for the millionth time.

"You were under house arrest…" You frowned.

"It was that, or I was going to come in guns blazing for you and get killed." Nico chuckled at the memory of his temper tantrum over Sergei's rules.

"Well, I'm glad you didn't." You reached over and rested your hands on his thigh.

The sound of his phone ringing broke the companionable silence. He turned and picked it up with a frown.

"You better get down to the station," said the stressed voice from the other end of the line.

"Why?" Nico shot off the couch and towards the kitchen as you looked on in confusion.

You could hear the muffled voice of the person on the other end of the line shouting, and Nico's low answers.

"I'll be right over. But how did we not know about this sooner?" Nico clamped the phone between his ear and his shoulder.

"They forgot to submit the paperwork. Pretty convenient, huh?" Nico grunted.

He shoved the phone in his pocket before turning to face you. "They just released Roxanne, the first gang leader I put away, so I have to go."

You leaned up to kiss him when he pointed towards your room. "Please pack a bag. For maybe two weeks, tops." Half of his face twisted up as he tried to remember something.

"Umm... Why?" you crossed your arms over your chest.

"Because she looks for those close to the traitors of her organization. And you're close enough to me to be considered a target." Nico pulled out the emergency duffle bag he kept under the bed and unfolded it.

"Have you forgotten... I was at Maxim's side during his so-called union meetings?" Your lips were pursed, and you raised your eyes at him. Then you laughed.

"Ok, fine. But that doesn't mean I'll allow the same

thing to happen to you that happened to Jess." Nico rubbed his hands over your upper arms.

"That won't happen." You protested.

"Sergei will drive you to an unspecified safe house location. No, if ands or buts." Nico fixed a stern gaze on you from the doorway, barely even acknowledging your feelings on the matter.

You didn't answer him and instead turned back the bag. You heard him sigh as he moved down the hallway, leaving you alone in the house.

Sergei and Andrei had gone out to help Nico with Roxanne, and you assumed Nico would send Sergei home once he got to the station.

Too bad you wouldn't get to say goodbye. You grimaced at the thump of the random clothes you were throwing and hitting the bottom of the overnight bag with.

Just enough to get away from here.' You thought about how you had enough running cash left over from helping out with Anna.

The bag now packed, you turned to your phone, charging on the bedside table. You wouldn't need something for Nico to be able to track you by. The SIM card and battery made a crunching sound between your fingers.

You swept up the shards and put them in the trash. The garage was almost empty, so you wouldn't be able to get away in one of the cars in there.

Luckily, you knew where Nico kept a nondescript

emergency car, and you slid open the hidden panel on the floor. The gleaming of a sliver Toyota shone back at you. You slid open the next panel that contained a ramp to drive it out.

After the sound of the car broke the overly loud silence of the empty house, you steered it into the driveway before closing the hatch up.

You glanced at the clock and an hour, and a half had passed already. It took a little over an hour to get to the station, and you were running out of time.

Back in the kitchen, you scribbled on a notepad: *'Sergei, I'll be back soon. Went to pick up some personal effects from my place. ~ (Jessica)'*

You got back in the car, and drove out of the long driveway, pulling out onto the main road in the opposite direction of the station.

The radio in the car couldn't get a signal, so you turned it off and the sound of the tires going round and round on the road droned on.

You passed the Rockford city limits before the two-hour mark was upon you. A friend of yours lived in the city and knew a large part of what you were involved in, between Maxim and now Nico. You kept her up to date knowing that when you would have to flee, you would inevitably end up at her place.

You swung the car into an empty spot and listened for the click of the automatic door locks. The top floor community balcony hosted splendid views as you looked out.

The loud ding of the doorbell could be heard through the white windowless door.

"Who's there?" A wary voice came from the other side of the door.

"It's me, your highness." Before you had even finished speaking, the door was flung open, and a flash of a head of bright red hair greeted you.

"Oh." Your breath was squeezed out of your chest by the force of her reed-thin arms wrapping around you.

"Can't… breathe…" you gasped out.

"Oh. Sorry." She released you before hoicking you into the apartment and closing the door.

"How have you been? Why are you here?" Small slim fingers shook you by your shoulders.

"Good, I guess. I need to lay low for a few days, and I need your help to keep an eye on someone."

She folded her arms across her chest in disapproval.

"Please…" You gave her a pleading look.

"It is going to depend on who you want to keep an eye on. But you knew that." She blew a bubble in her gum, then popped it.

She opened her laptop and followed your directions, as she traced down the camera systems.

Not even a half an hour later, Nico's worried face popped up on the screen, grainy and blurry, but his.

"He's not the usual type you go for." Jessica threw the open window up on the TV and fixed a coding loophole. The window was refreshed, and the image of the footage was much clearer.

"Well…" you sipped at your water as you wrote down as much as you remembered about him. The spilling of your emotions onto the paper was almost cathartic.

"Just saying. Not trying to be mean." Jessica spun around in her chair, her hair a flag of shimmering red.

"If I swung that way, I'd tap that. But I don't, so oh, well." She shrugged as the teapot whistled. "What does he do for a living?"

She poured the tea into a set of worn mugs, and handed one to you, before the couch creaked.

"He's undercover and working on putting Maxim away for a long, long time." You motioned at the screen.

"That's his brother, Sergei, and his partner, Andrei."

"How do you always find the most extreme men? I swear you have a sixth sense for it." Jessica shook her head and sniggered behind her teacup.

"It comes with being a bartender. Enough about me. What about you? Got a special lady in your life?" you minimized the video screen and turned on Netflix.

"Nothing yet. I got a promotion though. Kind of why my laptop is up to date." She pointed at the device in your lap.

You picked out a newer movie you hadn't seen and kept the video window opened in the screen's corner.

The rest of the week passed quickly with you keeping an eye on Nico, who seemed to be more and more exhausted the longer you watched and keeping up with Jessica.

Saturday night, you had just gotten out of the shower

and were rewrapping your leg and arms, when Jessica shouted from the living.

"Jessica! Get in here!" you ran into the room, foregoing clothes in the frantic rush to get to her.

"What happened?" you gasped at the scene on the TV.

"He got shot while visiting the bar, I think." She continued her ceaseless typing.

"Is he ok?" your voice squeaked out as you leaned over her shoulder, trying to read.

Your heart was racing in your chest as you thought about the amount of enemies Nico had probably made over the years.

"They can't tell yet." You pushed her away from the computer screen and stared at the grainy image of Nico.

"Can you get me anything else?" you stood up and faced her, your shoulders pulled tense and your cheeks stained.

"No." She closed the laptop.

"I'll bet on my life it was Maxim." You started to pace, tears forming in your eyes. "I need to get back there." You strode to the hallway before she stepped in front of you.

"On the contrary, I don't think that's the smartest idea. You being there would create more drama and draw more attention to what's going on." She glanced up from the floor and put her hands on your shoulders.

"Also, as much as I appreciate the view, I don't think

you need to handle this situation naked." She waved a hand at your form.

"Oh. Sorry. Give me a second." You backed out of the room and threw on some clothes.

"I need to go, though." You walked back out with your bags in hand.

"No. No, you don't." Jessica pushed you onto the couch, much to your chagrin.

"What should I do then?" you asked her.

"Wait, at least until they move him to a private facility or back home, then you can see him." Jessica paused on an article in the paper and read aloud to you. "Local man shot at most popular bar in town. Seems like the news is already making the rounds." She glanced at you.

"Yeah, I guess I'll stay here until they release him." You sat down on the couch, and your shoulder slumped onto Jessica's.

CHAPTER 22

"He's going to need heavier painkillers than that!" Nico could hear a loud growling voice arguing with a softer tone.

That must have been Sergei. Nico mused to himself as he struggled to open his eyes.

"Sergei…" Nico's voice felt like rocks grating, and he couldn't breathe.

"Hey. Easy. Take it easy." Sergei put his hand on his shoulder.

Sergei watched as the nurse disconnected the tube from the machine and the bulb above Nico's face sagged.

"Nico, I'm going to take the breathing tube out of your throat. Okay? On three, I need you to cough real deep for me." Another older woman came over and spoke to Nico in a soft voice.

"Ready. One. Two. Three." Then she pulled on the

tube as Nico hacked up his lungs trying to dislodge the obstruction.

As the plastic of the bed sheets crinkled, Nico could feel the throbbing waves of pain coming from in his lower abdomen and the open wound there.

His throat still felt scratchy, and someone held a cup of cold water to his lips. After a few moments, he smacked his lips together and tried speaking again. "Sergei."

"Yeah. I'm here." Sergei was sitting in the uncomfortable chair beside the bed. His eyes were red rimmed and lined with dark bags underneath.

"How long was I out?" Nico's head fell on the pillow, facing Sergei this time.

"A little over a day. You were non-responsive. They thought you couldn't breathe, so that's why… that was in you." Sergei motioned at the tube on the cart and then his throat.

"Ok… do you know when I will be released?" Nico took a deep breath and clenched his fists on the sheets.

"I can go ask. If you're okay alone for a few minutes?" Nico nodded; his eyes drooping shut already.

By the time Sergei had come back, sleep had reclaimed him.

* * *

The next time Nico came back around, Sergei was scribbling on a clipboard and being handed a short stack of papers.

"Hey, bud. You ready to leave? Or at least move to a private room?" Sergei handed the last clipboard to the nurse.

"I can go home." Nico's face lifted at the thought of getting back on the case.

"No. But we can keep working from the private room. They want to keep you here for a few more days for monitoring. They'll get you back to normal as quick as they can." Sergei reassured Nico, knowing he would want to get back to work and trying to find Jessica as soon as he was able.

A little while later, the nurses brought a wheelchair for Nico and moved him up to the mostly empty third floor of the hospital. The faux leather chair creaked under Nico's weight as his vacant eyes stared out the window.

"Have we made any progress? On the search for Jessica?" Nico didn't move from the window as he spoke to Sergei.

"I called Heather, and she thinks Jessica went to visit an old friend. And if she is there, then she will come back when she wants. We can't force her to come back."

"I know that." Nico clenched his fists in his lap, the pain of his nails digging into his palms, grounding him in a world without an anchor.

"The case is a whole another ball game." Sergei started. "Maxim has been asking after you and sent a food basket to the hospital for you. He must not have figured out that you were the one who put Anna away."

"So, we're getting closer to him?" Nico's voice is flat and hollow.

"The second meeting already happened, so that lead is closed. But we know there's a meeting where Dmitriy is going to be alone, so maybe we can catch him there." Sergei typed on his phone.

"Maybe." Nico closed his eyes and took a deep breath. "I'd like to sleep if I can." He limped over to the bed and collapsed into it.

"You want something to eat later?" Sergei paused in the doorway, hand leaning on the doorknob.

"Not really..." Nico heard the door click shut softly and squeezed his eyes shut and buried his face in the pillow.

A few days later, Nico was being wheeled out to the parking lot and stepping into the Thunderbird. Sergei watched as he limply sat in the seat and didn't fight the nurse fussing over him.

"You okay, man?" Sergei turned the key in the ignition and the car rumbled to life around them.

"Yeah, I'm fine." Nico wouldn't meet Sergei's eyes.

Sergei didn't say a word about Nico's obvious lies, just backed the car out of the spot and drove home.

"I remember who shot me." Nico's voice startled Sergei at dinner.

Sergei's eyes grew wide, and he frowned at Nico's untouched plate of food.

"It was one of Maxim's men." Nico spoke, as if the words were causing him great pain.

Sergei gaped at him in shock before opening the voice recording app on his phone. "You okay if I save this so you don't have to tell it more than once?" Sergei motioned at his phone now laying on the table.

"I went to Jessica's bar to talk to Heather and to get a drink. She wasn't there." Nico took a deep breath.

"I was sipping on my drink, and the gun pressed into the middle of my back. The man made me turn around and face him."

"Take your time, Nico. We got plenty 'a time," Sergei nodded.

"I didn't hear the shot or feel anything. Then my shirt was red, and the ambulances were there. Then I woke up to you arguing with the nurse about painkillers."

"Nico…" Sergei warned.

"I'm done." Nico watched through glazed eyes as Sergei clicked the recording to finish.

Nico got up and slunk away, feet shuffling on the floor, to his room, and sat down in his office.

Nico had no concept of time, just that it had passed. He knew Sergei brought him food twice a day, and twice a day the plate went untouched. The world lost its colors, and Nico's skin grew pale.

Sergei worried about his weight and his recovery.

"You have no right to be here!" Nico could hear Sergei yelling downstairs, at whom he did not know.

"I'm sorry! I left and I shouldn't have!" Nico recognized that voice. "He was going to lock me up!"

"No. He wasn't. He was going to protect you." Sergei's growling now.

"How? By sending me away!" Nico shook his head, trying to clear the hallucination.

"Whatever! If you want to help, go see if you can get him to drink something." The downstairs door slammed shut and rattled the railing in the house.

"Fine!" a lady's voice yelled at no one.

A faint knock sounded on the door before it creaked open. Nico's muscles locked and could sense *her*.

In the same room as him, watching him. Seeing him.

"Hey, Nico." Your voice sounded like you had been crying. He had hoped he would never have to hear it again after that day when he tried to fix the damage Maxim had done to you.

"I… uh, I know you weren't feeling too great, but I'm going to leave this right here." The plastic of the bottle landed on the table. "And if you drink it, I'll stay with you."

Nico turned the chair away from the hazy window and paused when he could see you. His hand darted out and snatched the bottle off the table.

You heard the seal break and the glug of the water against the bottle. You watched as a sheet of greasy hair parted to reveal the face you had grown to love.

"Hey." You reached your hand out and let it tremble

in the air between you. You closed your eyes, trying to appear non-threatening.

He didn't speak, just stared at you for a while. When you were about to pull your arm back in, you felt the tickle of his fingers across your palm. He pulled you closer and traced aimless patterns up your arm.

"Tell me a fact." You could hear the strain in his voice.

"I love you." You picked the first thing that came to mind.

"Your name is Nicolas Knight." You opened your eyes. "Your brother is Sergei. You have protected me before." You heard his sharp inhale and harsh exhale.

"Jessica?" He raised his eyes.

You smiled at him and curled your hand up in his palm.

"I missed you." He pulled your hand to his lips and kissed it softly.

The heat of his fingers pulled you closer until you were sitting in the chair with him. Your head was on his shoulder and his arms were cinched around you.

"I love you." He seemed to take comfort in the simple phrase. "I was afraid you wouldn't come back." His index finger tapped on your spine.

"I'll always come back for you." Your eyes overflowed and soaked into his shirt.

"Don't cry, baby. I'm right here." He pulled you.

"I was so stupid running away like that." Your voice broke again.

"I would have done the same."

"I should have known better. You wouldn't be hurt if it weren't for me. I hurt you." He curled a strand of your hair around his finger.

"This—" Nico pulled your head out of his shoulder and made you meet his eyes - "—is not your fault. Stop thinking that." He gripped your body.

"But I feel like it is." You protested.

"You said you were sorry, didn't you?" Nico's eyes were soft as he questioned you.

"Yes." comes your faint response.

"Then let's put it behind us. Okay?" He swept his lips across yours.

"Okay," you said kissing him back.

JIMMY

CHAPTER 1

Day One

"Come in Cassidy," Eddie O'Neal said.

Moments later, you were sitting on the most expensive leather couch you've ever seen in a sleek, designed office of Boston's biggest Skipper, Eddie O'Neal. He had ordered your father to send you because your father had borrowed a large sum of money and was trying to get out of paying it back. Eddie told you that you that you would be held until your father pays back his debt in full. You complained and cried, but Eddie told you that no harm would come to you and that you could go home to daddy as soon as your father paid off every penny. He then told you he was going to have you taken to one of his mansions outside the city by his one of his drivers, who walked in after Eddie sent for him. You had been protected all your life, held into innocence by a strict upbringing, and even at twenty, you had seen so little of the world. You were scared for your life, but there was also a tinge of excitement.

The driver is too attractive to be a part of the mob. *This man should be on the cover of Vogue,* you thought. Your eyes glide up him, taking in his formal but work uniform, all in black. He held a hat that was kind of shaped like a pilot's hat. It was also black and had a small sliver plaque on the front that had a symbol engraved into it. You assumed that was the symbol for the drivers. His dark hair is gelled, his eyes are dark brown, his complexion is fair, and his lips are a soft rosy color.

Eddie has a few words with his driver then turns towards you to introduce you.

"Cassidy," Eddie says, walking towards you, the driver a step behind him. "This is Jimmy. He's the most reliable of my drivers. He will keep you safe until you get to the safehouse."

He almost winds you by flashing you the best smile on earth when you stand up to greet him. You thank the gods it's harder than having a cute boy smile at you to make you blush. You smile back at him. "Jimmy, right?"

He nods, then he looks at Eddie as if he's checking that nothing further is needed before leading you out of the building and to the car. He walks with his hand behind your back but doesn't touch you. When the two of you get to the car, he opens the back door for you and waits for you to get in so he can close the door too.

You watch him walk around the car and get in the

driver's seat. He takes his hat off and drops it in the seat next to him before pulling his seatbelt on and starting the car. He looks up into the rear-view mirror at you. "Seatbelt please."

You had been so busy looking at him you almost didn't catch what he said. "What?" you look around yourself and realize what he was asking you to do. "Oh sorry," you say, pulling the seatbelt across you and buckling it up.

He waits for you before turning on his signal light and pulling out of the parking space. He drives in silence for a while before looking at you in the rear-view mirror. "Do you need anything before we leave the city?"

You had been looking out the side window when he spoke, his voice pulling you out of your thoughts. Your eyes move to the rear-view mirror where you can see his face clearly and notice he has a bit of color crawling up his neck. You stare at him for a moment before realizing he must not have many long trips with the opposite gender, and he isn't sure how to ask if you need any lady products. "No, I'm okay."

He nods, looking relieved, as his eyes focus back on the road. "Okay. I'll stop and get us something to eat before we leave the city and a few things for the road. Anything particular you'd like to eat?"

"Anything's good. I'm not picky," you say, leaning against the door and looking out the window.

The ride is quiet till he pulls into a gas station. Jimmy unbuckles his seat belt and turns in his seat to look at you.

"I'm going to fill up and get up a few things. Did you want to come in with me?"

You look at him, surprised he turned to look at you. You had been in a trance, curled up against the door while he drove to the outskirts of the city, so him leaning into the back seat to look at you was daunting. "Oh, uh ... sure," you say, shrugging.

"Wait here for just a sec, okay?" he asks.

You nod and he gives you one of those killer smiles again before putting his hat back on and getting out of the car. You push yourself off the door and stretch. When Jimmy is done filling the tank with gas, he hangs the pump up and opens your door for you. You take the hand he offers to help you out of the car. He closed the door behind you and walks with you into the gas station store.

You put your hand on his arm to get his attention and point towards the bathrooms before walking away from him, so he knows you aren't running off. He nods and, even though you'd never know it, makes sure he keeps an eye on the bathroom doors while circling the shop, grabbing more food than the two of you could possibly eat. When you walk out of the bathroom, he is at the counter.

He looks over at you. "Get yourself something to drink. I didn't know what you wanted."

"Are you sure? You don't need to spend money on me," you say, a worried tone in your voice.

He smiles again. *Oh god, how can anyone get used to that sexy smile?*

"It's okay. It's on the boss."

"Oh, okay," you say before walking away from him to go get a drink.

Jimmy is leaning against the counter, watching you when you get back with your drink, the rest of the things in white plastic bags waiting to be paid for.

"Sorry," you say, placing the beverage on the counter. "They have a lot of choices."

He smiles and holds money out to the man behind the counter without taking his eyes off you. "It's okay sweetheart," he hands you back your drink and grabs the bags, telling the man to keep the change.

Outside, the sky has grown dark with rain clouds. Jimmy grimaces at the sky as you and he walk back to the car. You open the door to the back seat because his hands are full. You scoot in and hold your hand out to him to take the bags and place them in the back with you. He hesitates for a moment, not expecting you to offer to help.

"Thanks," he says, bending a bit to look into the car at you.

You place the last bag on your left, behind the driver's seat, then look over at him, giving a little smile.

He closes the door and hurries around the car as the sky opens and rains down on him. He tosses the hat into the seat next to his and pulls the door shut. "Burgers?" he asks, putting the car into gear and rolling forward while he buckles his seat belt.

"Sure," you say, sliding into the middle of the back seat and buckling up.

He pulls into the Sonic Burger's drive-thru across the

road and orders a few cheeseburgers, handing you the bag when it's handed into his window. He pulls back onto the road toward the mansion before asking you to hand him one. You eat a double cheeseburger in the time it takes Jimmy to finish two. There is still one left in the bag, so you fold the bag around the last one and reach forward to put it on the seat next to his hat. He glances from the road to you a few times to see what you're doing. You lean back, watching him look from the burger to you in the rear-view mirror.

* * *

The drive is awkwardly quiet for nearly an hour. You notice Jimmy looking into the rear-view mirror at intervals, his eyes flicking over to look at you each time. You deduce the trip is going to take at least till nightfall, from the way he pulls his tie loose and the amount of food he picked up at the gas station. So instead of sitting in awkward silence, you decide to strike up a conversation with your *transporter or alleged driver*. You just had to come up with a topic.

You lean forward so your head could rest on his shoulder if you leaned to one side. "Is this job of yours dangerous?"

Jimmy jumps in his seat, moving closer to the door and looking at you. His eyes widen. He looks back at the road, placing a hand over his heart. "Don't sneak up on me!"

"Sorry," you say, leaning back a bit.

He looks over his shoulder at you. "Now, what did you ask?"

You move as far forward as your seatbelt will allow. "I was just wondering if your job was dangerous."

"Oh, well, on a scale from one to ten; ten being the most dangerous you can have mine is about a six," he says, looking at the road as he talks. "I take the boss all the time, but those jobs are less dangerous than you'd think."

You nod. "Oh, okay."

"Why?" Jimmy asks, looking over at you.

"It had been quiet for a long time, and that was the first thing I could think of," you say.

"Sorry about that. I rarely have passengers talking to me unless they are giving me directions," Jimmy says.

"That's okay," you say, grabbing his hat out of the front seat and putting it on.

He looks over at your arm as you snatch his hat, then his eyes flick up to the mirror as you straighten your back to look at yourself. You notice him grinning at you.

"It looks better on you than it does on me."

"I don't know, it's quite cute on you," you say, still looking at yourself in his mirror. You notice him look at the road with a stiff movement, and when your eyes shift across the mirror to look at him, you realize he's blushing. You smile and lean back in your seat. "Do you not think you look cuter than you in your hat?"

He shrugs. "I don't know, it's just part of the uniform, sweetheart."

You tip your head to the side, trying to see around his chair, wishing you were in the front seat. "Well, if no one has told you before, you look very good in your uniform."

You think you see him bite his bottom lip, but you can't be sure. His face is a rosy pink from the compliment, and he shifts uncomfortably in his seat. "Uh..." he clears his throat. "Thank you."

* * *

Jimmy ended up pulling over a few hours later at a pit stop. You both used the bathroom and then he moved some bags into the trunk of his car. When he saw you walking back from the bathroom rubbing your arms, he frowned. "Are you cold?" he asks

You shrug, "I'm fine."

He watches you get back in the car's backseat before closing the trunk. When he gets in the driver's seat, he passes a blanket back to you. You take it, grateful that he wasn't convinced by you telling him you were fine. You pull the blanket over yourself as you hear him open a bag of chips and sit it on the chair next to him. By the time he looks back at you to offer you some, you are asleep.

You don't know how long you were sleeping for, but suddenly there is a hand on your shoulder shaking you awake. You groan before cracking one eye open.

It's dark now. Jimmy has his hat on, so you assume

you are close to the location he's dropping you off at. But something is off. His expression is different, like when someone notices something is off but can't quite put their finger on what it is.

"Wake up, something's wrong," he says, pulling he sees you open your eyes.

"What's wrong?" you ask, pushing yourself into a sitting position. You had slid down till you were lying on the back seat while you were sleeping.

He looks around at the building outside. "There are no guards."

You look out the front window and suddenly, a dark figure runs by. You point. "There's somebody."

Gunshots ring out, leaving holes in the windshield. You yelp in surprise and Jimmy is already spinning the car around, the tires flinging mud as he goes. "Get down!" he yells at you.

You duck in the back seat as more gunshots sound behind the car. Smaller sounding vehicles roar to life and follow the car. You peek through the rear window and see two motorcycles pulling onto the road behind Jimmy's car.

"Put your seat belt on!" Jimmy shouts at you as he swerves the car from side to side.

You turn and buckle yourself in as the motorcycle pulls ahead of the car, advances, then stops sideways, the driver shooting at the car. You duck again as Jimmy rolls his window down and shoots the biker. The guy drops on the road and Jimmy swerves the car around the bike. You hear the other bike pull up next to your window. You look up to see a man pointing a gun right at you and you notice something. The crest on his jacket ... It couldn't be, could it?

The guy fires a few rounds into the window, cracking it but not breaking through. Jimmy fishtails the car on the wet road and hits the bike with the back end of the SUV, sending the motorcyclist flying. You look out the back window again and see a few cars in the distance.

"Are there more coming after us?" you ask.

"Yeah, looks like," he says. His foot is pressing down on the gas as and you can feel from the force of the car that he's driving way over the speed limit.

"Jimmy..." you say, shifting in your seat so you are looking forward again.

"Yeah?"

"Those were my father's men..." you say, looking down at your hands in your lap.

You can tell he's looking in the rear-view mirror at you. "How do you know?"

"I ... I saw my family crest on his leather jacket," you say before biting your lip.

"Are you sure?" he asks. You nod, and even though it's dark inside the car, he must have seen you because he curses under his breath. He pauses for a moment, looking at you in the mirror, before speaking again in a much calmer tone. "It's going to be okay. As long as you're with me, I won't let anything happen to you."

You sniffle and feel his hand touch your knee. "That

man had the gun pointed right at me. Why do you think my father would have me killed?"

Jimmy takes his foot off the petal for a bit. "I don't know..." he stops talking until he hears you holding back sobs. "Hey, no, don't cry. Come on up front with me."

"Okay," you say, taking a deep, shaky breath to try to stop the looming tears. It's not exactly a simple task climbing into the front seat of his car, but Jimmy helps you as much as he can without driving the car into the ditch, and eventually you are sitting next to him. You see his head twitch like he wants to comfort you but isn't sure where to place his hand. But before you can say anything about it, he takes your hand in his.

"I must call the boss and tell him what happened. I really don't want to upset you, but I need to know..." he looks over at you, his hand squeezing yours. "Do you think your father would have you killed instead of paying the boss back?"

Your chin trembles. "Yes," you say, looking down at your lap before he can see your tears spill over.

He sighs, looking back at the road. His thumb brushes over the back of your hand as he adjusts the car so it's back in the correct lane. He waits until you pull your hand away to wipe the tears from your face before moving his hand. First, he pops open the glove box and pulls out a box of tissues for you, then he shifts in his seat to get his phone out of his pocket and calls Eddie.

He swallows loud enough for you to hear as he presses the phone to his ear, his eyes on the road. He must not like calling his boss because he is uneasy. "I'm sorry for calling so late sir, I have some bad news..."

Jimmy explains what has happened, not excluding any details, then he's silent as his boss tells him what to do next. "Okay, I'll call you if anything changes."

You watch him hang up and sag in his seat, the tension of the call almost noticeably rolling off him. "Was he upset?" you ask.

"Hmm..." he hums, glancing at you. "Oh, he's always upset, but he took it well. He's sending us to a different location. He has a car set up for us to swap so we lose these guys," he points his thumb over his shoulder.

"They're still after us?" you ask, turning to look out the back window again.

"Yeah, they are most likely tracking us and following just far enough that they are out of sight," Jimmy says.

You look over at him, your eyes wide. His lips press together to hold down a smile your shocked expression was pulling from him and takes his hat off, dropping it onto your head. "Don't worry, I'm an expert at this."

CHAPTER 2

Day Two

You wake up, neck stiff from sleeping against the car door, the sun is blindingly bright. You squint over at Jimmy, who hasn't stopped driving all night, holding your hand over your eyes to block out the sun. He looks rough, to say the least. His clothes that were crisp when you first met him are crinkled, he has stubble on his chin and upper lip, and he looks dead tired. You feel bad for falling asleep when he's had to stay awake to keep both of you safe.

He grins at you, his own sleepiness melting away briefly. "Good morning."

You push yourself up in your seat, rubbing your eye. "Morning...Where are we?"

"Almost at the car, we are switching. We'll have to grab the things in the trunk of my car quickly and then it's about a half a day drive to the safehouse," he says, pulling on sunglasses as he follows the curve in the road, so the sun is directly in both of you faces.

"You can't drive that long," you say.

"We can't stop. I'll be okay," he says, shrugging.

"I can drive," you say. "And I promise I'll wake you up if anyone suspicious shows up."

He looks over at you, then back at the road, silent for a while. "That might be a good idea."

You smile and sit back in your seat. At least there was something you could do to help.

Jimmy points at a truck stop. "The car is there; we have five minutes. You grab everything out of the back seat, and I'll get the things out of the trunk. If you must use the bathroom, run in quick, then we must go."

You nod, looking in the direction he's pointing. Then you swivel your head around to look at the things in the back. A few bags, the blanket, and his hat. Easy. It's not long before he finds the car. The two of you rush everything into the back seat of the new car, race to the bathrooms, then get in the car, you in the driver's seat. After quickly adjusting the mirrors, you pull out of the truck stop. Jimmy has instructed you to drive straight until you get to a crossroads where the road straight across from you is gravel, then wake him if he's sleeping. Then, Jimmy leans his chair back and uses his jacket like a blanket. You turn the radio on low and he's lulled to sleep before the first song ends.

You drive for so long you aren't sure you're still in the

same state, but finally you come across the crossroads he was talking about. "Hey, we're here," you say, touching his arm.

He jumps at the touch, then apologies as he props the seat back up. He directs you through so many lefts and rights that even if you were crazy enough, you try to run away from him. You'd never find your way back to the road you came from. Finally, after one last left turn, you pull into the driveway of a little farmhouse. The farm itself is no longer there, but the house looks like it was pulled from time, perfectly preserved.

You turn off the car and push your door open, admiring the little one-family house. It's a soft yellow with white trim. A wraparound porch and little shutters and flower-boxes full of flowers on all the windows.

You stand and stretch, your body aching from being in a car for that long. Jimmy grabs some things out of the car and walks to the door, the car keys in his hand. He unlocks the door and places the bags inside, looking around quickly to make sure the house is vacant.

"Come on in," he says, standing at the door.

You take the bags with you, including a duffel that was very heavy. He takes the duffel from you when you get to the porch. "What do you have in there? Rocks?" you ask, rubbing the shoulder you had it slung over.

"No, not rocks," he says and unzips it just enough to stick his hand inside. He pulls out a gun and you take a step back. "Relax… it's not loaded."

He hands you the gun, showing you it's empty first.

Your father never let you hold a gun even though he had lots around, so you survey it while you've got the chance. Jimmy must put his hand on your elbow to lead you inside. He sits you down at the table, then tells you he'll be back. He's just going to hide the car. You nod, putting his gun on the table. Once he's outside, you get up and roam around the house, opening doors and closets to find this house is completely stocked for living in. There are clothes in the bedroom, food in the kitchen, soaps, shampoos, towels, shoes. You name it, it's there. The only thing you find odd is there is only one bedroom with a bed in it, the second bedroom has been made into a panic room. It's filled with monitors showing different angles of the property. Must be well hidden. You hadn't seen a single camera when you were marveling at the house.

You find the one in the garage and see Jimmy get out of the car and close the garage door before making his way back inside. He was walking like he was sore, and you didn't blame him. Your lower back and legs were still aching, and you longed for a few minutes in a hot tub.

Jimmy walks into the house and looks around for you. "Cassidy," he calls out.

"Yeah?" you say, stepping out.

"I was just wondering where you went," he says, sinking down in a chair and stretching his legs out.

"I found the panic room," you say, walking towards him. "It's cool, but that means there is only one bedroom."

He blinks, taking a few moments to understand what you're saying to him. Then his eyes widen. "Oh."

He gets up and walks around the house; you follow him, only now realizing how tall he is. You also notice, now that he's moving around without his jacket on, that despite how lean he is, he seems to have a muscular body. His arm muscles are visible under his black t-shirt and his shoulders are wide and fit.

He halts at the bedroom door, causing you to run into him. You grab his arm to steady yourself as you take a step back. He looks down at you. His expression makes you think he's not used to having a woman near him.

"Sorry," you say, taking your hand off his arm.

He nods, his eyes shifting away from you as color crawls up his neck. His movements seem stiffer now, like he's out of his element. "You're right...One bedroom..." His eyes land on the bed. "One bed..."

You look from the bed to his face and see Jimmy frowning. 'How can he be that attractive when he frowns, you wonder as your eyes view his face?'

Pink tints his cheeks as he notices you staring at him, and he hesitantly looks over at you. "What?"

A slow smile forms on your lips as you watch him. "Nothing, I was just thinking you're too hot to be in the mob."

His blush deepens as he breaks eye contact, sputtering incoherent sentences. All you caught were words like manly, tough, and killer. Your smile only got bigger as this gentle hunk tried to convince you he wasn't pretty. You secretly hoped your father's men looked for you for a long time, so you could stay here with this adorable goof.

You hold your hands up. "Okay, I'm sorry. I was mistaken."

Jimmy glares at you, knowing you're teasing him. Somehow, during his rant, he moved, so he was now standing in the middle of the bedroom facing you. Your eyes glide over him, and you still can't believe anyone working for a mob boss can be that handsome. You try not to stare at him because he seems uncomfortable with that kind of attention, but it's very hard to stop looking at him.

"Uh ... I'm going to find something to make for dinner," you say, breaking the small silence that fell between the two of you. "You can shower now, and I will after dinner. I'm guessing this house doesn't have a huge hot water tank, so I'll probably have to wait for it to heat up."

"Okay..." he says, looking a bit shocked at your offer.

You nod at him before stepping out of the room, pausing at the door to say; "Oh, I saw some clean clothes in the closet. I don't know what size they are, but they look like they'd fit you."

Jimmy smiles shyly, looking down. "Thanks."

You walk to the kitchen with a smirk plastered on your face. God, that man is so fine-looking. You knew you weren't a girl with the purest mind, and despite your father's rules against dating, you learned as much as you could about sex so that when you had the chance, you wouldn't be naïve. And right now, all that things you had learned in secret, you wanted to try on Jimmy. The problem was; Jimmy was shy and kept a distance between himself and you. That was something you weren't sure how to change.

You open the fridge and look through the contents, your mind still rolling on with its train of thought. There was no rush to get Jimmy to let you close to him, so you were going to start by making sure he had three home-cooked meals a day. Your mother, before she died, had always said food was the way to win a man's heart. You were a wonderful cook with lots of recipes stashed in your mind. You could make a meal out of just about anything and you knew the best deserts to complement the meal.

You didn't have time to start a desert from scratch tonight, so one of the boxed ones would have to make do. You pull out the meat and veggies you want for the meal and set them on the counter, then search for a cutting board and some pans to cook in. Once you have the veggies chopped and the meat cooking on low heat, you mix some cake mix. Unfortunately, you couldn't find a cake pan, but there was a cupcake pan and the paper wrappers to match. The pan is large enough to fit all the mix into it in one go. You stick it in the oven and put on a timer, then you toss the veggies and some noodles into your pan. Stir-fry was the easiest meal to make quickly. You add some seasoning and let it simmer for a few minutes.

You take a step back to check the cupcakes in the

oven, but bump into Jimmy. You jump in surprise; he hadn't made a noise as he walked into the kitchen, but now that your back was against his chest you could smell his shampoo.

"That smells good," he says, leaning over your shoulder to look at the food in the pan.

You look over your shoulder at him. "It's almost done."

"Already? Wow ... Anything I can do to help?" he asks. He's pressing into you now, not in a horny way, more like if you were there in the way he would eat out of the hot pan.

"Um…" you think for a moment, hoping your stalling will keep him this close to you longer. "I guess you could look for something we can eat this out of."

"Okay," he says, he doesn't move right away, but you're still a little sad when he moves away from you.

You open the oven a bit to check on the cupcakes; they are cooking thoroughly and should be done right as you two are finished eating. You close the oven door and turn off the burner as the stir-fry is on. Jimmy places two bowls next to you and toy fill them up, leaving the left-overs in the pan for now. You each grab one and walk over to the table to eat.

Jimmy is the noisiest eater you've ever met. Not in a nasty way, but like every bite is the best thing he's ever tasted. You ask him if it's good and his mouth is too full to speak, so he just makes a happy sigh as an answer. You smile, holding back a laugh.

"I don't think anyone has ever appreciated my food that much before," you say, picking up the dishes when you're both done and taking them to the sink.

"My mother can't even cook that well," he says, turning in his chair to look at you.

You smile at that as you take out the cupcakes just as the timer buzzes.

"What's that?" Jimmy asks, your back is to him so he can't see what you pull out.

You place the pan on top of the oven to cool a bit and turn the oven off. "Dessert."

You hear him get out of his chair and walk towards you as you pull the cupcakes out of the pan. He stops behind you, not pressing against you like last time, but you can still feel his heat. "You made dessert?" he asks, sounding surprised.

You place the last one on the counter before turning to face him. "Yeah, well, I have to pay you back for keeping me safe. Wouldn't want you running off and leaving me for dead."

He blushes and looks away from you. You only notice now that he's in a plain white shirt and plaid pajama bottoms. "I wouldn't do that, and you really don't owe me anything."

"Yes, I do," you say so quickly you almost cut him off. "If you hadn't been doubtful of where you were meant to drop me off, I'd be dead, and honestly, cooking for you is the least I can do."

He just nods. His blush has faded, but he's not making

eye contact. Your mind replays all the times he's blushed and every time it's when your eyes met his. Your mind is screaming."

"Just let them cool off and I'll put some frosting on them, okay?" you say, gesturing over your shoulders at the cupcakes.

He nods again. "Okay, I'll be in the panic room checking the monitors and alarms, unless you need help to clean up?"

"Go ahead, I'm fine," you say, moving away from him and searching for something to put the leftovers in.

He watches you for a second before walking over to the panic room. You find containers and put the leftovers in on, keeping the larger one out for the cupcakes. Then you take the knives, pan, and cutting board to the sink to wash them up. When you have all the dishes in the dish rack drying, you find a towel to dry your hands on and pull out the frosting kit you found earlier. You don't make them too fancy, but use a spout on the frosting bag, so it comes out like little flowers. You do one third of them in chocolate, one third in vanilla frosting, and the last third in both, not knowing what one Jimmy would like best.

You put one of each on a plate and take it into the panic room, setting the plate down on the desk next to him before letting him know you are going to take your shower. He nods and his hand hovers over the cupcakes as he tries to decide on what one he wants to eat.

You walk out of the panic room and into the bedroom, which is right next to it, to find something to sleep in. Looking in the dresser that's positioned against the wall across from the end of the bed, you find a long nightshirt and some underwear. You take them and walk back past the panic room to the bathroom. You don't bother to trying to lock the old door because you don't want to get stuck, and you know there is a zero percent chance Jimmy would walk in unless someone was going to kill you while you were showering. And in the case of someone trying to kill you, you would need to have the door unlocked to let Jimmy in to save you.

You turn on the shower, adjusting it to the right temperature before taking off the clothes you had been in for the last two days. Your body still aches from being in a car for so long, but the hot water seems to wash some of the discomfort down the drain. You wash your hair with the same shampoo Jimmy used before you can stop imagining him in the shower before you. You shake your head as you rinse the soap out. No, you don't want to lust over him; you don't even know if he'll like you like that, anyway. But your imagination doesn't stop there.

In your mind, Jimmy is soaping himself, a cloud of steam covering the naughty parts. Since you've never actually seen a man naked, your mind just cuts that bit out. His eyes are closed, and his head tipped back, so the water is washing his hair away from his face. His hand slides down his stomach into the cloud of steam and his expression changes slightly. His eyebrows pull together and his mouth opens slightly as his hand moves below the steam cloud.

You've stopped moving as your imagination takes over. Your hands are in your hair, mid rinse, your eyes have closed, so your imagination could be more vivid. Your breathing has picked up. There is a strange feeling growing in your stomach that you don't identify but you like.

There is a knock at the door. You jump in shock, your mind snapping back to your present surroundings. "Yes…" you say.

"Eddie just called in with an update. Come to the panic room when you are done," Jimmy says from the other side of the door.

"Okay, I'll be out soon," you say, hurrying to rinse the rest of the soap out of your hair. You find the razor Jimmy used and quickly use it. You rinse it out very well before putting it back and turning off the shower.

You get out, dry off quickly, pull the underwear and nightshirt on, then wrap the towel around your hair and drop your clothes in the hamper as you walk out of the bathroom. You go into the panic room and knock to get Jimmy's attention, even though the door is open.

Jimmy looks over at you, his eyes quickly taking in your exposed legs, and light night shirt. The muscles in his jaw work as he clenches his teeth, looking away from you. He directs your attention to a map on one of the monitors. He points to a spot. "We're here," he says and points to another spot further southwest from the first spot. "Eddie has located your father's boys here. They seem to have lost us, so that's good, but we've been ordered to stay put until further notice."

"So, we don't know how long we'll be here?" you ask, taking a step into the room.

Even though you are still quite a ways away from Jimmy, he leans away as you step into the room, and he noticeably tenses up. "No, but if I were to guess, I'd say we will be here for at least a month, unless your father's men get close, then we'll have to move somewhere else."

You sigh. "Okay... What's Mr. O'Neal planning on doing now that I'm not helping get his money back?"

"I think he's looking for your father, but no word on his location yet," Jimmy says, looking at the monitor.

"Will he kill me if he doesn't pay?" you ask. You knew your father wasn't a good man, but he was the only family you had.

Jimmy looks over at you with a sad look. "I don't know."

You sigh, looking down at the ground.

Jimmy gets out of the chair and walks over to you. "Come on, let's get you to bed," he says as he puts his arm around you and leads you to the bedroom.

When you two had dinner, the sun had just started setting, but now it was so dark the light had to be turned on to see the way to the bed. Jimmy walked you up to the bed, then pulled the blankets back and covered you. You caught his hand when he turned to go.

"Would it be wrong to ask you to stay with me just for tonight?" you ask softly.

You feel his arm tense up. "I—I…"

You let your fingers slip away from his and you pull the blanket closer. "It's okay, you don't have to…"

Jimmy stands there for a long while, looking down at you, his body still turned, ready to leave. He takes a deep breath, and you see his hand make a fist before he walks out of the room. You hug the blanket to your chest and shut your eyes, trying to block out the unwanted emotions for your father. You really didn't want to be alone tonight, but you also didn't want to pressure Jimmy into staying. Maybe he had a girlfriend, and that's why he was trying to keep his distance.

The bed sinks down behind you, and you look over your shoulder in disbelief. Jimmy is lying down as far away from you as the bed will allow.

"Just tonight," he says when he sees you looking at him.

You roll over; the bed is so tiny; you end up pressed right up against him, and give him a hug. "Thank you."

He tenses when you press against him. He lies still stiffly for a moment before putting a hand on your side and gently pushing you away.

"Sorry," you say, quickly pulling your arms away and moving back to your side of the bed.

"It's alright, just try to stay over there, okay?" he says.

"Okay," you respond.

CHAPTER 3

Day Three

You wake up before Jimmy. A few things are surprising about this morning. The first thing is finding out that both of you have somehow ended up in the middle of the bed. The second is that he's holding you, his arm wrapped around your waist. The last, and most surprising, is he's pressing into your rump. Your eyebrows shoot up when your brain registers what part of him is pressing into you. You bite your lip and look over your shoulder at him. He's still sound asleep.

You are torn. Your mind wants to know what it's like to touch him, but you also don't want to jump on the guy that's keeping you safe, not yet anyway. You're sure he's going to freak out when he wakes up and finds himself in this position, but you don't want to pull away from him because it feels nice being held. You decide to stay still, pretend to be asleep and play dumb if he asks you anything about his hard cock pressing against you.

It's not long before you feel him wake up. His body tenses against you before he backs his hips away. You pretend his movement is what wakes you. You groan and roll over, peaking at him through sleepy eyes. His face is red, and he's looking at you with wide eyes.

"What's wrong?" you ask, trying to sound worried.

He swallows hard. "It—I have a situation..."

You give him a confused look. "Are you okay? Do you need help?"

He shakes his head. "I—I'm okay...did...?" He looks away from your face, embarrassed. "Did you feel it?"

"Feel what?" you ask, letting your eyes close.

"My..." he pauses, trying to figure out the best way to say this. "Situation?"

You open your eyes again and give him the most confused look you can muster. "I don't understand what you're asking me."

He closes his eyes, his jaw clenching as he prepares himself to explain his situation. "In the morning, men get —um ..."

"Hmm…" you offer.

"Hard," he replies, studying you.

The surprise on your face is genuine. You never thought he'd actually say it. "Oh ... I guess it's normal."

He closes his eyes, looking like he's in pain. "Don't tell me that. Now, I feel like a pervert."

You chuckle. "Don't worry, you're definitely not one."

He smiles at you and the two of you lay in silence for a few minutes before you speak again. "I am made of questions right now."

"About what?" he asks.

"Your condition," you reply.

His eyes widen as he looks at you, his blush coming back. "What?"

You shrug. "I've never been this close to a man before. I'm just a little curious."

"Curious?" he repeats.

You nod. "Like you said 'in the morning', does that mean it happens every morning? If so, why? Are these morning situations so obvious?"

He stares at you. "Uh..."

Your eyes light up. "Can I touch it?"

"What?" he asks. "Why do you want to know these things? Why do you want to touch it?"

You shrug again. "I'm cur-"

"Right, curious, you said that already." Jimmy rubs his face. "Okay uh... yeah it happens every morning, I don't know why, I never actually thought about it before, and I guess it feels the same, I don't know."

You watch him happily as he answers your questions. "Interesting."

He looks at you, amused.

"Can I touch it, finally?" you ask again.

His amused look melts away, embarrassment taking its place. "I don't know..."

"Okay... well what if I just..." you say, moving so you're pressed up against him.

He freezes up at the contact, then tries to move his hips away again, but you stop him by placing your hand on his hip.

"Cassidy," he says.

You slip your fingers under the edge of his waistband and follow it around to the front of his pants. He sucks in a breath but doesn't stop you. You look up at his face as you slowly push your hand further inside. His eyes are closed and he's biting his lip. Your hand slide down further until you are almost touching his 'situation'. "Can I touch it?" you ask again lowly.

Jimmy's chest rises and falls quickly with heavy gasps. He anxiously pants, "Oh fuck..."

You bite your lip and wrap your fingers freely around his cock. His back arches as your fingers ghost over it, exploring its size and feel. You feel something wet as you explore a bit more. You find it's coming from the tip as you smear it down his shaft. It allows your hand to slide up and down easier. Your hand closes tighter and start jerking up and down.

Jimmy gasps while his hand makes a fist in the blanket. You stop, worried you are doing something wrong.

"Don't stop," he pleads.

You push his pants down until he's free from them, then you watch as your hand pleasures him. This is the first time you've seen a man's dick and you look at it in awe. You're not sure what you were expecting but it wasn't this. Jimmy looks at you, confused, as you stop jerking suddenly. You push on his hip till he's on his back. You sit up next to him, and he opens his mouth to say something, but you bend down and put your lips over his manhood. The only thing that comes out of his mouth is a moan.

You're not sure what you're doing, you just had an urge to do it. You shift your position, so you can rub him as your mouth sucks on the tip. He made a fist in your hair as he let out a profanity or two.

"Please Cassidy, suck all of me," Jimmy grunts.

You do as Jimmy asks, and he pushes your head down, plunging him into your mouth even further. You pull back in surprise, but he pushes your head back down, groaning your name. *Shit, that was exciting.* You slowly bob your head up and down, taking him in as far as you can, trying to get him to groan your name again. And Jimmy does over and over until his hips buck forward, pushing into your mouth too far, a hot gooey liquid sprays the back of your throat. You gag, pulling your mouth off his cock.

He sits up quickly. "I'm so, so sorry," he says, his hands flapping around you like he doesn't know what to do.

You wipe your mouth and your eyes are dreamy. "That was because it felt good, right?"

He nods, his expression full of emotions.

"It's okay," you say smiling.

He put back on his pants then flops back down on the

bed, his arm resting over his eyes. "I can't believe I let you do that. I'm such a wicked man."

"Why are you saying that?" Your eyebrows scrunch.

He looks over at you. "We hardly know each other, and you said that you've never been with a man, and I didn't stop you from doing what you did."

"But I wanted to..." you say.

He shakes his head. "I still shouldn't have let you do that."

You look down at your lap. "Is it because you have a girlfriend?"

"No, it's because we met two days ago," Jimmy pushes himself back up, so he's close to you but not quite touching you. "Don't be sad, you did nothing wrong, it's just, my job is to protect you and keep you safe not..." he looks away, struggling to find the words. "Not... doing those naughty things with you..."

You nod, still looking down at your lap. "I understand," you slowly look up. "Did I make you do something you didn't want to do?"

He looks at you in surprise as he rubs the back of his neck. "No... I just shouldn't have done that."

You nod again, realized that your inquisitiveness didn't force him into something he didn't want to do. You feel his stare and you meet his eyes.

Jimmy opens his mouth to say something but stops himself. After a few more moments, he tries again and succeeds to ask. "Was that your first time?"

You bite your lip, nodding again.

"Fuck," he mutters, closing his eyes.

* * *

The morning is awkward, and Jimmy hardly talks to you all afternoon. You bring him his meals in the panic room, and he just mutters *a thank you* without looking away from whatever screen he's looking at.

After you put dinner in the slow cooker, you walk into the small living room and sit on the couch. You had been so happy this morning when he let you touch and pleasure him, but he's avoiding you like the plague now and that really hurt. You understood that he can't do that again because he's working but he didn't have to avoid you. You could control yourself and not touch him if that's what he wanted.

You sigh and turn on the TV. You don't really feel like watching anything but it's better than sitting in silence. You pull the blanket that's folded over the arm of the couch around you and stare at the local news channel. Your eyes grow heavy and just as you're about to give in and catch a quick snooze, something shows up on TV that's a little shocking.

"Jimmy…" you yell. "Hurry, come check this out."

You hear his bare feet slap against the floor as he makes his way to the living room. "What?"

You point to where the breaking news live feed was playing. The camera angle was taken from a helicopter, an old brick building was on the screen, it had its top two floors almost completely missing. There were firemen on the ground trying to put out the blaze and police trying to keep people out of the way so the bricks falling off the building didn't hit bystanders. The employees of the building were gathered a few feet away. Just then the camera zooms into them and Eddie O'Neal's disgusted face fills the screen. The newscast lady's voice plays as pictures are shown. *"A devastating day for businessman Eddie O'Neal as an arsonist attempts to destroy his office building. Two that are listed in critical condition and dozens of others have suffered only minor injuries. No casualties to report at this moment."*

The newscaster keeps talking as you and Jimmy stare at each other.

"This is bad," Jimmy says.

"She said businessman, do they not know that Eddie runs the mob?" you ask.

Jimmy shakes his head. "Hardly anyone knows who's behind the ring. I think my boss has people working for him in the media, so they filter out what the public knows."

"Oh..." you say looking back at the screen. Eddie lifts his phone to his ear the exact second Jimmy's phone rings.

Jimmy picks it up. *"Yeah...we're watching the news right now, are you okay?...Okay...Yes ... Full lock-down? Are you sure? I thought they lost our tail...Okay, no problem."*

He hangs up and runs his hand over his face. You look back over at Jimmy with questions in your eyes.

"We are on full lock-down, no leaving the house. The

windows are all bulletproof and the walls are secure, I must lock the doors and then we wait," Jimmy says, not looking at anything.

"Maybe they figured out where we are hiding?" you ask, trying to keep the fear out of your voice.

Jimmy shakes his head. "No, I don't think so. All we know is that your father's men tried bringing down my boss's building."

You gasp. "I had no idea my father was that kind of man..."

Jimmy watches you as you pull the blanket closer around yourself and bite your lip. He sighs and walks over to sit next to you. He puts one arm around your shoulders and pulls you against him. You believe he's trying to comfort you, but his movements are too stiff, and he's so tense that it's more uncomfortable than calming. "I've heard of your father in some circles. He can be a son of a bitch but don't worry he won't hurt you."

"How do you know that?" you ask.

He sits back. "Because I'm here to keep you safe. Even the Feds would have a hard time getting to you with me watching your back."

You laugh as you go to hug Jimmy. He freezes up at your touch. You pull back. "Sorry, I didn't know you were going to be uncomfortable with me getting close."

Jimmy shakes his head, looking down. "It's not that..." he sighs. "I've never been close to women and after what happened this morning, I—"

He frowns, his jaw clenching hard enough for you to

see the muscle in his neck bulge. You rub his cheek. "It's okay, I'll try to keep my distance."

Jimmy catches your hand as your fingers still trace his jawline and he raises an eyebrow. You give him an apologetic look.

CHAPTER 4

Day Ten

It's been a week since you, and Jimmy got to the safehouse. You've mostly kept your promise of keeping your distance, but as the week went on, he became friendlier and more playful, making it harder. He spent the nights on the couch, giving you the bed, but the last two mornings he woke you up by climbing onto the bed, holding you down and tickling you. He seemed to like to tickle you, not just in the morning either. While you were doing dishes, he would sneak up behind you. And when you'd shriek and run around the small house trying to get away from him, it spurred him on, making him determined to pin you against the wall or hold you down on the couch tickling you till you were out of breath.

In fact, just a few brief moments ago you had been

minding your business, doing up the laundry as he checked in with his boss, then with no warning, he had snuck up behind you and tickled your sides. You had been briefly trapped in the laundry room but somehow got out and now found yourself on the opposite side of the table, watching his movements to stay away.

Jimmy had a devilish grin on his face as you pointed your finger at him. "Stop it or else!"

"Or else what?" he asks, calling your bluff as he slowly circles the table.

You mimic his movements to keep him on the opposite side of the table. "I... I'll tell Eddie!"

His grin gets bigger. "And you think he'll believe you?"

"Why wouldn't he?" your steps slow slightly.

"You think Eddie would believe that the man he's paying to keep you safe is chasing you around the house, trying to tickle you?" His amusement grows as your threat crumbles before you.

He places his hand on the table and, like a freaking ninja, hops over it. You scream and run for the bedroom, trying to get the door closed before he gets there. His foot wedges between the door and the frame, stopping it from closing. Your feeble attempts to keep the door shut fail, and he pushes it open easily. You back into the room, holding your hands out in front of you as he walks in towards you.

"No, no, please. Jimmy, please don't," you say as you back up.

Jimmy walks slowly towards you, backing you up until you almost trip over the corner of the bed. When you fumble, he swoops in and scoops you up. He climbs onto the bed and uses his body to hold you down as he runs his fingers up and down your sides. You laugh and wiggle under him, planting your feet on either side of him on the bed, trying to push yourself out from under him. He just laughs as you fail at getting away. You continue to fight his tickles, growing breathless.

Jimmy slips his fingers under your shirt, and you clutch his wrists. "No, please stop!"

His fingers stop tickling you and he uses his elbows to lift himself off you enough to look down at you. "What's the matter?"

"You're under my shirt..." you say a little shyly, unable to keep eye contact with him. It was strange being shy to have him touch you when just a few days ago you had him in your mouth, but you couldn't help it.

"I don't think I've seen anything make you shy before," Jimmy says, his palms pressing against your sides.

Your heart jumps at his touch and you look up at Jimmy in surprise. He's looking at you, grinning. He leans over so his weight is on one arm, and he uses his hand to slowly push your shirt up till it rolled under your bra. He shifts slightly again before bringing his head down and pressing his lips just under your belly button. You gasp, your hands grabbing the sides of his face to stop him.

Jimmy chuckles, turning his head to kiss your wrist

before saying. "So, you're okay putting your hands and mouth on me, but I can't return the favor?"

Your heart falters and your face gets hot. "W—What? I thought you couldn't do... that thing... because you're working?"

He gives you another crooked grin. "I said shouldn't, not couldn't," he reaches up to stroke your cheek. "Why are you blushing so much? You never blush like this."

"You just said that you were going to do..." You're too embarrassed to finish the sentence.

You have to look away from him to ease your awkwardness. It was such a bizarre feeling, being embarrassed. You didn't know it was such a powerful emotion, it made you want to run and hide. The strangest part was that you didn't feel this way when you were touching him.

While you were looking away from him, trying to control your emotions, Jimmy had bent down and left a trail of kisses down your stomach, getting closer to your pants' waistband with every peck. His hands were against your sides, holding your shirt up. His thumbs stroked the skin just below your bra cup.

"I don't know what it is about you that makes me want to behave badly," Jimmy says against your skin. "But if you want me to, I will do anything you want."

Your body is responding in all the right ways, but your mind is uncertain. *Despite your confidence when you had pleasured him the other day, you hadn't been with anyone before. You're sure he would understand if you told him. The problem was you didn't know what to say. Obviously telling him you had never been with a man before would be on the top of the list, but after that. Did you tell him to keep going? To stop? Something in between?* You had no idea.

"Cassidy?" Jimmy says, causing you to pay attention to him. "Are you okay? You look shaken up."

You bite your lip and shrug. He pushed himself up, looking at you with a worried expression.

"I..." you start, pausing for a moment to make sure you're wording this right. "I like having you close to me, and I don't think you'd ever do anything I'm not okay with. I just..." you have to look away from him. "I'm a virgin."

Jimmy says nothing, but you feel him pull down your shirt before his chest presses against yours. His arms slip under your back and his face presses against your shoulder. When he speaks, his voice is low. "I'm not asking you to have sex with me right now. I was just hoping I could do the same thing to you as you did to me."

You glare at the ceiling. "What do you mean?"

He looks over at you, a smile playing with his lips when he realizes you don't understand what he wants to do with you. "Pleasure you with my hands and mouth."

You stare at him. "Oh."

"Would you like that?" Jimmy asks, shifting his body off you and sliding a hand down your stomach, his fingers slipping just under the top of your pants.

Your hand slaps around his wrist and you close your eyes. "I-I don't know..."

He stops moving his hand as soon as you touched him

and, although your eyes are closed and can't see him, he looks at you. "Should I maybe kiss you first?"

You look over at him in surprise realizing you had done, and were talking about doing, very intimate things and you hadn't even kissed yet. Your glee rises till you're laughing like it's the funniest thing that's ever happened in your life and Jimmy joins you. The two of you laugh until your sides hurt and Jimmy's wiping tears from his eyes.

As your laughter dies down, you roll on to your side, so you are facing him. "That might be a good idea," you say.

His smile fades as his eyes shift away from yours and focus on your mouth. Your heart picks up its pace. His hand rests on your neck and he uses his thumb to tip your head up before slowly leaning in. You close your eyes as he leans closer, pressing his lips to yours. He moves back, and you whine, grabbing the neck of his shirt and pulling him back into the kiss. He smiles against your lips before kissing you more passionately.

The thumb that he used to tip your face up for the kiss now slides over your chin and pressed down. Because you can't tip your head down while he's kissing you, his thumb just pulls your mouth open. His tongue slides into your mouth and you flinch slightly. His tongue pulls back, and he kisses your lips a few more times before trying again. This time you don't flinch, but you also don't know what to do.

It doesn't seem to matter to him you don't know what to do with his tongue in your mouth because he just keeps doing what he's doing as he pushes you back so he's leaning over you again. He has one arm under your neck while the other hand rests on your hip.

Then his hand does the same thing you did to him before pleasuring him. His fingers slip under your pants, then slide around to your front before slipping further south. You pull from the kiss gasping, as his hand slip between your legs. His mouth moves to your neck and his fingers start stroking you. You clutch at him, gasping, but with the second stroke your gasp turns into a moan.

For someone who seemed so uncomfortable around you, his fingers sure knew what they were doing. He stroked you until your panties were soaked from your arousal, then he pushed a finger inside you. You tense up and he stops moving. His finger is long, and you can feel it deep inside you.

"Relax," he says, looking down at you. "This will not hurt."

You bite your lip and nod. His finger slips in and out of you and you moan. He keeps thrusting his fingers into you until you ask for more, then Jimmy pushes in another finger before you could even think to ask him.

Having two of his fingers push inside you is making you shudder in the best way. Jimmy slows his pace, and you beg him not to stop. You can feel him grin against your neck as he works you into your orgasm. You moan as you cling to him, his fingers still sliding in and out of you as your body clamps down over them.

After he's sure you are satisfied, he takes his hand out

of your pants and reaches over to the bedside table to grab a tissue to wipe his forehead. When he looks back at you, you are still laying down with your eyes closed as you try to catch your breath. He lies back down next to you and kisses you.

"Didn't that feel good?" he asks.

You nod, still breathing too hard to answer.

He pulls on your collar to expose your shoulder so he can kiss it. "I still didn't get to use my mouth on you."

"No," you say, shaking your head. "You'll have to do that next time."

"Next time could be right now…"

"I don't think I can handle that," you say.

"Okay, I guess I'll have to hold myself back from touching you more," he says, smiling at you.

Just then an alarm sounded, causing you and him to jump. Jimmy hurries into the next room to check the monitors. You take two minutes longer to get in motion, but you are soon at Jimmy's side. He is frowning at the screen.

"I think they found us," he says, tapping the keys on the desk to make the camera zoom in.

You see your father's men snooping around the yard on the screen and your hand clutches Jimmy's arm.

He looks over at you. "It's okay. I'm going to keep you safe. The car is already packed, we just have to make it to it and then I can get us out of here."

You nod, still looking at the screen.

"Put a scarf on and grab the long coat, we are going to pretend you are an old lady, and as long as they don't see your face, we should be good," he says, walking out of the room and handing you the coat and a scarf.

You pull them on as Jimmy instructed, and he pulls a Red Sox cap on, then the two of you make your way to the garage. He gets you in the backseat and makes sure his gun is accessible before he starts the car. He instructs you to sit slouched, with your head down so you look older, before he opens the garage and pulls out. You are holding your breath, trying not to look up as the car moves down the driveway.

"Shit," Jimmy says, slowing the car. "Don't say anything."

The vehicle comes to a stop, and you feel your heart trying to beat its way out of your chest. Jimmy rolls the window down slightly.

"Everything okay?" Jimmy asks the man outside the window.

"We are looking for two fugitives. A man and a young woman. Have you seen anyone in the area?"

You assume Jimmy shakes his head. "No, I haven't."

"Hmmm..." the man outside the window hums. "Where are you headed?"

"The hospital. My aunt here isn't feeling well," Jimmy lies smoothly.

The man outside the window is silent for a while before waving them on. You let out a sigh after Jimmy rolls the window back up. You are so relieved you almost forget to keep looking down and duck your head down again, but not before getting a glance at a man on a phone pointing at the car you and Jimmy are in.

"Buckle up," Jimmy says before spinning the tires in the gravel and sending the car lurching forward.

You get plastered to the back of the seat from the car's force and fumble to get your seatbelt buckled up before Jimmy drifts around the first corner. Gunshots ring out behind you, and you hear the bullets hit the back of the car. Jimmy drifts around another corner then circles around the tiny group of suburban houses before pealing down the dirt road at high speeds. He loses half the cars that had been chasing you before pulling onto a road that was more grass than road. It curved and split off into the woods in so many directions you could have sworn this was the way to a movie rather than an actual road. Just as you expected, you'd never see civilization again. Jimmy peals the car out onto a paved highway again. A few cars swerve to keep from running into this car as Jimmy speeds his way away from the dirt path your father's men are still trying to make their way out of.

You sag in your seat. And place your hand over your heart. "I'm really starting to hate car chases," you say.

Jimmy looks in his rear-view mirror at you, a smile playing with his lips. "What? You mean you don't enjoy having to run for your life?" he jokes.

"Yeah, it's a surprise to me too," you answer, turning

to look at the road behind you, and you thank God that you don't see anyone behind you.

"Well, at least you haven't lost your sense of humor," Jimmy says, speeding past the other cars on the highway.

CHAPTER 5

Nightfall has begun and the two of you followed the same procedures as last time for changing vehicles. This time you had an old camper van. Jimmy was taking you further into the countryside. You were lying down on the bench seat in the very back of the van. Sleep was calling your name, but you didn't want to leave Jimmy to drive all night again while you slept.

"Jimmy?" you say in a sleepy voice.

He chuckles as he looks in the rear-view mirror at you. "Yeah?"

"Are we almost there? I'm tired," you say.

"Not yet. Get some sleep. I'll wake you when we get there," he says, looking back at the road.

"No, I feel bad sleeping while you are driving us to safety," you pout.

"What do you want me to do? Hid the car and nap with you?" he asks, in a joking tone.

"Yes."

He looks at you in the mirror. "Seriously?"

"Yes," you repeat, meeting his gaze in the mirror.

Jimmy's eyebrows raise in surprise as he looks back at the road. "Okay, I'll find a place to hide the van."

* * *

After Jimmy found a place to hide the van, he showed you that the backseat could fold down like a futon to make a bed. Reaching over you, he pulled a blanket and pillow out of the back of the van for you. He covered you with the blanket as you tucked the pillow under your head. He leans down and kisses your forehead before shifting so he can move off the little bed.

"Wait," you say, catching his arm. "Stay here."

He sighs, "I shouldn't. I don't know if I can keep my hands to myself if you're that close."

"Then don't keep your hands to yourself," you mumble.

He looks over at you in surprise. You scoot over a bit and pat the bed next to you. He smiles at you, then shrugs out of his sweater and pulls off the baseball cap before lying down next to you. You pull the blanket over him and snuggle up to his side.

He is not tense like the first time he was next to you. You close your eyes and feel him kick off his shoes before turning towards you and slipping his arm under your neck. His chest presses against yours as he moves himself closer to you. His fingers slip up under your shirt and you squirm.

"What are you doing?" you ask, giggling as you try to move away from his touch, which is so light it tickles.

"I told you I wouldn't be able to keep my hands to myself," Jimmy says.

"Jimbo, stop that tickles!" you say, grabbing his wrist and holding his hand against your skin.

He chuckles. "What did you just call me?"

Your eyes widen. "Uh ... Your name?"

"No, you called me Jimbo," he says. His grip on your side gets stronger.

"I don't know what you're talking about," you say, struggling to keep your composure.

He pushes himself on top of you, wedging himself between your legs. "Are you sure about that?" he asks, as his fingers tickle your sides.

You squeal and grab at his hands to stop him, but he clamps his hand around both of your wrists and pins your arms above your head. He attacks your sides, and you laugh and beg him to stop as you squirm under him.

"Okay! Okay! I called you Jimbo, I'm sorry. Please stop!" you plea.

His fingers pause. "How sorry are you?"

"Very sorry. It was an accident. I didn't mean to," you say, trying to catch your breath.

You now realize the position the two of you are in. Jimmy's still holding your arms over your head as he kneels over you. You've shifted down in your attempts to get him to stop tickling you and are now laying with your knees pressed high against his sides.

He seems to notice the position the two of you are in at the same time you do because his smile fades and he lets go of your wrists. Your hands slide down the pillow, so they are next to your head instead of over it and the two of you look at each other as darkness creeps in around you.

"Should I move?" Jimmy murmurs.

You shake your head as you place one hand on his chest. Your hand slides up to his neck, then around to the back of his head. You see his jaw muscles work as you pull him down towards you. Your hand makes a fist in his hair as you reach up to kiss him.

Jimmy sighs into the kiss and pushes into you, so you are pressed into the bed. He slides down onto his elbows, holding himself over you so his chest is against yours, but he isn't crushing you.

You wrap your arms around his neck, returning every kiss he gave you, your eyes close to concentrate on how it feels to have him this close to you. Your legs slip up his sides and you receive a moan from him. You feel his hand slide down your side to grip the back of your thigh, can feel his arousal pushing against you as his hips press into you.

"Wait," you say weakly as his mouth moves to your neck. "This feels weird."

"What feels weird?" he asks, his mouth still leaving kisses on your neck.

Your hands move down to his hips. "This."

He pushes himself up with an eyebrow arched up. "What? Being between your legs?"

You shake your head. "No, this..." your finger slides down the front of his pants. "pressing against me like that feels strange."

A smile spreads across his lips as he's looking down at you. "You're cute."

"Why? What did I do?" you ask, looking up.

He leans down to kiss you again. "You're bold when you're touching me, but when I'm touching you, you get shy and embarrassed. Why is that?"

You shrug. "I guess when I was secretly learning about sex, I was more interested in knowing what guys enjoyed having done to them."

He lifts his head to look at you again. "Secretly learning about sex?"

"Well, my father would have burned me at the stake if he knew I was trying to find out how to jerk a man off, so yeah, secretly," you say.

His eyebrows raze at how straight forward you were being. "I see..."

Your cheeks warmed. "Is it weird that I told you that?"

Jimmy's thumb strokes across your cheek and he smiles. "No, I like how honest you are." He watches your face for a few moments before speaking. "You know I'm going to ruin your innocence now."

Your eyes widen. "W—what did you say?"

Jimmy grinds his hips against you, making sure you feel the length of him.

Your hands grip his hips to stop him, but it doesn't work. "Ah, Jimmy!" you shriek as you cover your face.

Jimmy laughs and does it again, causing you to shake your head while still covering your face. He smirks as he moves down to press his chest against yours again. "What's wrong?" he asks, pretending he doesn't know what he was doing.

You glare at him, and he can't hold back his laugh. "I mean, if you wanted me to touch you, you could have just asked instead of whatever that was," you say.

"I don't want you to touch me," he says, suddenly very serious. "I want to be inside you, but I also don't want to push you into anything you aren't ready for."

You blink in surprise and ask; "Like—you mean sex?"

He nods, not breaking eye contact.

"Really? Like right now?" you ask, staring.

"Yeah, but only if you want," he answers.

"Hmm—I guess I'll have to say yes," you respond.

"Are you sure?" Jimmy reiterates, giving you a questioning look.

"You'll go slow, right?"

"Of course."

You hug him for a bit, preparing yourself for what's about to happen before you loosen your grip.

"I think I'm ready."

Jimmy smiles at you as he pushes himself up onto his knees. He has to slouch, so he doesn't hit his head on the roof of the car. He leans to the side, reaching into the back of the van and pulls his bag onto the bed.

You watch him with a confused look on your face. "What are you doing?"

Jimmy chuckles at your use of the nickname, or at how innocent you are, before he pulls his hand out. He's holding something small and flat between his fingers, but it's too dark for you to see what it is.

"I was just making sure I had a condom before—" he says. "Hold on to this for me?"

You take it, about to question why he doesn't hold it himself. But then he unbuttons your pants and tugs them off with ease and you realize why he gave it to you. You blush as he moved between your now bare legs and begins pushing up your shirt. Your heart jumps into overdrive as Jimmy exposes your bra and moves your arms over your head so he can finish pulling off your shirt.

It shocks you how aroused you are from just being undressed. Jimmy leaves your panties and bra on and struggles to get his pants off while staying between your legs. You tuck the condom into your bra and wait for him to be free of his pants before grabbing the bottom of his shirt and pulling it up. He lets you take it off, then pressed down against you.

You can feel every bit of Jimmy. His athletic body fits perfectly with yours and the thin material of your underwear is soaked through as he pressed his hips forward into you. Your legs slid up his sides and you long for him to touch you.

"Okay?" Jimmy asks, his voice deep. He's grinding his hips against you, making sure you know what to come.

You nod, wrapping your arms around his neck. With one hand, he tugs on your panties. He reaches between your legs and palms you a few times before slipping a finger between your lips. He locates your clit and rubs circles around it. Your back arches and you exhale pleasured sighs.

"I almost forgot," he says, not stopping his hand. "I must give you some tongue."

Before you can reply, Jimmy shuffles down and pulls your panties off. He spreads your legs apart and all you can do is stare at him in shock. He dips his head down and his tongue slides over your most sensitive spots. Your head falls back against the pillow and your back arches high as you gasp. Jimmy reached a hand up behind your arched back to un-clip your bra as he continues using his tongue to pleasure you.

Your breasts free themselves from the cups of your bra as soon as he unlatches the back. You thought being this exposed would be uncomfortable or maybe a little embarrassing, but as Jimmy pulled the bra away from your chest you became more aroused than you thought possible. You wanted more. You needed Jimmy inside you.

"Please," you barely say as his tongue makes circles around your clit. "Jimmy, I need you," he moves so his body is pressed flat against yours and you wrap your legs around his waist. "I want you to be my first."

Without moving your legs, he slides his own underwear down. Then he grabs the condom, which was, thankfully, still sitting on your chest. He rips it open with his teeth and puts it on before pressing his tip against your opening. He pushes in a little too quickly and you wince.

Jimmy looks up at your face as he pulls out. "I'm so sorry."

He rocks his hips, just trusting a small amount of himself into you until there is no resistance, then he moves deeper inside you. You gasp and cling to him as he fills you, stretching you to accommodate his size. Your mind keeps repeating 'he's inside you, fucking you, filling you' and that is all you can think of.

He moans as he thrusts his entire length into you and holds it there. "I'm afraid that I'll never get enough of you," he breathes into your neck.

Your hips buck forward, pushing him into your G-spot and you gasp. "Don't stop," you plea.

Jimmy makes the most arousing groan and changes his position, pulling your legs over his shoulders as he pulls out and pushes all the way back to your G-spot. You moan as he continues to hit your G-spot with every thrust. Your body quakes and you moan out his name as he thrusts faster. Your body clamps down on him, but he doesn't slow, continuing to hit his mark until you cry out his name as your orgasm washes over you.

Jimmy's still hard inside you, but he's stopped moving. He's looking down at you as you catch your breath.

"Did..." You attempt to ask, "you...finish?"

"No," he says, laughing when you look up at him,

worried. "It's okay. When you catch your breath, we can go again."

"It's okay, I'm ready," you say, still gasping.

He smiles at you and pulls out. Your eyes flutter shut at the feeling.

The van was an older model, which is why it had the bench seat that folded back. It also had two seats in the middle of the van that could swivel around. Jimmy spun the chair closest to him around got off the bed to sit in it. He pushed the arm rests up and gestured for you to come towards him. You slid yourself over to that side of the bed and he pulled you onto his lap, sinking you down on his erection.

You gasped at the feeling of him re-entering you. The chair was wide enough and tall enough that you could only touch the floor with your toes. Your legs were spread as far as they could be and the only way you could move would be to use Jimmy's shoulders or the back of the chair to hoist you up.

His hands slid from your hips to your breasts, you looked down to watch him kneed them in his hands, his first and middle fingers catching your nipples and pulling at them. You gasp at the feeling and tip your head back. At that moment, he started thrusting up into you, freeing a moan from you. He had easy access to your G-spot in this position and he had you moaning in seconds.

"You feel so good inside me," you pant as you grab his shoulders.

"Oh god Cassidy, you can't say things like that when I'm trying to get you to come again," he groans.

"I'm sorry," you laugh, gasping as his thrusts become quicker.

You quake in pleasure again, and Jimmy's moans are matching yours this time, so you know he's about to erupt. Your cunt clamps down on him harder and he thrusts a few more times into your G-spot, holding that position as his release washes over him at the same time yours does again.

Jimmy whines and his delight makes you to hold him harder as you watch his facial expressions.

A minute later, you slump against Jimmy, and he holds you there until he catches his breath enough to move you onto your makeshift bed. He places you on the bed and lies next to you, pulling the blanket over you both. You roll over, place a hand on his chest as your eyes close.

"I love you," Jimmy says, kissing the top of your head as your eyes close.

"I love you too, baby," you retort.

CHAPTER 6

Day Eleven

A gloved hand clamps down over your mouth, cutting off your scream as you're dragged out of the back of the car. Jimmy jumps at the sound, sitting naked on the bed as the blankets are dragged away with you. A big, heavy man is pulling you away from Jimmy as he wraps you in the blanket. His voice booms out orders to the other men in a language you don't recognize, and the surrounding men avert their eyes and head towards the van.

Jimmy has tugged on his pants and is scrambling for his gun in the front seat when one man pulls the side door open, grabs him and yanks him out of the van. He lands on his side on the ground. You fight to free yourself from the big man, trying to get to Jimmy.

The man hoists you into the back of a black van you know belongs to your father and lays you down next to him. You watch as someone roughly forced Jimmy towards the van, his hands zip-tied behind his back. He's covered in dirt and his body is covered in red marks, you know, are from punches. They sit him down across from you and you see his lip is bleeding.

Your heart aches at the state he's in, but that feeling changes to fear when you realize the two of you will be brought to your father. First, Jimmy works for O'Neal, the mob boss, so your father would kill him just for that. But when he finds out Jimmy slept with you, he'll be so mad he might do something worse than kill, he might skin Jimmy alive or chain him to a post and burn him to death.

You clench your teeth. You had to find a way to keep your father from killing him. Had to tell him some lie that would buy time or get in contact somehow with Eddie O'Neal.

You lean forward, towards Jimmy, but the heaven man grabs your shoulder and forces you back against the seat. Jimmy moves to lunge at the man, but the two brutes next to him hold him down. He pulls his shoulder away from one of them, trying to force his way towards the big man. The man, Jimmy pulled his shoulder away from, swings his fist and it connects with Jimmy's jaw.

"Stop!" you shout.

To your surprise, they do. All of them, even Jimmy, stop and look at you. You stare at them at the reaction you got, sinking back in your seat. You hold the blanket closer to yourself now, hyper-aware that you're nude under it.

Your father's men talk among themselves in Spanish, and you feel Jimmy's gaze on you. You meet his eyes and instead of seeing a broken man, you see a man who's bruised and beaten but filled with fight. You know it would take a lot more than a few punches and a zip ties to break him. This both inspires you and frightens you. *You know your father. I mean, he tried having you killed, so O'Neal had nothing to hold against him. If Jimmy didn't bend to your father's will, then he wouldn't last long. The only way you could think to save Jimmy's life was to tell your father the two of you was getting married and to get Jimmy to pledge his life to your father until the two of you could think up a way to kill him and escape.*

You rub your forehead. *No, that wouldn't work. Your father would never trust one of O'Neal's men. Maybe if you could get these guys to stop somewhere, you could find a way...*

You let your trail of thoughts run off as you look up at the huge man next to you and tap his arm. He looks down at you. He's wearing sunglasses, but you can still tell he's entertained because you had the lady-balls to get his attention.

"Sir, I think we should stop somewhere and find me something to wear." You have to force yourself not to cringe at the word. "My daddy would be furious to know I was in a car with four men and had nothing more than a blanket covering his little princess. I hate to think what would happen to any of you if he thought his men, the men he's paying to take me to him, saw anything they weren't meant to see."

The big man's face loses some color.

"Mira, who would should he trust? The man who claims he saw nothing or own his flesh and blood? And of course, he would trust that if you had seen something that you were enough of a gentleman that you wouldn't have forced yourself on me, right?"

The huge man's facial expression looks like a fish, opening and closing his mouth without being able to say anything. The car suddenly comes to a stop, and he goes white as a sheet. "Estamos aqui," he says in Spanish.

Jimmy looks at you, impressed just as you gear up to let this man have it. *Fuck being the damsel in distress. These men, your father too, if they wanted to play dirty, then that's exactly what you'd do.* You let the blanket drop as the door of the van opened. The big man reaches towards you, grabbing the blanket and you lean back, so it looks like he's forcing himself on you, just as your father enters. You almost smirk as a furious look crosses his face and push him into sheer rage by screaming. "Get your fucking hands of me, you pervert!"

Your father pulls out his gun and shoots the big man in the shoulder before dragging him out of the van. *You do a purposely bad job at covering yourself. That way, your father is mad at anyone who looks in your direction, and let your eyes tear up. Fake crying was one of your talents. You didn't use it often, so your father always believed it was real.*

"Daddy—" you say, your voice cracking with the fake

tears you're summoning. "They..." you pull at the blanket, covering yourself a little more. "They're not going to hurt me again, are they?"

You watch as your father's head explodes with rage and shoots the two men next to Jimmy in the head, then turns to shoot the big man in the face. *Well, that would buy Jimmy some time, wouldn't it...*

Your father climbs into the van and covers you up. "What about this fucker?" your father asks, pointing the gun at Jimmy.

"He tried to stop them," you sniffle and let your father put his arm around you. "Then they beat him."

Your father keeps his gun pointed at Jimmy. "Is he one of Eddie's men?"

You don't want to let your father know you know who Eddie is, or that you've spent the last week with one of his men, so you just say in the most insecure voice you can muster. "Daddy, he kept me safe."

You can see your father hates the fact that he can't kill one of O'Neal's men. Out of honor, your father owed him for keeping you safe. He pulls the gun away and instructs his men to clean up this mess and bring Jimmy inside. He helps you out of the van and into the building. You didn't know where this place was, but you assumed that from the short drive it took to get you to him they had been moving from safe house to safe house like you and Jimmy had attempted. That would also explain why O'Neal's men couldn't find him.

Inside, your father leads you to a room and instructs

you to get cleaned up and dressed. He assures you no one will hurt you again. You stop him before he leaves. "No one will hurt Jimmy, right?"

"No one will hurt him unless we have a reason to," he replies before leaving, closing the door behind him.

You wash up and find something to put on as quickly as you can. You don't trust your father with Jimmy. He could twist the situation around easily and kill Jimmy while you are away, if that's what he wanted. You get dressed before hurrying out the door to find the nearest guard and ask for directions to your father.

"Excuse me?" you put on a friendly and shy act as you find a guard. "Can you tell me where my father is? I seem to be a little lost."

The man just nods and leads you down a few halls before opening a door for you. You step in and just as your eyes land on Jimmy, who is tied to a chair, your father's fist connects with the Jimmy's face. Your stomach leaps into your throat as you see how much violence was inflicted on Jimmy in the short time you were away.

"What are you doing?" you almost yell at your father. "He kept me safe and fought off your men and now you're doing what? Going to punch him to death for trying to save your daughter from those bastards?"

Your father sighs and grabs a rag as he turns to look at you, wiping the blood from his knuckles. "I know you think he's your rescuer, but he's still one of Eddie's men. I need O'Neal's whereabouts, so I can find that bastard before he can find me."

"But Jimmy has been with me for days… how would he know where this Eddie guy is?" you ask, playing dumb. You know Jimmy gave updates.

"This fucker has to know," you father says, and for the first time in your life, you see your father scared to death. He didn't handle fear well.

Wait. The boss and Jimmy made sure they got in touch at specific times each day, unless of course, there was an emergency. Jimmy had missed one of these, so his boss had to know he was missing. And he knew where they were last, so there was a very good chance he was about to blast his way in any moment.

Jimmy's head rolled forward, so he was looking at his feet, the split on his lip dripping blood onto the floor. "I don't know where he is. I send location updates. It's like a driver's log."

Your father grabs a chair near him and launches it across the room, yelling. "You're fucking lying, you piece of shit!"

You jump at the sudden show of rage and watch as he paces the room, running his fingers through his hair. You almost feel bad for your father. *Almost.*

"Daddy?" you murmur, careful of how you speak to him right now. "Did something happen between you and this Eddie guy? I've never seen you this stressed out."

"He's going to kill me, little one," your father says, looking out the window on the other side of the room. "He's the leader of the fucking mafia, and I've pissed him off."

'Yeah, no shit,' you think to yourself. "What happened? Is there any way we can fix it? Or you know, make him just leave this alone?"

Your father shakes his head. "No, I borrowed money from them, and I can't pay it back then..." he pauses. "I knew he had you, or at least one of his men did so...I sent a few guys to blow up one of his office buildings."

"You what?" you ask, pretending very well to be shocked.

"I know. It was stupid, but I didn't know what he was going to do to you to get me to pay him back," he says.

"And blowing up his building, and possibly me as well, was the best thing you could think of?" you ask, crossing your arms over your chest.

Your father hangs his head as you speak. Apparently having his daughter killed wasn't something he was taking lightly. Too bad for him, you were probably never going to forgive him.

Just then, something crashed through the window, missing your father's head. He ducks down, and you jump away from it as it bounces towards your feet, bracing for it to explode or shoot out gas or something.

Jimmy lifts his head to look at the small cylinder on the floor. "My boss is here. This is his way of giving you a choice."

"How do you know?" your father asks, just as you say. "A choice of what?"

"Open it. It contains a note for you," Jimmy closes his eyes as he takes a deep breath. He looks like he's hurting.

Your father stays still, looking at the container on the ground. The shooting starts outside and he doesn't move. He hardly even blinks. He just whispers. "How the fuck did he find me?"

You start inching your way towards Jimmy, hoping your father stays in this trance like state until you can get him untied. But just as you get to him, your father pulls out his gun and points it at Jimmy, well at you because you are standing in the way.

"Daddy…" you scream, eyes wide.

"It was you, wasn't it?" he asks, his eyes look unfocused.

The gunshots are now inside the building, and they're getting closer. You stare at your father with genuine fear. He tried to have you killed. It wouldn't surprise you if he took a shot at you himself.

"Daddy, please don't," you say, your voice louder than a whisper.

His eyes still seem glazed over, like he's not seeing you. His hand holding the gun at you trembles slightly. "He's not taking me alive," he says.

Just then, the door is kicked in and Eddie's men rush inside, guns pointed at your father. A few of them yell at him to drop his weapon, but you can see he's already made his choice. You squeeze your eyes shut and brace for the pain. A single shot rings out and the whole room falls silent.

Did you die? No? You crack one eye open and look down at yourself to find the wound, but there was none.

You look behind you at Jimmy and find he's no worse than he had been a moment ago.

Where did the shot come from? You swivel your head around and find your father on the floor, blood pooling out of the top of his head. Your blood runs cold. You may not have loved him like you should have, but he was still your father and seeing him on the floor with the gun still in his mouth and an ever-growing puddle of blood spilling out from his head was making you lightheaded. You turn away and see someone untying Jimmy, but everything seems to move in slow motion.

Jimmy is confused as he gets up. He mumbles something to you, but you can't hear him. The corners of your view start getting dark and the floor comes up and hits you.

CHAPTER 7

Day Twelve

"Will she be alright, Dr. Castell?" you hear someone say. They sound close, like they are right next to you, but you are disoriented and still can't figure out what way is up and down.

"Please Jimmy," another voice says. "I've known you for years. You can call me Rick. And yes, she will be fine. It's just a bump on the head. Nothing to worry about."

The first person, the one closest to you, sighs. "Thank you."

You think the person next to you is Jimmy because one, your father just blew his own brains out, and two, you didn't know anyone else.

"You're welcome, Jimmy. I'll be back in a bit to check on both of you," the other man, Rick, said. You can hear him put something down and his footsteps leaving the room.

You take a deep breath to let Jimmy know you are awake, not quite ready to open your eyes yet. You feel his hand cover yours and his lips press against your forehead. You have to pry your dry lips apart to speak, and your voice comes out hoarse. "Where are we?"

"A private clinic. The boss keeps this place so that his men aren't asked about the injuries they receive while working," Jimmy answers as he strokes your hair away from your face.

"Clever," you say. Your mouth is so dry you're not sure how you are managing to speak. "Is there any water around?"

"Yeah, hold on," Jimmy says, and you hear him move away. You put your arm over your eyes and crack one open. As you expected, the blinding brightness from the lights was beaming down on you. You groan, snapping your eye shut. *Why do these medical facilities think having that much light on a patient recovering from whatever ailed them was a good idea?*

Jimmy moves back to your side and helps you into a sitting position, you hold onto his arm as he adjusts the bed into an upright position. He leans you back against the bed and hands you the cup of water. You take a sip, your eyes still clamped shut. "Can you turn the lights off? They're too bright."

He doesn't even say anything, but goes to shut the lights off and returns to your side. You slowly open your eyes, squinting because the light outside the room is still quite bright to your unadjusted eyes. "Thank you."

"You scared me," he says, watching you worried.

"I'm sorry, I'm not usually squeamish like that when it comes to blood," you say, looking down at the cup in your hands. "I think it was the fact that my father took his life in that way that caused me to pass out."

Jimmy sits on the hospital bed next to you and wraps his arms around you. The two of you sit in silence for quite a while. Nothing needed to be said. You knew Jimmy was sorry you had to see your father kill himself. He knew you weren't attached enough to him to feel like you lost family today, so he couldn't say the only thing that could be said in this situation, which would have been 'sorry for your loss'.

After a few moments, you think of how Jimmy had been beaten up, and you had completely forgotten to ask how he was. "Oh my God, Jimmy, I'm sorry I didn't ask earlier. How are you feeling? Are you okay?"

You can feel him smile against the top of your head. "I'm sore, but I'll be fine."

Silence falls between the two of you again. It was strange how your life had flipped upside down in less than two weeks. And how, despite all the horrible things that had happened and the fact that you were currently in a hospital bed, you were so very happy.

You were so happy you started feeling guilty for being this happy. People died, you and Jimmy had to run for your lives several times, and then Jimmy was beaten up badly. But it was all behind you now and you knew things would never be the same and that's what made you happier than you ever remember being.

"Jimmy?"

"Hmm?" he hums, his chin resting on the top of your head.

"Are we going to do that again?"

"Do what? Run for our lives, killing people on the way?" he says, humor coating his words.

"Well, I was asking about the sex, but yeah, that too," you say, pulling your head out from under his chin so you can look up at him.

Jimmy smiles and even with his split lip and bruised face, he's still the most beautiful man you've ever seen.

"I'd gladly do all of that with you," he says.

"Well, that's good," a man's voice says from the doorway, breaking the moment. "Because, Cassidy, you've just inherited your father's place."

The two of you look over to see Eddie standing in the doorway. He's in all black like the rest of his men had been when they stormed your father's warehouse. He's just missing the bulletproof vest and gun.

"What do you mean?" you ask.

"The guy that would have stepped in after your father's death was found outside with a bullet wound to the chest. He stopped me and told me to make sure you take your father's place. Apparently, you have a knack for this line of work," Eddie says as he walks into the room towards the bed you and Jimmy are sitting on. "I was a little worried about telling you this, but after overhearing the conversation you two just had, I have an idea that should be beneficial for all parties involved."

You and Jimmy stare at him, waiting for him to continue.

"I was thinking, since Jimmy is like a brother to me, a younger brother that I can boss around..." Eddie starts.

"Even though I'm older that you..." Jimmy butts in, smiling a goofy smile.

Eddie shoots him a look before continuing. "...And you are now the leader of the ring that potentially could be my biggest rival. Why don't you two get hitched and we join forces?"

"M-married?" you ask, stuttering in surprise. "We've hardy known each other."

Eddie shrugs, "I met my wife the day of our wedding, and I can't yet trust where your loyalties are, so it's that or be my rival and pay off your father's debt."

The blood drains from your face a little at the thought of being saddled with the cause of your father's suicide. "Can't you just take over?" you ask.

Eddie smiles. "I can, but you would need to die for me to do that."

Your mouth hangs open.

Jimmy, thankfully, sees you are in no position to give O'Neal a proper response and says; "How about we talk over the marriage thing, and she'll have your answer—let's say tomorrow morning?"

Eddie nods and leaves.

You have to hold yourself back from expressing your shock and alarm before Eddie is even out of the room, which is a very hard task when your mind is racing in like ten directions at once. As soon as the door closes behind him, you turn to Jimmy, looking at him with wide eyes. You aren't even sure where to start, so you start rambling and you're sure you aren't making any sense. "Take my father's position? Marry you? What is he thinking? I can't do that! But if I don't then, he'll make me pay, and I probably won't be able to see you anymore. Unless we run away and leave him a note saying 'good luck with the law-breaking, you can have these guys-"

"Whoa, take a breath," Jimmy says, holding a hand up to stop you. "Okay, let's take this one step at a time. Okay?"

You nod at him, still taking deep breaths to keep yourself calm.

"Alright first things first. Do you think you can handle running things? There will be people to show you everything you need to know that is specific to your ring and its dealings, and you've got me for anything else," he says.

"I've got you?" you ask.

"Wedding or not, you've got me," he says, smiling.

You almost tear up. "Okay," you say, trying not to choke on your words. "I...I think I can do this if I've got you. I mean, I convinced my father those men attacked me, so he'd kill them just because they hurt you. Also, so he didn't think you slept with me because, clearly he would have killed you."

Jimmy doesn't say anything, but his expression changes slightly. Like he's just realizing something he hadn't noticed before. "Marry me."

"What?" you look at him in shock, "I can't-We can't … We've only known each other for like a week and a half," you sputter.

"So? We'll be engaged for a year while we plan our wedding and we can get to know each other better. Hey, we spent a week living together and didn't want to kill each other so that's a start," he says.

You stare at him, not knowing if he's joking or not. "Are you serious?"

"I've never been more serious. I've been looking for a woman who wouldn't run from this side of my life and have had no luck finding her. Only you… I wouldn't want anyone else even if I did find her," Jimmy admits.

You shake your head, rejecting the thought of being involved with the mob boss's favorite getaway driver. "Come on, Jimmy, would you want to stay with me if you found your Bonnie?"

"Since I'm Clyde, I've already had found my Bonnie," he says, leaning in to kiss you before you can say another word.

The End

www.ingramcontent.com/pod-product-compliance
Lightning Source LLC
Chambersburg PA
CBHW070339170726
48291CB00001B/110